KT-436-366

The Divine Conjuror

The Divine Conjuror

by

Miguel Ruiz Montañez

Translated by

Charlotte Palmer

CHARTERHOUSE LIBRARY

WITHDRAWN

**Beautiful
Books**

www.beautiful-books.co.uk

Beautiful Books Limited
36–38 Glasshouse Street
London W1B 5DL

ISBN 9781905636693

9 8 7 6 5 4 3 2 1

First published in Spain as *El Papa Mago* by
Ediciones Martínez Roca 2008.

Copyright © Miguel Ruiz Montañez 2008.

Translation © Charlotte Palmer 2009.

The right of Miguel Ruiz Montañez to be identified as the
author of this work has been asserted by him in accordance with the
Copyright, Designs and Patents Act 1988.

All rights reserved. No part of this publication may be reproduced,
stored in or introduced into a retrieval system, or transmitted, in any
form, or by any means (electronic, mechanical, photocopying, recording
or otherwise) without the prior written permission of the publisher. Any
person who does any unauthorised act in relation to this publication
may be liable to criminal prosecution and civil claims for damages.

A catalogue reference for this book is available from the British Library.

Cover design by Head Design.
Typesetting by Misa Watanabe.
Printed and bound in the UK by CPI Mackays, Chatham ME5 8TD.

To Beatriz

Then I saw an angel coming down from heaven,
Holding the key to the bottomless pit and a large
chain in his hand.

He captured the dragon, that ancient serpent,
who is the Devil and Satan,
And tied him up for a thousand years.

He threw him into the bottomless pit, locked it,
And sealed it over him
To keep him from deceiving the nations any more
Until the thousand years were over.
After that he must be set free.

The Book of Revelation, 20:1–3

The history

One thousand years ago, at the end of the first millennium, a series of events shook Europe.

People lived in fear of the dawning of the millennium, amidst prophecies of the end of the world, and strange happenings unsettled a barbaric society.

The events and historical figures found in this book are real, including the figure of Gerberto d'Aurillac, Silvestre II, the pope magician.

However, many enduring legends have also been included, since today it is difficult to look back on those times without touching on some of the mysteries that continue to obscure one of the most tempestuous periods in human history.

CHAPTER 1

Reims
Champagne-Ardenne Region

A sudden ray of light illuminated the Count's desk, casting a purple veil over the shadows of the room. The change distracted the nobleman, turning his attention towards the large, open window. A beautiful moon dominated the star-studded sky where, just now, the heavens had opened with another violent summer storm.

His study was in the highest part of the castle and, from the very moment he had settled there, Pierre Dubois, the Count of Divange, had made remarkable progress in his secret investigations. Now, the shades of light in the room—bluish, and dark like his complexion—seemed to confirm the fascinating discovery he had just made. The manuscripts, lit by the faint light, left no room for doubt: the talking head, the infernal machine created by the pope magician, was to be found right here in the castle where the Count's ancestors had lived for centuries.

Pierre rushed down to the basement, frantic with his realisation, shouting as he went. The walls of the basement were constructed from enormous, ancient blocks of stone, their size giving away the age of the cavern. More than one thousand years old, the castle had been used as a fort in the Middle Ages and required extensive restorations, after suffering a series of ravages during numerous battles. A nineteenth-century extension, partly attached to the medieval castle, now provided his home and servants' quarters, a modern residence in clear contrast to the medieval bastion.

The arrival of the Count in the left wing caused a great stir among the servants, who were astonished to see their master enter so visibly shaken.

'We must dig behind the south wall,' he shouted.

'It's three o'clock in the morning, Sir,' his assistant pointed out.

'I know it is. I've just discovered that we've been mistaken all this time. We have spent more than two hundred years looking in the wrong places.'

'Well, then perhaps we can wait a little longer…'

'How dare you suggest such a thing! Call the workers and make sure they are ready to begin a new search straight away. We will start as soon as the sun comes up.'

The Count had dedicated his entire life to this mysterious mission, the noble continuation of his ancestors' quest, and he was not going to waste any time after the revelation he had just experienced.

He needed to know if one of the greatest mysteries in history could really be unveiled.

Impatiently, he descended the steps down to the foundations of the castle. If his suspicions proved correct, the entire family vault would stir on this glorious night. This could not be delayed. With his bare hands he touched the wall at exactly the same position and height recorded in the manuscripts. The chosen stone felt ancient, a thousand years old. He considered borrowing his workers' heavy tools, used in yesterday's excavation, but thought wiser of it, ever aware of his declining health. While he waited for the workers to arrive, he decided a moonlit stroll through his vineyards would calm his nerves; to try to sleep now, for even a few minutes, would prove hopeless.

The Count had never wandered around his estate at this hour. Millions of stars created a breathtaking tapestry of light over the Champagne region. Like most of the neighbouring vineyards, the land that stretched out before him had been owned by the Dubois family for generations. His family had been linked to the production of champagne since the day that Dom Pierre Pérignon, the Benedictine Abbot whose tomb lay nearby, had by chance discovered the method of producing this king of all wines. Since then, the entire region had become dedicated to what would come to be the most desirable drink in the world. They would live forever in the shadow of the bubbling wine's fame.

He found a seat in the porch of one of the terraces and glanced at the rolling hills, full of vines, bowing under the weight of their fruit.

A good harvest, he thought to himself.

The grave of champagne's creator lay close to the castle, along with those of many other illustrious French men and women who had also given this region a name. General Charles de Gaulle, the man who had contributed most profoundly to the glory of France, rested close by. These thoughts did not interest the Count now.

Count Dubois had dedicated his professional career, indeed his whole life, to unravelling the secrets of the life of a mysterious, illustrious ancestral neighbour. Silvestre II had not been born in Reims but it was here that his now infamous studies had come to fruition. Originally from a small village far away from this region, Gerberto d'Aurillac had experienced his spiritual and scientific triumph in the heart of Champagne-Ardenne.

There was nobody more closely linked to the passing of the first millennium, the end of an ill-fated era, than this magician. He was the first French pope, and a remarkable mathematician. There were hundreds of rumours and mysteries about Gerberto, the pope of the year 1000. People had accused him of making pacts with the Devil, of practising witchcraft, and of gleaning scientific knowledge from the Arabs. An old legend had it that a cockerel crowed three times when Gerberto d'Aurillac was born, and the cry was even heard as far afield as Rome…

Only God could know whether Gerberto had ever practised the spells and black magic that he had been accused of while occupying the archdioceses of both Reims and Ravenna and, ultimately, the papal throne. These positions could not, at that time, have seemed fitting for a man who created machines, had an unprecedented command of mathematics and supported radical political ideas. It was not surprising that his peers took this intelligent man to be a magician. At the time, it was inconceivable that a mere peasant could not only be a genius, but also rise to the position of pope, without the assistance of the Devil.

If the Count's research proved to be correct, it would put an end to centuries of speculation. One thousand years on, the world might finally discover the truth behind the amazing secrets of a man who had laid the foundations for change during one of the most unstable periods in history.

Pierre Dubois looked up and saw that the horizon was beginning to turn orange. He did not know how much time he had spent gazing at the sky but was relieved that the painful lumbago in his waist, so acute when he had got up due to the cold of the night, had retreated.

With effort, he stood up from his perch and walked towards the basement, where the whole team of workers obediently waited for him. As soon as he saw the Count enter, his assistant stepped up to him, seeking instructions.

'Follow me,' said the Count.

'We have already tried hundreds of times over there.'

'Not the way we are going to do it today.'

With an unusual feeling of confidence, he ordered the heavy machinery to be moved to a retaining wall, one which led to nowhere.

'So far we have only been digging up the floor of the basement, thinking that what we looked for lay beneath us,' the Count said, pointing down at his feet.

'But where else if not there?'

'In the walls. Take this stone away immediately.' He touched an enormous slab that formed part of the massive foundation wall of the castle.

The labourers got to work with their hammers on the stone. The noise rang out loudly in the room but after a few minutes, lumps of stone began to separate from the main block. The foreman called a halt to the work. One of the men tried to see if a large piece could be moved when suddenly it came away easily in his hand.

A hole had opened in the thick mortar wall and the

Count ordered the workman to squeeze his rickety body through the opening. As the dust settled on the other side, a dim lantern revealed through the gloom a large room, strewn with what seemed to be hundreds of strange objects. It seemed as if, centuries ago, this place had suddenly been abandoned. A thick layer of dirt coated everything, making it impossible to identify most of the items left there. After a few seconds, the Count's eyesight adjusted to the deep darkness of the cavern, which was barely penetrated by the haze of the lantern's light.

In the centre of the room, Pierre Dubois, Count of Divange, found what historians, archaeologists and distinguished men of learning across Europe had searched for over a thousand years. Part of a gigantic machine, in the shape of a huge head, was raised up on a solemn, black, marble pedestal. Like hell itself, both monstrous and perverse, the enormous head looked at him.

CHAPTER 2

The Count took three deep breaths before making his decision. He would have to lay off most of the workmen, paying them for their help so far. Only a small group of trustworthy labourers could remain, to be given the task of creating a more accessible entry to the cavern.

The room was fully illuminated, with a multitude of unusual objects and inventions in view. Clearing away the dust and centuries of untouched grime, cataloguing items, making them function and understanding the use of so many devices would be a daunting task. The few people allowed to enter tried not to look directly into the eyes of the awful beast, whose looming presence created a tense atmosphere in the chamber.

Jean Luc Renaud, the Count's personal assistant, tried to inspect the machine from a scientific point of view, attempting to ignore the horrible appearance of the whole artefact. With all the courage he could muster, he uttered the question on everyone's lips.

'Is this the talking head of the pope magician?'

'It is,' answered the Count, an ambiguous expression on his face, a mixture of pleasure, surprise and fear for his prized object. 'Without doubt, this is the machine created by the wise pope.'

Those left in the room crowded into a circle around the incredible discovery, desperate to see the monstrous creation for themselves. Without taking his eyes off of it, Pierre Dubois told them what he knew of the bizarre relic.

'We have before us one of the most sought-after secrets of the last millennium. Since its creation, some people have always doubted its true existence but, after the death of Silvestre II, others wasted no time in starting rumours—some preposterous, others accurate. Even the Templars found a name for this marvel—Baphomet—and the extent to which they worshipped it was, partly, what cost them their lives. This head played an important part in the trial that put an end to the Order of the Knights Templar and, because nobody could explain the secrets of the mysterious head, the legend of its existence was carried down through the centuries until, in the mid nineteenth century, it reached our fellow countryman, Eliphas Lévi. He dedicated much of his studies to Baphomet and what it represents. By God, I still cannot believe that we have a wonder like this standing before us.'

'What does it have in its mouth?' asked Renaud, pointing to one part of the machine, a sort of orifice caged by many parallel metal bars. Each one was interlaced with a series of wires that disappeared into the dark interior of the invention.

'That is an abacus,' the Count responded without hesitation. 'The distant relative of the present-day computer.'

'But…if this horrible monster is an invention of our Pope Silvestre II, does this mean that they already knew of the abacus in the tenth century?'

'Even before then. It was invented at roughly the same time by several different cultures. There were European, Oriental, American and many other abacuses. Its origin is lost in time. Contrary to what one might think, humans were interested in counting before writing.'

'I really don't understand,' said Renaud. 'You have spent your entire life pursuing the famous talking head of the pope magician. In the last few centuries, many archaeologists from all over the world have searched for it and now this is, without doubt, a head but…how can it talk? It seems disappointing.'

'On the contrary. I am sure that the head talks and that it has many things to tell. This machine uses the profound mathematical knowledge of its creator. The mouth is the means of entering data, like a keyboard for a computer. Our task now is to make the ancient robot work.'

* * *

The stairs seemed longer than usual. Prompted by a call from the Countess, who was interested in her husband's find, Pierre came immediately. A break to gather strength would not hurt.

He watched his wife before entering her bedroom. Her beautiful blonde hair, recently washed, blew lightly in the breeze. From the window, it seemed that she was overseeing the radiant sun as it fattened the grapes of the next harvest. Véronique Dubois, the Countess of Divange, was a subtle woman. She smiled at her husband and kissed him on the cheek, the most she would do to express her happiness at his discovery.

'Last night we heard your shouts and thought it was another of your fleeting revelations,' she said. 'Our daughter didn't sleep a wink. You know how sensitive she is.'

'How is Guylaine?' The person he cared about most in the world.

'Worried about you. You have spent too many months immersed in that project—her whole life, actually. No one understands what's going on in your life.'

'Leave it now. We have finally succeeded in the search.'

'Oh no! Now you will have to work even harder.'

'We have found some remarkable contraptions. We have found the talking head. It's true, we have to start a rigorous investigation now, which will take up most of my time, but I will do it with pleasure. Let me show you that I can be a good husband, father and lover again.'

'Pierre, there are some things that never change. Miracles can't happen.'

The Countess crossed her room to the bathroom and closed the door. The conversation was over.

* * *

Despite some concerns and disappointments, the following days passed quickly, with the excitement brought about by the mysterious objects in the castle room. Their hidden secrets had yet to be revealed. Not a single device offered a simple, written instruction explaining its function, although some of the smaller objects, once cleaned and catalogued, had a clearly identifiable use. The astrolabes for example, of different shapes and sizes, were easy to identify.

The talking head was, without doubt, the most complex contraption. Made from bronze, you could still see the remains of the gold plating from an age ago, which gave it an even more sinister appearance. The Count measured it and noted down every detail possible. The head's sheer size gave it an imposing appearance, over two metres high and wider still. Its insides contained so many mechanisms that it was also surprisingly deep. It looked like an immense statue of the Devil; nobody could imagine why it had been created.

Its face was the most imposing. The features belonged to an indefinite being—half human, half animal—indescribable and disconcerting. The piercing gaze of that monster shot daggers at anyone who dared look directly in its eyes. The massively proportioned mouth, as the Count had explained, was where information would be entered into the machine. With its wires and counters resembling a traditional abacus, along with various strings inside the mouth, this part of the head clearly was a data entry point. Other strange mechanisms mounted on the back pointed to a very specific function, one that had yet to be discovered.

'Do you know what it is for?' Renaud asked the Count,.

'It's clear that it is used to do calculations and give answers to concrete questions,' he replied, his eyes fixed on the multitude of wires, bars, levers, wheels and buttons that were installed inside the machine.

'I believe we must study some of the other items in the room to understand how this machine works. What's clear is that, if Gerberto d'Aurillac himself constructed it before he became pope, he used secrets contained in ancient books, most likely Arabic or Hindu. Without those books it will be difficult to make it function.'

'And if Gerberto, Pope Silvestre II, really did construct it, why does it have this diabolical appearance?'

'Good question. You already know he was accused of practising sorcery and collaborating with Satan. I think that he constructed this monstrosity a little before the year one thousand. You know about the strange events of that time.'

The Count turned to look it directly in the eyes.

'I believe that our pope gave the machine this awful appearance to scare people. For some unknown reason, he knew that this invention would prove dangerous in the wrong hands.'

* * *

As the days drew on, the gloomy underground space became inhospitable. They had hardly advanced at all in their work and the humidity was seeping into their bones. Pierre could not remember how many days he had spent absorbed in the search, utterly dedicating himself to this quest. The dust that now covered his body made him look like a ghost.

Suddenly, light footsteps in the entrance to the cavern brought him back to reality. He saw her silent approach, as if she did not want to bother him. Guylaine had brought him something to eat for dinner.

'This has to stop. You have to get back to normal life and spend time upstairs resting. We don't know how many days you have gone without sleeping.'

'I couldn't sleep a wink, even if I wanted to,' he said, kissing and hugging her. 'You know how passionate I have always been about this subject. I have dedicated so much of my life to investigating the mysterious happenings at the end of the first millennium. If there is a country that contains the secrets of that era, it is ours. That period, the transition from the year 999 to 1000, unsettled millions of people, convinced that the most terrible apocalyptical prophecies would be fulfilled a thousand years after the death of Christ. People recorded strange phenomena, like great famines, sightings of marine monsters, exceptional lunar eclipses, showers of stars and comets and, most fearfully, a frightening meteor that was visible in the sky over Europe for more than three months. With so many unresolved mysteries, do you think I can stop now?'

Despite the passion he had for solving these millennial enigmas, the most important thing in his life was still his daughter. He looked her directly in the eyes and realised that she was crying.

'Listen, Guylaine, you know how fascinated I am in this subject,' he said, enveloping her in his arms and taking a lock of her blonde hair. 'Everything I need to resolve this great mystery is here. I owe it to all the generations of our family that have lived in this castle to continue.'

'All right, but promise that you will keep me updated. This is not my fascination, but I want to understand what intrigues you.'

The pure and transparent look in the blue eyes of Guylaine Dubois made it clear to the Count that he would always have the support of his daughter.

* * *

At nearly seventy years old, the Count's sparse, once straw-coloured hair was almost white and was now dishevelled and unkempt after days of incessant work.

Bit by bit he had managed to make the different parts of the strange machine work. A group of springs and a collection of buttons were clearly significant. When they were activated, the deformed creature performed a repetitive sequence of simple operations that the Count had learnt to identify. However, the exact process of transmitting orders from the mouth, through the abacus and into the interior proved to be more complex.

His main concern was whether the device only processed simple calculations or if it could be used to obtain answers to bigger, more significant, questions. Applying what he knew methodically, little by little, he managed to understand the use of each one of the pieces and fragments that made up the head. His excitement grew when he realised that practically all of the parts were connected. Now all that was left was to put them into motion at the same time.

He took a breath and tried his luck, pressing the ignition spring.

What happened next would change the Count's life forever. One thousand years after its creation, the machine creaked into life.

CHAPTER 3

In the last few days, Guylaine had felt a great sense of loneliness; worry succeeded in stealing another night from her. Her father had gone so long without sleeping, he had lost weight and probably his mind as well. She didn't know how her mother was coping with her husband's distracted temperament. To make matters worse, the huge expanse of her room added to her restlessness.

Guylaine had always believed that the living quarters attached to the castle were not conducive to a healthy family life, perhaps because since she was little she had endured the continuous quarrelling of her parents, who seemed doomed to suffer endless arguments in such an enormous space. In the last few years, the disillusionment and distance between the Count and his wife had become deeply rooted. On a number of occasions, Guylaine had unsuccessfully tried to bring them back together. She could remember the thousands of times that she had pondered over her parents' personalities, how different they were and the opposing ways in which they viewed life.

Her father—passionate, independent, a little timid, caring, studious and brilliant—had always treated her with respect and consideration, to such an extent that she had become his confidante in all matters. At almost thirty years old, Guylaine

Dubois knew that she owed much to her father, particularly her personality.

Her mother, while also passionate, was too vehement. In fact, each time that she tried to understand her, Guylaine came up against an impassable wall that she simply could not get beyond. More than once she had asked her mother, directly and openly, why she would not show her feelings and true personality to her family.

It was no surprise, then, that for years they had both lived in their own private worlds and that the relationship between them felt irreparable. Guylaine's attempts to strengthen her parents' marriage had been fruitless and it was now a lost cause.

Daylight peeped through the curtains. An intense pain in Guylaine's back reminded her that she had been tossing and turning in bed. She had a hard day at university awaiting her, as her pupils had an early examination, immediately after which she had arranged a teachers' meeting to prepare for the summer holidays and the following year's timetable. She gathered her strength and went into the bathroom. From there, she telephoned the kitchen to order her breakfast.

* * *

Guylaine was surprised to see her mother in the kitchen. Most of the servants were also crowded in the hub of the castle, and Guylaine did not want to miss the novelty of seeing her mother, the Countess, preparing food. Even Renaud, the Count's assistant, who was usually so serious and professional, looked amazed and slightly amused by the sight.

'I've never seen anything like this,' said Guylaine, smiling broadly.

'Your father has not been to this side of the house for several days and someone has to take charge…' began Véronique, holding a good piece of meat in her hands. 'I have decided to make chateaubriand, my style. Do you remember it?'

'Actually, I don't. Why?'

'We have to do something special so that your father will come out of that horrible dungeon. My recipe can't fail. With a bit of luck, he will eat up here today.'

'That's a good idea.'

'Well, go and tell him to come out of that hideout, shower and be ready to eat his favourite dish. I'll serve at midday.'

Guylaine descended to the gloomy workroom, smiling at the thought of her mother's ingenious idea. All of a sudden, the thoughts she had had during the night about the deterioration of her parents' relationship evaporated. It was as if they had been a happy and well-matched couple since the day they married. She squeezed her body through the small gap that they had opened in the stone wall. The narrow opening, and the shadows in the cavern, made her feel claustrophobic.

Inside the cavern, a sulphurous smell overwhelmed her for a moment.

They probably used some sort of chemical product in the experiments, she thought.

She looked behind the shelves where the strange items had been methodically organised. It looked like no one was there. Her eyes adjusted to the room and she tried to work out whether her father was behind the machine. The darkness and immense proportions of the beast prevented her from seeing if he was working around the back. But when she came closer to the monster, he was nowhere to be seen. He must have gone upstairs to have a bath and rest. Finally, some good news.

Only when she turned back to the exit did she see the note. A yellowish envelope, stuck to the terrible face, made her heart beat faster. Inside, in shaky handwriting, Pierre Dubois had written a clear message. He had gone in search of the truth.

* * *

Guylaine's crying disturbed everyone crowded in the kitchen, most of all her mother. Véronique abandoned her cooking and rushed over to her daughter, who held the letter in her trembling hands.

The Countess asked everyone, except Renaud, to leave before she began.

Dearest Véronique and Guylaine,

The last few days have been the best of my life. Although you have seen me distressed, I have enjoyed myself like never before.

The countless generations of my family who dedicated themselves to pursuing the work of our pope magician have, at last, been rewarded. I believe I have found the secret to solve this great enigma.

At first, no one imagined that the talking head was, in reality, a subtle combination of art, science and…I believe, sorcery. Therefore, understanding what this fearful artefact contained has taken weeks.

The mechanisms, pipes, devices and each and every one of the pieces that are inside this head were constructed by the best conjuror the world has ever seen.

Now I can confirm, without the shadow of a doubt, that what I discovered in the vaults of the castle is the authentic Baphomet, the idol adored by the Templars and searched for by academics for centuries.

I still do not know whether this thing was born with the help of the Devil, if it comes from ancient Arabic magic, or if it really was a product of Pope Silvestre's genius.

But what is certain is that the moment has come.

The machine has spoken.

The Countess stopped to breathe and, pacing the kitchen, tried to contemplate what she was reading. Out of the corner of her eye, she could see from her daughter's expression that she was also shocked. But Renaud, her husband's faithful assistant, concealed his thoughts.

She gathered her strength and continued.

It has been hard work understanding this terrible monster's various riddles to find their meanings—my mathematical knowledge is good but not as advanced as the mind of Pope Silvestre II.

For a while, I believed that the head would respond to simple and mundane questions.

But I was wrong.

A perfect mathematical model—half science, half sorcery—leads unambiguously to a final answer. The talking head first announced it in the year one thousand—it says the same now.

The end of the world has come.

Both women breathed quicker with fear. Guylaine had stopped crying, her face showing the confusion caused by the letter. She looked across at her mother and saw the same expression of disbelief. After a brief pause, the Countess read the last few paragraphs.

The world is ending. There is no doubt. The model is perfect and it has confirmed this. But there are still things we need to tie up.

There is something that we can do. I have to find the way to do it. I must find the answer before it is too late.

Don't worry about me. I have gone on this crusade voluntarily and must face up to it alone. For this reason, I beg you not to follow me and to stay calm until I return.

Take care of yourselves.

Pierre Dubois
Count of Divange

Jean Luc Renaud quickly left the room, not wanting to show any emotion in front of the ladies. He had spent his whole life working by the Count's side and his master's unannounced departure hurt him deeply.

Alone, the women embraced each other. Once again, Guylaine broke down in tears, while her mother let her gaze wander to the window, trying to prevent herself from welling up too.

The weather had changed. Thick, black clouds raced towards the castle, threatening a storm.

CHAPTER 4

Paris

Never before had he seen a traffic jam like the one in front of him now. Among the obstacles ahead, the exit towards Port Maillot was temporarily blocked. The noise of the horns made the situation all the more unbearable. If a thirty-year-old like himself, who had been born in this city, couldn't handle the continuous traffic nightmares, how could the millions of visitors to Paris endure it? Yet again, he would be late.

When the elevated roof of the Concorde Lafayette hotel came into sight, he managed to sneak down a short cut. By a stroke of luck he found a place to park. Perhaps things weren't so bad.

The restaurant, Chez Robert, was full. It was not going to be easy to find the person he had agreed to meet for lunch. He was met by the maître d'.

'Hello, Marc. Your uncle is waiting for you; he is not best pleased.'

The maître d' led Marc to the best table in the restaurant, the corner he always reserved for his most important clients.

Marcos Miñón looked at his watch, distracted from his phone conversation. On seeing Marc, he waved and gestured for him to take a seat. He seemed impatient.

'Well, you're here at last,' Marcos said to his nephew.

'Yes, you know what the traffic is like.'

'You should have left earlier,' he said curtly, looking up and down at what Marc was wearing.

'Well, I'm here now. Did you just want to have lunch with me or was there something else?'

Marcos took a breath before speaking. If it were not for his brother, he would never have included his nephew Marc in a matter like this. However, the memory of more difficult times made him think that, one way or another, he had to involve this young man, who was after all part of the family.

Seventy years earlier, after the war had split Spain in two, his parents, the Miñóns, had fled the country. He and his brother had been born there but, like so many other Spaniards at that time, they had been brought up in France.

'Although we are very different, your father gave you my name.'

'I can't believe that you've made me come all the way here to reprimand me again. Remember, I'm over thirty now.'

The two Miñón brothers had refounded the detective agency that their father had left them when he died. The first years were hard to begin with, the business suffering after Detective Miñón's long illness. Mignon was a name chosen to avoid the use of the ñ, which was too difficult for clients to pronounce. Eventually the whole family adopted this version of their name.

Marcos, the elder brother, was an efficient leader of the firm, and after ten years he had turned it into a reputable Parisian agency. He had dedicated his life to it, rather than to a family, but it had left him lonely; he had only his brother to give him comfort in difficult times. The arrival of his first and only nephew, Marc, was an occasion which all of the Miñón family celebrated. They were finally a happy family —until the day that Marcos's brother and sister-in-law died in peculiar circumstances.

One cold winter's day, an old man came to the agency. He wanted a detective to verify whether his children were caught up in drugs, because he wanted to leave his legacy to someone who could be trusted to continue the family business, a well-established imports and exports firm called Baumard. Although the assignment did not seem to have any complications, Marcos and his brother were attacked several times during their investigations. When they were about to hand over the final report to their client, the terrible accident took place.

After going to an opera in the Bastille, Marc's parents were returning home to Montparnasse, where they had just bought an apartment with a large and sunny spare bedroom, so that their son had a decent place to grow up and study. A terrible storm raged over Paris that night. The car lost control and crashed into the fence of the River Seine. Although the police blamed the accident on speeding in bad weather, several witnesses believed they saw a black vehicle pushing Marc's parents' car out of control. The police never found the suspect's vehicle, nor could they connect the incident with the case Marc's father had been investigating. The accident had happened more than twenty years ago, but the events of that day changed the family irrevocably.

'Well, are you going to explain what you want me for?'

'I'll tell you. A count in the Champagne region, near Reims, has disappeared. He has left a letter expressing his desire that no one follows him. The police report says that they are looking for him both here and abroad, and are optimistic. However, his wife, the Countess, and, above all, his daughter insist on our agency investigating his disappearance separately, just in case.'

'And how do I come into this?'

'It's an easy case that you can undertake alone and a good way of initiating you into the firm.'

'Don't take this in the wrong way, but have I ever said that I wanted to work with you?'

'The Mignon Agency is yours as well as mine. You are your father's only heir.'

'Well, that doesn't mean that I have to be employed.'

'Listen, my boy, you can't carry on being the young idealist going everywhere to save the world. Your adventures with Greenpeace were all very well when you finished studying but you can only take that so far. What I'm proposing to you is that you begin a career in the agency, your firm, and that you start taking the reins. I'm not as young as I was. What do you say?'

'I don't know. I'll think about it.' He looked outside, and he took a quick sip of his wine.

* * *

The traffic continued to bring the city to a halt. It would do him no harm to take a walk and wait for the thousands of cars blocking the Boulevard Périphérique to disappear. The Champs-Élysées was only a short stroll away. Paris was a city you could never exhaust; the more space you covered, the more you felt you could pass through its streets entirely unnoticed.

Lunch with his uncle had made Marc Mignon feel restless. Already a year had passed since he had left his job at Greenpeace. Pursuing boats in the Atlantic or photographing polar bears in the Arctic Sea would always be, for him, his best memories. Since then, he had intermittently worked with other organisations, and had enjoyed a brief spell with a non-governmental organisation offering aid to Africa. Full of intensity and activity, his youth had passed in a heartbeat. Hundreds of times, his uncle had told him to slow down, to be more like others of his age. Deep down, though, he knew that his life had been a continuous escape, an excuse not to think about his lonely adolescence without his parents.

He reached his destination, the Place de l'Étoile, with the imposing Arc de Triomphe dominating the top of the Champs-Élysées. Marc chose a brasserie with tables outside, close to his favourite place in the whole city: a vast music shop, where he whiled away whole afternoons looking for music from all of the countries he had ever been to. Watching the people go by, enjoying a refreshing cold beer, Marc reflected on his uncle's job offer. If truth be told, the only person who really understood him was his uncle Marcos. He had been like a father to him for several years, before Marc had flown the nest, hastily and without any real direction.

Although he managed to complete his studies, Marc then spent more than ten years living a nomadic life, wandering, pursuing lost causes against giant corporations, corrupt states and various other people causing harm to the environment. From a practical point of view, his uncle's offer didn't seem all that unattractive. It would mean a stable job and, perhaps, a chance to find the happiness he had never found chasing unobtainable goals for a decade.

It was not that he cared particularly about the detective profession, but he had wanted to change his life for a while. All in all, the proposal to enter into the world of private investigation was not a bad one. His father had been a detective: one of the best, Marc had been told. It was evidently a good job, one in which you could travel, meet people and above all, receive a salary; something of a luxury in the last few years.

Maybe this job would give him the stability that he had longed for deep down. The painful memories in his past had made him flit from one job to the next, never feeling settled. Undeniably, his uncle's offer was a challenge, because Marc would have to prove to himself and others that he wanted to grow up and take control of his life. On the other hand, the work that he had been offered came loaded with unknown factors. He knew almost nothing of crime, he did not know the techniques of investigation, and in all likelihood he wouldn't know how to act in the unfamiliar situations he would face. However, it was evident that the case was not difficult. Chasing a crazy old man, a barmy count, did not appear to be a difficult assignment for a novice investigator.

One way or another, the idea that this first challenge would give way to new adventures took root in his mind. Without realising, Marc Mignon had decide to become a detective.

CHAPTER 5

Reims

Behind a group of thin cypresses, the imposing silhouette of the castle suddenly appeared.

Marc had left Paris early to have lunch with the Countess and her daughter. The journey to Reims took less than two hours, although towards the end, he had to search for the castle among hundreds of hectares of vineyard. He was growing tired of driving through so many identical and ordered rows of vines. The knowledge that those grapes would end up as champagne, however, was a pleasing thought.

He was met by the butler.

Marc Mignon looked around at the marvellous surroundings. From the outside, the Count's home was a red stone building, crowned with a steep, pointed, black slate roof. The great whitewashed, wooden windows were decorated with rich carvings of vines and gave the building a romantic air.

The inside of the castle was luxurious but practical. Portraits of the Counts of Dubois across dozens of generations hung beside the main staircase. As far as the eye could see, impressive slabs of black and white, perfectly polished marble decked the floor. He was still examining the place when the sound of heels coming down the stairs startled him.

'Good afternoon. You must be Detective Mignon,' said

the Countess, offering him her hand.

'The very same. And you must be Madame Dubois, Countess of Divange.'

'That's right, but do call me Véronique.'

The woman was younger than he had expected, and not at all as he had imagined. His uncle had said that the Count was around seventy and, as a result, Marc had instinctively imagined his wife to be a woman of similar age. The Countess could be no more than fifty and clearly took care of herself. Her beautiful blonde hair and firm, tanned skin gave her a youthful air, a far cry from the image he had had in his head. Her fitted red dress accentuated her narrow waist. Most striking of all was the intense, crimson lipstick with which she had painted her lips to match her outfit.

'Follow me, please.'

She guided him towards one of the back rooms. A heavy wooden door, engraved with lavish reliefs of bunches of grapes, led to the dining room, where the Countess's daughter was waiting.

Great. Two blondes for the price of one, thought the aspiring detective.

Guylaine Dubois was the spitting image of her mother, though younger, a little shorter and lacking in her mother's aristocratic gait. The Countess gestured for each of them to sit, positioning herself in between them.

'I imagine that you have hundreds of questions to ask us,' began the Countess, lighting a cigarette.

'Yes I do, but perhaps it would be best if you both tell me the whole story from the beginning.'

'As you wish. My husband is a millennial expert…'

'What's that?'

'You don't know about millennial theories? You've never heard of mysterious happenings from the year 1000?'

'Actually, no I haven't.'

'This may take us a little longer than anticipated, then. Do you have to go back to Paris today?'

'No, I'm going to stay in Reims until we work out where your husband is,' said Marc, who was still looking the two women up and down and thinking about the Countess's pungent perfume.

'I see that you are convinced of your success,' expressed Véronique. 'It pleases me to hear it. Guylaine can explain the background of Pierre's investigations better than I. She is a professor in history and has collaborated in her father's work.'

'That's right,' said the daughter. 'Although he hasn't always involved me in his research.'

'Which research are you referring to?'

'Generations of my family have spent centuries investigating the same subject. My father has pieced his ancestors' knowledge together but, although I grew up here, I haven't always had access to his investigations.'

'Let's talk about you first, Mr Mignon', said the Countess. 'Then my daughter will take you to see the monstrous talking head and will tell you all about my husband's investigations.'

It took Marc a few seconds to realise that this was not a suggestion but a demand. The Countess was used to getting her own way and he wondered how this had affected her relationship with the Count.

'Well, I belong to the Mignon Agency, which my grandfather founded and my father and uncle developed after him. Before working for my family's company, I worked for Greenpeace, doing all kinds of things like saving whales and taking care of bears in the North Pole.'

'How interesting. And where do you intend to begin your investigation?' asked the Countess, lighting a second cigarette.

'For cases like this, our agency has an established procedure. However, firstly I need to understand the background of the Count's investigations…'

'Of course, but do enjoy your lunch first. Then you can talk to my daughter, who will explain in detail the Dubois family's unique obsession.'

* * *

As Marc Mignon and Guylaine descended to the basement, the detective realised that the castle contained many hidden spaces. For the first time since he had arrived, Marc could no longer smell the Countess's distinctive perfume, which made him think that she had never come down here before.

The basement was very different to the rooms upstairs. The luxury of the living quarters above sharply contrasted with the medieval architecture and old grey stone found in this part of the castle. The gloom of this place reminded him of dungeons he had seen in American films about knights going into battle. He considered asking the young woman for a flaming torch like the ones he had seen in adventure films, where the hero explores the darkness of an ancient tomb. He stifled a laugh as Guylaine turned to him.

The detective's expression surprised her; he seemed to be smiling.

'I don't know what you find so funny.'

'Forgive me. This place makes me think of old adventure films.'

'I hope you're not a detective who imagines things. We need to concentrate on finding my father.'

I'm already putting my foot in it, thought Marc.

The light from inside the cavern was weak and golden. Marc saw part of the stone wall had been hammered away to make an opening.

'Why did your father choose to create a door right here?'

'He found old manuscripts revealing that there was a hidden room just behind here. My ancestors have been exploring the hidden recesses of this castle for centuries. My father is the first Dubois to work out that the great secret of the pope magician could be found just here.'

'Who is this pope?'

'Let's go in first and then we can talk,' said Guylaine. She was beginning to think that their choice of detective had not been the wisest of decisions.

Without touching the bare sides, Guylaine squeezed through the improvised door between the stone slabs. Marc followed her. Being larger than the young woman, his shoulders got wedged in the door, so he had to push himself through by kicking with his legs. He burst out of the gap into the cavern, bumping into Guylaine, who looked at him disapprovingly.

Just as he began to apologise, he finally saw the incredible contraption. He had not prepared himself for a sight such as this. Guylaine was pleased to see that the monstrous machine had managed to wipe that ridiculous smile off his face.

'I've never seen anything like it,' said the young man, finally.

'Well, start preparing yourself for more surprises. My father spent decades searching for this creature and, when he found it, he suddenly vanished. We need you to find out where he is.'

'Yes, of course…'

Marc could not look the cruel face of the monstrosity in the eyes.

He found a strange-looking chest, dragged it in front of the beast and invited Guylaine to sit down next to him.

'When you're ready, you can start explaining to me what the hell that is…'

'It's probably Satan himself. What do I know?'

'Just start from the beginning, please.'

'I'm sorry. My father's really very important to me. I'll try to explain the nature of his investigations and, if you wish, I will show you the letter he left before his disappearance. I think you should know all the ins and outs of my ancestors' studies before you read the note, as there are several references to my family's work in it.'

'Thank you. Please, carry on.'

'It all started one thousand years ago…'

CHAPTER 6

For the fourth time, the Countess dialled the same number. She looked out of the window. The grey afternoon had turned into a fierce storm. The lightning must have knocked the telephone station out of use. Her mobile wasn't working either, which added to her frustration. She had spent more than three days trying to get in touch with him.

She watched dazzling colours looming on the horizon. Although she was used to afternoons like this, the loud noise of thunder and the stark colour of the leaden sky disturbed her and allowed her imagination to indulge in fanciful ideas.

She had met Bruno two years ago. She thought his name sounded Italian. He certainly had a distinctive accent, which she had always attributed to his Moroccan roots. Young Bruno had explained to the Countess that he came from a poor background. He boasted that he developed his muscular physique at the expense of his studies. She was not sure she believed him—Bruno was the most sophisticated man she had ever met.

Her efforts to hide the secret of her young lover from her husband seemed to have worked; but above all, she did not want her daughter, who now seemed to be in the castle all the time, to find out about her affair. The Count was always travelling, either in the name of his investigations or to give a paper at some conference. Guylaine often had to stay overnight in Paris because of her job and, thanks to their combined absences, Véronique Dubois had enjoyed a second life with her young lover.

Bruno was truly unique. He was a tender, affectionate, subtle man and, best of all, he showered her with little gifts. In return, she had given him hundreds of presents over the course of their affair and he was always appreciative of these tokens of her affection. Bruno often took books from the castle library but would always return them to their original place and, on many occasions, commented on how much he had enjoyed what he had found there. Archaeology and medieval history were his favourite subjects; it was surprising how much he had in common with her husband.

While the Countess knew that Bruno liked her, sometimes, like the Count, he often seemed more interested in studying millennial subjects than in paying her attention. At first, Bruno would ask tentative questions about the Count's investigations, but over time he grew more confident and interrogated Véronique about her husband's discoveries. Every bundle of papers and manuscript he happened upon sparked his interest, as he tried to decipher their significance.

When the Countess realised that he had not phoned her for several days, she tried to call him. His phone always seemed to be disconnected. A sense of guilt began to creep over her.

She began to suspect that her young lover might be linked to her husband's disappearance.

* * *

Out of the back pocket of his trousers, Marc took a simple, leather-bound notebook that his uncle had given to him when he joined the agency. Guylaine watched as he recorded the date and hour and sat poised, ready for her to start recounting her family history.

The man finally seemed to be behaving like a proper private detective.

'It all started at the end of the first millennium,' she said, adopting a serious tone of voice. 'There are a series of people you should know about.'

'Please go on.'

'Halfway through the tenth century, around the year 950, one of the greatest geniuses that the world has ever seen was born. His name was Gerberto and he was born in the village of Aurillac. This man's wisdom astounded the people of the time, dazzling the aristocracy and Catholic Church alike. He captivated nobles and bishops to such an extent that when he was still very young, he became one of the most influential people of his day. In fact, he came to be so powerful that, backed by emperors and archbishops, he reached the position of Supreme Pontiff and, before the end of the millennium, became Silvestre II—the pope of the year 1000.'

'Very interesting,' said Marc, taking notes continually, genuinely engaged in the story. 'And was it this man who constructed the monster?'

'That's right. That's how the legend goes.'

'So, we have a pope who invented an incredible machine. When exactly was he pope?'

'His papacy lasted between 999 and 1003. At the end of his term, he died inexplicably. No one was able to determine the cause of his death, it was surrounded by mystery.'

'Yes, this seems to be a recurring pattern, but tell me more about how such a strange man came to be pope.'

'Gerberto was incredibly intelligent.' Guylaine tied her rich, long, blonde hair in a thick ponytail to make herself more comfortable. 'His mind demonstrated his mathematical brilliance through several groundbreaking discoveries. It was Gerberto who introduced the Arabic numerical system to Western culture.

'But I'm getting ahead of myself. I should start at the beginning. Our pope was born in a shack, to a humble peasant family. Legend has it that on the day he was born, great events took place. In his village, a pagan, cave-dwelling druid called Andrade predicted a great future for the child and passed on his Celtic knowledge.to him

'Instead of taking care of his father's herds, the young Gerberto spent hours studying the stars, and his mind began to blossom. One night, the abbot of a nearby monastery came across Gerberto, who was surrounded by animals, analysing the movements of the stars. The abbot asked him what he was observing and was struck by the young boy's intelligent response. Impressed by the young boy's mind, the abbot invited him to come to the abbey to complete his education. In those times, monasteries were the true home of scholarship. Under the supervision of the monks, our little peasant soaked up all the knowledge he could. He undertook the studies of a typical Benedictine monk, attending liturgical services and working in the school. He learnt to write on small boards and to sing through lessons with a precentor. The school also taught him Latin grammar, prompting his interest in Classics. His eagerness for learning stunned everyone, and, after only a short time in the abbey, he began learning the ancient discipline of Trivium—that is to say, grammar, rhetoric and dialectics.

'The time came when the abbey could no longer provide a suitable education for this exceptionally intelligent young man. However, due to the dangers involved in travelling at that time, it was not easy to send a monk from one place to another. A stroke of luck befell Gerberto though, and not for the first time in his life.

'Count Borrell of Barcelona passed through the town on one of his trips to France. He had come to marry Ledgarda, the daughter of Raimundo Pons, the Count of Rouergue. Fortunately for Gerberto, the Catalan nobleman stopped at the abbey when he visited the tomb of Saint Gerardo. During a conversation with the abbot, Count Borrell was told of the most gifted pupil in the whole monastery and how the young genius could go no further by studying with these monks.

'Spain at this time was practically all Muslim. Catalonia existed as a borderland, soaking up Arabic culture. In many of the Catalan monasteries, the monks had translated works from Syrian, Persian and other ancestral languages, texts that referred to astronomy, arithmetic, geometry and many other underdeveloped sciences in Europe. Gerberto was invited to Vic, in Catalonia, where he stayed for three years. There he continued his studies, furthering the education he had received through the study of the other sciences of

Quadrivium, composed of music, geometry, astronomy and arithmetic. It was at that time that the young pupil developed an exceptional mind for numbers, a passion that would stay with him for the rest of his life.

'At the end of this education, Gerberto travelled with Count Borrell and the bishop of Vic to Rome. In the holy city, extraordinary things happened to the travellers: the bishop was assassinated and Gerberto had a chance encounter with Emperor Otón I, a meeting that radically changed the young student's life. An exceptional friendship was born between Gerberto and the Emperor, a bond that he would share with the emperor's two descendants, Otón II and Otón III, men who became heavily involved with Gerberto's ascent to the throne of Peter.

'In Rome, Otón I asked Gerberto to give lessons to his son, the young heir, who was about sixteen. Gerberto's role as a teacher proved crucial in forging a close union with the future emperor. From there, Gerberto moved to our city, Reims. He stayed here for twenty-five years, driving forward the intellectual development of this region, initially as a teacher and then as a bishop. The education of the seven arts of the Middle Ages, those of the Trivium and the Quadrivium, would never be the same again.'

'And is there a relationship between his teachings and the ferocious machine that we have before us?' the young man asked, looking out of the corner of his eye at the malformed creature's horrifying face.

'Of course,' she responded quickly. 'In Reims, Gerberto wrote a treatise about tools of calculation using Arabic numerals, called *Regula de abaco computi*. Although it seems incredible that he could write this groundbreaking manual back in the middle of the tenth century, he did so, as well as constructing complex abacuses using no less than twenty-six positions, with which he could count up to four million. No one knows why he would have wanted to calculate such high numbers.'

'I didn't know any of this.'

'Well, it's all set down in fascinating detail in historical manuscripts.'

'And did Gerberto write down anything else related to this machine?' asked Marc, still taking notes.

'Well, not directly but in another way, yes. He compiled notes on geometry with remnants of Boecio's *Ars Geometriae*. In this text there were some practical guidelines, which he must have applied to some of the instruments in this room. He also wrote many treatises that were lost.'

'You mean, he wrote his own manifesto…'

'Yes, but he didn't show any interest in religious subjects. He was even less interested in sacred literature. He loved profane texts though, and secret books. In Spain, Rome and here in Reims, he ordered scores of treatises, considered immoral by the Catholics, to be sought out and translated.'

'Interesting.'

'Indeed. That's why my ancestors have been so keen to find the writings and inventions of Gerberto.'

'Has anyone else shown interest in this subject? Any individual or organisation?'

'As far as I know, there are many universities and professors, as well as writers, who have followed the work of Gerberto.'

'Well, I would like you to make me a full list of all of them.

Especially those who have shown a great deal of interest in the things we have in front of us.'

'OK. I'll prepare it for you straight away. I've finished my teaching at the university, so I have a bit more time.'

'Thank you. But you still haven't answered my question. How did a man like Gerberto come to be pope?'

'As I told you, after his meeting with the Emperor in Rome, he established a very strong friendship with the man. Otón I, and subsequently Otón II, gave him all the support he needed to become bishop. From Reims, Gerberto helped Hugo Capeto, Count of Paris, become King of France in the year 987, and so the old Carolingian dynasty was replaced. The Emperor accepted Gerberto into his court in 997, entrusting him with secretarial work and assigning him the role of personal advisor. Despite so many duties, Gerberto's papers from this time assure us that he continued working on his studies. For example, he constructed a nocturlabium[1] at that time, which impressed the members of the court greatly. When Pope Gregorio V died, Otón III tried to gain control of the pontiff and managed to instate Gerberto as pope.'

'I see. And Gerberto chose the name Silvestre II?' Marc interrupted.

'Correct. The name is very significant. If you remember, Silvestre I was the confessor for the Roman Emperor Constantine; I imagine Gerberto wanted his title to be Silvestre II because his protector, Otón III, was looking

---

[1] An instrument that calculates the rotation of stars to measure time.

to create a Roman Christian unified empire, an order of Catholic Europe.'

'So, this is how the monk came to power, at this pivotal moment?'

'Yes, precisely in the year 999, when humanity lived in fear of the end of the world.'

'But the world didn't end…'

'No, but strange events took place that this machine might be able to explain. Are you ready to hear about them?'

CHAPTER 7

Jean Luc Renaud felt sick as he thought about what had happened. He wasn't certain, but he believed that a group of people he had had contact with had something to do with the Count's disappearance.

He noticed that a storm had broken outside. It was an oppressive and dark afternoon. He crept into the darkness of the cellar, where the pungent smell of wine, thousands of bottles arranged neatly on wooden shelves, testified to the success of the Count's business. In the last few years, at least two, if not more, of the Count's champagnes had sold the largest amounts recorded by the Dubois family for years.

Jean Luc had spent his whole life with the Dubois family, ever since he finished his degree in medieval history, the same subject the Count had studied. The job of assistant to such an important medievalist as Pierre Dubois was one that Jean Luc couldn't refuse; the Count had an incomparable library, a family history filled with fascinating research and, above all, a genuine medieval castle to explore. His relationship with the Count had always been good. The Count treated him well, tolerated his flaws and paid him fairly. The idea of changing job had never even occurred to him.

Indeed, if any feature characterised Renaud, it was precisely his inability to make decisions. When faced with difficult circumstances, it was as if shackles bound him, stopping him from putting thought into action. Jean Luc liked to think that it was his perfectionism that held him back. It was during one such bout of indecision that he had first received help from two unexpected sources.

The Count and Renaud were carrying out an investigation in one of the oldest neighbourhoods in Reims. They had found original manuscripts from the Middle Ages that had pointed to a potential discovery in this part of town. The Count was away in New York, lecturing for a fortnight, but by phone he ordered his assistant to evict all the residents of an old property, which he believed sat on top of a site where invaluable and ancient papers could be unearthed.

To get to the hidden manuscripts, Jean Luc would have to throw a group of old-aged residents, who had lived on the estate for several generations, out into the vineyards. While he wondered about the best course of action, two mysterious young men, both dressed in tailored suits, offered to resolve his quandary out of the blue. The mysterious pair somehow persuaded the families to leave their homes without putting up the slightest resistance. The two men never asked Renaud for money in return for their services, only for information about his and the Count's investigations.

At first, he had thought they were either students of the Sorbonne interested in the Count's medieval research or journalists from some prestigious historical magazine, lying in wait for an exclusive. Now he wasn't sure. This was why he had come down to the cellar.

A bottle fell from one of the shelves in the cave and smashed on the floor, shattering into hundreds of pieces. The noise startled him and made him look up. It was then that he saw people at the back of one of the wine-ripening rooms.

'Is that you?' asked Renaud, directing his voice towards where the glass had broken. He could not see well in the darkness.

'It is us. We are here to help you again.'

'What do you want?'

'We have something to ask you,' said a cold, monotonous voice.

'Do you know where Pierre Dubois is?' The assistant's tone gave his nervousness away.

'Today we ask the questions, Jean Luc. We have come to hear about the information you have extracted from the machine and…'

'I don't know anything. The Count carried out his investigations alone, in secret.'

'Don't lie to us. We've come for your boss's papers and then you will help us take the mechanical head away from this castle.'

'I won't help you do that. The deal we made never extended to this,' cried Renaud.

'We've never asked for anything from you. The time's come for you to repay your debts.'

The echo of the hidden man's words made Jean Luc realise: the Devil had come to reclaim what was his.

CHAPTER 8

Marc had spent all afternoon working on the case. Outside, a storm was flooding the vineyards but the detective felt protected by the thick walls of the medieval castle.

'What you're telling me seems like the behaviour of a rational person,' Marc reflected.

'Exactly. What I have told you so far is, let's say, the documented part of Gerberto's life. However, the legends surrounding this pope, many of which have a sound historical basis, are very different,' explained Guylaine.

'Go on. I'm all ears,' he said, picking up his pen.

'To start with, the actual cenotaph of Silvestre II in Rome—the funeral stone erected in his memory—sweats when the current pope in office is going to die. Legend has it that, when a pontiff is close to death, the marble plaque secretes a substance similar to sweat and, inexplicably, grows moist. They say that this has happened upon the death of all the popes who have passed through the Vatican since Silvestre II himself died in mysterious circumstances.'

'I don't believe it,' said Marc, looking sceptical.

'Well, that's how it is. In fact, Silvestre II is very well known in religious circles because of this so-called miracle and, every time a Holy Father is taken ill, people flock to the stone in Rome to see if it really sweats. There are even those who say that when the pope is going to die, not only does the air grow humid around the tomb but noises, like the crack of bones against each other, can be heard from behind the marble plaque.

'And this is not a new phenomenon. Some centuries after the death of the French pope, in 1648, there were so many rumours about Silvestre II that they decided to settle the matter and open the tomb. What they found shocked them: the body was intact, with the pope's hands crossed over his chest. But suddenly, his remains turned into ash and a pungent smell spread through the air all about them.'

'I've never heard that.'

'It's a very old myth. And it is not the only one surrounding him,' Guylaine added. 'After his death, he was accused of making a pact with the Devil and practising witchcraft, although it's not possible to prove any of these things.'

'Of course.'

'After the death of Silvestre II, the attacks against him started. People grew suspicious of his exceptional intelligence. A humble man would never have been able to attain such intellectual brilliance had he not had supernatural assistance, people thought.'

'What do you mean?'

'They accused him of being involved with Satan. The first person to attack him was Cardinal Bennón of Osnabrück, who claimed that the pope magician asked the Devil to tell him the day that he would die and the Devil replied: "It will not be before you have celebrated mass in Jerusalem." This response calmed him for a while, but when they sent him to Santa Cruz of Jerusalem, which is the Roman basilica not far from Letrán in Rome, he suddenly felt unwell and realised that the prediction was coming true. And that was indeed where he died.'

'Rumours of witchery connected to the Vatican itself!'

'Well, it seems that suspicions of witchcraft were even more prevalent inside the Vatican. Do you remember I told you that Silvestre II died in unexplained circumstances?' asked Guylaine, continuing once Marc had nodded. 'Well, Sigberto, the Abbot of Gembloux, accused him of practising black magic and said that he was assassinated by the Devil.'

'Do you believe in Satan?'

'I'm Catholic so I believe in God and, yes, I also believe in Lucifer. They are two sides of one coin. How about you? Do you believe that a diabolical being lies in wait for us?'

'I'm not very religious, for want of a better word, and I've never believed in the Devil.'

'Well, for many people, including me, if you believe God exists, then so must the Devil.'

* * *

The telephone rang with a shrill tone. It seemed that the Countess would finally be able to speak to Bruno. She held her breath, waiting to hear her lover's voice.

'Hello, Véronique.' Bruno greeted her in a quiet, impersonal voice.

'You've abandoned me for days and now you greet me like this?' she cried.

'I've been very busy.'

'You know that my husband has disappeared and that my

daughter and I are going through a difficult time. I don't suppose *you* have anything to do with the departure of my husband?' she demanded.

'I don't understand how you could ask me that.'

'Because you're always snooping into Pierre's affairs. You've asked thousands of questions about his work, books and studies. And just when he finds that damned machine, you disappear as well. What did you want all that information for?'

'Purely for curiosity's sake.'

'At times I think that you've being stringing me along just to get closer to my husband's investigations. You've never been interested in me, have you?'

'That's not true. I'm very tied up at the moment. I'll call you when I have more time, I promise.'

'I want you to come here right now. I beg you.'

'Honestly, I can't,' he said, and ended the conversation.

The Countess threw the receiver against the wall. The broken pieces scattered across her marble floor.

CHAPTER 9

'Do you really believe that we ought to entertain the idea that the Devil is somehow involved with the machine and the disappearance of your father? It's odd that one of the prime suspects of my first case is Satan himself,' Marc thought, aloud.

'This is your first case?' Guylaine asked, clearly shocked.

'No, of course not. I was joking.'

'Oh. Well, I think that if we want to find my father, we have to understand what he was trying to say in his letter so we can trace the clues it contains. That's the normal procedure for detective work, isn't it?' she said.

'Yes, of course. But what makes you suspect that the Devil could play a part in this case?'

'I can't get this strange thought out of my head. When I found my father's letter, there was a strong smell of sulphur in the air. People say that sightings of the Devil are always preceded by a sulphurous stench.'

'Yes, I've heard that. Obviously, though, that's not easy to prove. People don't come across citizens of hell every day.'

'I thought I should let you know,' she warned. 'There are many references to the Devil in millenarianism as well.'

'Tell me all you know.'

'As I told you, my father is a millennial historian. At that time, Europe found itself going through a period of great change. The West had been in a tense period of stagnation ever since the collapse of the Roman Empire. Europe was a place of forests, tribes and witchery, where neighbouring kingdoms hated each other, constantly threatening one another's destruction. However, positive changes began to creep in towards the end of the tenth century. A cultural awakening, principally in writing, took place in the monasteries, as the monks dedicated themselves to translating ancient texts. Europe surfaced out of its profound depression, leaving the years of massacre, despair and death behind them.'

'But what are the historical facts that make you believe that the kind of extraordinary things you talked about actually happened in this period?'

'A French monk's work gives us the answer. His name was Raúl Glaber, a Cluniac clergyman who, in his scriptorium, recorded the millennium in great detail. He lived in many French monasteries but never settled; people described him as a vagabond and a wanderer. He wrote a series of five books, called the *Historiae*. Their value today is incalculable and through them he became one of the major scholars at the end of the first millennium.

'Throughout his life, he wrote in the shadow of the prophecies told in the Book of Revelation, which contained the message that one day life on earth would end. He believed that the apocalypse would take place on the one-thousandth year after the imprisonment of Satan and the birth of Christ. At this point, evil would invade the earth, disasters would blight the world and everything would cease to be. This is the basis of millennial thought, as chronicled by Raúl Glaber.'

'I've never heard of him,' declared Marc Mignon sceptically. 'Which particular mysterious events does he write about?'

'Horrific events,' answered Guylaine. 'According to him, God gave signs to everyone through dreams, visions and even miracles. The *Historiae* says that these signs predicted things to come, striking terror among thousands of people.'

'Can you give me a list?'

'A series of comets appeared, an event many scholars recorded. It was believed, throughout the Middle Ages, that sighting this phenomenon foreshadowed great change. One of those comets, which Glaber described in great detail, stayed visible in the sky for more than three months. It shined so brightly that many thought that God had sent a new star to announce the end of the millennium and the astonishing new times that were to come.'

'Well, yes, that does seem mysterious. But there could be several explanations for that comet.'

'I would agree, except that other things happened. There were extraordinary eclipses that different authors reported. Glaber says that the sky turned a sapphire colour as never seen before. As if this was not enough evidence for the apocalypse, there was an extraordinary lunar eclipse during which the moon turned a blood-red colour, which was followed by an abundant shower of meteorites.'

'How frightening it must have been for those poor people, so ignorant at the time.'

'And it didn't stop there,' she added. 'There were great epidemics that led to widespread starvation, adding further toil to those years, and also repeated sightings of sea monsters. Massive whales which had never before been known to travel to the Mediterranean waters brought yet more fear to the already panicked population. In other places, wolves terrorised the inhabitants of cities; people looked on in amazement as churches burst into flames when these animals approached them. Glaber describes a crucifix in a monastery that shed real tears in response to these events.'

'It doesn't surprise me that all of that caused panic. But where does the Devil come in?'

'Hold on. The Devil is one of the key figures in the work of Raúl Glaber. All his words stem from the sacred scriptures and, especially, the Book of Revelation. In Chapter 20, the text says, and I quote: *"Then I saw an angel coming down from heaven, holding the key to the bottomless pit and a large chain in his hand. He captured the dragon, that ancient serpent, who is the Devil and Satan, and tied him up for a thousand years."*

'This prophecy persuaded the people of the first millennium that, in the realm of the invisible, two forces were going to clash: Good and Evil. This supernatural war would take place at the end of the millennium, the moment in which satanic powers would be unleashed. The Devil would free himself from the ties of angelic forces. Millenarianism, above all, predicted the failure of divine forces and the return of the Devil, who would come back to earth to reclaim what was his. Raúl Glaber not only speaks of the Devil in his writings but also of three occasions where he witnessed evil apparitions. These encounters always happened at night or in the dim light of dawn. Lucifer showed himself to our monk in diverse forms as well. On one occasion, he appeared in the guise of a deformed dwarf, dark and infernal with a rough face, full of wrinkles and growths, a squashed nose, bulbous lips, a goatee and canine teeth. Another time, he presented himself in the guise of an Ethiopian and instructed Glaber to give up his work, leave the monastery and give in to earthly pleasures. This particular demon tried to dissuade him from sacrifices, penitence, fasting and vigils.'

'This prophecy of Revelation, is that what your father is referring to in his letter?'

'Yes, that's right.'

'And what point is he trying to make?'

'I've no idea. The part of the Book of Revelation my father is referring to says that an angel restrained the Devil, so he could not lead nations astray; yet, after one thousand years, Satan would be released. The truth is that I can't see a connection between the talking head and any of the topics of investigation carried out by generations of my family.'

'I see, but it's a clue that we have to investigate,' the detective noted.

'Yes, it's a good start,' said Guylaine. She pointed to an anagram etched into the marble stone pedestal beneath the enormous monstrosity. 'I haven't noticed that before; look at the symbol at the front.'

Marc approached and saw that someone had inscribed a pentagram there: the five-pointed star.

'Satan worshippers use this sign in rituals to invoke the Devil,' he said.

'Exactly, now you really *do* have a clue.'

'Yes, but it does make you shudder a bit.'

* * *

Véronique knew that she should not do what her heart asked of her. A woman with a social status as high as hers, in a relatively small city like Reims, should not go out into the street in search of a lover who had scorned her; especially one with a lost husband, who was God only knew where. Such ideas were useless, though; she had made the decision the very moment the young man had abandoned her. She stopped agonising over the correct course of action and grabbed her bag, determined to find answers.

CHAPTER 10

'There are things in all of this that I can't get my head around,' reflected Marc. 'Maybe the Devil helped the pope with many of the things he achieved in his life, but…where did he get the knowledge to construct the machine that we have before us?'

'Good question. In recounting the whole dark legend of Silvestre II, I haven't told you about his supposed contact with the Arabs. We know that the young Gerberto lived in Vic, Catalonia for three years, between 967 and 970. There he had great teachers and met wise mathematicians. The monastery's library had a good reputation at the time: Santa Maria of Ripoll was where Arabic works of arithmetic, astronomy and geometry had been translated. During his years in Spain, the future pope acquired a great deal of knowledge from the most transcendental books of Middle Eastern and Indian culture.'

'That all seems understandable.'

'I know, but don't forget one very important thing. At that time in history, Spain was a melting pot of different cultures. Arabs, Jews and Christians lived among one another. Of all of them, those who excelled at science were, by far, the Arabs. And the border to the Arab world lay next to Catalonia.

'The story goes that Gerberto crossed the border and

there first acquired his Islamic wisdom. The young monk's thirst for knowledge was unquenchable and his first contact in Christian Spain could have been with Muslims, who convinced him that, in order to procure deep wisdom, he would have to travel to Córdoba, the great metropolis of the West, taken from the Romans by Muslims in 716. By the middle of the tenth century, the capital of Andalucía, and of Spain itself, was a powerful place, attracting all the great thinkers. Many languages were spoken there, although Science, with a capital letter, had at that time only one language: Arabic. Over centuries, the Muslims had become particularly attracted to Greek and Persian sciences and translated into their own language the majority of ancient works that had been lost in Europe. Moreover, these people had always been in contact with India and China, while in the West, they had to wait for Marco Polo, who, two hundred and fifty years later, embarked on the first commercial voyages to those foreign lands. The Arabs spent many years absorbing the scientific advances of those distant climes.

'So, their knowledge of astronomy was centuries ahead of ours; while we were involved in horrific wars, they dedicated themselves to naming stars that we didn't even know existed. They already used terms such as "zenith", "azimuth" and "astrolabe", amongst others. Their arithmetic and mathematical knowledge was also considerably more advanced than ours at that time. Most significantly, it was the Arabs who began to use the concept of zero, which had been imported from India and enabled the use of a numeric system similar to the one we use today.

'Gerberto probably travelled to Córdoba hoping to

study at its most famous library, which, in those days, had more than three hundred thousand volumes, probably the largest collection in the world. The Caliph Abderraman never stopped buying books, especially those by classic authors containing ancestral wisdom. Furthermore, he had hand-copied versions of the valuable texts from Baghdad, Alexandra and Cairo, the other centres of learning at the end of the first millennium. The greatness of Muslim Europe spread to the rest of the continent. Most European leaders sent ambassadors to make contact with the source of this advanced learning. In the year 974, the German Emperor Otón II, who, as I have already told you, was closely linked to Silvestre II, decided to send a delegation to a recently constructed palace in Córdoba: Medina Azahara. They say that when the Emperor's ambassadors arrived, they knelt before the people they thought were receiving them at the palace. It was explained to them later that they had bowed to the servants of the prince's secretary, who had probably given a false impression of their rank because of the ostentatious clothing they were wearing.

'Aside from all this, there were those who said that Gerberto may have robbed the most hidden secrets of this ancient world collected in the city of Córdoba.'

'You mean the machine could contain secrets stolen from the library in Córdoba,' he repeated, trying to keep up with Guylaine's narrative.

'That's right. We probably have here, before us, the machine that a French monk constructed with the plans, books, texts and knowledge of ancient wisdom, which he plundered from the Arabs.'

'I think I'm beginning to understand,' said Marc.

'In fact,' Guylaine continued, 'there is evidence that very sophisticated machines were constructed from the knowledge of old civilisations. A two thousand-year-old astronomical calculator has recently been found in Greece. It's called the Antikythera mechanism and the device contains one hundred cogs and pieces that can calculate the orbit of many stars with surprising precision. The scientists who are studying this discovery believe it is the oldest example ever found, but it's not as old as the example we have in front of us.'

'So Leonardo da Vinci was not the first man to develop such strange machines?'

'That's right. Incredible contraptions like this had been around for centuries. Gerberto may have robbed plans from the Arabs but perhaps he exchanged them for some of his own fascinating discoveries. It doesn't surprise me that, although he may also have acquired some occult knowledge, Gerberto ended up making a much more elaborate artefact than that found in the original plan.'

'Well, I've got a good understanding of the subject now: the Devil, the Arabs, the ancient wisdom…it's about fitting the pieces of the puzzle together,' said Marc.

'But don't forget that your main task is to find my father.'

'Of course, that's my job. Do you want to tell me anything else?'

'Actually, as you can imagine, there's a lot more. I've only given you a summary of a turbulent period of history. Millenarianism is a movement that studies the uncertainty caused by the passing of a thousand years. Do you remember the 2000 effect, the last change of century and how—'

'Yes, of course. I was in the United States then. People there were concerned about what could happen to computers with the change to the year 2000, everyone thought it could bring the world to its knees.'

'Then imagine how people would react in a medieval, uncultured society, dominated by religious fear,' she added. 'When the year 999 approached, people started to think that the end of the world was just around the corner, that everything would end there. Superstition was rife and even the Book of Revelation in the Bible predicted the apocalypse.'

'But it's nothing to be scared of. In the end, it would simply mean exchanging one set of numbers for another, going from 999 to 1000,' reflected Marc.

'No, you're wrong, I'm afraid it wasn't that simple. Don't forget that in those times, they still hadn't introduced Arabic figures to any European country. With the 2000 effect, yes, it was just a case of passing from one figure to another, but during the change of the first millennium, things were very different.'

'Why?'

'Because Roman numerals were still in use. It meant passing from the extremely long figure DCCCCXCIX to a new value.'

'So you believe there was a "1000 effect"?'

'Of course.'

'And what number did they pass to?'

'To a simple, single Roman number: the year M.'

CHAPTER 11

The Countess had decided to follow Bruno. She knew that she ran a big risk, pursuing a man through a city where the Dubois family were so highly regarded. But in the busy bar in the centre of Reims, an old tavern from which she could see the impressive Notre Dame cathedral, she could go unnoticed while observing the group of friends Bruno had met up with. They seemed to be a group of young North Africans talking about girls, football and motorbikes. There wasn't a woman among them. This calmed her jealous temper.

The storm had passed, leaving behind a mild, starry evening. The Countess thought she would enjoy a glass of vermouth at one of the outside tables. She chose a comfortable seat from which she could watch the movements of the group through a window. She tried to relax, tried to convince herself she was doing nothing wrong sitting there; if she met anyone she knew, she'd have to make up some excuse for why she was drinking alone.

The tranquillity of the tavern and the calming qualities of her drink set her mind back to the evening that she had first met the Count. She had not been much older than twenty. They met at a charity event on the top floor of the Hilton hotel in Paris. She had never seen the Eiffel Tower before, and from such a privileged spot. The Countess aspired to a life of luxury. So when a nobleman, from one of the most famous champagne houses, offered her a glass of the celebrated wine, she quickly accepted the first, second and even fifth glass—as far as she could remember.

Back then, Pierre Dubois was considered one of the most eligible bachelors in the whole country. On a drunken whim, the Count reserved a room for them both in the Hilton. The couple didn't emerge from the opulent suite until lunchtime the following day. Their first night together was one of the most important in the Countess's life. The room that the Count had chosen that night was magical; they made love for the first time in the shadow of that illuminated tower, the symbol of Paris.

The rest all happened very quickly. After a little over two weeks he asked her to marry him and, in the space of three months, they wed and set up home together in one of the most well-known castles in all of France. She relished the luxurious pleasures that she had always desired and dreamed of as a little girl, which the city of her birth, Bordeaux, had never given to her.

A year later their only daughter, Guylaine, was born, and from then on their lives continued rather routinely. Their marriage suffered as her husband indulged the same obsession as his ancestors, trying to unravel the mysteries of the end of the first millennium to find that absurd head created by the French pope.

She had forgotten the last time she and the Count had been intimate, since he had devoted himself almost exclusively to his studies. For years, she had thought about asking him for a divorce and starting her own independent life. She was always dissuaded by how well Pierre had drawn up their marriage contract; he had been careful to ensure that any such separation would return her to the poverty of her life before they had married.

Into her lonely life, young Bruno had come along, elegant, refined, sweet and, above all, possessed of free time in which to make her happy. He helped her to forget the afternoons, nights and weekends that her husband spent in unpronounceable places looking for traces of that damned pope magician.

The waiter came over to see if she wanted another drink. She nodded and then turned her head to look carefully at each one of the members of her lover's group. Two of them were a similar age to Bruno. Another, with grey, curly hair, must be a little older, she thought. The third, a mature man with dark skin and thick, healthy hair, looked familiar. She tried to remember where she had seen him last. Her heart skipped a beat when she realised that he was one of the workers from the castle, a labourer who had been employed to repair the cellars and had left of his own accord, on the exact same day Pierre had disappeared.

Véronique managed to calm herself with a second glass of vermouth, almost downing it in a second. She scrutinised the members of the group again, establishing that it really was the man she feared it was. Should she report what she had seen to the detective? It was evident that there was some kind of connection between that man and her lover. But in order to do so, she would have to reveal her relationship with the young man, exposing her affair. She felt deeply uneasy.

She took a last sip of her drink, but the glass was already empty. She realised that the men were exchanging papers. She paid special attention to a scruffy blue file that Bruno was holding. Inside, there were old leaves of paper that had been ripped out of books. From a distance, she could make out a couple of manuscripts that could have been taken from the Count's own immense collection of papers. Damn the day that she allowed Bruno access to her husband's office!

She left the tavern in a hurry. She knew that she was not going to be able to sleep all night. She would have to come up with a plausible explanation so that the detective could spy on these people without him discovering the secret of her shameful relationship.

Out of nowhere, an idea of how to tackle the problem dawned on her and she began to smile.

CHAPTER 12

Marc took one last look around, as he left his hotel room, in case he had forgotten something. The Countess had offered him a suite in the castle where he could work in comfort without wasting time on pointless journeys. She had also given him an interesting lead. Weeks ago, one of the North African labourers employed in the cellars had asked lots of questions about her husband's investigations and had then left, of his own free will, on the exact same day the Count had disappeared.

He closed his bedroom door and made his way outside to the Boulevard Paul Daumer. He had chosen this place as it was really close to the motorway and only a few minutes from the cathedral of Reims. His car was parked on the road in the next block.

From a distance, he could see that someone was inspecting the inside of his car, a dirty, old, black Peugeot. In fact, it was covered in such a thick layer of grime that the man looking over his car could barely see in through the windows. Marc watched him, trying to guess what on earth he wanted. He supposed it was just another Parisian crook trying to rob him.

Marc ran over as quickly as he could. The noise of his footsteps startled the man, who ran swiftly away down a side street. Marc followed him down Rue Venise, his heartbeat quickening as he gave chase. He was closing on him when he realised that the crook was very young, almost a child. The boy looked scared to see someone bigger, and considerably burlier, pursuing him. Marc stopped to let the boy go, thinking it was obviously some local tearaway, a young Moroccan or Algerian boy. The boy took this lucky break and tore down Rue de Capucins.

It was only while he was catching his breath that he recalled what the Countess had told him about the North African worker employed in the castle, and the possible implication of Islamic groups in the Count's disappearance. He couldn't get the idea out of his head. It was clear that someone had been following him.

* * *

Although the incident had unsettled him, Marc still had a whole day of investigations ahead of him. He had to interrogate the Count's assistant, Jean Luc Renaud.

From the very instant he had first met him, Jean Luc had made him feel uneasy; he seemed timid and reserved, one of those people who always seemed to be hiding something. Marc knew that he should patiently try to coax information out of him, as he would definitely know more about the Count's activities than anyone else. Even though the Countess maintained that Jean Luc was devoted to his superior and would collaborate wholeheartedly, Marc still had his doubts.

Renaud bounded in with a bulging file under his arm. The detective noticed that he was dressed in a rather old-fashioned manner and that his oversized, checked bow tie lent him an aristocratic English air.

'I would like to carry out this meeting in your office and also visit the Count's workplace, if you don't mind,' said Marc.

'Absolutely,' Renaud replied immediately. 'If it will help you, it would be my pleasure to show you to our offices.'

Marc followed him to a maze of rooms in the upper parts of the castle. He noticed that this part of the medieval fort looked very different to the rooms in the living quarters. It seemed that, on coming up here, they had gone back in time by about a century.

'The Count wanted to move our offices here some months ago. He said he was convinced that if we were surrounded by all this medieval architecture, we would be inspired to find new clues. And he was right...' the assistant said, looking melancholic when recalling his master.

'Why, what did you find?' asked the detective, constantly looking around him. He felt nervous.

'We found some tenth-century manuscripts written by a monk who had worked side by side with Gerberto d'Aurillac, the pope...'

'...magician. Yes, I already know who he was.'

'These documents contained a large amount of data about public spaces in the ancient city of Reims and the surrounding area, including plans of all the historic buildings. The Count later investigated each and every one to discern exactly where the talking head could be found. Thanks to those papers, he had a breakthrough that came to him while he was working at dawn in the highest tower of the castle.'

'Could we go there now?'

'Of course, follow me,' responded the Count's assistant without hesitation.

They passed through Renaud's impeccably kept office. The masses of papers piled up on his table were arranged in perfect symmetry, as if he had measured the distances between the files in millimetres. A group of pencils lay neatly aligned on the table, each placed at the exact same distance from one another.

'The cleaning lady doesn't move your things then?' asked Marc, gently mocking the man.

'No one comes in here except me. And the Count, of course.'

They continued into Pierre Dubois' office, Marc realising that the assistant's room acted as an antechamber to the space where his master worked. The nobleman's office was much larger than that of his employee and radically different. Disorder and anarchy dominated. Hundreds of manuscripts, documents and papers were strewn haphazardly everywhere; not even the computer screen was properly visible under the yellow reminder notes stuck to the edge of the monitor.

'We could sit here. It seems comfortable enough,' proposed the detective, carefully moving a group of papers.

'Yes, this is the Count's favourite place,' said Renaud.

'Well, make yourself comfortable and tell me all you know,' Marc said.

'Look, Monsieur Mignon, you can rely on me. There is nothing I want more than to find my master and discover the truth about what happened to him. I have always stood by the Count of Divange's side. I have dedicated my professional career entirely to him.'

'Good, as I expected. Please explain to me everything that has happened in the last few weeks.'

The assistant's account sounded convincing and backed up the statement given by the Count's daughter. The story was familiar to Marc so his attention began to drift and, just as he stopped listening to the assistant entirely, Renaud said the word 'devil'.

'What did you say? Could you repeat it? Start from the beginning of that last bit, please.'

'For some years now, we have been receiving special help in our investigations…'

'Tell me in minute detail.'

'It arrived unexpectedly. It was in the course of some inquiries into Gerberto's time as a cathedral teacher in Reims.

'On one of these occasions, we needed to demolish a very old building in order to excavate the ground beneath it. However, the property still had people living in it. By chance, I met two people who quickly solved the problem, without the need for the Count or myself to intervene. It was incredibly lucky meeting them like that. They helped us considerably. All I can tell you is that when we finished removing the foundations of that extremely old building, we found some of the manuscripts that enabled us to find the precise location of the talking head.'

'And who were those people? Could you describe them?'

'Truthfully, I know very little about them. They always appear as a pair and, on all of the occasions in which we have met, they have asked to carry out their tasks without much light, in partial darkness, although I couldn't tell you why. They dress well and are highly educated. We've always needed them to help us achieve the goals of our investigations and they have never asked for anything. Well, at least until now.'

'What are you talking about? What have they asked for?'

'Nothing... I didn't mean to say that.'

'But you did say it. Please answer the question. What did those people ask for?' The detective tried to look him in the eye, but the Count's assistant evaded his gaze.

'Please forget what I just said; I didn't express myself very well. These people have helped us and that's all that matters.'

'I don't believe you. Do you know where I can find them?'

'No, I haven't the faintest idea, but I promise you that, when it comes to them, I will tell you all I know.'

The assistant tightened his lips; he had decided not to say another word for the moment. The detective gave him a hard look to put pressure on him. When the silence became unbearable, Renaud got up and hurriedly left the room. Marc jotted down in his notebook the obvious: Jean Luc Renaud knew something.

* * *

Marc walked down the corridor which led to the living quarters of the castle. While he considered what he had learnt from his interview with Jean Luc, the detective bumped into the lady of the house, who asked him how his investigations were progressing.

'Countess, I already have some solid clues.'

'Please, call me Véronique, I don't like to seem so distant and aristocratic. I'm not much older than you. Besides, noblemen and women are flesh and blood too. I don't come from a blue-blood family myself. Let's say that I have been adopted by this lavish world. Just a little piece of advice: don't let titles impress you for one second.'

'Don't worry, I've met people from all classes and orders in my life.'

'Really? You'd make an impression on anyone, I suspect. Are you happy in what you do?' The woman lit an American cigarette; her crimson lipstick stained its white tip.

'Yes. I'm very optimistic about this case. I believe we're going to find your husband soon. Why do you ask?'

'I don't know. Perhaps there's an ounce of wickedness in me.' She took a deep drag and slowly exhaled the smoke. 'I like to disconcert young people.'

She left him to retire to her room. Behind her, the air in the hallway was suffused with the smell of cigarettes and her characteristic, subtle perfume.

* * *

He let himself into his room in the castle; a pleasant surprise. The room was large, light and, above all, comfortable. Over the years, he had become accustomed to sleeping in makeshift beds, like a narrow sleeping bag on the deck of a boat, so he couldn't have been more pleased with the bedroom he had been given. It was comforting that the Countess, his client, had shown her support over the course of the investigations and her daughter seemed convinced that he could solve this complex mystery.

Plus, he already had two decidedly solid leads.

Firstly, it was evident that there was a North African group who, in one way or another, were interfering in the investigation. He couldn't stop thinking about that young boy trying to look inside his car, probably to see whether there was something to steal…the Count's documents perhaps. They had probably got someone to follow him; somewhere there was someone who was interested in knowing the movements of a detective contracted by the family of the missing Count. But there was more to investigate. Since Guylaine had explained to him the complete history of the pope magician, he couldn't forget the possibility that Silvestre II had robbed secrets from the Arabs in Andalucía and that now, much later, someone could be trying to reclaim them. Was that possible? The idea was difficult to get his head around, but not crazy.

Secondly, he had an equally important clue in the assistant Renaud who, he was convinced, was hiding something significant to the case. As soon as possible, he must investigate the people who had helped the Count find the mechanical creature. It seemed absurd to think that the Devil to be behind all this; Marc did not believe either in him or in the existence of paranormal beings. The loss of his parents at a very young age had made him understand how harsh the world could be. As a result, he was more concerned with earthly matters than possible dark underworlds. Either way, the clues available opened various doors that made him think that the case—his first—could be solved.

But there was something else. Guylaine had made a real impression on him. At first, he had thought that she was the typical daughter of a nobleman—an aristocrat who was remote from normal citizens. For a nomad like him, it was important that the people around him were in touch with the real world and understood life's everyday problems. The Countess and her daughter appeared down to earth to him, especially Guylaine, with whom he had spent many hours. Now he couldn't get her out of his head. He lay down on the large bed and let his imagination run free.

CHAPTER 13

Light shone faintly through the middle of the black clouds. Jean Luc Renaud peered out at the overcast sky. The storm that had raged for several days showed no sign of respite and it looked like the impending downpours would flood the countryside for yet another day.

He thought about the predicament he had somehow got himself into. He hated situations he couldn't control, so he couldn't understand how he had landed himself in this mess. But that's the way things now stood and he had to get out of it as best he could. The two strange men had decided that their new meeting must take place near the city of Epernay, a few kilometres from Reims; the exact location they had chosen for the appointment was the Abbey of Hautvillers. The site was truly original: the tomb of the Benedictine monk, Dom Pierre Pérignon, who discovered the method for producing champagne, was found there.

Renaud entered the city through a narrow road, bordered on both sides by millions of vines belonging to one of the most prestigious cellars of the area. He imagined that under these lands there must be hundreds of tunnels that wine-producers would use to mature wine. It was a drink he knew little about; in fact, he had never even tasted a single drop of alcohol.

He did not fancy meeting up with these people again, although, after that difficult meeting with the detective, who had got practically everything he knew out of him, he should keep in touch with them until they revealed the whereabouts of the Count. It was evident that the detective employed to find the nobleman was shrewd and would constantly be hot on his heels.

As before, the site chosen was dark—perfect if one wished to pass unnoticed. It would never have occurred to him to arrange a meeting in a spot like this. It was incredibly secluded. The meeting was to be held at the tomb of Dom Pérignon himself.

Although he had arrived on time, as he always did when he had an important appointment, Renaud did not see anyone outside the abbey. He couldn't tell in the faint light whether there was someone there or if they had already entered and were waiting for him next to the monk's enclave. He slipped into the darkness of the chapel and looked for a stone plaque announcing the resting place of the man who invented champagne. Eventually, he found an enormous, black marble plaque. Minutes passed and nobody appeared. He looked at his watch again and saw that he had already waited for half an hour after the appointed meeting time. To pass the time, he read the memorial stone to learn something about a renowned person about whom he knew very little. The silence was broken by the whistle of the church door. Someone was coming in. He turned around and that's when he saw them.

Through the shadows of the altar, two men advanced towards him. Trembling and suspicious, Renaud cleared his throat. Although he was afraid, he confronted them.

'You're very late.'

'We had a spot of trouble on the way. You're in good company though: no less than the monk who put the bubbles in champagne.'

'I know little about wine.'

'Well, you *should* know the story of Dom Pérignon, who has enabled your master to make a lot of money. His wine cellar is one of the most lucrative in France.'

'I dedicate myself to other matters. What is it you want from me this time?'

'The same thing that we asked you for at our last meeting. We want the notes that the Count has made about the machine, the results of his investigations in the days after the discovery of the talking head. We also want you to help take all of the contraptions out of the castle cavern without raising suspicion.'

'That's impossible. To begin with, the Count did not leave a single note before his departure, except the letter, which only explained that he had left. Also, it would be impossible to take the head from there; it is far too big to fit through the entrance that has been made in the castle wall. It would be dangerous to open up the hole even more—it's a retaining wall for the foundations of the ancient fort. The machine measures more than two metres wide and high; it would be impossible to remove it from there without destroying it. And I understand that you don't want to see it destroyed.'

'Absolutely not. We want to help you resolve the problems that could arise when the machine is set in motion. For years, we have assisted you with everything we could and now we want no more than to carry on being helpful in your search for the Count. Whatever you need from us, you only have to ask; we will always be nearby. Don't forget that.'

'Are you holding the Count? Do you know where he is?' asked Renaud, distressed.

'We ask the questions. You ought to dedicate yourself to furthering the Count's investigations and making the talking head work. That's our aim and it should also be yours.'

'But I don't understand,' whispered the assistant. 'You could at least tell me why that machine is so important to you and why you're so desperate to make it work.'

'It seems incredible that you can't see something so simple,' one of the men said. 'More than one thousand years ago, that mechanical creature you have in the castle was just a collection of inanimate objects, empty tubes and buttons that could do nothing. Back then, it was a machine without a soul.

'Silvestre II found answers to millennial secrets, having dedicated his life to the study of ancient wisdom. He then applied his findings to the talking head, which he had constructed years before without being able to make it function as he had wished. With that knowledge, he set the perfect being in motion, inside which thousands of years of scientific learning can be found.'

'I just don't understand,' repeated Renaud.

'That's obvious. God and the concept of Good have dominated human history; you can't see past it. Anything in opposition to these things has always been considered evil.'

'And how does the machine fit into all this?'

'We believe that it is the Antichrist,' the man replied. 'Its power is immeasurable.'

CHAPTER 14

The day began with splendid sunshine that pierced through the lavish curtains of one of the larger rooms in the castle.

If all of my detective jobs are like this one, I might carry on in this career, Marc was thinking.

A quick jog around the grounds would do him good and would give him a chance to reflect on the course of events after the Count's disappearance. In the hall he bumped into Guylaine, who was on her way to the dining room. The girl kissed him on the cheek, wishing him good morning.

'If you want, we can meet when you get back from your run to analyse my father's letter, as we discussed,' she said.

'Of course. I'm only going to run for a couple of kilometres and I'll come right after. Will you wait to have breakfast with me?'

'Yes, I'll wait in the kitchen with my father's note.'

* * *

When he had covered a resasonable distance, a strange noise from behind his back surprised him. Véronique was driving a little electric car that reminded him of a golf buggy. The woman gestured for him to get in.

'I'll take you back. You've already run far enough,' said the Countess, smiling. 'I imagine that maintaining that body of yours takes a lot of work.'

Marc stepped in next to her, thinking she looked very refined at the wheel.

'I enjoy exercise. It keeps me in shape and—'

'And helps you get kisses from the girls, like the one my daughter gave you today?'

'What? That was just a polite greeting. That's how I took it anyway,' he replied, slightly annoyed.

'Don't worry. I love to wind people up. Perhaps it's because I get envious seeing people younger than me getting close to one another.'

The Countess's hearty laughter made him realise that here was a woman free from the strict codes of noble behaviour.

* * *

After a reviving shower, Marc met Guylaine for breakfast.

'Here's the note my father left. Would you like to see it?'

'Of course. It's an essential clue to help us find him.'

The handwriting was shaky. The almost illegible script didn't seem fitting for a person of noble upbringing.

'Is this his normal handwriting?' asked the detective, taking a bite of croissant.

'That is his handwriting but it's clear that the letter was written in haste. There are paragraphs that even I find difficult to read,' she said, passing her finger over the spidery writing.

'Why did he write it so quickly? That's something I don't understand: if a person had decided to leave, for whatever reason, they would write much more than this. Don't you think?'

'Yes, I agree. I don't remember any of my father's writing being so rough. They are definitely his words though.'

'So, you're sure he wrote the letter?' the detective asked.

'Yes, I think so. The signature leaves no room for doubt.'

'But could it have been dictated? Might someone have pressured him to write these strange words?' asked Marc.

She took a few seconds to respond, so the detective poured himself more coffee.

'I don't know,' said Guylaine, although she had understood what he meant. 'His messy handwriting could be down to his sense of urgency. Perhaps he was desperate to follow the trail of his investigation wherever it was about to take him. When my father is excited by something, he is unstoppable. He's a very special man.'

'Yes, I can imagine. But he could have been coerced. Don't take it badly, but it is a possibility. Someone could have entered that cave downstairs and made him write these words by threatening him. Does that seem absurd?'

'No, not at all. My mother and I have both considered it and we told the police our concerns. It's hard to believe that my father would leave without saying goodbye, to me anyway, so I've not discounted that possibility. In fact, I explained it to the inspector on various occasions in the days after my father's disappearance, but he took no notice.'

'Well, it can only be one of two things: either he left or he has been kidnapped. And what about the contents of the letter?'

'Yes, there are some interesting ideas in there,' the

Count's daughter responded. 'My father calls the machine Baphomet.'

'What's that?'

'The talking head of Silvestre II disappeared when the pope died. Nobody knew what became of it or whether it had even ever really existed. Numerous legends about its existence were dreamed up over the following centuries until the inquisition of the Order of the Knights Templar on Friday the thirteenth of October 1307, when many Templars were arrested and subjected to a trial lasting several years. Over the course of the interrogations, some of them referred to a head *in figuram baffometi* or "in the form of Baphomet". Not all of the Knights Templar worshipped the deity; it seems that only some people high up in the ranks of the Order knew of its existence. Unfortunately, we know nothing more about the Baphomet of the Knights Templar. The word reappeared centuries later, when a scholar of dark arts, Eliphas Lévi, painted an image of Baphomet.'

'What else does the letter say?' asked the detective.

'To begin with, it says that the creation of the machine is a product of witchcraft, which is strange because my father didn't believe in the occult. He also says that the machine works through a combination of art and science, under the spell of a powerful sorcerer.'

Marc read the text carefully.

'The note doesn't really say much at all. I reckon he's trying to tell us that there is a witch inside the creature that makes it work.'

'Yes, but my father writes things here that don't fit with his character. He didn't believe in the supernatural. He has always taught me to believe only in that which can be demonstrated through science,' added Guylaine. She looked sad and uncertain. 'Let's focus on the next part of the note, which blames the Devil for all of this mess.'

'I didn't want to tell you but I think you have a right to know,' said Marc, adopting a more serious tone. 'You must keep it to yourself. Do you promise?'

'Of course, you already know you can trust me.'

'I believe that the Count's assistant, Jean Luc Renaud, has been in contact with people who could be involved in satanic circles.' He stopped to watch the woman's reaction.

'That's absurd.'

'It might sound so, but it isn't. You know that I don't believe in such things either, but he has told me himself that for some years he has been in contact with people who have offered him free, special assistance, which has helped the Count to find that damned machine.'

'Renaud is a faithful employee to my father. I find it hard to believe that he has done anything dishonest.'

'That's exactly it. He hasn't done anything wrong. He has only tried to help his master with what he wanted most in the world: to find the pope's strange machine. In the process, Renaud has been in contact with a group of people we should keep an eye on. According to him, they may be close to the Devil. The Count even refers to this in his letter. It was you who first spoke of the Devil and his relationship with Silvestre II.'

'And what are you going to do about it?' she asked. She began to cry.

'We'll investigate them. I need to know who they are and

what information they have. They could be a key piece of this puzzle.' He picked up a fine linen napkin to dry Guylaine's tears. 'Please don't cry. Let's try to move the case forward. I think that we are close to finding the truth. Trust me.'

'OK,' said Guylaine. 'The next sentence in the letter I consider to be the most worrying.

'*It has been hard work understanding this terrible monster's various riddles to find their meanings—my mathematical knowledge is good but not as advanced as the mind of Pope Silvestre II. For a while, I believed that the head would respond to simple and mundane questions. But I was wrong. A perfect mathematical model—half science, half sorcery—leads unambiguously to a final answer. The talking head first announced it in the year one thousand—it says the same now. The end of the world has come.*'

'What did he mean by this?'

'It's the most important part of the letter, but it doesn't tally with any of my ancestors' investigations. As far as I know, Silvestre II was a great mathematician. But I don't know how he devised a model to predict the future—to predict the apocalypse.'

'I know,' Marc replied. 'I can't understand how a man with the scientific mind of the Count would believe this piece of junk and come to the conclusion that the world would end. What kind of information did he get out of that damned machine?'

'If we knew that, we would have solved the case and perhaps my father would not still be missing,' she said, bursting into tears again.

'You must try to keep calm. We are going to find him, don't doubt it for a second. Please carry on. How does the letter end?'

'In the last lines it says that we are not to follow him, because he must sort things out alone,' said Guylaine, wiping away her tears.

'It seems that your father donned a superhero's cape and has decided to save the world.'

'I've thought about it a lot. I think he has obtained intelligence from the pope himself, perhaps millennial secrets, and knows where he can find other information to solve the mystery, which could be a prophecy or something like that.'

'What a muddle! What the hell could that invention contain?' exclaimed Marc.

'That's what I'd like to know.'

'Could you make the machine work?'

'Definitely not.'

There was a pause in the conversation. A waiter offered them more orange juice, interrupting the silence. He left when they both declined.

Marc took the opportunity to analyse the woman's face. Her nose, small and well proportioned, was an exact replica of her mother's. However, the full lips of the Countess were not mirrored in her daughter; Guylaine had the same sensitive mouth as her father. In any case, both women's hair, blonde, elegant and noble, crowned them perfectly. The intense fragrance of the Countess's perfume, which trailed behind her wherever she went, was not at all like the sweet, youthful aroma on her daughter's skin.

She realised that he was examining her. She arched her eyebrows reproachfully but with a faint smile on her lips.

'And now what are you going to do, detective?' she enquired.

'We have various clues to follow up. We have to investigate Renaud's peculiar friends and some strange people that have been following me for some reason. They must have something to do with the Count's disappearance.'

'That all seems worth exploring,' said Guylaine. She was pleased with the man's work.

'Yes, but first I have to get everything straight in my head.'

CHAPTER 15

One by one, Renaud listed the exact locations where his meetings with the strange men had taken place and, when the detective put more pressure on him, added that they had always chosen dark, private and gloomy places for these conversations, places where they were protected by shadow. Now Marc Mignon had five precise locations where he could investigate sightings of them. He had planned to make a number of inquiries in the North African areas of the city with the intention of finding the boy who he had caught looking in his car. He had also come across a potentially significant piece of evidence: a photograph of the worker mentioned by the Countess. The detective took to the road.

He drove though the vineyards that were familiar now, compared with how disorientated he felt when he first arrived. Marc felt settled in the castle; the Dubois family were treating him well and had provided him with two solid clues to help find the lost nobleman. The case seemed like it wouldn't be all that difficult to solve. He thought he would find the Count soon. He parked near the cathedral, right in the centre of Reims.

Marc went into a bar and ordered a black coffee. The décor was no different to any typical French café. Behind the bar, an affable-looking waiter seemed like he might be willing to help the detective with some of his inquiries. When he saw that the waiter had finished serving all of his customers, Marc took the opportunity to ask him some questions.

The waiter helped the detective pinpoint the North African neighbourhoods on a map; helpfully, he also marked the places where he had seen Renaud meet his contacts. Marc bid him goodbye and walked down the city's ancient, narrow lanes, reading the map as he went, trying to find some of the locations he had been shown. His sense of direction was impeccable.

Marc had to decide which of his suspects to pursue first. The idea had occurred to him that the North African groups and the Satan followers might have something in common, but from looking at where he was hoping to track these people down on the map, it seemed that there was probably no link between them. The day was getting warmer; again storms threatened. Marc noticed that there were large sweat stains on his shirt. Perhaps he had walked too quickly. He decided to head over to a nearby restaurant for a cold drink.

Out of nowhere, a blow to the nape of his neck suddenly blurred his vision. As he fell to the ground, he could just see two men appearing from behind him; he could feel them grabbing him and lifting him off the ground with surprising strength. He had still not taken in what was happening to him when a third man, whom Marc had not noticed, hooded him with a thick, black cloth, shrouding him in darkness and blocking out his senses.

* * *

When Marc came around, his whole body was in pain. He struggled to think clearly because of an intense headache but he managed to remember that the kidnappers had put him to sleep with some kind of narcotic. It seemed as if only a few minutes had passed since they had attacked him. He thought he was in a pitch-black room, but in fact he still had the thick hood over his head. Battered and anxious, his breathing became increasingly strained. What fate lay in store for him now?

He couldn't be sure where he was, having no idea how far they had taken him from Reims. The idea that someone he couldn't see was watching over him unsettled him even more. Unnerved by the thought, Marc jumped when he heard footsteps of two, perhaps three, people approaching—from which direction he could not tell. His heartbeat quickened at the thought that worse was still to come.

They left the hood on him and the interrogation began.

'You already know what we want from you,' barked one of the captors. 'We can do this gently or hard. You decide.'

'I don't have a clue what you want from me,' said Marc. His voice sounded odd, muffled by the material that covered his head.

'If you tell us absolutely everything you know about the machine, the way to make it function and the secret it hides, we will let you go and nothing will happen to you.'

'But I don't know how the machine works. I've been employed to find the Count and investigate what happened to him. I haven't the faintest idea how to operate that piece of junk.'

After he had finished speaking, he was hit for the first

time. His face felt like it had exploded after a fist landed squarely on his nose. An intense taste of blood filled his mouth, making his breathing even more laboured. He didn't understand how these men could hit someone who was blindfolded and defenceless. He started to worry about what other brutal acts they could carry out.

'Monsieur Mignon, this is a very simple process; it will only last as long as you dictate.'

A long silence followed the stranger's words. Marc tried to dream up a reply that would buy him a few moments' thinking time.

Another blow, sharp and precise, hit him in the stomach, winding him and making him retch. Intense pains in his abdomen made him suspect that he had snapped a rib. Just as Marc was on the cusp of losing consciousness, a new voice, from the back of the room, threw a direct question to the captive.

'You know we are going to kill you if you don't collaborate with us. Do you understand?'

The detective nodded vigorously, to ensure his agreement could be seen.

'Well, start telling us the secrets you have learnt from that machine.'

'I'm going to tell you everything I know but I beg you not to hit me any more.' His voice was drowned by the blood soaking the black hood.

'Now we're on the right track. Begin.'

He started to explain at length what he had done since arriving at the castle. The words poured out of his mouth in desperation. When he had finished, he held his breath, awaiting further interrogation.

'We don't believe that the Count has not left even one document about his investigations behind. He must have left his discoveries somewhere. If his letter says that the machine has been made to work, and that he has gone in search of the truth, it's obvious that he has obtained knowledge from the contraption.'

'But nobody, not even his daughter nor his assistant, has those papers,' Marc explained, trying to convince them he was telling the truth. 'If he did note down his ideas, he must have taken them with him, wherever he went.'

Another blow struck his head from the side. These people would not think twice about killing him, regardless of what he said. A cold chill went down his spine. He tried to put fear out of his head and concentrate on the conversation; he had no other option.

'I'm telling the truth. Why would I hide things from you when I know if I don't collaborate you'll kill me? Believe me, there are no papers about the machine. Only the Count knows how to put it in motion; he must be found first.'

A fist sank into his stomach again.

'You'd better be telling the truth. Where could the Count be?'

'It's a mystery,' stammered the detective. 'The police don't know either. We can only guess that he found a riddle within the machine, which made him leave in a hurry to find more answers.'

A long pause heightened the tense atmosphere. All of a sudden, when he thought he had but a few moments to live, a softer voice spoke to him.

'Listen, I reckon you should retire from this case. You don't fit in here. If your agency carries on poking its nose into this, you could meet the same fate as the unfortunate victims in the Baumard case. And you already know how that turned out…'

His blood suddenly froze.

That was the case in which his parents were killed.

CHAPTER 16

Marc woke up in the middle of nowhere. Every muscle in his body ached. A searing pain in his head prevented him from opening his eyes straight away, although the dim light allowed him to open them slowly. The taste of blood still filled his mouth, making him spit. He tried to sit upright but his trembling legs made it difficult. Getting to his feet was like trying to lift a puppet without strings.

On the ground next to him, he found the hood that had made it impossible to see the thugs who had brutally beaten him. He hadn't ever experienced pain like this and still wasn't sure if the beatings had caused any lasting damage; his muscles were not responding when he willed his body to move.

After a while—he had no concept of how long—he managed a few, unsure steps which brought him to the edge of a field. The moon weakly lit some thickets that were blocking his path. With difficulty, he reached a small hillock from which he could just make out the back part of a house in the distance. When he got there, it seemed uninhabited. He walked around the house and stumbled upon a motorcycle that was lying on the ground. He started it up and drove down the dirt track that led towards a narrow, tarmac road. After a few kilometres, it met a motorway. When he had figured out the way to the Dubois family estate, he opened the throttle.

The castle seemed more comfortable and familiar to him than ever before when he reached the front door. He left the motorcycle at the front of the building and rang the bell several times, calling for help. He was received by the butler, who, like a true professional, didn't react to the ghost-like figure that stood before him but, instead, called for the Countess to come down as quickly as possible.

She appeared immediately and was horrified by Marc's battered body.

'Oh my God! What's happened to you?' she asked, without taking her eyes off him.

'Someone wanted to know what has happened to your husband. It seems there are some people who are very interested in his whereabouts and the secrets he's discovered from the machine downstairs.'

'Good God! I'm going to take you to hospital right now.'

'No, I think that what I need is a good bath and to try to forget about all this. I need to think about what has happened,' he said.

'Well, all right. Go to your room and get comfortable. Let's hope you haven't broken anything; I'll come up and treat the wounds on your face.'

Marc slowly climbed the steps to his room, wanting to get to the luxurious bathroom as soon as possible. The last few hours had been the most frightening of his life. The sound of water filling the bath calmed the irregular beats of his heart, which, little by little, slowed down as he immersed himself in a restful cloud of foam.

The Divine Conjuror

* * *

The Countess had been alone all afternoon. Her daughter was giving a university seminar in Paris and would not return till the following day. The solitude had prompted Véronique to call Bruno again. This time, the Countess had dreamed up a solid plan to revive her affair. She was going to yield to all of his requests and even forgive him for the documents she suspected he had stolen from her husband. She planned to leave her husband, once she found out the reason for his disappearance. The memory of passionate nights in bed with her energetic lover and of sheets damp from the sweat of two people in love, pushed her to make the hardest decision of her life.

Even though the divorce would be costly, her desire to be with Bruno had convinced her that she must act. Determined, she had left him several messages on his answerphone early in the morning and, having heard nothing back, had called him again at midday, finally managing to speak to him.

At first, the conversation had been sweet and amiable. She had deployed her kindest words, her most delicate phrases. But when she suggested to him that they should continue their relationship, he had ended the conversation abruptly. Véronique had pleaded with him but Bruno had been determined to finish the discussion.

The Countess had taken comfort in a drink.

* * *

Submerged up to his neck in warm water, the detective

relived the events of his kidnapping in his mind. He tried to forget the blows he'd received and focus on the words of the interrogation, words that drove daggers through his heart. The men knew that the machine existed but they had no idea where the Count could be found. However, all of these thoughts hung at the back of his mind; the word Baumard had struck him hardest: the name of the case the Mignon agency never solved, in which his parents had died. The idea that those bastards had something to do with it made his stomach turn.

A knock at the bathroom door disturbed his thoughts.

'Hello, Marc. How are you? I've come to treat your cuts. May I come in?' inquired Véronique.

'One moment,' he said, drying himself and putting on an enormous white bathrobe, the emblem of the Divange family embroidered in gold on his chest.

He sat on the bed and waited for the Countess to enter.

'Let me put a bit of disinfectant here,' Véronique said to him, sitting beside him and opening the small case.

Her slightly slurred speech made Marc realise that the Countess had been drinking.

'Don't look at me like that; I have problems too. Tell me if I hurt you.' She placed a light plaster on his forehead, while pressing cotton wool soaked in water on his cheekbone.

'You don't have to justify yourself to me. It's your house after all.'

When the Countess had finished cleaning up his face, Marc went over to a mirror to see how he looked.

'Not too bad at all,' he said, turning his head from right to left to look at the Countess's work.

'I was a nurse before I became a countess.'

'I'm as good as new. You must have been a great nurse.'

'I didn't do badly. So, are you going to tell me what happened?'

'Of course I will. This morning I was investigating various leads and—'

'Would a drink go down well? I think it might make you feel better, relax you a little.'

'Thank you.'

Véronique left the room and returned a few minutes later with an elegant black bottle of champagne, which she opened immediately. She filled two glasses with the exquisite wine; both were drunk very swiftly. She refilled them and then asked Marc to begin his story.

He told her what had happened, avoiding any reference to the death of his parents. When he finished, Véronique sighed.

'I'm sure that the Count has gone somewhere of his own accord, to carry out his investigations without being disturbed,' explained the detective.

'But he could have told us where he was or, at least, left us a little clue. Don't you think?'

'Not necessarily. He said in his letter that he went voluntarily and we shouldn't try to follow him.'

'That bloody machine and that damn pope. What can this piece of junk possibly be worth for people to resort to violence to get their hands on it?' she reflected, filling up both glasses again.

'I don't know but this case is definitely starting to intrigue me more than I ever would have thought.' He lowered his gaze and finished the sparkling wine with one deep swig.

Véronique could see that Marc was unsettled by the case and suffering the effects of his kidnapping. She took advantage of the young man's situation, giving him a light kiss on his wounded cheek. Taken aback, he turned his head and met the woman's warm and sensual lips. Within a few seconds they had thrown back the bed sheets and sunk into a deep embrace. Given the delicate state she presumed he was in, she tried not to be too rough with him. She began to kiss him all over his body, tenderly but with no restraint or timidity. Marc let himself get carried away by the caresses, her hands deftly removing his bathrobe and placing him on the bed, submerged in pleasure. The mixture of Véronique's intense perfume and the fine bubbles of the excellent champagne transported him away from the horrors of his day. Véronique led their lovemaking with a firm hand, leaving him no choice but to submit.

CHAPTER 17

Guylaine arrived at the castle at an odd hour. Whenever she went to Paris and knew it would be a late return, she preferred to stay in one of the central apartments belonging to her family. She had even planned to stay in the city this time. However, she needed to let Marc and her mother know about the call she had received and the information she had been given. She quickened her pace up the stairs of the castle. She had phoned her mother's mobile several times without success, nor could she get through to the detective, whose phone was turned off. Her news was urgent, so she went into her mother's room without knocking.

But the Countess was not there. Without thinking, Guylaine made her way to Marc's room on a different floor of the building. She ran up the stairs and bumped into her mother coming downstairs wrapped in a bathrobe.

'Where you have been? I've been trying to get hold of you all afternoon. I have very important news.'

'I had to sort something out. What are you doing here? Weren't you supposed to be coming back tomorrow?'

'Has something happened? Why are you dressed like that? I've never seen you outside of your apartments in your nightclothes.'

'Give me a few minutes. If it's news about your father's

disappearance, call the detective down so he can hear too. We'll all meet in the kitchen; I'm going to get dressed.'

Guylaine watched her mother go down the stairs, confused by her behaviour. She went in search of the detective and knocked at his door. He sounded tired but called out that he would come down straight away.

* * *

Guylaine made tea and waited for them to come. Twenty minutes later the detective appeared, followed by the Countess.

'What a day! I didn't think it would be so difficult to find you both,' said Guylaine. 'I've been calling you all afternoon.' Then she looked up. 'Marc! Your poor face! It looks terrible.'

'I ran into some trouble today,' Marc explained. 'Some thugs kidnapped me, blindfolded me, drove me out into the country and beat me. They wanted to know where your father was and to find out more about the machine.'

'Oh Marc, that's shocking,' she said, looking at him properly for the first time since she had arrived. 'Did they hurt you badly? How are you feeling now?'

'Don't worry. I've tended to him as well as I could,' the Countess reassured her daughter. 'There doesn't seem to be anything broken. I think he just needs to rest and to forget what has happened.'

'But Marc, are you in pain?' asked young Guylaine, truly concerned. Softly, she touched his swollen wounds.

'Thank you, Guylaine, for your care, but your mother has

given me her healing hands.'

He looked at the Countess, who avoided holding his gaze. Guylaine noticed the strange glance that passed between them and instantly suspected something. She looked to the ground, crestfallen. Surely nothing had happened between them behind her back?

'Well, and…what news do you have to tell us that is so important?' asked Véronique, trying to lighten the uncomfortable situation.

'The police called me. Europol confirmed that my father has been seen in Barcelona this morning.'

CHAPTER 18

Barcelona

An express flight from Paris took them to Barcelona the next day to attend an appointment with the Spanish superintendent. It all seemed very hasty to the Spanish police but the matter was of such importance—to Marc as much as Guylaine. During the journey, the detective had tried to see if any of the passengers resembled the suspicious individuals he had seen in Reims or even if he recognised anyone's voice as belonging to his captors of the previous day.

It was difficult for him to look Guylaine in the eye after what had happened with the Countess the night before. Although he enjoyed reliving the passion of the previous night in his head, he sensed that Guylaine would never understand it.

They were met by Inspector Casals de Carrer Balmes close to Diagonal Avenue. The man seemed conscious of the importance of finding the Count; the French police had let him know the urgency of the matter. The case file he had in his hands was sizeable; he appeared to have the information he needed regarding the Count. He picked out a photo of Pierre Dubois and began the interview.

'Is this your father?' he asked directly.

'That's right. I think that is a recent photo,' Guylaine answered, feeling slightly emotional.

'He was seen just yesterday in the monastery of Ripoll in the province of Girona.'

'Where's that?' inquired Marc.

'Close to here, about a hundred kilometres away, a little over an hour,' answered the inspector.

'And to get there, you have to pass through Vic, don't you?' remembered Guylaine.

'That's right. I see that you know our region well.'

'Yes, I have been here several times. I'm a historian and I know that Pope Silvestre II studied in Vic for some time and used the fantastic library at the monastery of Ripoll to read books translated from Arabic.'

'Yes indeed. It's a magnificent building with a fascinating history.'

'Then that must be why my father is there. He is tracing the steps of the pope magician...'

The detective and Guylaine agreed that she would drive to Ripoll. Both of Marc's legs hurt, he was suffering from intense abdominal pain and he couldn't see properly. He needed time to clear his head. The words of one of his delinquent captors, warning him not to continue with the case if he didn't want the same fate to befall him as had his parents, still echoed in his head.

For his grandfather, a citizen of Madrid, who had been forced to flee from a Spain ravaged by civil war, the death of his son and daughter-in-law cost him what war could not take away from him: his own life. He had died the following year, suffering deep depression. The tragic event had also had a profound effect on his uncle Marcos: since that day, he had become incapable of establishing a stable relationship with any woman. His trust had evaporated. Marc didn't remember his grandfather—he had been very young when he passed away—but his uncle had, on many occasions, spoken to him about the Baumard case. He had even shown him the file once or twice when his little nephew visited the agency offices.

The Baumard case had begun in Paris twenty years ago. The founder of a respected merchant family, Monsieur Baumard had employed the Mignon agency to watch his children, to confirm his suspicions they had set up a drugs business on the side, using the family trade network. Marcos was involved as much as his brother in the initial investigations. Their work failed to expose even the slightest trace of illegal operations. When the Mignon Agency was about to hand over the final report to their client, Marc's father called his brother saying that he had discovered some new elements in the case that needed looking in to. That same night, he asked Marcos to take care of little Marc, as he and Marc's mother were going to the opera.

Marcos never managed to find the vehicle that crashed into his brother's car. Nor could he link the accident to the Baumard case. After twenty years, the matter was filed away in the Mignon Agency archives. Now those thugs in pursuit of the machine's secrets had given Marc a clue about the accident in which his parents died. Was there a link between the Baumard case and the Dubois case?

Thoughts kept running through his head. Perhaps sleeping with his client at the end of such a stressful day had not been such a good idea. Obviously he had enjoyed himself—

Véronique seemed to really know how to please a young man—but if his uncle Marcos, or even Guylaine, were to find out, what would they think of him?

Guylaine noticed that Marc kept shifting in his seat. Was her driving making him uncomfortable? she asked.

'Not at all. Sorry, it's just that I can't get the case out of my head, that's all. I'm going over something one of those thugs said. Can you keep a secret?'

'Yes, of course. I am nobility after all.'

They both laughed. He told her how settled he felt in the case and how much he appreciated the kind treatment she and her mother had both given him, but he thought better of telling her about his parents and the kidnappers' threat.

'In what way has my mother treated you well?' she asked him, taking her eyes off of the road for a few seconds to look directly at her passenger.

'Well,' Marc hesitated, desperate to sound nonchalant, 'the Countess is a good woman but she's not typically aristocratic; she knows how to treat others as equals. I always imagined nobility to behave differently.'

Marc looked at Guylaine attentively, trying to find similarities to her mother. Until the previous day, he would have sworn that the daughter was gentler than the Countess, but now he was not so sure. Guylaine's sense of humour, original ideas and youth were all her own.

Their exit to Vic was approaching. Guylaine reminded the detective that Vic was the city where Silvestre II, when he was still just the young Gerberto, had ventured to further his knowledge of mathematics and other disciplines.

'Yes, I haven't forgotten. I have it all here: "*From Vic, the monk went to the monastery of Ripoll to look for ancient books in its enormous library.*"'

'That's right. And that must be the reason for my father's visit. He must think there is something to discover here,' she said, looking out of the rear-view mirror.

'What's wrong? Why do you keep looking behind so often?'

'I think someone is following us. I can't stop thinking about what you said to me on the plane and I'm pretty sure a red car has been behind us since the Barcelona exit.'

Marc turned his head and tried to see the vehicle. A medium-sized saloon car with two people inside was pursuing them at a close distance.

'Let's see if they turn off at Vic. If they don't, we'll get off this road at the next exit and see if they really are following us,' Marc suggested.

Guylaine followed his instructions, branching off their planned route. They went through a small, quiet village lined with new red brick houses. Marc asked her to slow down. The red car was nowhere to be seen.

* * *

It was midday. The bright sun illuminated the old city. They approached the entrance to Ripoll in the car with Marc still looking behind him in case they were being followed.

'The red car seems to have gone,' he said, fixing his gaze on the road in front again.

'Remember that we've come to find my father.'

'Of course. But if they are following us, we'll need to take every possible precaution, don't you think?'

'Yes, I'm sorry.'

They parked the car close to the city centre. A sign indicated that the millennial monastery was close by, so they left the car and set off in that direction. Marc took one last glance around. Just as they were about to set off to the abbey, he clocked the same car again. It was turning right at the end of the avenue and it was clear that the driver and his companion had seen them park.

'They're following us. There's no doubt about it,' he said.

'Right, well, we'll be careful. Let's visit the temple now and look for my father.'

'Very well, but we must be careful.'

They entered a square in front of the monastery. A beautiful example of Roman architecture, the two towers of the monastery rose up in front of them, the highest part of which housed the abbey bell. Guylaine noticed that her companion was moving hurriedly, nervous of his surroundings.

A busy group of tourists waited for the guide to usher them inside. Guylaine pulled at the sleeve of Marc's shirt, directing both of them to join the group of visitors, as if they were just two more tourists. They entered the sanctuary, shrouded by dozens of tourists armed with cameras.

'Nice work,' he said to her, still looking around in case he spotted anything else suspicious. 'We mustn't let our guard down for one second. They're following us and it's possible that they're doing the same thing as us.'

'OK. You watch out for them and I'll look around and figure out why my father has come here, agreed?'

Marc nodded.

The tour guide lifted an umbrella, indicating that the group should gather around her, so she could begin the tour.

'We have before us the spectacular façade of the monastery of Santa Maria de Ripoll,' the guide recited, as if rehearsed word by word. 'The origins of this magnificent temple are linked to a famous figure in Catalonia. In the year 879, Count Wifredo el Velloso, or Wilfred the Hairy, decided to repopulate the entire region, founding this monastery. Although decisions for the design of the building were not initially clear, some years later, in the year 888 to be exact, its builders decided to rebuild it and consecrate it as Santa Maria. This was done in the presence of the Count himself and his wife, who willingly offered their own child to the order, admitting him as a monk and donating a considerable sum of goods and money to the monastery.'

The guide paused to check that the group understood her explanation. When the flash of cameras stopped, she moved forward to a new position and continued the talk.

'The laws of reinstating the population made Ripoll a safe place protected from the Arabs. Wifredo's other children were determined to expand the monastery; in the year 935, the bishop of Vic consecrated this fabulous complex. Not much later, Abbot Arnulfo designed and expanded the basilica into five naves and enclosed the complex within a wall. Pope Agapito approved the protection of the building in the year 957 and, thanks to this, the construction of the cloisters and the expansion of a number of monks' rooms commenced. It was also Arnulfo who stimulated the development of the scriptorium and he greatly improved the library's collections, converting the monastic school of Ripoll into one of the most important centres of learning at that time.'

Guylaine elbowed Marc to make sure he was paying attention to the guide.

'This is really important. She's talking about the years in which Silvestre II must have been here. Remember, I told you about the excellent library in this monastry.'

'I'm listening, but I've got to keep on the lookout for those men,' he said, looking at the scores of people in their group, in case he saw something strange. 'Do you think the reliefs on the doors might contain clues that your father would have found interesting?'

'The doors are from the middle of the seventeenth century. We ought to focus on the parts of the building that are from the end of the first millennium. The rest isn't relevant.'

The guide moved through the central part of the nave and, when the group had gathered around her, she continued the tour.

'Having been Count, the Bishop Oliba, great grandson of Count Wifredo, renounced the obligations of his position to take the holy orders of this monastery in 1008; he did this in response to the events which took place at the end of the first millennium.'

Guylaine nudged Marc again, startling him.

'Did you hear that?' she asked.

'Of course. Why?'

'Sshh.'

'Abbot Oliba,' the guide went on, 'gave a new and definitive purpose to the scriptorium through the acquisition of certain manuscripts. He ordered the addition of the bells on the back of the temple. After years of work, around the year 1032—that's to say, almost exactly one thousand years after the death of Jesus Christ—they had built a majestic building, the largest and most magnificent of that time. In the presence of counts, bishops and the high orders of the Church, Oliba consecrated this temple.'

'There is something here,' Guylaine announced, in an inappropriately loud tone of voice.

Marc looked around. There were so many people that it was impossible to know whether the couple of men who had been following them had infiltrated the group. The detective was still considering this when he heard a voice that made his stomach turn. It belonged to one of his kidnappers from the day before and now he could see his face.

CHAPTER 19

Marc broke out in a sweat. Strings of beads laced his forehead. Being so close to one of his kidnappers made him feel deeply uneasy. He pulled Guylaine away by the arm, guiding her forcefully towards one side of the temple's main nave. Away from the group of tourists, they found themselves in an entirely separate part of the millennial building. Marc scoured the nave for an exit leading to the cloister, famously enclosed by a double layer of pointed, ogival arches. Despite the impressive spectacle of the galleries, Marc felt intensely anxious that their pursuers were but a few metres away.

'Have you seen them?' Guylaine asked.

'Yes. One of them, I would say, is average height without any distinctive features. He's with another taller, thinner man. As soon as I spy them again, I'll let you know.'

'I have a good hunch about what my father came here to do, so can we hide here for a while until it's safe, then carry on with our investigations.'

'Good idea. That far corner of this gallery seems most concealed and if they come looking for us, we'll be able to see them first.'

They ran to the back of the cloisters and hid behind some columns. After a few moments, the group of tourists entered the immense cloister. Marc felt sick when he saw that the two men were still attached to the group. The taller one, dressed in a beige cotton suit and brown hat, looked like any other tourist. The other man, who wore a waistcoat, was constantly taking photos. He wasn't hiding camera film under his waistcoat, but a gun. Guylaine immediately picked out the two criminals in the tourist huddle. The detective's gaze was fixed on them.

When the group began to leave the cloisters, the two men broke off to take a stroll around the galleries. Recognising their pursuers' intentions, they edged to the other side of the galleries, crouching low. By the time the thugs got to the south side of the cloisters, Marc and Guylaine had stumbled upon a door, which led them to some simple rooms that originally must have been the monks' accommodation.

There seemed to be no exit to the outside. Marc might as well have led his client into a net. He grabbed Guylaine's hand and dragged her back into the cloisters. He ducked his head, signalling for her to get down again and together they sneaked round the edge of the galleries, reaching the same door through which they had entered the cloisters. Out of the corner of his eye, Marc saw that his kidnappers were still there, inspecting the rooms they had left moments before.

Without losing any more time, they ran back to the road and hurried towards the car. Their relief was short-lived: the four wheels of their car had been punctured.

CHAPTER 20

Marc and Guylaine looked at each other, not knowing what to do. Two thugs were following them in a city they didn't know and one from which they couldn't immediately escape. Guylaine noticed that the men had also broken one of the car windows to steal the papers they had left inside. Even the road maps they had used to get to Ripoll had gone.

'Follow me.'

Guylaine dutifully did, trying to keep up as the detective rushed towards the side streets around the monastery.

From the safety of the smaller roads, they glanced around and realised that they couldn't even see the monastery from where they were, so they must have put a good distance between themselves and the kidnappers.

'Are you sure that they're the ones who beat you up?'

'I will never forget the voices of the men who interrogated me. They treated me so brutally, their voices are imprinted on my memory forever. I'm absolutely sure it's them.'

'You were right to suspect that they followed us on the plane.'

'That's what I feared. I'm convinced that they have been following me since the day you contacted the Mignon Agency. I have a feeling that they may have broken into the castle somehow. While I can't be certain, I think that they may have been watching your father's progress for many years, in case he succeeded in his search for the machine. Once he found it, many people clearly wanted to gain access to the secrets of the pope magician.'

'So what do we do now?'

'First and foremost, we need to stay alert. We have to find out where we are and get hold of another car. We also need to ask people around here if they have seen your father.'

'Sounds good to me. Let's divide the work.'

They booked into a small hostel. Staying somewhere like that would attract less attention; they had dismissed the idea of reserving rooms in a bigger hotel, where the men would definitely think to come looking. Swiftly, Marc prepared a list of hostels and hotels in and around Ripoll. Although the police had been tipped off that the Count had been seen near the monastery, they didn't have any news on his current whereabouts. It would not be difficult to check each hotel one by one, simply asking if they had seen a crazy, restless old man and, as Guylaine had brought several photos of her father with her, Marc should be able to secure a reliable identification within a few hours.

Night crept up but the couple had made little progress. They had booked into a double room, passing themselves off as a young married couple; that way they would go unnoticed if anyone asked after them as separate individuals, and also they thought they should probably stick together given the violence the men had previously demonstrated. When she had asked the owner of the hostel if she had a room with twin beds, Guylaine was quick to add that her husband had a habit of tossing and turning in his sleep. Marc felt uncomfortable discussing sleeping arrangements with the Countess's daughter.

They decided to look for somewhere for dinner; the lady at the hostel had recommended a small restaurant serving simple Catalan food. They walked for a few minutes and found it without difficulty, stepping tentatively inside. They picked out a discreet table, sat down and tried to relax. Not every so-called tourist looks for the obvious restaurant.

'I still can't believe that my father might be somewhere nearby.'

'I know. I'm sure that he's not far, still on his quest for new information.'

'There's no doubt about it. If I've inherited anything from that man, it's his obstinacy. He won't give up until he finds what he's looking for. Do you mind if I phone my mother?'

'No, not at all.'

She took her mobile phone out of her bag and tried to call the Countess. Her mother's phone was turned off, so she tried the castle's landline.

If Guylaine somehow knew about what had happened between him and the Countess, he ought to think of a reason to excuse himself pretty sharply, Marc thought.

Taking the phone from her butler, the Countess immediately asked after the detective. Marc felt on edge, and swallowed slowly. Guylaine replied that he was fine but this didn't seem to satisfy her mother, so she passed the telephone to Marc so that he could tell her himself.

'Hello. Yes, thanks for asking. I'm a bit better; my body still aches a bit though.'

'Well, I hope the treatment I gave you made you feel

good. Did you enjoy it?' the Countess asked.

'Of course. I don't have any visible scars now; only the bruises are still there.'

'I imagine you'll be left with something else after the treatment I gave you… I want to do it again.'

'So do I.'

Marc frenziedly passed the mobile to Guylaine, who wished her mother good night.

Halfway into the first course, Guylaine told him that she had had a brainwave about why her father had come there.

'What are you talking about?'

'The Abbot Oliba.'

'Why? I don't see the connection. That great grandson of Wifredo gave up his position in the nobility and ended up in the monastery praying to God. What more is there to learn from that?'

'You haven't paid attention properly. Let me explain it to you. Oliba was a Count and a descendant of the most important lineage in Catalonia at that time. Do you know what time I'm referring to?'

'I don't remember.'

'The end of the last millennium, the years prior to Silvestre II's papacy, when he built the machine with all the knowledge he gained from reading thousands of those books in the monastery. At that time, Oliba was a very influential nobleman. But what happened?'

'He shut himself away as the Abbot of Ripoll.'

'Exactly. Moreover, with the pope already dead and the machine somewhere in France, he dedicated himself to writing, translating and buying more documents for the monastic library. But that's not all. He also extended the building and presented it to the public in 1032 exactly as it stands today.'

'I don't understand. What significance does this date have?'

'The year 1033 was exactly one thousand years after the death of Christ.'

'And what happened then?'

'The coming of Parousia.'

Marc's confused expression made it clear that he had no idea what she meant. Before he could open his mouth, she started to explain everything.

'In the Middle Ages, people were fearful of what the end of the millennium would bring. People believed in the apocalyptic symbols found in the sacred scriptures.

'In Catholic millenarianism, Christ must govern for a period of one thousand years. Even though this was not recognised by the apostles in the Gospels, the Book of Revelation by Saint John does speak of it. Moreover, he dedicates his most evocative passages to explaining that, after the time had passed, the beast of the seas would surface, the heavens would open and the world would come to an end.'

Guylaine took a sip of her wine and continued.

'As I've already told you, the tenth century has always been recognised as a dark period in European history. Remember the strange events I told you about?'

Marc nodded.

'Although the end of the millennium was officially in the year 1001, there were many people who believed that, in reality, the prophecy of the Book of Revelation wouldn't happen until a different time altogether.'

'When?'

'The year 1033.'

'Really?'

'And Christians believed in the Parousia—the second coming of Christ—a time in which God would come back to earth to deliver the human race from earthly disasters. The Gospels too contain various predictions about the Second Coming.'

'So, the fact that the Abbot Oliba was interested in redesigning the monastery of Ripoll has aroused your suspicion.'

'Exactly. My father believes that 1033 was the starting point of millenarianism. Today the guide told us about the work of Oliba, who devoted his life to remodelling and expanding the monastery that inspired the pope magician.'

'What can we look for there, then?'

'At that time, the manuscripts and books were only accessible to those who knew how to read. To communicate with more people, images were carved into the stone of the monastery, spreading ideas visually. We must go back there and read the signs found on the walls of the monastery.'

'Perhaps if we go at night we'll avoid any unwanted encounters.'

'Perfect idea, fitting of a good detective. Let's go tonight.'

* * *

In subtle colours, and more practical attire than they had dressed in for dinner, Marc and Guylaine looked quite the part as a detective couple. Setting out with two torches that the landlady had offered in order to fix the hire car, they found the path that led back to the monastery. The temple, illuminated by a powerful full moon, was an imposing sight as it suddenly came into view. They stopped for a few seconds to admire the façade: masonry over one thousand one hundred years old.

As Guylaine scanned the silhouette of the building, she remembered what the guide had said. The Abbot Oliba built part of the temple, ordering the construction of the slender bell towers at the south-west corner. By the time he had finished, he had contributed significantly to the majesty of this grand building. In the presence of counts, bishops and the high orders of the Church, the reformed monastery, one of the most impressive works of the Romanic era, was offered up to Jesus Christ.

Marc impatiently pulled her onwards. The main door, through which they had entered that same morning, was locked. Looking for an accessible smaller door, they decided to try to enter through the cloisters. Near these, there was a large door made of dark wood with an old and visibly crumbling lock. Marc gave it a firm push; it didn't give. He got a screwdriver out of the back pocket of his trousers—part of the repair kit the landlady had also lent them. He forced the tool in the enormous lock but it had no effect. He tried pushing the implement in all directions but had no luck.

'I thought they taught these skills to all detectives,' Guylaine said ironically.

'It's a really old lock. It's not a model I'm familiar with.'

'Let me try.'

Guylaine knelt down in front of the large door and

inserted the screwdriver, putting her ear next to the lock to listen to its clicking sounds. Within a few seconds, the door opened in front of her.

'In the Dubois castle there are dozens of doors like this that I have opened hundreds of times. When I was young, I used to try to find secret rooms in the castle, hidden behind old, unused doors.'

'I see,' he murmured, a thin smile crossing his face.

They went inside; it was pitch black. They must be in one of the rooms attached to the main nave, thought Marc. Torchlit, the room looked like it was a meeting point for priests and clergymen as scores of habits, traditional tunics and cowls, perhaps worn for mass, were hung up on wooden clothes racks.

Guylaine had a good sense of direction. She tapped her torch on Marc's shoulder and gestured him to follow her through one of the interior doors, which opened with a handle as old and rusting as the last.

'Where are you going?'

'I want to see the bell tower.'

Guylaine raced up step after step, and they emerged into the cool night air at the top of the tower. Marc shivered at the thought of standing there while the bells were tolling. Guylaine walked round the room several times. She touched the stone walls, trying to guess how old they were. She inspected every nook and cranny but found nothing, not even one inscription.

All of a sudden, a flash blinded them. As soon as their eyes adjusted to the intense light, they saw that a monk had turned on the powerful halogen lamps in the main part of the church. Before they could open their mouths, the friar addressed them.

'I warn you: I've called the police. I've been watching for a while, in fact since you came in. In a few moments, they'll be here seeking your arrest. Clear off!'

Guylaine and Marc both wondered how they could convince the poor monk that they meant no harm.

'Forgive us. We haven't come to steal anything,' the detective began. 'We mean no harm. We're here because we need to resolve a problem and we hope that the solution might lie within these walls.'

'Do you think I'm stupid? It's obvious that you have come to take one of the monastery's relics. Get out of here if you don't want the police to catch you!' he shouted from the top of the nave.

'Please believe us. What we're doing here is very important to us. I beg you to listen,' Guylaine implored.

'Well, come back tomorrow and book an appointment for the guided tour.'

'We can't. Some people are following us. We were here today but we need to check some things that may be able to help us find my father, the Count of Divange.'

'Are you joking? You're Pierre Dubois' daughter?"

'That's right. I am Guylaine Dubois and my companion is Marc Mignon, a detective. We're here following the trail of my father, who disappeared some weeks ago.'

'I pray to God that you're telling the truth.'

'Why?' she asked.

'Because I know the Count. He stayed in the monastery for over a week.'

CHAPTER 21

The monk invited them to sit in a room that was so dark it was difficult even to find a seat.

'My apologies. I spend lots of time here alone. I like the darkness; it helps me pray in peace.'

He lit a worn candle lamp, which did little to improve the dim lighting of the room.

'Is that better for you?'

'Yes, thank you,' Guylaine answered. 'Shouldn't you call the police so they don't come?'

'Don't worry. That was just a little lie I told you to get you to leave; I didn't have enough time to call the police. But as a warning, it succeeded, no?'

'Without doubt,' Marc had to admit. 'Could you tell us when and how the Count of Divange came to the monastery of Ripoll?'

'Well, it happened all of a sudden. One morning a man came here asking if anyone could help him with some very important investigations he had to carry out. My superiors chose me to accompany the scholar, who knew the illustrious past of this temple so well and told me things even I didn't know about the monastery as a whole. It was extraordinary meeting him—we have never met anyone in this holy place who was so well versed in millennial themes.'

'Yes, my father has spent his whole life studying the Middle Ages and particularly the coming of the first millennium, whichever year it was supposed to have been most feared.'

'But what surprised us the most was when he told us he was the Count of Divange and that he lived in a castle from the age of Silvestre II. That's incredible!'

'It's the house I live in too.'

'You're very lucky, señorita. Your father is one of the most cultured people I have ever met. In fact, when my superiors spoke to him, they invited him to eat with us. Lunch went on for so long that we invited him to dinner and it got so late that we proposed that he stay the night and, indeed, for as long he wanted.'

'So he was here for a whole week?' checked the detective.

'That's right. It might even have been a bit longer than seven days.'

'Well, my family have been looking for him since he disappeared. My mother is seriously concerned about him, isn't she, Marc?'

'Undoubtedly. The Countess has been through a lot in the last week.'

'Really? I'm sorry to hear that. We didn't know that Pierre hadn't left an account of his intentions behind.'

'Did he come alone? Has anyone asked after him while he was here or after he left? Sorry to impose and then ask these questions, but it's just that this matter has got quite serious,' apologised the detective.

'Don't worry; I understand. Yes, he came alone. Nobody asked after him while he was here but, yes, people did ask after him—this morning, in fact. Two men, whom I didn't like the look of.'

'And what did you tell them?'

'Nothing at all. They asked whether the Count had been here and I said that he had. But that was all I said. I didn't tell them what Pierre had done during the week he spent with us.'

'Thank you. And what did my father do for a whole week in this monastery?'

'Pray. He is a very religious man.'

'I already know that. And what else?'

'He was investigating all sorts of strange things. We know this temple better than anybody does; the monks have been here for centuries. He set about measuring distances, touching the stone of the walls, reading and rereading each and every one of the inscriptions in this building. He also looked over the extremely old books and documents we have preserved within these walls.'

'And did he come to any conclusions?' Guylaine carried on questioning.

'Yes. He showed particular interest in the Abbot Oliba.'

'I knew it!'

'At the beginning of the eleventh century, after the year one thousand, our Abbot Oliba ordered the reconstruction of the existing church to convert it into one of the most elaborate in the entire Romanic period. He constructed no less than five naves, a façade with two tall towers and a tall cross, topped with seven apses.'

'It's an astonishing and mysterious building. It's obvious that the Count has found clues here…' The detective tried to coax more information out of the monk.

'I don't know what to tell you. The truth is that Pierre left without telling us what he found. He thanked us for our help in the monastery, and said that he had resolved half of the questions he had to clear up in relation to the mysterious millennial theories.'

'And do you know what they were?' inquired Guylaine.

'No, he didn't tell us. He explained many things about the end of the first millennium to us that we didn't know, but he didn't share anything else about the discoveries he made in our temple. He's clearly an exceptional scholar, passionate about the secrets of that French pope, but I can't tell you anything about the conclusions he came to during his week here. As I said, he didn't mention anything before he left to go to—'

'To where?' the pair blurted out together, giving the monk a real fright.

'To Córdoba. Your father has gone to the south of Spain, to the city that was once the centre of the world. Oh yes, when the Count left, he said that he knew the pope had been there. When he told me that, I couldn't believe it. How would a man like Silvestre II have crossed the borders into a heretical region? Why did he go there? What dark intentions could he have had to warrant such a risky journey?'

* * *

At midnight, they made their way back as carefully as they could to the hostel. On the walk back they saw no sign of their pursuers. Once inside, Guylaine took the opportunity to call her mother again and tell her the good news. She quickly recounted the meeting with the monk and the news that her father had been staying with them since he had disappeared and had been well, which the Countess listened to with joy and relief.

After hanging up, Guylaine realised she had not told her mother that her father had left for Córdoba. She turned her head and saw that Marc seemed to be asleep; she quietly slipped into the adjacent bed, trying not to wake him.

Even though he was exhausted, Marc kept going over and over the same thing in his head, which was infuriatingly keeping him awake. During the night he weighed up whether or not he should tell his uncle about the shocking threat the thugs who brutally beat him up had put to him. Instinctively, he felt he should tell his closest relative the news, but another voice inside him told him that it was his own problem which he should resolve alone.

He had been waiting for the thugs to kill him but what had happened didn't make sense. For some inexplicable reason, out of the blue, someone had threatened to kill him in the same way someone had killed his parents twenty years ago. The Mignon family had continually tried to work out whether an assassin was to blame for Marc's parents' death or if they had suffered a terrible accident because they were speeding. Now, thanks to the threat of a thug whose face he had not been able to see, he knew for certain that his parents had been assassinated. Even if it was just to make them explain to him what had really happened all that time ago, a burning desire to go out and look for them was growing inside of him.

Despite his confusion, Marc's heart was showing him a clear path. He should figure out this problem on his own. Or at least, that's what he thought he should do.

* * *

Marc woke up to find that Guylaine was not in the room. He dressed as quickly as he could and went downstairs, still putting on one of his shoes. His anxiety was quickly overcome when he saw her chatting to the landlady at one of the tables in the foyer. Both women were deep in conversation over a glass of orange juice. Female chatter no doubt; he couldn't begin to imagine what they were talking about.

A quick greeting was enough to get Guylaine's attention.

'Hello Marc. I was just telling this lady that we finally found a clear trace of my father yesterday, that he was here for a week and has now gone to Córdoba.'

His expression of surprise and anger made it clear to Guylaine that she had stepped over the mark.

'Please don't take any notice of what my wife says. She's a bit put out by the trip to Spain; we should probably get back on the road today, in fact. If anyone asks after us, please tell them that we were never here.'

The detective took the landlady's arm and whispered something in her ear.

'My wife is a little unbalanced; we've been following my father-in-law, who disappeared with a young girl, abandoning his inconsolable wife. We can't be sure, but we think that she has managed to employ some thugs to find her husband and his young lover. That's why I'm begging you to say that we were never here if anyone asks after us, or my wife's father. Could you do that for me?'

The woman looked seriously worried. She believed Marc's explanation, even though it was quite different to what his wife had said.

While they were packing their suitcases, Marc reprimanded Guylaine, who admitted that she had been reckless, giddy with the news that her father was alive and well.

'You've forgotten that there's one, if not two, groups of men not far behind us who will beat us to a pulp if they catch us. This isn't a game. I believe they will not stop at killing us, and also your father, to get hold of the secret that that bloody machine conceals. Do you understand what I'm saying to you?'

She nodded. Marc's grip was hurting her as he held on firmly to her arm. She tried to free herself but he would not relent.

'We're being tracked down by organised groups who would kill us without batting an eyelid.'

Guylaine whimpered when he shook her vigorously. He let her go and tried to apologise. It had all got too much for him.

'I've got to tell you something important about the case.'

She nodded, taking a paper tissue out of her bag and dabbing the tears that had started to roll down her cheeks.

* * *

They said goodbye to the landlady, thanking her for their comfortable stay. Marc gave her a friendly wink on his way out. The landlady smiled back broadly.

Once again, they walked towards the monastery. They had left their unusable car there yesterday. Just as the car hire company had promised, they found a new vehicle ready for them next to the old one. A young man, dressed in company colours, saw them approaching and asked if they were the clients who had called him. Once established, he explained proudly that he had brought them a premium model with better features than the damaged car by way of compensation. They said goodbye to him and prepared to begin their journey.

'So, now, how do we get to Córdoba?' Guylaine wondered aloud.

'If we drive all the way, it will take us nearly twelve hours, or we could leave the car in Madrid and catch a high-speed train there. There are no flights to Córdoba.'

'I think we should go by car. We can get there directly. What do you reckon?'

'Let's go. The Muslim city awaits us.'

For the first few kilometres, Marc could not stop looking into the rear-view mirror, desperate to know that they were not being followed again.

'They followed us all the way from Paris to here. When do you think they will give up the chase?' wondered the detective.

'I don't know.'

'Believe me, they will try to catch us and to get to your father too. They are not going to stop until they get him.'

'Then we'll have to be careful.'

'I know I've asked you before, but do you know what secrets the pope's machine might contain? Why is there so much interest in deciphering it?'

'I don't know what these people are after. We have to stick to what my father told us in his letter. Remember what he wrote about witchery, spells and the bizarre information stored in that contraption. In all honesty though, I don't have a clue.'

'Well, we'll just have to carry on looking for your father and hope he can explain everything to us.'

'I know. By the way, are you going to tell me what provoked you to shake me like that this morning?'

'Yes, I will.'

A sudden change in Marc's mood made Guylaine sit upright in her seat, ready to hear what he was going to say.

CHAPTER 22

By the time Marc had finished telling her about his parents' death, his mouth was dry.

Guylaine thought carefully about her next words, hoping they might comfort him in some way.

'Have you thought that maybe they said it just to scare you and distract you from the search for my father? Perhaps there's no connection and they only investigated your background and used what they found out to threaten you.'

'Yes, I considered that. But the hatred in the guy's voice when he said those words clearly gave away that he had been involved in what he was talking about and that my parents had been assassinated by this same group of thugs.'

'And why might they have done something so brutal?'

'That's the thing. I can't find even the slightest connection between the Baumard case and the disappearance of your father.'

'What's wrong with your voice?'

'Don't worry, I just need to stop to get something to drink.'

He found a place for them to stop and rest, an enormous service station where dozens of trucks were parked—and it had a large self-service restaurant. The road towards Madrid had been quite clear so far; they should reach the centre of the country before dark.

He left Guylaine in the car, parked in the visiting area, telling her not to get out of the vehicle under any circumstances. He walked up to the garage, dodging between vans across the middle of the car park. Turning around, he saw one of their pursuers standing right in front of him, staring, impassive. By the time he realised that he was in danger, the man had broken into a fast run, coming straight towards him.

Shocked but acting quickly, Marc kicked the man hard in the stomach as he neared him; the thug fell into a ball on the dirty tarmac. All he could do was to stare up at the detective, surprised by the blow. Marc turned on his heels, trying to get to the white vehicle and Guylaine as quickly as possible.

On reaching the car his eyes grew wide with shock; Guylaine was not in the car.

* * *

Trying to contain his panic, also caught up with anger, Marc looked over the car to see if those bastards had broken in by force and snatched Guylaine. Her bag was nowhere in sight. Had it been discarded, after a struggle, beside another car perhaps, or were there any other traces of her nearby?

It was impossible to scan the whole car park, as drivers had haphazardly parked their lorries everywhere and several heavy vehicles were arranged in a line across the middle of the concourse, forming a perfect barrier against any quick exit attempt. It suddenly occurred to him that, if they had forced her to get out of the car, it was likely that their getaway car might still be in the vicinity. He began to run as fast as he could to check for the battered red saloon. His heart beat violently as awful images of what those savages might do to Guylaine if they had got their hands on her flashed across his mind. Marc weaved in and out of the enormous haulage lorries, never getting a clear view between them, constantly fearing that he was one step too slow.

Without any forewarning, Marc crashed heads with someone, with a noise that must have rung out across the car park, not just between his ears. The person he had knocked into fell to the floor with the strength of their collision, and Marc's legs also gave way beneath him. When he managed to stagger back on to his feet, he realised that it was one of the lorry drivers. The man threw a string of insults at him, accusing him of not looking where he was going. Marc didn't lose a second in apologising but after a couple of hasty words carried on running. The sunlight at that time of day was so blinding that he had to shield his eyes to see any distance. There was no trace of the red car whatsoever. Nor could he see Guylaine anywhere.

Peering into the dingy cafeteria there was no one he recognised; in the garage shop, again, no one. Now worried almost beyond logical thinking, his heart pounding and his head throbbing, Marc could not even spot the kidnapper he had punched in the stomach only a few minutes ago. She had definitely been taken. It must be them.

* * *

Marc had no idea how to find Guylaine. With his head down, weakened and disappointed with his failure to protect his client, he took himself back to the car. On his way back, out of the corner of his eye he saw a woman very similar in appearance to Guylaine waiting in the queue for the toilets. Could it really be her, standing by the garage he had just searched? For a brief moment he was overwhelmed with joy. He had imagined the terrible situation he would have had to face up to if she had been kidnapped—as if he didn't already have enough problems.

He had not even reached the line of women snaking in front of the toilets when he saw the taller of their pursuers making his way towards her at full pelt. He knew he must get to Guylaine first. It wouldn't be easy, seeing that the other guy was already considerably closer. Adrenaline pumping hard, he yelled to Guylaine to leave the queue and run to the car. With frantic gestures, desperate that he wouldn't be able to help her escape in time, he pointed out to her the kidnapper.

Guylaine saw that, just metres away, a tall man was rushing towards her from behind, arms open, hands out, ready to grab her. She leapt out of the queue and ran, ran as fast as her legs would take her until she reached Marc. He grabbed her by the hand and pulled her towards him in the direction of their car. He told her to run as fast as she could, and she obeyed without saying a word.

Seconds later they reached the hire car, both silently shocked at how quickly they had reacted in the last few moments. Marc shot a glance over to where the man had been and saw that, although he had fallen some metres behind, he was rapidly making the distance across the car park. Marc started the car in first gear, the engine shuddering reluctantly to life. The vehicle jumped on to the pavement, at the same time lifting the criminal onto the bonnet, smearing his face against the windshield.

Marc thought he would never forget the image of that face pressed up against the glass, centimetres from his own face. Marc looked him directly in the eye. The stranger held his gaze unflinchingly with a coldness that would make blood freeze. All he could think about was that this man might well have killed his parents.

His pulse did not slow down as he accelerated through first gear, forcing the man to the ground. Despite the loud crunching of the motor as he drove away, the sound of the body hitting the pavement cut through the noise and made him shudder. He looked out of the rear-view mirror just to make sure that the immobile heap on the pavement behind them was not about to give chase.

CHAPTER 23

After speeding away from the car park, even the dozens of kilometres they had covered didn't calm their fear that the red car was still somewhere behind them.

'Do you think they will have given up?' asked Guylaine, Marc's endless glancing into the mirror unnerving her.

'Hopefully we're a good way in front of them. But I do think that we should catch the high-speed train from Madrid to make sure we get to Córdoba before them and can shake them off our tail.'

'Good idea.'

Comfortable in their seats on the train, for the first time in days the detective and his assistant exhaled a deep breath in unison. They smiled at each other thinking, about the mad journey they had undertaken to get on this train.

Marc decided to be frank with Guylaine.

'I want you to know that we are in grave danger.'

'You think I don't know that?'

'I fancy spending a few days on some faraway beach; this is making me think about my time with Greenpeace. I'm exhausted.'

'I expect that's because of the beating you suffered the other day. We've got a bit of time until we get to Córdoba.

Do you want to tell me about your life before you became a detective?'

'All right. What do you want to know?'

'I would like you to tell me why a young guy like you decides to waste the best years of his life protecting whales from Japanese fishermen.'

'What a question! I saw it as a positive investment of my time, not a waste.' He stretched out his legs as much as he could and crossed his arms across his chest.

'As I've told you, my parents died when I was about ten. It's difficult to imagine what goes through the mind of a child who loses their family in one fell swoop. It was an awful thing to happen, an event from which I have never recovered. The following years were really hard for me; I had been a well-behaved child—shy, in fact—but I became a rebellious adolescent. My uncle took care of me and supported me as I, with great difficulty, managed to finish the baccalaureate and my degree. I owed it to him after he had dedicated his life to raising me, his nephew. He never married nor seemed to have any girlfriends; I think it was down to the worries I gave him. That's why I was determined to finish my studies to honour him.

'After that, I dedicated the rest of my life to doing what I wanted to do and, instead of looking for a job related to my degree, I took a rather non-conformist route. First of all, I travelled round North America, from north to south, using the little money sent to me from France, supplemented by some minor jobs. On my travels, I realised that the world was in a real state. One particular event persuaded me to take a more activist stance in life. It happened in a Chilean fishing factory, where I worked for some months, having covered the entire Pacific coast by this time. It was there that I realised multinational companies had no scruples in the pursuit of cheap fish which they wished to sell at as high a price as possible; they plundered the sea and had no respect for endangered species or awareness of the damage they were doing. Every time we received a shipment of fish, I felt sick about what was arriving. After a few weeks, I came into contact with some people from Greenpeace who were trying to track down the fishing boats that supplied the unscrupulous guys with all the fish they asked for. I decided to unite with them and ingratiated myself into their circle.

'The following years were incredible. I have seen so much of the world and have visited countries that I would never have imagined going to. Do you remember the barrels of nuclear waste that were thrown into the sea and the people that went out in motorboats to try to stop them? Well, I was there, in one of those little unprotected boats in the middle of the ocean. I enjoyed those adventures; I ended up chasing bear hunters and people who slaughtered seal cubs in the North Pole.

'After a long time immersed in these crusades, I suffered an injury when I was tracking down some animal slaughterers on an ice plain. The blood left an enormous red stain in the snow. They had to treat me in a filthy hospital in a place I don't even know how to pronounce. When I could travel again, I returned to Paris to rest for a few months and—'

'And what?'

'Well, my uncle Marcos Mignon offered me this job. I have to confess that I lied to you. This is my first assignment as a detective. I'm sorry.'

The silence in the cabin, interrupted only by the soft whistle of the train as it travelled at great speed to its destination, was finally broken by her first words after his confession.

'I already knew that. My mother investigated your agency in the first few days you were on the case, as there were some things that didn't make sense to her about your manner of dealing with the case.'

'What did she find out?'

'That nobody in the world of private investigations knew you. The Mignon Agency is very famous but you were absolutely unknown.'

'So why didn't she say this to my uncle? Why did she let me stay on the case?'

'It's pretty simple. My mother warms to people she considers "nice". She must have had her reasons.'

Guylaine was still suspicious about the detective's relationship with her mother; she asked herself whether she thought he would have been capable of going to bed with the Countess. If that was what had happened, she would never forgive him.

* * *

A train attendant approached them with a cart full of drinks. Marc bought a small bottle of water to clear his throat. He let his mind wander and considered the possibility that Guylaine knew about the slip-up with her mother. Through the glass door that separated one carriage from another, he could make out the figures of two men approaching from the back part of the train.

He took Guylaine's hand sharply and pulled her to her feet. He put a finger to his lips, asking her to come with him without saying a word. They left their seats, stealthily heading towards the back of the train. After they had gone through the restaurant, he decided to speak.

'They're following us again. Those guys have caught wind of our plans and they know where we are going. I think there must be something else we don't know. I think someone is passing them information.'

'I don't know what you mean. How were they been able to follow us here?'

'We've got to find out, but first we have to get off this train.'

They saw that their pursuers were checking the different compartments one by one. Marc bumped into a stewardess and asked her what the next stop was. The blonde girl flashed him a big smile.

'Córdoba, Sir. We will be there in five minutes.'

He pulled Guylaine by the hand again and dragged her to the back of the train. When he was convinced that there was no more passageway he could go down unnoticed, he pushed her into the bathroom. Peering through the door, he checked no one had seen them and closed the bathroom door. The narrow compartment was barely big enough for both of them so, squashed up against each other, they held each other's gaze in silence. After a while, they noticed that the train was slowing down; it was drawing into the station. He whispered to her to keep quiet and half opened the door to check where their pursuers were.

As the train reached a complete standstill, he glanced down the passage and pushed Guylaine out of the toilet.

When he had checked that no one was following them, he grabbed her hand again and led her to the seats where their luggage was. They snatched their cases and ran to the exit.

On the platform, they found themselves in a line of people heading out of the station. They joined them and saw that the exit of the station was not far. They walked in that direction as casually as possible. With no trace of the thugs who were pursuing them, they reached a large area in front of the railway station. Although it was possible to hire a car inside the building, they chose to walk to an adjacent street and lose themselves in the maze of roads. As they only had a small suitcase each, they were able to move swiftly on foot.

By a stroke of luck, they happened upon a medium-sized, modern-looking hotel in which they could discreetly spend the night.

They agreed to use the same story as they had done in Ripoll: they were a couple in search of a crazy old father-in-law, who had gone mad in his pursuit of a young woman. If anyone asked after them, the concierge would say that he knew nothing, thanks to the generous tip he had accepted from the secretive guests. They found their room and quickly closed the door.

Guylaine went over to the window and looked outside to check that no one was watching them from the road. She told Marc that it seemed like they were safe at last. Marc asked her not to be so complacent because, if the thugs had followed them to Córdoba, someone close to them must have tipped them off.

When he finished speaking, they realised with surprise that there was only one bed in the hotel room.

CHAPTER 24

Reims

Véronique Dubois felt claustrophobic within the four walls of her bedroom. Alone, bored and frustrated with the Count's wild behaviour, she threw herself into alcohol. She had never drunk like she had done in the last few years. It was the only refuge from her problems though. With Pierre away from the castle, her child out of the country and, above all, her lover lost to her forever, what else could she do but drink?

Having drunk a fair amount of the family champagne, and with nothing to do that afternoon, the Countess decided to tour the empty rooms of the castle, which now seemed more than ever like a dungeon. She went into Guylaine's bedroom and opened one of the wardrobes. She liked to wear her daughter's dresses and, on more than one occasion, she had borrowed one to go and meet Bruno, in an attempt to look younger. As she had said many times before, she thought there was nothing good about getting old. She believed that her affair with a young lover was some form of compensation for the years her husband had taken away from her.

She left her daughter's bedroom and made her way to the rooms upstairs, where the Count had relocated his offices some time ago. She couldn't remember when she had last been there; it must have been more than five years ago. It was an unattractive space, because of the grey stone walls and the old-fashioned installations. She noticed that some windows didn't even have panes, as they were in the highest tower of the Divange medieval fort, the exterior aspect of which was listed and protected from renovation. She sat down at Pierre's desk and reclined in his favourite old armchair, which was covered in leather that had to be older than he was, and tried to work out what it was that had kept her in this castle all these years.

She opened one of the drawers; it was an absolute mess inside. Dozens of pencils, biros and fountain pens had been abandoned. It was like a cemetery for writing implements. She opened another of the Count's drawers in his desk; this time she found a bunch of different-coloured files that had been piled up in a disorderly fashion. Picking up one of the files, the Countess saw that it contained documents related to the buying and selling of land. Pierre had been constantly having land excavated in search of information about the location of the great thing that was now in the basement. She opened a yellow folder and what she found made her feel very anxious.

It was a hand-written letter addressed to her husband in the familiar script of her lover's writing.

Impatiently, the Countess checked that it was the only paper in the file. Seeing that it was, she placed it on the empty table and started to read.

Dear Pierre,

First and foremost, I would like to thank you for the interest you have shown during our negotiations and for accepting my proposal.

I know that it can't have been easy for you. The development of your family's investigations over hundreds of years has been carried on most admirably by you.

That is why, once more, I must tell you that your decision has been prudent. You have not made a mistake.

For reasons that I cannot explain now, I know about almost every aspect of your millennial search. I believe I can bring significant insight to the investigation as we embark on the next stage together.

Yours sincerely,

Bruno

Her initial thought was to rip that awful piece of paper into a thousand pieces. She had to breathe deeply before thinking about what to do with it. With her pulse still racing, she realised that the letter had an envelope attached to it. Still unbelieving, she turned it over and saw that there was Bruno's address perfectly written on the back.

Véronique swore out loud.

For years she had been the faithful lover to this young man. In that time, she had had the best moments of her life. She had even toyed with the idea of leaving the Count to form a stable relationship with Bruno. In the last few days, after he had broken up with her, she had started to mull over what happened over the course of their relationship before the dreadful day that he left her. Among many other things she remembered that, despite her asking several times, he never wanted to show her his apartment—the flat he said he rented in Paris—and they had always made love in the castle or in one of the other flats which, spread across the country, made up the property empire of the Dubois family. She remembered bitterly a number of passionate nights they had enjoyed in secluded hotels in the French countryside.

The envelope displayed an address on the Boulevard Haussmann, extraordinarily close to the Paris Opera House. It was an expensive area in central Paris that did not tally with the lowly social position Bruno had always claimed he came from.

Why had he lied to her?

Who was her lover really?

She went to pick up her mobile phone but remembered that she had broken it in a rage. She let a few minutes pass and meditated on her next step. She picked up the phone in the Count's office and dialled the number of the Mignon Agency. She would use the detective firm to find out what was behind this deception.

* * *

The Countess demanded to speak to Monsieur Marcos Mignon himself, the person whom she had entrusted with the search for her husband. The receptionist informed her that the general director of the firm was investigating a case in Strasbourg, but that he would probably be back in the office the following day and, if her matter was not very urgent, he would call her on his return or another of the many detectives at the large organisation would deal with it.

Véronique Dubois barked down the telephone that only the head of the agency would do. The Countess left her number insisting that it was urgent. Three minutes later, the phone rang.

'Good afternoon, Countess. My secretary has explained how keen you were to get in contact with me. Has something happened?'

'You could say that. The detective that you sent to us has gone to Spain with my daughter and, although things are otherwise progressing well, I have discovered a new clue that is really important for the case. It has to do with a suspect who lives in Paris. When do you get back to your office?'

'I had planned to return tomorrow on the last flight of the evening, but I can be there first thing if you would like?'

'Yes, please. I would like to see you as soon as possible.'

He agreed and said goodbye politely. Once she had done as she had planned, she hung up the telephone and set about packing a suitcase.

If her manipulative ex-lover was in Paris, she would go there and expose him.

CHAPTER 25

Córdoba

They had waited for it to get dark before going out and inspecting the city. A tourist map from the hotel helped them to identify the main historic sites of the old town. It was obvious that the Count would be searching for millennial monuments here, so anything that didn't date from the Middle Ages could be immediately discounted. A faint ray of amber twilight filtered through the room's thick curtains. Marc and Guylaine looked at each other and knew that it was time to go out. Their first destination was the Great Mosque of Córdoba.

The impressive monument had, in fact, been constructed long before the end of the millennium and had gone through successive stages of extension and development. They decided to go for a long walk around the roads near the mosque to look for the Count. Anyone who had come to research millenarianism would be in the grounds of the mosque-cathedral for sure. They went to their destination on foot.

'We needn't go so fast,' suggested Guylaine. 'We have time to take a leisurely walk and look around calmly.'

'Sorry. It's just that I can't get the thought out of my head that those guys must be around here somewhere. It's obvious they'll be heading to the same places as us.'

She nodded and carried on, eyeing up people around

her more suspiciously, in case they were their pursuers. She paid particular attention to the people having dinner at the many terraces scattered around the mosque; it seemed as if everyone was eating outside on this warm night.

'In Andalucía people practically live in the street. It's cooler in the evening, so the locals prefer to go out at night. Wouln't it be nice to sit down and have a nice, cold beer at one of those terraces…' suggested Marc.

The mosque appeared at the end of the road, imposing like a barrier.

'I expected a more spectacular monument,' Marc pondered. 'I always thought that this building was one of the largest and best-conserved buildings from the Middle Ages.'

'It is. It's much more impressive inside than outside. Don't forget that, even though the Christians converted it into the cathedral of Córdoba some years after the acquisition of the city, it's designed for Muslim prayer. But there's no doubting it's an imposing monument. I visited it some time ago and can still remember its huge interior…'

'I don't reckon it will be open at night.'

'I don't think so either. But if you agree, we could take a walk around the building, in case my father is anywhere nearby.'

'Of course.'

They walked away from the entrance through which thousands of tourists entered every day and went around one of the corners of the rectangular building.

All of a sudden, Guylaine bumped into a man who was walking about absentmindedly; his head was lifted as he contemplated the highest part of the building. By the look of surprise on Guylaine's face, Marc thought that it must be her father whom she had run into. The detective helped the man up, who had fallen to the ground with the force of the impact.

He now saw that it wasn't the Count. Nevertheless, the person in front of them was a great surprise.

A speechless Jean Luc Renaud looked up at them in disbelief.

* * *

Marc's first reaction was to grab Jean Luc by the lapels of the bottle-green jacket he was wearing and demand that he explain what the hell he was doing there. Guylaine intervened, stepping forward calmly.

'What a surprise! What are you doing here?'

'Well, the same as you. Last night I spoke to the Countess and she told me you had got hold of information that the Count was in Spain. So, that's why I have come here.'

'And have you seen my father?'

'No. I haven't stopped looking since I arrived but I haven't seen the Count anywhere. I think that he must be following an important clue in one of these places.'

'And how do you plan to find the Count?' the detective interrogated.

'Well, I don't know… I think I'll come here tomorrow morning and ask the guards if they have seen any sign of him. If he really has been in the mosque, I'm sure that he will have carried out an exhaustive investigation, so he must have interviewed the staff to get more information.'

'That was our plan too,' Guylaine told him.

'Well, if you don't mind, I'd like to join you in the search. I have a hunch that your father is nearby.'

* * *

Marc watched the enormous full moon from their hotel room. They had returned at midnight, leaving Jean Luc behind; he had arranged to stay at an old Spanish university friend's house.

They didn't see any sign of the two thugs on the way back. They had also warned Renaud to keep an eye out for the two men who had been following them since Reims.

Due to the suffocating heat, Marc stayed by the window for a while to cool down. The noise of a motorbike speeding up the road in front of the hotel woke Guylaine up, who was sleeping in bed. She saw that Marc was lost in thought, gazing at the sky.

'Can't you sleep?'

'No. I'm going over something in my head.'

'Only one thing? Thousands of things are going through my head these days.'

'Mine too, but one thing is especially bothering me now.'

'And what's that?'

'Renaud lied to us. You didn't tell your mother that we were coming to Córdoba. How did he know we were here?'

'You're right,' she murmured. 'I didn't tell my mother we were coming here, so someone else must have told Renaud. Who do you think could be behind this?'

'I fear that the thugs following us could have been in

contact with him. You already know that I'm suspicious of him because he admitted he had had some involvement in satanic groups that have been helping your father in his investigations.'

'Yes, but I still don't understand how a man like my father's assistant, who has spent his whole life with us, could go about soliciting help from demons.'

Marc didn't answer, watching the moon's slow movement among the buildings of the old city.

'Stop looking at the sky and tell me your suspicions. If Renaud is in some way connected with the brutes who interrogated you or with the Devil's helpers, if they are the same people, however small this connection may be we need to get more information out of him. We should keep him close and find out if it's true,' said Guylaine, waving her hand in front of his eyes, trying to break the trance he was in.

'Exactly. I already had that in mind. There are lots of loose ends in this case and they're making me nervous.'

'Don't worry. Everything points to the fact that we're close to my father.'

'If only that was certain. Don't you think you ought to call your mother to ask her if she has spoken to Renaud?'

'It's a little late but I will.'

Guylaine called the castle, knowing that she was going to wake up the staff, but she was unable to get through on the Countess's mobile. The butler answered straight away, insisting she did not need to apologise because he had not yet been asleep. Guylaine's question surprised him though; he assumed she knew about her mother's movements.

'Miss, the Countess left the castle this afternoon. She took a suitcase, as if she was going away for a few days, and she didn't leave an address. I thought you knew.'

Guylaine's silence said it all. Something had happened to call the Countess away.

CHAPTER 26

The day dawned without a cloud in the sky. Marc and Guylaine had already been around the mosque several times that morning in search of the Count. Although the morning was cooler than the warm night, they already had sweat patches on their shirts. While they scoured the building, conversation turned to the inexplicable departure of the Countess and their sudden, chance encounter with Renaud.

After a while the pair settled down for a rest. The Count's assistant appeared on time; they had agreed to check the interior of the mosque with him. They bought three tickets and chose not to go round with a tour guide. Jean Luc had offered to give an in-depth explanation of what they were going to see. He had been there dozens of times, sometimes as a tourist and, on many other occasions, as a historian. Jean Luc promised that his research on the mosque would help them find clues from the age of the Umayyadd Empire, which could help them uncover secrets of the first millennium.

In the entrance to the mosque, Marc's eyes widened.

'Your reaction doesn't surprise me, Mr Mignon,' Renaud said to him. 'Everyone looks equally in awe when they first set foot in this fabulous building.'

Having passed through the Gate of Forgiveness, the Count's assistant planted himself in front of the Orange Tree Courtyard and cleared his throat, ready to begin his talk on the Great Mosque of Córdoba.

'This courtyard conserves a good deal of its original appearance and is a good place to start. The Visigothic basilica, which was previously the most important Christian temple in the city, originally stood on this site. When the Arabs, under the first Umayyadd Emir Abderraman I, invaded the Iberian Peninsula, they decided to destroy the previous building, probably between 780 and 785, and constructed this mosque in its place, on the foundation of the Christian church. Furthermore, he changed its orientation so that, unlike other mosques, the new temple was south facing. Nobody knows exactly why he did this, although it could be simply down to error. Politically speaking though, the builders of this impressive work might have wanted to imitate the Great Mosque of Damascus, another of the Umayyadd's marvellous works that faces south.'

Inside, they saw a massive forest of columns; Marc thought they looked like the palm trees he had seen on a trip to Saudi Arabia. The place undoubtedly cast a spell on them, enhanced by the dappled light that filtered through the lattices and domes of the great space. Marc's surprise grew as he walked through an immense room full of marble shafts that branched off into richly sculpted arches, in which colourful carvings created a spectacular visual impact.

'This space has been through many extensions and

remodellings, some of which were very significant. For example, Hisham I constructed a minaret, which was then knocked down by Abderraman III. Today its remains are inlaid into the Christian bell tower of the cathedral.'

Guylaine and Marc looked at the part of the mosque the assistant was pointing to.

'As I have said, this mosque was developed gradually but the greatest reforms took place in the tenth century, coinciding with the splendour of the Caliphate era. After Abderraman III, Almanzor decided to put the final redevelopments of that period into effect, carrying out the biggest extensions of the mosque of all those undertaken in this millennial building,' Renaud explained.

'Obviously there could be many clues relating to our investigation here. But…what exactly could my father be looking for here?'

'I don't know for certain. This mosque is an extraordinary synthesis of European history; it contains thousands of clues that we are unable to see, despite them being right under our noses. A good part of what we are looking at is conserved from the millennial period and has been enjoyed in this form by travellers, scholars, ambassadors and, of course, the Muslims who prayed here over the centuries. I think the Count will be searching for a clue that came up when he was examining the talking head.'

'I think that, since we don't have any firm ideas, we should have a look around the mosque for him.'

'Yes, but with caution. It's likely that our pursuers are nearby,' warned Marc, who pointed them in the direction of a more isolated part of the building where they could proceed more discreetly.

The detective observed that Renaud didn't bat an eyelid when he mentioned the thugs. Although this didn't necessarily mean anything, Marc thought that he should keep an eye on him.

* * *

A little over an hour passed. The many circuits they had done around the columns had made the three of them dizzy, so they decided to take a seat on a small bench.

'Why is this mosque so important to the case?' asked Marc. 'How is it connected to the end of the first millennium?'

'We must look to the Umayyadds for the answer,' replied Renaud. 'There is no firm evidence that Silvestre II was in Córdoba before he became pope, but there are signs which indicate that this could have been the case. And why did a monk like Silvestre want to come here? The answer is simple: this city was the centre of the world in the tenth century. The Umayyadds converted it into a centre of power admired by all of Europe. Do you know the history of the Umayyadds, Mr Mignon?'

'No, I must admit that I don't.'

'Well, it's very interesting. It all started with Abderraman I, also know as "the Immigrant". Today millions of people from all over Africa immigrate to Europe in search of a better life, but centuries ago this was very unusual, especially for one such immigrant to come to this land and fill it with wealth. Do you realise how odd that must have been?'

Marc nodded, as did Guylaine, who was following Jean

Luc's explanations with increasing interest.

'Well, Abderraman I was the first Umayyadd of al-Andalus. He came to these lands in the year 755, fleeing from the slaughter of his family in Damascus at the hands of the Abbasids, who had become the new caliphs of Baghdad. When he arrived south of the peninsula, delegates of the East governed these lands and there were swarms of Arabs and Berbers here, as well as Christians, Jews and other races.

'With time, Abderraman I grew in social status and was awarded the post of Emir of al-Andalus. Back then the Moorish mosque was a small and modest building, an old basilica that had been used by the Visigoths for a long time. As Emir of this region, Abderraman I had to prevent the caliphs that governed in the East, the Abbasids who had wiped out his family, from taking control of these lands. He declared this part of Europe independent, founding an Independent Emirate.

'The next logical step was to found a great mosque to show the world that the rise of the Umayyadd lineage had begun and, of course, to build a place where Muslims could pray. The monument we are standing in now can be attributed to Abderraman I, who died in 788 or thereabouts.'

'I guess he wasn't the only Umayyadd to make this land prosperous?'

'Indeed. His dynasty in the city of Córdoba lasted for many centuries. One of his descendants, Abderraman III, proclaimed Córdoba as an independent caliphate in the year 929, putting an end to the Emirate state. Abderraman III proclaimed himself Caliph to set himself up as the political head of state and spiritual leader of the Muslim people; his family came from the Quraysh tribe which Muhammad belonged had to. He also succeeded in preventing the northern Christian kingdoms' attempts to re-conquer al-Andalus. As Caliph, he began to build a palatial city not far from here, the stunning Medina Azahara, just as his namesakes in the East had constructed for themselves.

'By the middle of the tenth century, as the end of the millennium was approaching, the Caliph of Córdoba had made the city the centre of the world. His influence extended beyond the borders of al-Andalus across the whole of Europe. The Holy Roman-German Empire exchanged ambassadors with Córdoba and Emperor Otto himself sent distinguished representatives here. The power of the Caliph in military, economic and cultural fields had no bounds.'

'And this is why our pope must have come here,' added Guylaine. 'If there was a city in the whole of the Western world that was rich in scientific knowledge, as well as housing these millennial secrets, it was Córdoba. There are those who say that this city's library contained hundreds of thousands of books from the most diverse sources, conserved and translated from Greek extensively into Latin, and also into Arabic and Hebrew.'

'Yes, indeed. Muslim intellectuals like Averroes, Abubekar, Ibn Masarra, or the Jew Moses Maimonides, made this city world-famous in the scientific fields of astronomy, medicine and mathematics.'

'But you still haven't answered my question,' insisted Marc. 'What connection could all this have with the end of the millennium and, above all, the Count's investigations?'

'There is a date that I still haven't given to you, Mr

Mignon. The Umayyadd Empire existed until the year 1031, disappearing a little before the one-thousand-year anniversary of the death of Jesus Christ.'

'Ah yes, the Parousia and the prophecy of the Book of Revelation proclaim that the Devil is unleashed one thousand years after the death of Christ.'

'Indeed. I am pleased to hear that you are becoming increasingly well-informed…'

Renaud's subtle yet intense stare as he said these words did not go unnoticed by the detective, who realised that he was hiding a secret, but as yet was refusing to share it with them.

CHAPTER 27

Marc was worried; he couldn't work out what Renaud, who had appeared from nowhere and who was now directing the search for the Count, was hiding.

Hearing that they spoke his language, a French tourist asked them for the exit to the mosque. As Renaud was directing him, Guylaine saw two men running towards them at great speed. Before she had time to think, she found herself shouting to Marc and Jean Luc, warning them desperately, but causing several visitors to turn their heads in surprise at her outburst in the holy temple. Marc took her by the hand and urged their guide as forcefully as he could in the direction of the exit.

The next second, Renaud tripped over the root of a tree in the courtyard, staggered and, unable to control his fall, landed in a bed of yellow and red ornamental flowers. The detective didn't know whether to follow Guylaine, who was already outside the mosque, or help the Count's assistant, now awkwardly struggling to get to his feet. When he saw that their pursuers had thrown themselves on top of Jean Luc, he ran after Guylaine, putting himself between them and her, taking one last glance at Renaud, who was being lifted up by one of the thugs. The man looked directly at Marc, his eyes full of hatred. Marc and Guylaine held hands and ran towards one of the narrow streets that led away from the millennial mosque.

* * *

After a few minutes of darting up and down the narrow streets branching off the mosque square, surprising the tourists enjoying quiet drinks in the *terrazas*, Guylaine felt her heart beating uncontrollably. She begged Marc to stop, at least for a moment. Given that they couldn't see anyone following them, they slipped into the nearest doorway, concealed from the street by an enormous column, and only then did Marc let go of Guylaine's hand.

He was the first to speak when their breathing had calmed down.

'I think we've lost them.'

'And Renaud as well. Good God! What will happen to him? After what they did to you, I don't even want to think about what they'll do to him. I don't think he'd survive even one attack or round of torture. I've known him some time and he's weak. He'll break and tell them everything they want to know…'

'There's little more he can reveal than what they already know. We haven't really told him anything else.'

'What now?'

'I suggest we go to the police to report Renaud's disappearance. We have to try to find him.'

'Now we have two missing people.'

'Strictly speaking, there are three, if you count your mother…'

Tears began to fall down Guylaine's cheek. They were lost

in a city they didn't know, pursued by two characters with dark intentions, and they were currently without a coherent plan.

Marc drew her towards him, holding her close. Holding her in his arms, he couldn't help but think how he had become attracted to Guylaine. She was intelligent, sharp and affectionate – all qualities of a woman he felt he could be able to share his life with, after the loneliness of his childhood and adolescence. But there was no point fantasising. If she ever knew, Guylaine would never forgive him for his foolhardy encounter with her mother. There was absolutely no excuse. He had taken what the Countess had offered him with pleasure. Not even the brutal thrashing he had been given that day could be justification for his actions. He resolved to abandon all hope of a future in which she featured. Guylaine noticed that Marc was squeezing her tightly. She pulled away and, wiping her tears with a tissue, promised not to cry again. It was clear that her father's life was in danger and she had to be strong.

Marc was impressed by how quickly Guylaine regained her composure, suddenly ready to move on in search of a police station. He owed it to her to banish all romantic thoughts of her from his mind; he must, for once, be strong.

CHAPTER 28

Paris

Even though she had to been to Paris countless times, a woman as cosmopolitan as the Countess could always find new entertainment, so much more stimulating than Reims. Véronique left the Hilton hotel. She had booked on impulse the day before, perhaps because it evoked a comfortable feeling of nostalgia.

She walked up the street and headed towards the central offices of the Mignon Agency. Within a few minutes, she reached the smart, four-storey building on Avenue Hoche that housed the finest organisation dedicated to private investigation in France. From the reception, she was personally accompanied to the meeting room on the top floor. The Countess saw that the company was far larger than she had imagined.

Someone offered her coffee. Then out of one of the many doors surrounding the reception room, a man of considerable stature, with a tanned complexion and tidy black hair, appeared. The Countess guessed him to be about fifty years old. He looked good for his age and immediately made an impression on her.

'Good morning, Countess. I'm Marcos Mignon.' He spoke directly, with extreme confidence, while taking her hand to kiss it. 'Please, do step into my office.'

She sat down on a large leather sofa from which she could see the Trocadero and the Eiffel Tower through the agency's large windows.

'You have offices worthy of a fine institution. I've always imagined that a detective agency would be housed in a dark establishment, with an old fan and a glass door with the investigator's name on it.'

'I think you have seen too many Hollywood films. Nowadays, there are lots of modern agencies like ours; although, thinking about it, there are also still one or two left as you mentioned.'

Marcos waited for the Countess to finish her coffee before beginning his questions.

'What was the urgent matter that you wanted to speak to me about?'

'Firstly, I would like to thank you for sending us that fabulous young detective to find my husband. He is a great help and it appears that he now has some very solid clues in connection with the possible whereabouts of the Count.'

'It pleases me to hear that. My nephew is just starting in this job but I can assure you that he is going to be one of the best in the business. I am convinced that Marc has the makings of a top detective, just like his father. Does that have anything to do with why you have come?'

'Not exactly. He is with my daughter in Spain right now. The problem is here, in Paris, which is why I decided to get in contact with you.'

'Go ahead.'

'Are you obliged to keep the information your clients give you confidential?'

'Absolutely. You can trust me.'

'Good. It's very difficult for me to explain what I have to say, but it is of vital importance that I do. Might I have some water?'

Marcos opened a panelled door, behind which there was a fridge full of drinks. Seeing that he also had quarter bottles of champagne, Véronique thought that a glass might calm her nerves and loosen her tongue. He agreed and opened a bottle for her.

'Some years ago I met a young North African man who, for reasons that are difficult for me to explain, had a big impact on my life.'

'You don't have to tell me any more than that.'

'Unfortunately those extra details are important. The thing is that, during this time, I have been having an affair with him under my own roof, in the castle. In my husband's office, where he carries out his investigations, there is a lot of information about all his studies.'

'What's the young man called?'

'Bruno.'

'And his surname?'

'He never told me,' answered the Countess, taking another sip of her drink and lighting a cigarette. 'Nor had I any need to know it. He was certainly a cultured boy and, over time, he asked me to lend him some books from my husband's library. Later on, he even asked me for some plans and papers about my husband's most recent investigations regarding this damned old machine that the Dubois family have, for centuries, been looking for. I didn't think anything of it. I thought that my lover was simply fascinated, and wanted to learn for his own personal interest. He's an archaeology student in Paris, you see.'

'Could you tell me why this might be connected to the disappearance of your husband?'

She didn't say anything in response but, instead, put her hand in her bag and took out a folded letter. She passed it to him to read. The Countess told the detective that she wanted his help to get into Bruno's apartment, even if he was not there.

The detective took a large gulp of his drink before answering the Countess.

'I cannot break into someone's apartment just like that, with no cause for entry. Only the police can do that and even then only with the authority of a judge.'

'I have employed the best agency in Paris. I'm sure that you're accustomed to doing such things on a daily basis, or so I've been led to believe. I'm going there right now; if you want to accompany me, do so. If not, I'll go alone.'

Marcos had little choice but to give the benefit of the doubt to the Countess.

They left the building by a lift that took them directly to the underground car park where the detective had a car ready. A little over twenty minutes later, they reached Boulevard Haussmann, managing to park right outside the block they hoped included Bruno's apartment. The door was open and there didn't seem to be any sort of concierge guarding the entrance, so they made their way up to the fourth floor. As they slammed the gates and the lift cranked into action, Marcos told Véronique what he wanted her to do.

'Ring the bell and wait for someone to answer it. If he's

inside, I imagine he'll invite you in. I'll wait on the landing of the stairs. If he's not in, we'll try to pick the lock. Agreed?'

She nodded.

In front of Bruno's apartment door, Véronique was again curious that the boy's description of himself as a poor student did not match this smart Parisian apartment style. She rang the bell once and waited briefly before pressing it again. When there was no reply, she signalled to Marcos to join her by the door. He brought over an enormous set of keys and lock-picks on a sturdy brass ring. He knelt down and, with his ear glued to the lock, started to insert the various keys one by one. After just a few minutes, the door to the apartment was flung open. Marcos got out his gun and edged into the apartment first.

Marcos checked the rooms one by one to make sure they were alone. Only then did he speak, asking the Countess to tell him exactly what they were looking for.

'I'd like to see if there are any letters, documents or any other paperwork that could tell us who Bruno really is.'

Véronique opened the top drawers of an ornate antique desk in one of the corners of the room and found a large bundle of papers, which she began to look through. She was searching for two things: any possible correspondence Bruno could have had with her husband and messages from other women. Marcos couldn't see anywhere else in the apartment that would be likely to contain the man's papers. Looking behind the front door, he saw that there was a box hanging on the wall, containing several sets of keys. One of the keys was tied with a small label, reading simply: Storage Room.

'I'm going to go downstairs for a minute to take a look

at the entrance and also the building's basement. It seems he has a small storage space somewhere, so it's possible that there could also be documents there.'

'Go on then. I'll carry on here.'

She finished looking through the young man's papers and kept two letters that might contain interesting information. She had become quite close to Bruno over the years and she considered had a right to know about his private life, which he had always hidden from her. Taking the opportunity to look over his bedroom, she found a simple but well-decorated room. Inside one wardrobe he had a rail of good-quality, designer suits, unlike the casual clothes he used to wear for her, befitting of a penniless student. The Bruno she had known seemed to be a completely different person to the one who owned this apartment. She sat on the bed and tried to imagine all the other women Bruno must have made love to here.

Suddenly, she heard a loud noise from the living room. Thinking that it must be the detective, she went out to find him, but couldn't see anyone there. She stepped back into the bedroom. As she turned around towards the bathroom, she was struck, hard and sharply, on the head. Everything went black.

CHAPTER 29

Córdoba

Marc was wrestling with the problems that faced them; Guylaine's voice brought him back to reality. They had got back to the hotel safely. Out of exhaustion, they decided to eat in the hotel room and continue their search.

With no time to spare, Guylaine made three phone calls. First she checked that the police had no news of Renaud, who had vanished without a trace. Not even the guards of the mosque could recall two men forcefully dragging another man out of the building. After the guards had checked the monument thoroughly, it was also clear that the Count's assistant was no longer there.

In her second call, Guylaine tried to get through to her mother, who still wasn't answering her mobile. Her mother must be trying to avoid contact, but why? Finally, however, she did manage to get through to the castle staff. The butler confirmed that they still had no news of the Countess, who had not contacted them since the day she left the castle.

'Do you have any idea where this wild hunt will take us next?' she asked Marc.

'No, but I'm sure we'll find out soon. You mustn't lose faith.' Marc buried himself in a large map of Córdoba. 'We should think about what Renaud told us today and look for answers. What did he say the city Abderraman III ordered to be built in the tenth century was called?'

'Medina Azahara. It's a palatial or court city, built by the Caliph to make room for all his state officials and their departments. It was also a place for him to take up residence, of course. I went there some years ago. By chance, my visit coincided with a magnificent exhibition about the art and culture of the Umayyadds; it left a great impression on me. Before my visit, I didn't have a clue about the exceptional archaeological work that had been carried out there.'

'What do you mean?'

'I mean that no one could possibly imagine what is inside Medina Azahara. Historians and archaeologists never tire of unearthing the treasures of that buried city. Until 1911, the great work of the Caliph had remained lost, hidden under layers of earth and meadow. Restoration work only began relatively recently, given its one-thousand-year-old status, carried out over the course of the last century. As each part of the palatial city was uncovered, the world marvelled at one of the best-kept secrets in human history. Even today, perhaps only ten percent of the city, which is more then one million square metres in size, has been excavated. Imagine what could still be discovered in the vast majority of the city that remains underground.'

'That's fascinating. Might your father have chosen to pay a visit to that site during his investigations?'

'Yes, I think very likely so. If he has come to Córdoba and we can't find him in the Great Mosque, it wouldn't surprise me if he is heading for the legendary Medina Azahara.'

Tired by their final conversation at the end of a long, intense day, they both rolled over to their respective sides of the bed and politely said good night.

* * *

Hiding behind sunglasses, Marc got out of their new hire car to inspect the perimeter archaeological site for any sign of their pursuers. When he was sure there was no one suspicious in view, he signalled for Guylaine to follow him.

'I see that here they call it Madinat al-Zahra,' pronounced the detective thoughtfully, reading a big sign announcing that they had arrived at the famous buried city.

'That's its original name. It could mean "the city of Zahra" one of Abderraman III's concubines, to whom he felt a particular attachment. He may even have been deeply in love with her. Although there are those who cling to the poetic story that he built this city in his sweetheart's honour, the truth universally accepted today is that when he announced the Caliph of Córdoba independent, he wanted to demonstrate his power to the world. If the Caliphs of the East had a palatial city, the Córdoban Umayyadd had to have one too; above all, to demonstrate to his enemies that his force and might were immense. Amazingly, Abderraman III built this city in less than forty years, starting in the year 936.'

'Is it possible that Silvestre II was here at some point, then? Could he have gathered ideas here to construct that horrifying head in your castle?'

'When our pope was still a Benedictine monk, he lived in Spain between the years 967 and 970. This city and all its installations were recently constructed and in full use by then.'

She deliberately took a brief pause so that he could absorb what she had said.

'Moreover, we must not forget one very important thing. Before Silvestre arrived here, Abderraman III had decided to hand over power to his son, al-Hakam II, who succeeded him while he was still alive. That was in the year 961. Therefore, if Silvestre actually did travel to Madinat al-Zahra, he would have found a most cultured leader, a lover of ancient books held by the Umayyadd Empire. It was al-Hakam II who treasured their ancestral, secret and prohibited texts held in Córdoba.'

'So our man, the French monk, travelled to Córdoba, drawn here by the enormous library of a reigning caliph, who so happened to have an interest in the dark arts.'

'Yes, but that's not the only reason. Al-Hakam II was a sensitive person who loved all the arts. He was impartial, treated all ethnic and religious groups as equals, respected Christians and Jews, and even gave them posts in the caliphate administration. He rejected the sectarianism of other leaders who wanted a purely Muslim Córdoba, free from other races and religions. He was a highly intelligent leader who has perhaps been overlooked in the history of al-Andalus, since he governed between two rather more memorable and notorious figures: his father, Abderraman III, and al-Hakam's distinguished successor Almanzor, the scourge of the Christians.'

'So, if our Silvestre was here, surely he would have been well received by al-Hakam II, the pious man you have described.'

'I think so, and al-Hakam II would probably even have granted him access to the immense caliphate library. The monk had been educated in the most distinguished Benedictine monasteries and completed his education in the most important disciplines of the time. It would be hardly surprising if the doors to an establishment like this were not open to such an intelligent man.'

'And how did Caliph al-Hakam II die?'

'I seem to remember learning that, in the year 974, he suffered a bad stroke from which he never recovered, so he handed over power to his son and dedicated himself to what he loved most in life: books. They say that he shut himself away in his own temple, the library. Illness brought him even closer to his workshop of copiers, bookbinders, writers and students. Given that he had bought books from practically all known countries, he dedicated his final years to reading and interpreting hundreds, among thousands, of works that had come from Baghdad, Damascus and Cairo.'

Guylaine paused for breath before they started to walk around the lost city.

'The day al-Hakam II died, the world lost one of the most illustrious libraries ever established.'

* * *

On entering the site for the first time, a look of disappointment crossed Marc's face, as he expected to see magnificent palaces excavated, ornate carvings and impressive garden designs.

'Don't forget that all of this had lain underground for about nine hundred years and formal excavations only began less than a century ago. There's also evidence that it has been constantly pillaged over the centuries and that the inhabitants of Córdoba have traditionally used materials from Medina Azahara for their own dwellings. This city was something of a quarry until it was rescued by archaeologists,' said Guylaine, trying to lessen his disappointment.

'What a shame! I imagined an opulent and luxurious building, like the one we saw yesterday at the Great Mosque.'

'That's how it was before the year 1010, when the city of the Umayyadds was sacked and brought to the ground. However, there are some relatively well-kept areas that show the splendour that Abderraman III and his son al-Hakam II gave to the palaces. Follow me!'

Guylaine took them to the layout of a large mosque with three spacious naves running its length, flanked by another two, each separated by a central door and a main portico that led inside. She clearly wanted her companion to agree that this place of worship was part of the buried city's glorious past.

'If you were to shoot *Arabian Nights*, you would do it here, wouldn't you?' she asked, spinning around with her arms wide open, delighted to have returned to a place that brought back such fond memories.

'Without doubt. And what was this enormous room used for?' asked Marc, lightly stroking a solid marble column crowned by a splendid arch.

'We are now in the Rich Lounge, or the Rich Hall of Abderraman II. Legend has it that there was such a profusion of gold, silver, pearl and precious stone in the ceiling carvings that, when sunlight shone on them, they produced a magical light display. The Caliph received his guests here to dazzle them with the impressive carvings, which made the room the talking point of the new city.'

'I'm beginning to see the hidden splendour of this place. This building must have been magnificent.'

'Well, wait until I show you the rest... As I told you, Medina Azahara is a palace or court city. It was the administrative centre of the caliphate and the government was transferred here from Córdoba in 947. As well as homes for the high dignitaries and their entourages, the city would have included staff quarters, rooms for the military and so on. The area over there is where the best homes were, a group of buildings surrounding an enormous central patio. Another important area was the military base; that part of the city was dominated by an elevated tower to defend the palatial complex. It would have been quite austere, fitting to a military life, I imagine. Do you want to see more?'

'Of course; that's why we're here.'

She took Marc's hand and led him towards the far end of the site where, behind some small trees, there was another building with beautifully constructed arches.

'This is the House of the Viziers, the Caliph's main residence. It is made up of a magnificent collection of five naves that run the length of the building near the boundary wall of the site. Look at the contrast between the building and its backdrop.'

The detective saw that the green of the enormous fir trees behind the building and the brown hues of the stone walls catching the sun created a stunning image. The two carried on around the site, ignoring the itinerary marked up on the guide map. After a few minutes, they reached another remnant building, the façade of which had enormous arches over the entrance doors.

'This is the Great Portico, the eastern entrance to the area fortified by the Alcázar. In front of here was the military base. You have to try to visualise regiments of horsemen gathered here, wearing beautiful tunics with the half-moon flickering on their ornate uniforms.'

'It's enormous. I didn't expect it to be this impressive...'

'There's more to come. If you look over there, you'll see some older-looking ruins. These are the remains of another Moorish mosque. Such was Abderraman II's devotion to the Islamic religion that this was the first building constructed in this city. It must have been as magnificent as the mosque we first found. As you can see, hardly anything of this temple has been preserved: only the foundations of the building and parts of the pillars have remained standing.'

Marc suggested they take a break. The oppressive heat and constant sun beating down on them had made it hard to breathe. Guylaine led him into the shade where she could explain one of her favourite features of the ancient city.

'This is the "pavilion garden". There is not a palace in the world, an architecturally sumptuous building or even an individual manor house that is complete without an ornamental garden. It was here that Abderraman III won the love of his wives and made them romantic promises.'

She let her companion look around slowly. She found another shady spot and beckoned him over. They sat down on a little wall.

'Did you say that this was the palace garden?'

'That's right. This would have been an enchanting spot, one of the most romantic in the city, where the Caliph could bring his lovers and dazzle them with his luscious vegetation and unusual species of birds, while they listened to the murmur of the hundreds of fountains and ponds that surrounded it. It was a paradise within the most luxurious city in the world.'

'This place is designed for falling in love.'

Guylaine didn't answer; she was still gazing at the ruins. It took a few long seconds for her to register his words.

'Well, we haven't come here to enjoy the landscape. Where could my father be?'

'Right behind you, my child.'

The voice came from between the columns.

Marc and Guylaine turned around and saw that Pierre Dubois was there, right behind them.

CHAPTER 30

Guylaine burst into tears. She leapt forward to embrace her father, taking him into her arms for what seemed like an eternity. Marc had not imagined the moment when they would finally find the Count. He settled for a simple introduction.

'Hello, I'm Marc Mignon, a detective your wife employed to track you down,' he said, offering his hand.

The detective inspected the nobleman. He had only seen photos of the Count of Divange in the castle; he was not prepared for the sight of a dirty and dishevelled man, in ragged clothing. It was hard to believe that here was a nobleman and the owner of one of the premier champagne houses in the world. As soon as Pierre Dubois began to speak, Marc realised that in spite of his unkempt appearance, his manner was entirely fitting of his status and heritage.

'It is a pleasure to meet you, M. Mignon. May I thank you for accompanying my daughter here and for the protection I imagine you have given her.'

'Don't worry, it's just my job. Are you all right?'

'Perfectly, except that I am yet to root out what I came here to find.'

'You have to tell us the whole story,' said Guylaine, controlling her tears.

'It really is perfectly simple,' the nobleman announced. 'I left Reims because I knew that there were plenty of people interested in my discoveries. For a while I have known I was myself being investigated; I was even offered money to unveil my studies. Ridiculous! I have dedicated my life to this research and then someone comes along and proposes that I hand over my investigations in exchange for money I do not need. There are many foolish people in the world, it seems. They have been chasing me ever since I left France. That's why I look like this; it is my form of camouflage. If I booked into any one of the hotels in this city, my pursuers would soon be at my heels, demanding I reveal everything I have discovered to date. How despicable people can be!'

'It's true. Start from the beginning, Father. You have no idea what we've been through since the day you left. I'd like to know why you made such a rash decision to leave the castle. Do you know that Renaud has been in Córdoba and that two thugs have captured him? Do you know that your wife has disappeared too?'

'I had no idea these terrible things had happened,' answered the Count, visibly upset. 'Can you fill me in?'

Guylaine began retelling what had happened since the day her father had disappeared from the castle and tried to convey what she and her mother had been through. She told him that Véronique had contacted one of the best detective agencies in Paris and so Marc had joined the search for the Count. She described in graphic detail the brutal beating some thugs had given the detective simply because of the case he was involved in. She recounted their journey to Ripoll, where they had met the monk who had taken the Count in, their arrival in Córdoba, and the strange disappearance of Renaud. Finally, she recounted their conversations with the police, who had not made any progress whatsoever in their search. She could not give her father any further information about where the Countess might be.

'But despite all that, we made it here. Shall we talk about you now? There are lots of things we ought to know. First of all, what did the machine say to you once you got it to work?'

CHAPTER 31

Looking out beyond the city of Medina Azahara, the Count took a deep breath before beginning his tale. He sat on the low wall next to Marc and Guylaine, and began to explain all he had learnt about the talking head.

'At first it was difficult to understand the mechanisms of the contraption. The machine was created at a time when mechanics were very basic, which means that the principles by which it operates are unknown to the majority of people. A long time ago, when the Greeks dominated the world as well as other early cultures, simple machines with cogs and springs were already in use. Silvestre II acquired complex knowledge from old texts to devise the idea of the head. It was here, in Córdoba, that he came upon a text that contained information on how to put his creation in motion. Essentially an instruction manual, this book gave his monstrous invention a soul.

'And he did not acquire it by conventional means: he stole it.'

'That's the theory of William of Malmesbury, who wrote a ridiculous history of Gerberto a century after the pope died,' Guylaine pointed out. 'I can't believe it's true.'

'Only to a degree. Malmesbury gave quite a strange explanation. He said that an Arabic philosopher demonstrated

179

the magic arts to Gerberto but refused to give him the mysterious book. So, Gerberto plied the philosopher with alcohol, seduced his daughter and stole the book. Legend has it that when Gerberto came to a very large river he apparently invoked the Devil for his protection in exchange for an oath of fidelity. Malmesbury argues that it was because of this pact with Satan that Gerberto became successful over the following years, going from being a lowly monk to reaching the archdiocese of Ravenna and finally obtaining the throne of Peter. In that same legend, Malmesbury recounts a fantastic story in which the pope casts in bronze an awesome head which, through the art of dark magic, would respond to any question asked and also contained important secrets from the most diverse cultures of the world.'

'So, he was right…'

'In part. The bit about the head is obvious. But I have been unable to confirm any pact with the Devil. It is one of the things that we have to investigate. Even though I admit that the machine looks like the work of the occult, the involvement of Satan in this story is something that still has to be clarified.'

'That brings me to ask you if you have any idea who the men who on our trail are,' interjected the detective. 'As far as I am aware, there are two groups of people following our investigations. One set are Arabs and the others are potentially connected to satanic circles. Do you know anything about these people?'

'A lot actually. And I know what they are looking for…'

Marc was amazed. 'You have no idea how grateful I'll be if you can tell me who beat me up and what their interest in the machine is.'

Dubois continued. 'There are indeed two groups of people that have been following me for some years now, perhaps even longer. I would be lying to you if I said that I know exactly who they are but I *can* tell you what they're looking for.'

'Well, Father, don't stop there! You're making me nervous.'

'The machine guards a transcendental secret for all humanity. Our world is in danger and the talking head holds the key to preventing catastrophe. If it falls into good hands, there is a chance we can save the world. If it falls into bad hands, I don't even want to think about what could happen.'

CHAPTER 32

Guylaine saw that her father was weary from wrestling with all the mysterious questions surrounding the pope's machine. What the Count had told them about the talking head's secrets was enough to condemn him as a madman.

'You seem tired,' she said. I suggest we go to the hotel and sort out another room for you without raising any suspicion. Marc can be very resourceful. He's been good to us.'

The detective had a flashback to his passionate night with the Countess and felt deeply disappointed with himself. If it got back to the Count, he didn't want to think how he would react. He struggled even to look the man in the eye when he considered his betrayal and instead, tried to banish these thoughts and concentrate on securing Pierre Dubois a room in the hotel without alerting any watching eyes.

* * *

At the hotel there was no trouble getting the Count in, as Marc managed to reserve the room in his own name. He thought continually about the threatening words of the thugs and wondered whether the Count would know anything about the Baumard case. He must ask him soon; he must take the first opportunity.

'I ought to congratulate you on your achievement, Monsieur Mignon,' expressed a satisfied-looking Pierre Dubois.

Guylaine smiled, a smile that showed that she too was pleased with the detective for bringing them all here together.

'That's my job. By the way, since we've found you now, do you want me to continue with the case?'

'But of course! You are a great investigator and the Mignon Agency has a very good reputation in Paris; moreover, you have taken care of my wife and my daughter brilliantly. It would be foolish to dispense with your services now when we need them most. You know how to handle yourself in dangerous situations and find solutions to problems. Please do carry on and keep protecting us as you have done until now. More than asking you, I beg you.'

'Of course, that was what I hoped you'd say. You must understand that it is my duty to ask you, but I do feel very committed to all this and would like to see it through to the end. Please forgive me for any mistakes I may have made along the way.'

'What do you mean?'

'Nothing in particular,' answered the young man, blushing. 'In a case as complex as this, unwanted situations can arise.'

'I have no idea to what you refer; however, you can rest assured that, until now, your work has been most satisfactory.'

Guylaine looked equally confused by Marc's words. Given that her father had his own room, it made sense for her to share it with him for the rest of their stay, so she moved her belongings across the hall.

On his way back to the room, Marc felt somehow downcast by the new arrangement. Could this possibly be a symptom of falling in love? He daren't even contemplate such an idea.

CHAPTER 33

Dinner in the restaurant on the top floor of the hotel gave Guylaine and Marc the chance to listen to the Count's investigations further. From the table that they had reserved they looked out at the beautiful city of Córdoba, wonderfully illuminated at night.

'This city has a unique charm,' Guylaine whispered to Marc, staring at the old buildings in the distance.

'Yes it does,' the detective replied. 'How's your new room?'

'It's the same as the one we had. My father is in the shower and will be here in a few minutes. After living rough for so many days, he seems to be enjoying the luxuries he has always been accustomed to once again,' said Guylaine, laughing.

'Why do you say that?'

'The first thing he did was ask for a bottle of champagne. And he ordered the best bottle he could find!'

'And how about you? How are things between you and your father?'

'Fine, of course, he's my father. Here he comes…'

He was dressed in an immaculate marine-blue suit, complemented by an elegant red cravat and similar handkerchief that protruded ever so slightly from his breast pocket.

'You look a new person, M. Dubois,' exclaimed Marc.

Dressed as he now was, no one would have guessed that the man had been roaming the streets for days, sleeping rough in shelters or outdoors, and eating poorly when at all.

'Sit down next to me and we'll pick up the conversation where we left off this afternoon,' Guylaine asked him, gently taking his arm. 'I'm anxious to know about your discoveries in detail; you still haven't told us what the talking head said.'

'True. Let's order first and I will then tell you everything I know,' said the Count, who was eagerly poring over the menu. 'Apologies, but I have gone for many days without eating properly and I am desperate for something substantial.'

He chose *foie de canard* as a starter, followed by *maigret* with a confit of apple.

'I see that you're reacquainting yourself with French delicacies.' Marc was surprised that the Count had ordered two duck courses. 'Together with some champagne, this meal should certainly remind you of your former life.'

'I see that my daughter has told you about my love of champagne. You two get on well, don't you? That is lucky as we have a long way still to go in this case.'

When the image of the Countess cavorting in bed came to mind again, the detective suddenly felt empty. He had to try to dismiss the images in his head, no matter how long it would take him to forget what he had done, as he could not bear to see the Count betrayed now that he was found.

'I think the time has come for you to begin your tale,' Marc said.

'Very well. I will start from the moment the machine first cranked into motion.'

'Do you mind if I record what you say so that I can use it when I return to Paris to help me find clues to further our investigation?'

'No, not at all.'

Marc pushed the record button.

'The days I spent analysing the machine were, without doubt, the most satisfying of my life. No one looking for something as long as I have could have slept peacefully for a single night while they were trying to solve such a mystery. It would be like finding a box which contained secrets that could change the course of history, yet leaving it unopened.

'I must admit that my actions in the days following the discovery of the talking head were unacceptable. That dark basement, full of history, and the intense presence of the machine would intoxicate anyone. I spent days and nights constantly plagued by the thought that Silvestre himself had been in that same room and that he had placed all those devices inside the head to perfect the complex mechanisms. It was extremely difficult for me to work out how to make the machine start, as the pope of the first millennium had hidden any instructions before he died. He knew that what he had discovered must not fall into the wrong hands. Even though he left some references so that, with some effort, others could make use of his discoveries, our pope tried at all costs to avoid it being operated for ends other than those he created it for. At least, that is what I deduced...

'It is important to note that our Silvestre died only a few years after he was elected pope and could not complete the task he had set himself when he constructed the sophisticated machine. Also, it is likely that the distance between Reims and Rome proved unmanageable for him. Although the cause of the pope's death is not known, many people believe someone with dark motives poisoned him.

'When I started to connect springs, link tubes and repair the different buttons on the immense machine, I realised that, in order to make it all work, I had to apply the same principles that Silvestre had used and recorded in his treatises, such as the *Regulae de numerorum abaci rationibus*, which gives a fascinating insight into his mathematical mind, and the study of Euclides's geometry, translated by Boecio, who was his main point of reference. As soon as the whole machine began to work, I started to extract ideas from it. The revelations it gave me did not cease to surprise me. After a while, it became clear that Silvestre's machine contained a vast amount of ancient knowledge, which was believed to be lost. He had wrestled with all the great questions. Was there a civilisation before ours? Are we the first intelligent beings to have inhabited the earth? To what extent has Mother Nature governed the evolution of planet Earth?

'We will probably never obtain answers to these questions, but there have clearly been many cultures before ours who also pondered these subjects, and produced their own theories and secrets. However, during the turbulence at the end of the first millennium, such secrets were irretrievably lost. Imagine the quantity of books, manuscripts, papyruses and all kinds of scientific works containing ancient knowledge that have disappeared throughout human history. Over the course of his life, Gerberto d'Aurillac, Silvestre II or, as we like to call him, the pope magician, gathered together much of this marvellous ancient learning, not only interpreting it, but also constructing the machine to house and project the teachings of our ancestors for the future. The talking head contains a vast amount of information from the oldest ages, particularly relating to Mother Nature.

'Although the end of the first millennium has often been considered one of the darkest periods of history, it coincided with a gradual cultural awakening, a resurgence of writing and the dissemination of learning. Fortunately for us, there was such a gifted mind to gather that information and use it to benefit future generations. In essence, the talking head is a storage and recovery system that Silvestre built for people like us.'

Marc touched the stop button on the recorder. He asked his first question in a state of astonishment.

'But, what is the magical part of the machine? I am talking about the sorcery you mentioned in your letter. And not just that... Why did you write that the end of the world is near?'

'Yes, I also thought the machine was linked to witchcraft, demonic forces and secrets that go beyond the realm of science,' added Guylaine.

'These are valid questions. Up until now I have only told you the scientific background of how and why Silvestre II built such an extraordinary talking machine. As I have said, he used it to store a great part of ancient knowledge, gleaned from Ripoll and the fabulous library in Córdoba. By applying that knowledge in a certain way, he found a model to predict the future. The machine comes to the conclusion that life on earth is cyclical and at the end of the next cycle a cataclysmic event will take place, after which life on this planet will be take a different form.'

'And when will it happen?' his daughter asked him, concerned.

'In the year 2033.'

'So, two thousand years after the death of Jesus Christ.'

'Correct. And this time it can be scientifically proven that the prophecy from the Book of Revelation is going to come true.'

CHAPTER 34

When their courses arrived, the only person capable of eating anything was the Count. Both Marc and Guylaine had lost their appetites after hearing the Count describe such a terrible prophecy. The nobleman, however, seemed to be enjoying the succulent little pieces of duck dressed in a delicious apple sauce. Every so often, he took a sip of the glass of champagne he had ordered to accompany his meal. When the Count had put down his knife and fork after the final mouthful and taken a sip of champagne to finish, Marc asked his next question.

'But you can't be certain about the supposed apocalypse, surely? I understand that there is profound knowledge contained in that machine but…how can life on earth possibly end?'

'If you let me explain, Mr Mignon, I will tell you more about the prophecy. The Book of Revelation is one of the most mysterious works in the New Testament. Do you know the background of the book?'

'No—remember that I'm not very religious. Although I'm Catholic, I don't go to Mass and doomsaying has never affected me. I live a life in tune with nature, which doesn't leave me much time to contemplate the heavens.'

'Well, that in fact complements what we are dealing with.

Mother Nature is at the heart of the prophecy,' responded the Count, now with an empty glass of champagne, ready to ask for more.

Guylaine suggested that maybe he shouldn't have any more to drink while they were discussing matters of such great importance. It was clear that she adored her father and that he was her role model. The Count agreed with her. 'I will moderate my optimism and my alcohol intake, if that's what you want, my child. But it's hard to hide my excitement that I could be on the way to resolving a very old mystery that could avert global disaster.'

'Thank you, Father,' she said, offering a brief glimpse of a beautiful smile that did not go unnoticed by Marc. 'Please, go on.'

'The Book of Revelation contains mysterious references to millenarianism that form the basis of debates about the apocalypse. To explain, Mr Mignon, although it is generally accepted that its author was a man named John, traditionally identified as the apostle Saint John, personally I think that the text was written by a community founded by him, which continued his work after his death. That collective was strongly influenced by the apostle's predictions and, among the people in the group, there could have been a visionary who contributed the fearful prophecies the book contains. What is actually more or less confirmed is that the Book of Revelation was written at the end of the first century or possibly the beginning of the second century, at the height of the Roman persecutions of Christians as advocated by the Dominican emperor. This may be why the text includes advice for followers of Christ, encouraging them that by enduring the agony of torture their souls would receive a great reward.

'It is considered by far the most controversial book in the New Testament and its inclusion in the Bible was widely opposed. Due to the multitude of possible interpretations and the hidden symbols it contains, the text has had, for many centuries, both its defenders and detractors. In Europe, the Book of Revelation was accepted by decree of Pope Damasus I around the year 382, even though there is evidence that people like the Roman Cayo had previously rejected it for promoting the fear of apocalypse. In short, its origin was without doubt controversial and few scholars truly understand what the book intended to prophesy. Due to its complexity, many schools of thought have offered interpretations of Revelation over the course of time. The Preterist School holds that the text must be read from the point of view of the people of the first century and that it should only be framed within this context. In contrast, the idealists see the work as an allegory of the spiritual combat between good and evil. Of course, there are more advanced movements, like the futurists, who see various historical figures clearly identified in the Book of Revelation, like Napoleon and Hitler. There is a whole host of possible explanations for a book that demands a response yet polarises opinion.'

'I've never heard it explained so clearly. And which part of the book speaks of the dates that concern us?'

'For us, the important words are to be found in chapter twenty, verses one to eight, which I can recite from memory. I have read and reread the mysterious lines hundreds of times in my days.'

'Yes, Guylaine has already spoken to me about that passage.

Will you allow me to turn on the recorder?'

'Yes, please do.'

The red pilot light of the Dictaphone glowed at the occupants of the table.

'I refer to that strange chapter, which is uncharacteristically defended by the Catholic Church, despite the fact that its content is difficult to decipher and harder still to explain. In the verses that concern us, the Book of Revelation says:

Then I saw an angel coming down from heaven,
Holding the key to the bottomless pit and a large chain in his hand.

He captured the dragon, that ancient serpent,
Who is the Devil and Satan,
And tied him up for a thousand years.

He threw him into the bottomless pit, locked it,
And sealed it over him
To keep him from deceiving the nations any more
Until the thousand years were over.
After that he must be set free.

Then I saw thrones, and those who sat on them were given
The power to judge.
I also saw the souls of those who had been executed
Because they had proclaimed the truth that Jesus revealed that is
The word of God.
They had not worshipped the beast or its image
Nor had they received the mark of the beast on their foreheads
Or their hands.

*They came to life and ruled as kings with Christ for a
Thousand years.
The rest of the dead did not come to life
Until the thousand years were over.
This is the first raising of the dead.*

*Happy and blessed are those who are witness to
The first raising of the dead.
The second death has no power over them.
They shall be priests of God and of Christ,
And they will rule with him for a thousand years.
After the thousand years are over,
Satan will be let loose from his prison,
And he will go out to deceive the nations scattered
Over the whole world.*[2]

The Count gestured with his hand, indicating that he
wanted to end the recording. Marc obeyed and the red light
flickered out.

'And how should we interpret these verses?'

'Silvestre had a great interest in this prophecy, as it
has clear references to millenarianism and the year one
thousand drawing upon them. He knew that he needed to
understand the significance of that age, the time closing in
on his generation, for the future of humanity. Feudal society
came about at this point, when certain social structures
were formed that would over time advance civilisation.

---

[2] Revelation 20:1-8

The chaos and division that Europe had suffered under the fall of the Roman Empire gave way to a new system that brought about positive change. The renaissance of Europe in the fifteenth, sixteenth and successive centuries would not have been possible without the foundations laid at the end of the first millennium.'

'I don't understand,' murmured Marc, embarrassed to be showing his ignorance.

'Silvestre understood that from the tenth century, things were going to change. He had the courage to look into the past to decipher what the prophecy of the Book of Revelation was trying to communicate. That is why he spent his life painstakingly searching for old books, the content of which could only be seen by very few people. In Córdoba, for example, he examined documents that are still unknown to us today. From Egypt, Babylon, India, Greece, Rome…how many ancestral books have disappeared in human history, I wonder? The prophecy of the Book of Revelation was the first thing that drove Silvestre on his adventure to predict the future. But most important was the construction of the machine, which allowed him to mathematically predict what was going to happen many years later.'

'Unbelievable!'

'But true…'

* * *

While the dining party ordered coffee, a call was made by a waiter, from his mobile phone, concealed behind the elaborate fabrics dividing the restaurant from the kitchen. He had paid special attention to the conversation he had heard from this table during the course of the meal. As best as he could remember, he relayed the intriguing words the Count had spoken and agreed to a meeting as soon as he finished his shift. A smile crossed his face when he received the news. The operation was in motion.

CHAPTER 35

When the moment came for him to reveal the terrible prediction of the machine, the Count became visibly tense.

'Now that I have told you almost all of what I know, I think you are ready to hear the fatalistic predictions that Silvestre made around the year one thousand.'

'Go ahead, Father. Please spare us the suspense. So many terrible things have happened in such a short space of time that I'm a complete wreck. My mother is missing, two thugs are probably holding Renaud still, and will have done God knows what to him by now, and there are people out there following you and we don't have a clue who they are. Tell us now how we can avert Silvestre's prophecy.'

'Gaia,' said the Count with an air of circumspection. 'That is the key.'

'That's the theory that says that the earth is a living, self-regulating organism,' explained Marc. 'I've read the work of the English scientist James Lovelock plenty of times. At first, no one gave it a shred of credibility, but now it seems to be coming back into fashion.'

'I see that you are well informed, Mr Mignon. In that case you will find what I have to say easier to understand.'

'May I switch the recorder on again?'

'Certainly.'

'The ancient books that Silvestre had access to, many of which gathered wisdom from extinct civilisations, pointed to the fact that the earth, Mother Nature, venerated as a goddess, has a personality of her own. The idea that our planet is capable of self-regulation or being guided by her own principles is something that human beings have forgotten. Cultures prior to ours saw the earth as an organic entity and worshipped her as a divinity, naming her Gaia. They believed that our planet has the same characteristics as a living being, capable of altering its own behaviour. However, the appearance of monotheistic or polytheistic religions in the last few millennia distanced people from this idea and consequently from the earth we inhabit—the planet that sustains us and facilitates human life.

'We pray to our gods but forget to pay homage to what keeps us alive.

'Even long before the death of Jesus Christ, in the first century BC, Cicero wrote something very illuminating. He said the following:

'"*We are the lovers of the earth. We enjoy the mountains and the plains and the rivers. We sow the seed and plant the trees. We fertilise the land and even correct the course of rivers. With our hands, and through our actions in the world, we dare to create another natural world.*"

'These words are not the only ones to prove that our ancestors comprehended the power of the earth and what might happen if humans substantially altered the environment. At the end of the first millennium, the most lucid mind at the time was that of Silvestre, who was capable of predicting that life on this planet would end when Gaia ceased to tolerate human interference. His research from ancient works would even shock many modern-day scientists, despite all the advanced scientific technology at our disposal. Silvestre realised that the population in his generation was growing at an alarming rate, and would continue to do so after the end of the tenth century until the earth would no longer be able to sustain a growing population, and our future would be severely altered.

'It was precisely here, in Córdoba, that Silvestre began to devise a mathematical model capable of calculating how life in our society would evolve. When he saw this immense caliphate city, with its irrigation channels, bridges, aqueducts, sewer systems, and its scholarly advances in medicine, astronomy and other sciences, he was convinced that human beings were going to multiply out of control and that the earth would struggle eventually. He collected information from the many ancestral texts I spoke of earlier and converted it all into a mathematical model which he then installed inside the giant head, inputting the mathematical data using the abacuses in its mouth. This is how the pope magician came to the conclusion that no later than 2033, the earth would wage a tremendous war on its own inhabitants.

'This is where the prophecy of the Book of Revelation comes in. Now that two thousand years have passed since the birth of Christ and we have entered into the third millennium, another one-thousand-year cycle, we humans, the inhabitants of Earth, are debating what will happen to our planet with the advent of climate change.'

The detective instinctively pushed the stop button. A faint beeping sound was enough to startle them all and break their concentration.

'What does all this mean?' Marc asked immediately.

'Exactly what you think it means. It is what we scholars call "the 1000 Effect", a strange pattern found in nature, the next cycle of which will have a major impact on humanity and everything else on the face of the earth.'

CHAPTER 36

'It's an interesting theory,' said Guylaine. 'But I find it difficult to believe that a phenomenon like that can be predicted mathematically every one thousand years. Nothing catastrophic took place at the end of the first millennium nor at the end of the second.'

'True. When Silvestre spoke of the 1000 Effect, he, like the Book of Revelation, was referring to the elapsing of a large number of years that doesn't necessarily have to be exact. In fact, when the Book of Revelation says "a thousand years", as it does so many times, what it really means is "a very high number of years". The book was written in the first century; we must try to understand how the Christians would have read it at that time. For example, the number 1 was used to refer to God. The number 4 signified the universe and creation. The strangest number is 6, which denotes imperfection because it comes just before 7, which is the perfect number. That is why the notorious beast of the Book of Revelation, whose number is 666, would signify a gross imperfection.

'Finally, the numbers 12 and 1000 are used extensively throughout the Book of Revelation. The first chapter refers to the twelve tribes of Israel, to the city of God and also the twelve apostles. Twelve, therefore, is the Christian number for excellence. As far as 1000 is concerned, it is probably the highest number that many people were aware of at the time, so the author simply wanted to convey the passing of a large number of years.'

'How strange!' Marc exclaimed. 'I've always wondered why the number 666 is related to the Devil in the Bible.'

'We can never know for certain, because the number 666 is only mentioned once in Revelation. The prophecies have been a source of much controversy and made people believe that inexplicable things were going to happen. There are a group of people who are convinced that the beast—or 666—is not Satan at all, nor any strange being with feathers or scales that breathes fire through its mouth. There is a wide belief that this number actually represents the Internet. They believe that www is equivalent to 666. The reason for this is based on archaeological excavations around the cities of Sodom and Gomorrah, close to the Dead Sea. There, they found Semitic remains that identified the end of the world with three letters corresponding to a derivative of the Greek letter omega, pronounced *uom*. It was soon linked with *waw*, which is found in Aramaic and Hebrew alphabets and equates to the letter *w* of the Latin alphabet. The parallels don't stop there, as it is also the sixth letter in the Aramaic and Hebrew alphabets. Because of all this, the famous triple w of the web is linked to 666.'

'Extraordinary! Some fascinating conclusions can be drawn from analysing these numbers.' Marc was intrigued.

'Indeed. In our case we must recognise the 1000 Effect as the effect of cycles, cycles that threaten or are actually harmful to our planet. There is no doubt that the earth is in grave danger and that unbelievably, the pope magician was capable of predicting this a very long time ago. The only thing we don't know was whether he achieved this under the guise of scholar or dark magician.'

But the detective was not so awed by this statement.

'The strange thing is that humanity has already realised the serious effect of climate change on the planet. It's taken us a long time but we're finally aware that we must remedy the situation, or life on earth as we know it will end.'

'But it's not that simple,' said the Count. 'Climate change has unleashed a series of changes to our atmosphere that are now irreversible. Our world is deteriorating and, although we have taken our foot off the accelerator, it is not going to stop. There is no one who can stop it.'

'Supposing all of this was true,' reflected Guylaine. 'I'm doubtful that Silvestre's model and proposals could solve the problem. I remember you said in your letter that the only way of preventing the cataclysm the ghastly head in our castle predicts is to find something else that is not held inside it. Your note hinted that something is missing...'

'That's right. The talking head contains immense knowledge but the pope magician did refer to something concrete that is not found inside. We need to find another element in order to obtain the ultimate answers from the machine.'

'And what is that thing?' Marc interrogated.

'I don't understand either.' Guylaine couldn't see how another part, a cog, bolt or wheel, could solve a global issue. 'How can Silvestre's invention save the world?'

'I don't know exactly, but what I can tell you is that when the machine refers to this missing component, it calls it the Power.'

CHAPTER 37

At twelve o'clock sharp the maître d' told the diners tactfully that the restaurant was closing. The Count looked tired and sated but both Guylaine and Marc insisted that he explain the talking head's prophecies.

'Let's go to my room and take a look at my personal notes. You can read them while I rest. They are very descriptive and should tell you everything I know.'

The other two agreed. When they left, none of them noticed a waiter frenziedly entering a number into his mobile phone. He told someone that the Count's notes really did exist. All they had to do now was to get hold of the papers that had travelled all over the country.

* * *

Visibly exhausted, Pierre offered his daughter a large folder of notes, drawings and comments written in his hand.

'Treat this as an instruction manual for operating the talking head,' said the Count, unable to muster more than a murmur. 'If you read it carefully, you will gain a good idea of how the pope magician's machine works and what he based his terrible predictions for this planet on.'

'Thank you, Father. We'll let you rest and look over your

notes in detail.'

'Good,' concluded the Count, giving his daughter a kiss on the cheek and wishing them both goodnight. 'Be careful with those papers; they contain very valuable information.'

'I know; I was beaten up on account of them,' Marc said.

The Count nodded in sympathy. He knew there were people out there who would do anything to get their hands on those notes.

On the way to Marc's room, Guylaine whispered in the detective's ear that her father seemed older all of a sudden, and that perhaps age really did have no mercy. This, in marked contrast to her mother, who was abnormally energetic. Marc sheepishly agreed with her analysis. The click of the door unlocking saved him from having to hear a string of Véronique's virtues, which he was not prepared to endure. They walked into Marc's room and he offered Guylaine a seat. He thought about getting a spirit from the minibar for them both, but the task of having to sift through a thick file of the Count's papers was daunting enough to make him think twice.

Marc spread the Count's documents out on the bed so they could scan them all at once. Among them, the detective found something personal that the Count had written – almost a journal. Overlooking the technical diagrams for now, they chose to read these notes first.

CHAPTER 38

Castle of Divange
Pierre Dubois

First day of the finding

Today, I have made the most important discovery in the history of my family, the long generation of heirs to the dukedom in Champagne-Ardenne.

At approximately 7.30am, we knocked through a make-shift door adjacent to the foundations of the south wall of the castle. We revealed a dark room that, I believe, was deliberately closed and covered up by my ancestor, Silvestre. I have found there a large collection of mechanical inventions and all kinds of devices that must have been used in the construction of the immense bronze machine in the shape of a head.

The legend is true: Baphomet exists. There were those who decided that Baphomet was, in fact, the embalmed head of Saint John the Baptist, who, after death, was able to answer the most profound questions that were posed to him.

People also claimed that this divine power was a bearded head, for which the Knights Templar searched for centuries. The Knights' strange beliefs and worship of this monstrosity led them to be accused of heresy.

It was not until the nineteenth century that a plausible theory of the existence of Baphomet was written by a

Frenchman, Eliphas Lévi, in his book *Transcendental Magic, its Doctrine and Ritual*. From inspecting my discovery, I can now see that Lévi's investigations have been greatly underestimated.

I still don't know how to make it work. Furthermore, there is also no way of knowing if the creator of this machine himself could make it work. The legend of Baphomet has been sitting in the basement of my castle all this time, for a thousand years.

At first I was horrified by the head. Even in my worst nightmares I could not have pictured such a strange appearance. Anyone who sees the head would think it was the work of the Devil. I believe that its creator gave it this terrifying appearance to ensure that the machine would only fall into the hands of those wishing to use it for good reasons.

Second day

I have started to examine the hundreds, or perhaps thousands, of wires, buttons, cogs and other mechanisms contained in the medieval machine. Given its age, I must try to see the machine through the eyes of its creator to comprehend how it functions.

It is essential that I analyse each element to understand its use. I believe after a couple of days I will be able to advance more quickly in my investigations.

Third day

I have gone several days without sleep; the progress I am

making demands my full attention. But centuries of dust and dirt in the basement are settling in my lungs, making it difficult to breathe.

I am already able to work a large number of the mechanisms that make up the machine. I have deciphered the abacus and now completely understand how I can enter data into the apparatus. As it has twenty-seven bars, each one having ten counters, the device is capable of calculating up to the value of four million. I will annotate diagrams in this diary so that other people can operate this marvellous invention.

Fourth day

My most significant discovery today has been the rudimentary system through which the machine stores information. The language that it uses is Latin and I have found many passages from Silvestre's books in the cavern that were thought to be lost. The books are written in code, in a rough though effective system, but I have been able to recover, letter by letter, word by word, the information they contain.

Fifth day

I have now found passages of text written by classical authors of ancient Egypt, Greece, Rome, India and even older civilisations, which have an incalculable value, as they were also believed to be lost.

I believe that the pope would have stored this information himself as guidance.

Sixth day

The references to Mother Nature and our planet in Silvestre's books are innumerable. There is a lot of information here that would surprise any biologist, geologist or chemist of our time. It appears that Silvestre was fascinated by producing calculations based on ancestral hypotheses in order to predict the future. His interest in Mother Nature is my greatest clue.

There are still some extremely dark aspects I am uncovering that I don't understand and that worry me.

Seventh day

Today has been an amazing day in my investigations. I have finally worked out how to bring the machine back to life; once I have finished cleaning and placing each and every one of the mechanisms in place inside the head, I will soon know why our pope dedicated his life to the construction of this machine.

The operating method is relatively simple: one has to turn a big cog under the abacus with considerable force. Once it is in motion, instructions must be inputted through the counters on each bar on which the letters of the Latin alphabet are coded sequentially. The machine only recognises Latin and responds in the same language. Once the question has been set, one must pull a lever to change the direction of the wheels. The machine answers the question through the same process: by lining up the encoded words on the bars. The device is rudimentary but effective.

Once my tests are finished, I will begin to introduce

simple questions myself.

Conclusions

I have finally managed to get the talking head to reveal its terrible secret, the same question that the pope magician sought an answer to so desperately at the end of the first millennium.

I have interrogated the artefact with different questions relating to Silvestre's studies of millennialism, in particular his fears relating to the catastrophic prophecies of the Book of Revelation.

The years 1000 and 1001 passed by with Silvestre carrying out his duties as pope. What sort of earthly catastrophe were his ancient books capable of predicting? How could his machine produce such powerful calculations? And when would the feared disaster happen?

These questions formed the basis of my studies of the machine. In the last millennium, earthquakes and world wars waged with destructive technology have devastated our environment, as have powerful tsunamis destroyed extensive areas of our habitat. Events such as these have threatened the destruction of the planet; indeed there are nuclear weapons in at least five different countries that could annihilate the human race at the push of a button.

The pope's invention spoke to me about Christ, the Antichrist, the Messiah, the apocalypse and the Final Judgement, but none of these caught my attention. Whatever question I put to the machine, it always referred to the power that the earth has over human beings. I discovered many unknown facts about our planet, its development and the way it has evolved. As far as I know, some of this information cannot be found in any other ancient texts.

I put a direct question to the machine today: what is the date of the end of the world? A clear response came back to me: the year 2033. I have asked this question several times and the number is always the same. When I interrogate the artefact about the causes of the end of the world, the reply is equally clear: Mother Nature will rebel against the children of God.

Time and time again, I have rephrased the question but I am always given a similar answer. The machine consistently speaks of air, water, plants, sky and all natural elements rising up against humankind…a process we could now call climate change.

It was an enormous shock to confirm that in the year 2033 a great earthly disaster will take place, based on the knowledge found in Silvestre's collection of ancient texts.

My curiosity was sparked yet further when I asked the machine to describe the earth, the world we live in today. Its reply was most strange. It said that Mother Nature is alive and is a being in her own right with her own needs, flaws and conflicts. It continued to describe her as a living organism that, if not treated adequately, can die. That is precisely the theory that we know today as Gaia, the worship of the goddess of the earth.

Through his old books and his ancient calculator, Silvestre made a brilliant prediction of the path of human history. He spoke of ages where our planet was covered by water and others in which the lands that came to be known as our country France were completely covered with ice and stalked by great mammoths. Some of these radical changes in our habitat are known today from recent archaeological discoveries. But how could Silvestre know about those former states of the planet, prior to the scientific developments we have since made? Without doubt, his ancient books contained all kinds of information that was somehow then lost.

I don't whether this is science or sorcery but the machine contains astonishing and infallible truths.

It seems that the earth is approaching the end of a cycle in which climate change will radically alter the natural world. When I ask for a solution to this catastrophe, it says something unprecedented: it is not prepared to answer the question because it lacks information. Silvestre clearly did not manage to get hold of some essential Arabic texts and in particular it is in need of information that he could not bring back from Spain.

When I ask the talking head where I can find the solution so that its prophecies are not fulfilled, time and time again it simply produces the words 'the Power,' an enormous force generated by nature that if used correctly could save the world.

The missing pieces of the jigsaw must be found in order to find suggestions of how to avoid the apocalypse the machine speaks of. On discovering the head, I believed that I had reached my destiny and my investigations were over, but I was wrong.

The true search for the millennial secret begins now.

CHAPTER 39

Breakfast for the Count was just as indulgent as dinner the night before, still replenishing the empty reserves from his days in hiding. When Marc and Guylaine questioned why he had filled his plate with eggs and Spanish ham, his defence was that he foresaw a hard day of work ahead and should eat a hearty meal.

Having read the diary, they were even more curious about the Count's investigations and weren't sure what to do next.

Guylaine had made a couple of important calls in the last two days: the police still didn't know what had happened to Jean Luc Renaud and there was still no sign or news of the Countess at the castle. They had left Jean Luc in the hands of two thugs whose methods of interrogation were known to be violent, and they were now particularly concerned for his safety. They waited patiently for the nobleman to finish his breakfast and then the detective began the next round of questioning.

'We read your diary last night with great interest. As you can imagine, there are still some things we would like to ask you that your notes don't resolve.'

'Well, go ahead. Quickly though; we have to leave as soon as possible. We have lots of work to do today.'

'My first question is obvious. How could Mother Nature end life on Earth?'

'Well, that is obvious, Monsieur Mignon. We don't need a wise pope to show us the critical problems we have created for our environment. In the last few years, climate change has become an accepted scientific reality, which all countries must unite to combat together. Some states choose to ignore this and that's why the predictions of Silvestre's machine are doubly important.

'The head predicts the moment that the disaster will occur, which, until now, scientists have been unable to confirm accurately, even though many anticipate a natural catastrophe in the middle of the twenty-first century or even slightly sooner. In my opinion, the main contribution that Silvestre's investigations can make is in furthering our knowledge of the planet, what he calls Mother Nature or the goddess of the earth. Do you realise that scientists cannot agree on how certain natural features like marine currents or polar icecaps work? Despite all of our advances, we still know very little about the functioning of the earth as a whole. No one left us a manual for how to live on Earth; the global behaviour of our planet is still unknown to humans even at the dawn of the third millennium.'

Until then Guylaine had remained on the fringes of the conversation, but now she chose to express her worries.

'And Silvestre found information about that…'

'That's right. That is why Silvestre's findings are of such importance to contemporary civilisation.'

'And what could the Power you mentioned in your diary be?' Marc interrupted. 'You know I'm passionate about ecology and sustainable development.'

'I am glad to hear it, Marc. Even though every little helps, I fear that the sideline actions of many governments and organisations are not going to curtail climate change. To do that, one must find something much more effective. I don't know what this is but I know that Silvestre was working on it before he died and, what's more, I believe that someone killed him in 1003 when he was on the verge of finding the core of his subject, that he called the Power.'

'I don't understand,' Guylaine picked up the questioning again. 'Why were Silvestre's discoveries so important to someone?"

'Because the potential of his findings is immense. In the wrong hands, it could be catastrophic.'

'And why is there a group of Arabs on our heels? And why are we also being followed by what we believe to be Satan worshippers?' inquired the detective, forcefully this time.

'I have some ideas, Monsieur Mignon, but I cannot be sure that I'm right.'

The closure in the Count's voice as he settled that conversation made Guylaine return to another unresolved issue, to change the direction of their discussions.

'And what are the key pieces you talk about in your diary, which we still need to find?'

'Silvestre could not finish his investigations because of this missing element and because the machine would not answer certain questions because of its absence, whatever it is...'

'And I guess that's why you're in Córdoba,' reflected

Marc. 'Have you managed to find anything here?'

'I found some inscriptions engraved into a wall in the monastery. A bas-relief made it clear to me that, on his way through, Gerberto the monk, as he was then, left a clear and concise clue regarding his search.'

'And what did it say?' Guylaine was impatient now. 'I diligently searched for any detail leading us to Gerberto, and also to you, but I didn't find anything at all.'

'I can imagine, my darling,' he replied, taking her hand and kissing it. 'The thing is that, when you were in the millennial monastery of Ripoll, you didn't know what you know now. I expect that by reading my diary, and from what I told you yesterday, you will now see history through different eyes.'

'Yes, definitely.'

'Excuse the interruption, Monsieur and Mademoiselle Dubois, but where must we go now in search of new traces of the pope magician?' Marc asked.

'Well, that's obvious!' exclaimed the Count, surprised that the detective did not clearly see the way forward. 'The key is hidden in Medina Azahara; we must go there immediately. We will probably have to dig for it.'

'Not so fast,' Guylaine stopped him. 'I should change if that's your plan; I'll have to dress for the sweltering heat out on those plateaux.'

'Let's go upstairs and change,' Pierre Dubois said with a smile, glad that now he would have company on his great search.

* * *

Father and daughter headed to their room while the detective, who thought that his outfit was suitable for hard work in the sun, decided to wait for them in the hotel lobby. After a few seconds, Guylaine burst out of the lift. Her flushed expression made the detective think that something bad had happened.

'What's happened?'

'Someone's been in our room. They've taken all of my father's papers, including his diary.'

CHAPTER 40

There was no point in asking why they had left such important notes lying open for all to see in the hotel room, but the disappointment was written all over their faces and, in the car park next to the entrance of the Medina Azahara, they allowed themselves one final reproach.

'Now we have no advantage in this bizarre race,' said the Count.

'Or we may even be at a disadvantage,' added Marc. 'Those thugs have methods of obtaining information which we would never think of using and could now overtake us in the search. They would also obtain what we can't with force, if it came to that.'

'I don't think we should be so pessimistic,' Guylaine took the pragmatic approach. 'They may have our papers but we know a lot more than they do about the machine and the theory around it and we also know where to look for the missing element. Let's cheer up and head out there; I'm determined to find what surpassed the pope magician. Shall we go?'

The energy she exuded had an immediate effect on them. The men got out of the car and set off to the main gate of the caliphate city.

'You're right, my child. The answer to the whole enigma

could be here. Why worry about the information our enemies have now?'

At the entrance to the palatial city, the father and daughter showed their identification documents, proving they were archaeologists. With this authority, they could wander around the ruins without any restrictions, even through the parts of the city that had not been unearthed. They introduced the detective as a university companion who would be helping them in their investigations and without hesitation the attendant signed the necessary permission form for him to enter.

From where he stood, Marc could, once again, see how beautiful the buildings in the complex were. He asked the Count why the city had deteriorated to such an extent.

'It's a shame, isn't it? The destruction of this city is linked to the fall of the Caliphate of Córdoba. The decline really began when al-Hakam II, leader of the Umayyadds, died. His *de facto* successor Almanzor was indirectly to blame for recruiting a large number of Berbers into his army with the intention of consolidating his power as ruler. The Arabic leader showered them with gifts and supported them in order to further the military power of the caliphate, creating a kind of elite personal army. A little after his death, al-Andalus broke out into a bloody civil war between the Umayyadd followers and the Berbers.

'This war culminated in the collapse of the caliphate between 1010 and 1013. When the Umayyadd Empire of the West fell, the Berbers left Medina Azahara for good and moved on to Córdoba. By the time they left, they had either taken or set fire to everything in their path. That's when the pillaging of sites of architectural wealth started. Ornately carved wooden doors, capitals, timber, column bases, as well as the exquisite marble in the palace, were all ransacked and sold between the years 1043 and 1062. Isolated groups from al-Andalus and various palaces in North Africa received the best pieces from the caliphate city. The largest mosques in Granada, Fez, Marrakech and even the great Giralda tower in Seville, were among the buildings that were plundered.

'They say that, in the eighth century, some families still lived around these ruins and, by the time Córdoba was passed into Castilian hands, the old Medina Azahara had become the quarry for new Christian buildings. The fact is, Monsieur Mignon, that with the passing of time, the area was completely forgotten and has been partially buried over the course of centuries.'

Listening hard, Marc had a question about how they would uncover any clues. 'Guylaine told me that its architectural restoration started at the beginning of the twentieth century. If there is something of use in our investigations, I imagine that it will have been either pillaged or buried under tons of earth. Isn't that right?'

'Good point, detective. Those are indeed the two poss-ibilities we are faced with.'

'But I imagine my father has a hidden card up his sleeve,' Guylaine winked at him. 'He always does in situations like this. Don't you, Father?'

'Of course, my darling child. I must tell you that since the restoration work began under the conservation architect Ricardo Velázquez in 1911, the Dubois family received and kept each and every one of the investigation summaries and other documents that have been drawn up over the years of the excavations.'

'Well that card certainly works to our advantage.' This should make his own employment significantly easier, Marc thought.

'Indeed it does. As a result, we know the few places where the information we want could be and most importantly for now, where to search.'

'And what exactly are we looking for?'

'That's the problem. I don't have the faintest idea what the legacy of the wise Arab could be. It could be a simple book, parchment or something of that nature. In my investigations I did find a letter written by a Muslim doctor promising to safely store some of the information relating to Silvestre's investigations in his house, while Medina Azahara was still standing. The truth is that, although the buildings have severely deteriorated, there *are* areas that are still standing, either on the surface or underground. Our search must focus on finding that house; we have its rough position drawn up on an archaic map by the surgeon himself.'

'Brilliant, Father! But how can we access a site that hasn't been officially excavated? I understood that that part of the golden city, where the supposedly intact houses you mention can be found on the map, is off limits as it still hasn't been restored. And besides, I think it's impossible for us to gauge the exact position of the surgeon's house marked on this map.'

'Perhaps I can help you.' A skinny and well-dressed young

man came up from behind her. 'Excuse me for interrupting your conversation but I'm passionate about this subject.'

'And who are you?' the detective asked him, surprised by the eavesdropper.

'I'm an archaeologist. My name is Bruno.'

CHAPTER 41

The young man had startled the Count and his two companions. They had been so absorbed in their investigations that they had paid no attention to other people on the site.

'And what exactly do you think you can help us with?' There was a note of scorn in the Count's voice.

'I know about every excavation that has been undertaken in this city. My family has worked here for decades. One of my uncles worked under the architect Velázquez in the initial, groundbreaking restoration. If anyone can help you, it's me. However, if I've bothered you, forgive me and I'll leave you to your own work. I have no interest in what you were discussing, it's just that this city is my passion and so anything that happens here inevitably interests me. That is the only reason I offer my help.'

'Well, it doesn't seem like such a bad idea,' said Guylaine, eyeing up the stranger. His manner and presentation had not gone unnoticed. 'He seems sincere. Don't you think, Marc?'

'In principle, yes.' He was a little suspicious of the un-expected archaeologist. 'But what's your view, Monsieur Dubois?'

'Well, we will explain what we are looking for and the young man will tell us if he has a simple solution to our problem.' The Count was not taking any chances on the security of his labours. 'Although I warn you, Bruno, we cannot include you in our investigations. Do you understand?'

'Of course,' replied Bruno with a wide, convincing smile.

Pierre Dubois showed him the small map he held in his hand. Without hesitating, the young man pointed out where they should go on the site.

'If you look closely, this map seems to indicate that the Arab doctor's residence lies next to the famous House of Ya'far, the residence of the well-known prime minister under al-Hakam II, whose full name was Ya'far ibn Abd al-Rahman. He was a key figure in the Caliph's plans to extend the Medina Azahara. In fact, he oversaw the work on the central pavilion of the city in person, even working on the rebuilding of the Great Mosque of Córdoba.'

'Can you just take us to this house?' inquired Marc.

'Well, south of the servants' buildings there were built various residencies of great importance. One of these is the House of Ya'far and the other, the so-called Pool House. These are the only two large mansions excavated to date; there are more of them but there is still a lot of work to do in this marvellous city. Next to them stand a line of servant dwellings and, although deep restoration of the area is planned, only a superficial excavation has been completed to date.'

'You don't seem to have understood, Bruno. We have to get there as soon as possible. Do you know how to get there? If you don't, please leave us in peace.'

'Marc, please, let him finish,' Guylaine tried to calm his rising temper; Marc semed agitated by the archaeologist's sudden intrusion.

'Thank you, mademoiselle. The map you have leads us to an area north of Ya'far's house, between the larger buildings and the military base. Please follow me.'

Bruno marched ahead, looking out of the corner of his eye to check that the three were following him. He led them slowly to their destination so the group could see that their route reflected everything he had explained about the area. There were stone remains everywhere, lonely piles waiting to be restored. Scaffolding and various tools used by the archaeologists were scattered all over this part of the site, out of view from the main tourist spots. Marc recognised some of the places that he had visited with Guylaine the day before. He gave her a small wink, pleased that he had remembered all of her guided tour. The Count spotted this lack of subtlety.

When they reached a patio strewn with tiles, Bruno stopped.

'This is the House of Ya'far, of which I spoke a few minutes ago. At the moment it is in the middle of the restoration process. The flagstones are made of violet-coloured limestone. Many of them are missing so there is obviously a lot of work to do before this beautiful paving is restored to its former glory.'

The front patio, covered by three imposing arches, was at a similar stage in the restoration process. Some of the workers must have known the young archaeologist, as they didn't seem at all fazed by him striding onto their site.

Pierre Dubois was beginning to think that this stranger actually might know what he was doing and he had not put a foot wrong during his explanations. Moreover, the map was not easy to decipher, and the exact position of the house marked on it was not easily recognisable for someone who had not directly participated in the excavations, so the Count decided to trust Bruno in the search for the Arab doctor's residence. It hopefully contained the secret that Silvestre II never managed to find.

'Come this way,' beckoned Bruno, who had gone into an annex room and was pointing to a marble pillar that had been reconstructed, a mixture of original and new stone.

'If you look at the beauty and size of this room, you will understand the luxury the citizens of this city must have enjoyed. Even before the end of the first millennium, significant technological advances like the hydraulic system had already been made at Medina Azahara. The water circulation in these buildings for drinking, bathing, irrigation and many other uses had no equal in the year one thousand.'

The year one thousand. The archaeologist's words gave Guylaine a sudden fright. The direct reference to their investigations made her suspicious. However, since he was proving such a knowledgeable guide to the mythic spaces of Medina Azahara, she dismissed her misgivings as an automatic reaction to the phrase.

Bruno stopped under a group of arches that towered over an empty pool.

'This is the Pool House, the most recently restored building. It is built around a garden full of fountains, ponds and pools. As you can see, a path goes north from this house up some steps to the servants' dwellings. The surgeon whose house you are looking for must have lived in that part of the city.'

He pointed to an alleyway, much narrower than the wide lanes they had come through to reach the gardens.

'I do remember that part of the medina,' said the Count. 'As I recall, there are smaller houses dotted amongst these mansions we are passing through now.'

'That's right. They were built so that attendants could immediately and constantly serve the needs of those in the high posts of the caliphate. Clearly, this part of the palatial city was not designed to display the Caliph's wealth but to house the workers adequately.'

'Then,' questioned Guylaine, 'the doctor's house surely won't be found next to a worker's house?'

'Exactly,' the archaeologist replied. 'The location marked on your map is a little beyond the workers' houses to the south-west, but slightly further north than the big mansions, a spot to erect the home of a surgeon befitting of his status. Unfortunately, that part of the city hasn't been excavated yet.'

CHAPTER 42

The investigating party were excited to be told that the area they had reached was still covered by centuries of layers of earth, and studies had not commenced.

'This is promising!' exclaimed Pierre Dubois. 'We could be standing on top of the house of the Arab doctor, whose secrets could provide the key to my mystery and the end of our search.'

Marc grabbed the Count's arm, warning him to be cautious with his words in the presence of the stranger. After all they had been through, they needed to be very careful.

'You can all trust me,' said Bruno. 'I have brought you here as promised and you need me to excavate this site. I know all the workers on this archaeological dig and you can be sure that nobody will ask us what we are doing here. Believe me.'

'And why are you so willing to help us in our search?' asked the Count.

'I am a student of Arabic culture and, in particular, I am fascinated by Medina Azahara. Any new discovery in these lands keeps my passion for my work alive. The archaeological study of the Umayyadd era is my life.'

'I understand and share your enthusiasm. One only needs to look into your eyes to know that you are trustworthy.'

'Thank you very much, Sir.'

* * *

Confident that he had gained their trust, the young man made several calls to various colleagues who, according to him, were working nearby on the conservation of a large raised garden. In a matter of minutes five workers arrived, the team armed with picks, spades and all sorts of tools needed to work on the site. Marc was surprised when they got straight to work without saying a word to any of them. It was as if they had not even noticed the three strangers in their midst. After a while, the workers had opened an extensive hole that revealed the top part of a rickety stone wall. From then on, progress slowed down to a careful pace to avoid damaging the new remains.

The Count was riveted. Despite his daughter's insistence that he should stand out of the midday sun that bore down on them, the nobleman could not tear himself away from the dig for even a second. Pierre sat on a ramshackle wooden chair that the workers brought him and, with wide eyes, watched the excavation develop.

* * *

This was a moment as good as any to bite the bullet and question the Count about his parents' death, Marc thought. He had been mulling the opportunity over for several days now. If his captors really did know about the Mignon tragedy—or even worse, if they had been responsible—and they had also been following the Dubois investigations for years, there could be a connection between the two, however small. Marc took the Count to one side for a few moments in confidence. They walked back over towards Ya'far's house and found a seat.

'I want to talk to you about something that's not directly related to the case we're working on but that is important to me. I can't be sure that it has any connection to the Dubois family, or any of the events of the last few days, but I still want to clarify a couple of things.'

'Detective, you seem tense suddenly.'

'What I'm going to say affects me very personally.'

'Well, go on. Tell me what it is and I will try to help you. After all, I am indebted to you.'

The detective blushed; he didn't want to think about how the Count would react were he to find out about the liaison Marc had had with his wife. A man of his standing could drive the agency into the ground if he were to learn of the scandal. His uncle Marcos didn't deserve a blow like that; he had given Marc so much. Putting aside these thoughts, Marc blurted out his other pressing anxiety.

'My parents died working on what seemed like a simple case for the Mignon Agency. They were investigating a family business called Baumard. Do you know anything about it?'

'Of course I do. I am the owner.'

CHAPTER 43

Marc's blood froze. His prolonged silence unnerved the Count.

'Please forgive me,' murmured Marc. 'You must understand that this affects me very deeply. My parents were killed when I was still a young boy.'

'I understand. Look, Monsieur Mignon, I want to help you with your personal inquiries as recompense for your work on the case. What exactly is it you want to know about Baumard?'

'Everything. My parents were investigating it, under the orders of the owner, when they died. How long have you been the proprietor?'

'I bought Baumard Société Anonyme exactly nineteen years ago, when its founder, Monsieur Serge Baumard, wanted to take his money out of a company that had been in his family for generations. The Baumards had been working with our family for decades. One day, I received a call from Serge telling me that he was closing down the business, and so I decided to buy it from him. Had I not, I ran the risk of losing the distribution of several million bottles of champagne to south-east Asia. The company was a very efficient importer and exporter to the Far East, therefore the business was essential to our trade in foreign markets.'

'And do you remember the Baumard children being at all implicated in the drugs trade or anything like that?' inquired Marc, remembering the story that his uncle had told him so many times.

'No, I'm not sure about that,' responded the Count with an arched eyebrow. 'What I do remember is Serge telling me that he left the business as he could no longer fight battles on several different fronts at the same time. I think he was referring to his children, whom he thought were being led astray, but he didn't mention anything to do with drugs.'

'What was he referring to, then?'

'If I remember correctly, the old man told me that his children had got involved with a bad crowd.'

'Thieves, swindlers, con men? What type of friendships are you talking about?'

'No-one like that. I remember now. He said that his children had come in contact with a particular set that in some way or another had ruined their lives. But that was a long time ago, so I would forget about it if I were you.'

* * *

It was almost an hour later that the Count and Marc returned to the dig and were surprised to see that the workers had made visible progress. Bruno explained that they had found an area of soft earth, mainly loose sand, that had been deposited on the doctor's house over hundreds of years. This part of the caliphate city could have been excavated in the past but later filled back in to leave it as it was now.

'I have a theory. I think this earth was dumped,' said the

Count. 'Someone has consciously buried this area in sand.'

'It's possible,' considered Bruno. 'It is unusual to find this type of soil in these spots. You could be right.'

'Why should it make any difference, at least at the moment?' Guylaine was still fixed on the excavation pit. 'It's helping us with the dig as it's so easy to clear. If we continue at this pace, we might have finished by tomorrow.'

'It's very likely, mademoiselle.'

The Count called the detective and Guylaine into the shade, away from the party. He thought that although the dig would carry on into the night, it was unlikely that they would come across anything that needed urgent attention, so now would be a good time to leave the workers, rest for a while and come back very early the following day.

Marc wearily nodded his head in agreement and they made their way back to the hotel.

* * *

Marc's hotel room felt cold and inhospitable. The space seemed different without Guylaine. He plucked up the courage to phone her to ask her to go for a drink. She agreed to meet him at the bar after she had refreshed herself from the day.

While he waited, Marc sank in to a comfortable seat on the roof terrace, looking out over the city's stunning evening skyline stretched out before him. The peace of the city below gave him a chance to reflect on what the Count had said to him earlier that afternoon. Although he had not revealed anything that could help him resolve the mysterious death of his parents there and then, it was a promising step forward. As soon as he returned to Paris, he would look for the Baumard children. Twenty years was a long time to have to wait to make sense of the tragic accident but, although his uncle Marcos had investigated it in depth, the new clues from the Count could now be enough to give him closure at last.

Guylaine stepped out of the lift and glided towards him with a slight sway in her step. After several days spent on the run, her fitted black dress and the elegant necklace nestled into her chest caught the detective by surprise. With a faint smile opening across her face, the nobleman's daughter sat down opposite him and quickly glanced over the cocktail menu. He ordered a Manhattan and she did the same. When the drinks arrived, they raised their glasses to one another.

'It's been a long day, did you not want to sleep?' she asked.

'Yes it has been, but I couldn't sleep, I wanted to talk to you. It's strange…'

'What is?' she asked, taking a sip of her cocktail.

'That I miss having someone in my room. I have been alone for most of my life and now on my second day without you I can't get to sleep.'

'When was the last time you were intimate with someone?'

Not expecting the question, he spluttered in an un-gentlemanly way. He apologised and tried not to think of the Countess. 'Oh I don't know, how about you?'

'I asked the question.'

'I know. The thing is, I have reason to hide my past from such an intelligent woman as the one in front of me.'

'Well, the detective is a flatterer! Perhaps the ecologist inside you is more honest. What's the Marc Mignon from two months ago like? I feel like you act differently in front of my family to how you really are.'

'Jesus! The young heiress is a professional psychologist, as well as a historian. Does my life really interest you?'

'I don't know. You've told me about your experiences around the world as an eco-adventurer, but you haven't told me anything personal about you.'

'Does it matter to you what I'm like?'

'It's difficult to spend a continual amount of time with someone, as we have recently, without being ever so slightly curious as to whom they are. Don't you agree?'

'Of course but now you're avoiding my question.'

'I get on well with you and one could say that you interest me as a friend. If you're referring to us becoming more than friends, the truth is that the thought has not crossed my mind. It's been impossible to think clearly during our adventures of various sorts recently. Does that make sense?' she asked.

'Yes.'

Guylaine deliberately left a pause in the conversation to think back to the night that she had seen her mother coming down the stairs suspiciously. When the Countess drank it was usually a sign that her mother was out of control over something. It wouldn't surprise her if her mother had been coming from the detective's bedroom, having made an unforgiveable mistake. Guylaine would never be able to forgive Marc either, if that were the case.

From the wide terrace, Marc could see millions of shining stars, an incredible tapestry of the night sky blanketing their silence. After a few minutes, he broke the shroud.

'Can you imagine how vast the universe must be? Every one of those stars is an inconceivable distance from us.'

'Yes, and what is your point?'

'I've slept out in the open many times and whenever I've witnessed a night like this I've found myself travelling towards a distant star in my mind, wondering what life might be like in a different world.'

'And?'

'I always end up realising that happiness shouldn't lie far away but here, where it is all around us, if only we could find it.'

Marc looked at the girl in front of him; she was one of those distant stars he would never reach.

CHAPTER 44

Bruno called, informing them that they had already reached the floor of the Arab doctor's house. Without delay, the investigation party left the hotel. If they reached the site within half an hour, he said, they would be in time to see the small mansion revealed and at the same time, witness the exhumation of that final millennial secret that had escaped the world for so long.

The Count didn't wait for Marc to stop the car before jumping out of the back seat and, without saying a word, he ran inside the caliphate city. On arrival at their site, he found the same frenzied activity as the day before. At the foot of the excavation, Bruno was keeping a close eye on his chosen workforce.

'Welcome, Sir. I'm pleased that you have arrived at this point, as we are cleaning the floor of what was once a medium-sized house, probably the dwelling of a doctor or surgeon, a professional with an important role of looking after those in power. From the carvings we have found on various walls, it's clear that it's not the house of a servant; we might have got hold of what you are looking for.'

'I'm delighted!' It was a privilege just being there, watching as the home of a Muslim man of learning came out of the earth before his eyes.

The arrival of Guylaine and Marc caught the archaeologist's eye.

'Ah, I see you've here as well. Mademoiselle, I have told your father that we're about to finish cleaning the floor in order to carry out a detailed exploration of what we've recovered. You have arrived just in time. Take the tools away!' he shouted at the workers.

They dutifully finished brushing the sand away from a very deteriorated white marble floor. Without the instruments and work in progress, the image of the site completely changed. Much to their surprise, the remains of the house were more beautiful than the larger mansions they had seen on their wanderings. Although the roof had nearly disappeared completely, the walls appeared in a good state. They were as lavishly carved and as beautiful as the palatial buildings of the city, but with the wonderful benefit of being fresh – and seen only by their eyes.

'One thing is clear,' the Count's murmur caught the attention of the group, 'this dwelling has remained just as it was left back then.'

'What do you mean?' his daughter asked.

'Do you remember what we talked about yesterday, about the earth that covered these walls? My theory is that someone covered this house before it could be pillaged.'

'How can you be so sure?'

'This whole city has been the subject of many lootings over the centuries; however, look at the untouched timber and copper plating here. Someone deliberately hid this house, covering it with earth. The walls, floors and, in fact, everything about this house is much more intact than some of the conserved official buildings.'

'And what do you think whoever it was who covered this could have wanted to hide?' asked Bruno.

'That is precisely what we have to find out. That's why we're here.'

* * *

If they found something, it must remain secret. Marc whispered to the Count that everyone had to leave so they could investigate alone now. Pierre Dubois agreed with the detective and asked Bruno to order the workers to leave the site. The Count offered them all an excellent salary for the hours they had worked and went up to each of them personally to shake their hands and thank them for their hard labour.

'With all due respect, Sir, I'd like to ask you for permission to join in the investigations with you,' the archaeologist requested. 'You already know how passionate I am about this subject.'

'Of course—without your help it would have been very difficult for us to get even to this point. That much is undeniable. We would be honoured for you to accompany us. Incidentally, what's your surname?'

'Don't worry about that. Just call me Bruno.'

Guylaine looked across at Marc, who now had a deep frown across his brow. The Count was becoming impatient to begin the investigation. 'The time has come to start our inquiries.'

'How shall we divide the work?' wondered Guylaine. 'If we divide the space into three areas, we will find what we're looking for more quickly.'

'Even quicker as we'll do it between four. This young man is very capable of helping us. I will begin in the living room. You, my child, will go to the bedroom and Marc will take the bathroom. Bruno, you can check the exterior façade.'

'Sounds good to me. I hope you'll tell me what we're looking for, otherwise I won't know where to start.'

'Excuse my impatience. Strictly speaking, we have to find a book, a manuscript or some form of text that sheds light on our investigations.'

The archaeologist nodded and each of them made their way to the area they had been given without saying a word.

* * *

Pierre Dubois stood in the centre of the floor. He noticed that, beneath the exposed walls, you could see remains of the stone with which the retaining walls were built. It had been built using large, square-cut stones, and the joins between them were almost perfect. It was not like the stonework of the servants' residences, where the walls were laid with uncut stones, and rough-looking mortar. This home had clearly been built for someone of importance. More interesting still were the remains of the carved stone plaques, still attached to the walls, testament to the fact that the house had never been looted. Although somewhat deteriorated, the ornate and geometrical drawings stunned the nobleman.

After a few seconds, the Count saw that the doors had been adorned with beautiful horseshoe arches. The keystones alternated between shades of red and white, and had also been engraved with intricate carvings, part of an elaborate arabesque on a stucco wall, decorated with leaf and fruit motifs, a favoured style of the time. The small amount of roof that remained showed a glimpse of a remarkable coffered ceiling with its vaults formed by elegantly arranged beams.

Several columns were topped with beautiful ornamental detail that flowed into delicate decorations. These intricate carvings, which he remembered were known as a wasps' nest because of their numerous tiny orifices, must have been carved with a fine-pointed chisel by a skilled hand.

Finally, the Count turned his attention to the floor, seeing that not even one of the slabs of white marble was missing. In one corner, it appeared that one of the pieces had broken in various places. This was the detail in the room on which he focused first. He tried to lift the whole slab but it was firmly stuck to the floor, so he removed one of the smaller pieces and squeezed his hand through the small hole it left. Nothing. Removing every other broken piece one by one, the Count was disappointed still to find nothing. This initial setback was not going to slow him, so he gathered his thoughts and continued inspecting his allotted room.

* * *

Guylaine's eyes adjusted to the dark gloom of the room after the glare of the sun outside. In front of the bedroom, there was a small patio with a red marble fountain in its centre. She thought of the soothing sound of fresh, clean water that must have flowed around the palatial city at the end of the first millennium. The floor of the room was made up of baked clay flagstones and contrasted with the violet limestone slabs of the tiled patio outside. The limestone was inlaid with geometric drawings, simple decorations. It occurred to Guylaine that this room was designed for meditation since it lacked the luxuries of the main room used to receive guests. A room as inconspicuous as this would make a good place to hide something.

She felt along the walls, thick with the dirt from the recent excavation, and found no obvious recess or secret door. When she had checked all four walls, she turned her attention to the floor. Although some tiles rocked or wavered slightly, none of them gave way when she attempted to dislodge them. No success here.

* * *

Marc Mignon took out his notebook and wrote down his thoughts about what had happened that morning. When he finished, he headed inside and found two rooms. One of them appeared to be the bathroom; its fountains and tanks were clearly used to heat water for relaxation and therapy. It reminded him of a Turkish bath he had once visited, although this version was much more primitive and, now, deteriorated. It did not take him long to work out that the smaller, adjoining chamber was the latrine. He walked round both rooms several times and touched all the walls in search of a possible secret hole.

Nothing seemed out of place, or gave any suggestion

that the Arab surgeon had left his millennial secret in the bathroom.

* * *

They met back in front of the entrance to the house, where an expectant Bruno waited. The disappointed faces of all three of the group made it clear that the search had not been fruitful.

'Have you found anything? We haven't had much luck,' asked the Count.

'No. I was hoping that you had been more successful; there's nothing outside here. It is the façade of a house of a man with a certain status but it is far from containing the pomp or excess of the House of Ya'far or the Pool House. I can't think of anything that could contain a text, a message or whatever it is you're looking for.'

'No, it seems not.'

'If you can at least tell me what you want those words for, then maybe I'll be of more help to you. But without knowing the background to the case, it's very difficult for me to be of use.'

'Yes, I know. It is the key to a matter we are investigating, which we have to be discreet about,' explained Guylaine.

'I see.'

'Perhaps we could put our heads together over lunch.' Marc's stomach was summoning him. 'I think that we should eat something.'

There was a general agreement. Bruno bid them goodbye, saying that he had some business to attend to and they agreed to meet each other back at the site after lunch.

CHAPTER 45

Sitting in a comfortable restaurant, Guylaine took advantage of the time before their food arrived to talk about Jean Luc again. The police had told her that there was still no sign of him and that they had issued instructions to the train and bus stations, as well as airports in the region, to look out for a man who fitted his description. She told her father and Marc that the castle had no news of the Countess, who was still not answering her mobile phone.

'We must not lose hope of finding him,' the Count rallied. 'I'm sure that Renaud is fine and that he has just disappeared by chance. You already know how absentminded he is. I imagine that he is simply with a friend, talking about old books, completely oblivious to all our concerns. As for Véronique, something similar could have happened. It would not be the first time that she has gone to visit her family in Burdeos unannounced. She left the castle with a suitcase under her own steam. We should not worry about them any more. At least, not for the moment.'

'So what do we do now?' asked Marc.

'We talk about what we have seen again and see if any good ideas spring to mind. Let's all set out what we think is significant in the case,' Guylaine proposed.

The Count began. He described his findings in the

Arab doctor's house and the conclusions he had drawn. His biggest surprise had been finding an example of the opulent coffered ceiling that had disappeared from the rest of Medina Azahara.

Guylaine related the characteristics of the bedroom, which required less analysis, being considerably more austere than the reception room.

As far as Marc was concerned, the rooms he had investigated didn't reveal anything; the bathroom had no visible ornamentation and was in disrepair, and the other room was simply a latrine. There couldn't be anything hidden there.

'We must first consider what we are looking for,' suggested the Count. 'At times, to get to the bottom of things, it is best to start from the beginning and take a step back from the matter in question. We must situate ourselves between the years 967 and 970. Gerberto d'Aurillac was working in the city, searching for books and any new knowledge in the field of scientific advances. It is known that he came into contact with people who gave him such learning. Old books could be found here, which many people believed were lost, and the city also housed texts describing advanced scientific practices that would shock any Christian in Europe.

'We know that the doctor of Medina Azahara treasured such knowledge and that there were people who were willing to do anything to get hold of it. This man dedicated his life to healing others through practising the most traditional methods; living as close as he did to the centre of caliphate power, he would have had direct access to Abderraman III's library, which was greatly enriched by the acquisitions of his son, al-Hakam II.

'One part of the library houses texts translated from classical languages, another contains extensive collections of rare books from lost cultures. These would have been the most secret of all the caliphate archives. Our French monk managed to talk his way into both parts of the library to gather the most authoritative texts in the land on the subject of Mother Nature. According to William of Malmesbury, he stole a precious book that contained all the knowledge and profound magical arts documented by a wise Arab. Malmesbury also claims that, to avoid the book being discovered by others, Gerberto made a pact with the Devil that took him to Rome. If all this is true, which I doubt, what happened to the missing book?'

'Why are you so sure that he was missing a book needed to conclude his investigations with the machine?' Guylaine asked him.

'Simply because the talking head can do calculations beyond the conclusion that the earth is going to suffer a great catastrophe. However, it can't tell us what the remedy is, because it lacks information. The results of the machine are incomplete.'

'Our task then is to find a book, text or any kind of written artefact that contains this missing information to make the head work at full capacity,' concluded Marc.

'Exactly.'

'If we haven't found it in the walls, ceilings or floors of the doctor's house, where could it be?' Guylaine wondered out loud.

'Could it be behind the adornments in the principal room?' asked the detective.

'It could be, detective. Normally, it would upset a historian like me to consider removing a plaque, a coffered ceiling or even the smallest detail of a house that is now more than one thousand years old. But, in these circumstances, I think that it's the right course of action.'

'It seems barbaric to me,' Guylaine said.

'Darling, we are not going to destroy anything that can't be restored. We have found and recovered this building, which nobody would have known about if it were not for us.'

'I don't know. Maybe you're right, but I don't want to touch so much as a brick in that house.'

'That's what we have this strapping investigator for...'

Marc looked from father to daughter, not knowing which side to take.

CHAPTER 46

It wasn't until mid afternoon that they got back to the site. The young archaeologist was waiting for them patiently, leaning on a solid, striking white marble column. When Marc saw him, he realised that they would have to consult Bruno about the Count's plan. Sensing Marc's unease, the Count assured him that he would take control of the situation.

With a broad smile, Pierre approached Bruno.

'Have you eaten well today, young man?'

'Very well.'

'Good. Let me tell you my plan...'

Pierre Dubois took the archaeologist by the arm and led him inside the ruins of the Arab doctor's house. After a few minutes, they both re-emerged with serious faces.

'It was difficult to convince him but I managed. Our young friend now understands how important it is to find what we're looking for. Isn't that right?'

He nodded and pointed resignedly to the tools propped up against the exterior wall.

'I think that we should proceed with great care,' added the Count. 'There's no need to destroy anything, we just need to know whether there is anything written underneath the decorations. We'll just lift certain parts of the wall up and restore them straightaway. Well what are you waiting for?

Take an instrument each!'

The nobleman's drive surprised Marc, and he obeyed without saying a word, taking up a pick and making his way over to the area that the Count had signalled.

* * *

Pierre Dubois ordered Marc to start with some thin carved plaques that formed a spectacular mural on one of the walls. He instructed the detective to separate two of the pieces to see what lay underneath. Marc did as he was told and, with great care, using the point of the pick, managed to lever out two slabs. With Bruno's help, they removed these and placed them delicately on the floor.

Behind the slabs, they found bare brown and grey stone without any sort of inscription. With a brief gesture, the Count urged Marc to pull out two new parts at the other end of the wall. Again, the same surface blank surface was revealed. Marc and Guylaine were clearly nervous about destroying these rare artefacts but the Count insisted that they should carry on. The coffered ceiling or the beautiful arches over the doors did not seem like suitable places to leave any kind of inscription. They decided to go through to the bedroom.

A simple skirting board was the only decoration in the doctor's plain bedroom; otherwise the walls were smooth and bare. Prising away one part of the skirting, once again, all that lay behind the piece of marble was the stone with which the house had been constructed.

However, still the nobleman did not lose heart and, with

unwavering energy, instructed the others to follow him.

The bathroom, containing only a couple of basins and a small cistern, did not appear out of the ordinary or a likely prize-giving candidate. Just then, the Count looked as if he were on the verge of toppling one of the marble pillars. Guylaine saw no amusement in his acting, if it was a joke, and told him not to even think about creating such mayhem. Her father's growing excitement, now bordering on hysteria, was starting to worry her.

In an attempt to improve his erratic search method, Guylaine offered what she thought was a sensible clue.

'It occurred to me that if someone wanted to hide important and intimate knowledge, they would probably keep it in their bedroom – the room in which any person feels safest, a place where they are free to give themselves over to contemplation. Let's go back there.'

The men followed her unquestioningly.

She proposed that they gently bang the floor with a blunt handle of one of the tools to see if there was a gap underneath; a hollow sound would give this away instantly. Each member of the group took up a tool with a rounded handle, and all four found themselves kneeling on the baked clay tiles, the only sound the strike and echo of their tentative taps in the bare room.

None of the tiles seemed to be covering anything below.

When he came to the end of one length of the room, Marc turned and found himself face to face with Guylaine, who looked at him in confusion. They held their gaze for a while, until the Count, who noticed the sudden silence, asked them if they had found something. Without saying a word, they continued tapping their separate lines. There was no more than two square metres left of the floor to examine when the Count, who was on the verge of despair, knocked a tile that sounded different. He tapped it again and, compared to the dry, dull thud the adjacent tile made, this gave a fuller, more rounded sound. The space beneath this tile was hollow.

Encouraged by the promising resonance, he asked the detective to chisel at the tile with the pick. Reluctant to damage something of beauty, a relic of the past, Marc checked that the Count was sure that this tile was different from the others. The Count urged him on.

'Come on, hit it harder!'

This time Marc took a smaller pick and kneeling this time, gave it a sharp hammer that smashed it to pieces, scattering splinters to the edges of the room. They all gathered around to see what had happened.

Where the piece of clay had been before appeared a black hole, the bottom of which could not be seen.

* * *

The Count was in a visible state of shock; he looked up at the ceiling and closed his eyes, as if he was thanking God for the discovery.

Marc put his hand into the hole to work out how deep it was. He soon realised that even with an outstretched arm he could not reach the bottom of the space, so he asked for a torch. With the beam of light, he could make out another floor approximately two metres beneath where they were kneeling.

'We'll have to break a few more tiles, so we can get down there.' This time Bruno put his hand inside and felt underneath the floor for tiles that would be easy to lift in order to create a sizeable hole through which they could descend. The detective began to break three more tiles, giving them a small square entrance.

Outside, Guylaine had found a thick cord that could be used to lower them down into the hidden room.

Bruno offered to go down first, but the Count quickly interrupted; how dare the young archaeologist think he could take that opportunity away from Dubois? The Count gingerly tied the rope around his waist and ordered the detective to hold on to one end firmly. His daughter passed him the torch and, blowing a kiss, wished him luck.

* * *

The dark room must have been no more than four metres square and substantially smaller than the bedroom above.

The stone with which it had been built was a dark brown colour and had been left plain, not decorated at all, and the bare floor seemed neglected without tiling. The Count planted his feet on the ground and signalled up to the group that he was safe. He untied the cord from his waist, asked his daughter to follow him down and told the two men to remain so that they could haul them up again.

Silently, just as she had obeyed every order her father had given out in the short search, Guylaine did as she was told and followed him down the rope. She saw that there wasn't a single piece of furniture, object or tool in the dark, escapeless room. She was most disappointed to find no book in sight, not even a single manuscript.

In the gloom, she asked her father what the use of this peculiar hiding place could be. The nobleman shrugged his shoulders. Swinging the torch around, Pierre and Guylaine Dubois asked the two men what they could make out from above. Then, before they had become fully accustomed to their surroundings, they turned around to see that the fourth wall was completely covered with Arab symbols.

A long text had been etched from floor to ceiling, from one side of the wall to the other.

CHAPTER 47

The pallor that overcame the Count's face scared his daughter. Not knowing what to do, she waved her hand in front of his eyes.

'Father, are you all right?'

Guylaine remembered how her father had been in the days after his discovery of the talking head, when he looked like a ghost due to the thick layer of dust that covered his hair and shaded his appearance. History was repeating itself.

'Yes, I am perfectly well; do not worry. You have no idea what we have just found here.'

He pointed to the wall in front of them, composed of countless Arabic characters, etched in perfect rows on a massive plaque of white marble, the surface fully covered.

'You must realise that I'm not as good as you at everything and I didn't inherit your passion for languages, including Arabic.'

'You're right, I forgot that such an important language as this has never interested you,' he answered, reading constantly as he spoke. 'It's your loss because it is fascinating.'

'Indeed,' she replied, wiping dust out of her hair. She then realised that her whole body was covered in a fine layer of white sand.

Marc's voice, powerful and with a loud echo, came from above.

They asked him not to shout and to throw down the cord so they could come back up. When Guylaine re-emerged from the hole, Marc saw that for some reason, she had left her father below.

The detective helped her up and on to the bedroom floor. As she stood up, he saw that her hair was covered in dust and, without thinking, he gently brushed it away.

'You've looked better,' he said, smiling.

'Don't joke. We've found what we were looking for.'

'Seriously? What is it? Have you found a book?'

'Almost. There's an entire wall full of Arabic characters down there. As I don't understand the language, I've left my father to interpret the text. We must now get paper, a pencil and a good camera for him. Shall we go now? We don't have much time.'

Marc looked at Bruno, who immediately offered to take care of the Count.

They mustn't worry, he said—the Count was in good hands.

* * *

They reached the car in a couple of minutes. They had a few hours until it got dark, so there was time to buy the new instruments they now required. Marc wanted the drive so that he could talk to Guylaine about what was to happen next. Perhaps he was no longer needed, now that the search was over. His job was technically done.

'I have no idea what's going to happen now but I desperately want to go back to Reims and find my mother,' said Guylaine. 'First I lose my father for several days and then the same thing happens to my mother. Nothing like this has ever happened to me in my life; it's really thrown me.'

'I know. This isn't easy for anyone.'

'And I haven't stopped worrying about those horrible men either. The worst of this situation is that we don't know what has become of poor Renaud. Given everything that has happened, if we could catch a plane home today, I would do it gladly.'

Marc felt slightly disappointed but he understood. He nodded reassuringly in agreement before they parked the car.

As they returned to Medina Azahara with supplies, most importantly a camera with a good-quality flash, he asked himself if this would be the last trip he would make with Guylaine.

* * *

The sun was now only shining weakly when they got to the ruins of the doctor's house; there was hardly enough light to see the narrow path. When they went into the bedroom Bruno was not at the top of the opening.

The detective's heart raced as he threw himself towards the hole, shouting for the Count. In desperation, he considered jumping straight down, but prudence kept his feet on the ground. Pierre Dubois answered him in a trembling voice, saying that he was fine and that what he was reading was very interesting. Bruno heard their voices and came running through immediately, appearing behind the detective.

'Where have you been?' Marc shouted angrily.

'I was making some calls. Has something happened? You should calm down, or you'll lose it.'

'You shouldn't have left him alone down there. Anything could have happened.'

'Don't worry,' Guylaine interjected. 'Everything's fine. Please help me down there.'

She felt settled being back by her father's side. He started to tell her what he had learnt so far. She asked him to take the best possible photos and write down everything important because they should get out as soon as possible; night was closing in on them. With a deep breath, the Count got to work. This was one of the biggest events of his life, second only to the discovery of the talking head. Standing before such an exciting discovery, he wondered if the end of his long journey could be close at last.

* * *

In the hotel lobby they planned their evening. The Count was confident that in the space of two hours he could interpret the entire text and discern whether it was what they were looking for or not. So, they would meet for dinner to hear his findings. A cheeky smile gave away the fact that Pierre Dubois, historian and millennial expert, already knew that they really had found the key.

Marc Mignon made the most of this time to sort out his suitcase, in case his return home was imminent. While he gathered his clothes and folded them neatly, he thought back to the day his uncle had called him to talk over the Dubois case and the proposition Marcos had decided to make him. It wasn't that long ago, but it seemed like an eternity now. Despite the danger he had faced along the way, he was sure about one thing; from now on, his new life would be as a detective. At barely thirty years old, he finally knew what he wanted to do: his father's profession. He never would have imagined it. He finished tidying his room and made his way to the top floor of the hotel, to the Count's favourite restaurant. With a Manhattan in his hand, Marc sat and watched the other guests.

Half an hour later, the elegantly dressed pair of father and daughter appeared. Once more, the detective wondered whether this would be the last time they would all sit down to dinner together. They chose a discreet table so that they could speak, the same one they had sat at the night before. Eagerly, Marc awaited the Count's discoveries.

'In short, it is what we were looking for. We have been lucky. Very lucky,' said the nobleman, with a sparkle in his eyes.

'Do you mean that we've come to the end of the case?'

'Yes and no.'

'Can you explain what you mean?'

'Of course, that's why we're here. But first let us order. I am hungry and the menu here really is very good.'

They greeted the waiter in mutual recognition and listened to his recommendations.

The Count waited for him to leave before beginning to explain his findings.

'I'm almost certain that the information we have found today is exactly what we were looking for and that it is the missing element from Silvestre's machine that it needs to reach its final conclusions.'

'How sure are you?' his daughter asked.

'Not entirely. Next to the long text, engraved in the wall of the hidden room, I found an unexpected inscription that has unsettled me.'

'Can you tell us what it's like?'

'Of course, I'll draw you a diagram. Next to the text, there is a mysterious phrase that I cannot unravel. I know that the French monk stole, took or somehow got hold of a book or manuscript with information unknown in Western culture and that it probably provided the foundations needed to create the talking head.'

'We all already knew that,' interrupted Guylaine.

'Yes, that's right. The thing is that this phrase, which I am yet to understand, seems to indicate that someone had taken a fragment of the text and that the engraving in that room was the missing part.'

'Then everything is complete,' suggested the detective. 'Now we have the final piece of the jigsaw, that even Silvestre didn't manage to find.'

'No, because the phrase seems to suggest that no one should think that this piece of sublime knowledge completes the puzzle.'

'You mean that there is yet another part missing?' asked Guylaine in disbelief.

'Yes, that's what it seems to say and, what's more, there was also a symbol on the wall.'

'What do you mean? What does the symbol look like?'

Pierre Dubois copied on to a scrap of paper from his

breast pocket exactly what he had seen that afternoon in the underground room of the doctor's house:

R

R   R

The detective was confused by the strange arrangement of letters.

'And what could it be trying to say?'

'I found it difficult to understand but I have finally managed to grasp what our friend, the Arab, wanted to say. First and foremost, we must be clear about the dates; the monk was here before the year 970 and died in 1003. The palatial city was destroyed in 1013. But, from what we have seen, someone took the trouble to cover the doctor's house with a layer of sand to preserve a secret that must not be lost to civilisation.

'One must focus on the fact that whoever left this valuable information for the future did it by engraving it into a solid wall, on a marble slab, that is resistant to the ravages of time. It would not have lasted in the same way had they left a simple book or manuscript.'

'I really don't understand,' Guylaine sighed, a look of vexation on her face.

'Well it's obvious, my child. The wise Arab knew the holder of the first part of the book, wrote the second part of the ancestral secret for future discovery and even had time to leave a clue as to where the third and last part of the valuable revelation can be found.'

'And where could that part be?' the detective asked.

'You have to focus on the three Rs. It is brilliant, don't you see?'

'Not for me because I don't know what they mean,' Guylaine said, now exasperated.

'Well, my child, it is really very clear. This diagram with the three Rs refers to the most respected thinker at the end of the millennium, Silvestre II, the person who revolutionised mathematics and the sciences. Here is the R of Reims, your city, in which the French monk was archbishop for a long time. Then there is the R of Ravenna, where he was also archbishop and, finally, there is the last and most important R.'

'With all due respect, please tell us now where you mean,' Marc demanded.

'The career of the pope magician, who moved from one R to another throughout his life, ends here, so it is the decisive location.'

'And where is it?'

'Rome, of course.'

CHAPTER 48

'But that's incredible, Father. What you're saying is that the person who wrote the message knew that Gerberto d'Aurillac had taken valuable knowledge from here and had passed through Reims, Ravenna and, finally, Rome.'

'That's right. The person who engraved that phrase and symbol drew a cryptic map, so that people in the future could follow the footsteps of this man. At the same time, he made it clear who it was who possessed the necessary information. Everything contained within the machine, plus what we have discovered today and a third key element we have yet to find, are part of a legacy that these men of learning were trying to protect.'

'If I'm not mistaken, this means that we still haven't finished our search,' added Marc. 'The third R leads to Rome, where we must go to retrieve the missing text.'

'Indeed, monsieur, but there are various things to be done now in order to finish our investigations.'

Marc and Guylaine looked at one another, neither understanding what the nobleman was implying.

'We have no choice but to split up. Someone must go to Rome. It's obvious that Silvestre took the final information with him and kept it there during the years he was pope. He definitely must have left a record of it. But, in order to be certain of how to obtain what we are looking for, someone must use the machine to get that information.'

'What do you propose?'

'I will go back to Reims to activate the talking head. I will enter the data we have found today and try to get as much from the machine as I can. It's going to take a good few hours to translate the extensive Arabic text into the code required by Silvestre's abacus. And, in addition to all of that, I must look for my wife.'

'And what about us?' his daughter asked him.

'Well, there's only one option. I propose that you go to Rome.'

Pierre Dubois, pleased that he was going home to resume the most important investigation of his life, called the waiter over and asked him to charge the meal to his room. The waiter gratefully accepted his tip, watched the group until all three of them had left the restaurant, which was already empty that late at night, then immediately made a call to relay the good news. If everything proceeded to plan, the end was in sight.

* * *

When the detective got to Guylaine and her father's room, he noticed that it was immaculate. Here, they would plan the next stage of their separate journeys, in complete privacy. Marc pulled up a chair and, while he waited for the Count, worried about how they could travel to Rome safely if the dangerous men were still pursuing them. It was obvious they had to be cautious and stay alert.

'Something seems strange,' he thought aloud. 'I don't understand why those criminals who were following us have suddenly vanished. Renaud's disappearance also still disturbs me.' And I've lost the best clue I had about my parents' death, added the detective to himself.

The Count emerged from the bathroom and responded to the detective's latter comment.

'I keep assuring myself that Renaud must be somewhere safe. As I have said, he is a very sensitive character and will probably be resting after the trauma of my disappearance.'

'Perhaps, but given that we don't know where those thugs could come from again, we must tread carefully.'

'I had already thought about that. Before we do anything, you ought to know that there are no scheduled flights to Rome or Reims from Córdoba. I have decided that we should travel quickly, safely and comfortably.'

'What do you mean, Father?' Guylaine asked.

'I have made some calls and hired two private planes that will be ready first thing tomorrow morning. You will go to Rome in one of them. That way you will be there with plenty of time to start your investigations during the day. I will fly to Paris and will be home very early to start inputting information into the machine.'

'Just one more thing, Sir. I'm apprehensive about you travelling alone to France. I wouldn't want you to go missing again, for whatever reason.'

'I am grateful for your concern, son. But don't worry because the young Bruno has offered to accompany me. He really wants to see the talking head; he is fascinated by its history. I'm positive he's going to help us. You'll soon see.'

CHAPTER 49

There was not a single cloud in the sky and the view of Córdoba was breathtaking. After a few minutes, Guylaine could make out all the spectacular monuments inhabiting the city. She recalled the moment she found her father in the mythical city of Medina Azahara, a joyful reunion and a relief that she would remember for the rest of her life.

The private aircraft, with just nine seats on board, was extremely comfortable for its two occupants. Guylaine shifted her position and saw that Marc was dozing.

'Don't you want to look at the view?'

'Yes, of course, but I'd rather look out when we can't see the mainland any more. We have to cross over the Mediterranean on this route and I imagine we will be able to see islands like Mallorca, Corsica and even Sardinia. You know how much I love the sea.'

'It looked like you were asleep.'

'I was actually thinking about your father's plan to take that young archaeologist with him, whom we know nothing about. He has certainly been a great help but I don't think it was wise to let him go with the Count.'

'So, it isn't because you're ever so slightly jealous? I think that you want the case all to yourself and don't want anyone to overshadow you.'

'Don't talk nonsense! I'm very involved in the case, that's all. I don't want anything to happen to your father and that's why I am concerned for his safety. By the way, have you phoned your mother today?'

'Yes, but she still doesn't answer and it is now really starting to worry me. We have never gone without speaking for this long. Even when I'm giving classes in Paris, she calls every day to see how I am. Surely, something bad must have happened to her?'

'Don't worry, she'll turn up, you'll see.'

Guylaine tried to imagine where her mother could be. The first theory that she had been going over the day before was not at all appealing. For some reason, she thought that Véronique had finally decided to leave her husband and start a new life on her own. Although that was a reasonable explanation for her disappearance, it didn't make sense that she hadn't phoned for several days and hadn't even informed her own daughter.

If that wasn't the case, the other option didn't bear thinking about.

She looked out the little window and saw that they were flying over an island, but Marc was now sound asleep. She could make out golden coasts bathing in turquoise green seas, beautiful beaches and secluded coves in which small boats were anchored, which looked like small dots on a vast green canvas. She asked the pilot which island they were flying over and he confirmed that it was Palma de Mallorca. She reclined in her seat and, like the detective often did, tried to imagine what her life would be like on one of those marvellous beaches, when everything that was happening to her had run its course.

* * *

Touching down in Rome, both thankfully rested from the comfortable flight, they passed effortlessly through the airport and headed to yet another car rental office, where they hired a brand new sports car.

'With this car we'll be in the same league as the Italian racer boys!' Marc was awake now and excited.

'You have to drive carefully in Rome. People are crazy here on the roads.'

'I know. And I love it.'

Unlike in the other cities they had been to together, they decided to get a room each at the hotel, as they were no longer in any apparent danger. They had arrived in a private aeroplane and no one knew when or where they were going. After dropping their luggage off in their rooms and having a light lunch in the café, the couple began in earnest their search for the last part of millennial information the machine needed. In the car Guylaine took out a list of places they needed to visit, arranged in order of priority, which her father had prepared the night before. She called her father, as he must have arrived in Reims by now.

Pierre Dubois answered the phone immediately and greeted her warmly.

'Hello, my child! You are not going to believe how much progress we are making. This young man, Bruno, is an expert in millennial history. He is an invaluable assistant.'

'That's great. We're going to start our tour of the city. If you have nothing new to tell us, we are going to start with Silvestre II's cenotaph as planned. We're on our way there right now.'

'Perfect. If we discover anything, I'll call you.'

The façade of the Basilica of St John Lateran was bathed in the mid-afternoon sun and between the immense white columns a throng of people were preparing to visit the Bishop of Rome's residence. The enormous statues on the attic of the building seemed to be standing sentinel over the worshippers as they entered.

'Do you know this temple?' Guylaine asked Marc.

'No, I have to admit that I've never been. You can be my tourist guide again and I'll listen patiently.'

She started to explain to him that it was one of the four main basilicas in the sacred city and was the most important because it had been the principal Christian church in Europe for a long time, since the third century to be exact.

'Do you know who consecrated this temple?'

'No, I don't have a clue.'

'Silvestre I consecrated it in the year 324. You mustn't forget that Silvestre II was buried here as well.'

Guylaine carried on explaining that the basilica had suffered a number of setbacks while it was built over the years, including terrible fires. In 846 it was severely dislodged by a large earthquake, so it had to be rebuilt and was subsequently dedicated to St John the Baptist, the key figure linking the Old Testament and the New. This was the papal residence from the election of Silvestre I until 1376, when the Vatican was established as the centre of power for the Catholic religion, and the pope's new residence.

'Shall we go in?'

He nodded and followed her without saying a word. The interior, with five naves, was extremely well conserved for its age, he thought.

'The majority of what you can see is relatively new. Very little remains from the original third-century basilica; what survives was constructed over the following centuries, and then restored in the nineteenth century. I think what we see today is down to Borromi, who renovated it in the sixteenth century. He embellished the rooms of the apostles and everything that you see at the sides of the building. Shall we take a look at the tombstone of our pope, Silvestre II?'

Two enormous white marble plaques, placed one on top of the other, surrounded by a beautiful and elegant border of golden stone and crowned with a triangular capital, stood in front of them. The higher section of marble showed a relief with various images depicting the pope addressing his priesthood. A brief Latin inscription explained the illustrations. The marble plaque below held a longer text, also in Latin.

'Here we are. This is the cenotaph of Silvestre II.'

After so many days investigating the plans of the first French pope, Marc Mignon felt a shiver crawl down his spine as he stood before the grave.

CHAPTER 50

Guylaine understood Marc's silence; she was suddenly introducing him to the person responsible for everything they had been through and the core of his case.

After a few minutes, he managed to speak.

'So, this is the tombstone that secretes sweat when the current pope is going to die?'

'Exactly. When any pope becomes ill, people come here and touch this marble plaque to see if it is leaking a strange liquid, and if so, the pope will surely die. It's a paranormal phenomenon they attribute to the pope magician, a fitting legacy for a life full of riddles and strange spells. There are also those who say that if you put your ear to the marble, you can hear bones knocking together. Isn't it chilling?'

'It appears that, even after death, he hasn't stopped leaving behind mysteries.'

'Indeed. Now, perhaps there is another clue in the gravestone text.'

'Well, I'm afraid you must read it. I don't understand a word of Latin.'

Guylaine looked at him out of the corner of her eye then took a small piece of paper from her pocket and wrote down anything that seemed important as she read the cenotaph. A few minutes passed and, while she wrote endless notes, Marc sat down on a small ledge in one of the apostle's niches in the central nave. From there he had an exceptional view of the whole basilica. He looked to the right and saw a long line of people walking slowly, poring over the majestic reliefs and fascinating engravings that portrayed different scenes involving the apostles. He turned his head to the left and almost choked with disbelief.

Once again, there were the two men who had been pursuing them, hard on their heels still. He held his breath, took an enormous leap forwards and dragged Guylaine out of the temple, promising that he would explain everything to her later.

* * *

As quickly as they could, they made their way to the car park behind the Basilica of St John of Lateran. Inside the car, Marc began to explain what had happened, telling her that the very same pursuers had reappeared.

He stepped hard on the accelerator to take advantage of the sports car's strength. Within a few seconds, they were already several blocks from the basilica. Marc headed towards the Via dell'Amba Aradam and, from there, to the Baths of Caracalla where, on the open roads surrounded by gardens, they could easily see if they were still being followed. Trying to reassure himself that they had shaken the others off, he looked into the rear-view mirror but again the red car appeared behind them, just as it had for the majority of their expedition.

Marc drove faster, jumping traffic lights, swerving past

mopeds and edging around tight corners, and came to the Circus Maximus. He didn't have much time to think, but chose the narrow streets in an attempt to shake the pursuers off their tail.

The red car accelerated behind them, not allowing them to gain any distance, then pulling up next to them. Marc had time to glance through his window and see the driver's face. It was the same man whose voice he had recognised in Ripoll, the same who had threatened him with his parents' death during their first encounter. A deep feeling of uneasiness crept over him, but adrenaline kept his mind clear: he had to get Guylaine out of this dangerous situation.

All of a sudden, there in front of them, unexpectedly, loomed the silhouette of the Coliseum.

'A beautiful place to walk, not to run,' he said. He couldn't drive very fast around these roads because speed over cobblestones is a noisy drive.

He drove cautiously, without taking his eyes off the rear-view mirror. After a while, when they had come to the north-east of the city, he found himself in the Piazza Vittorio Emanuele II. He asked Guylaine if she thought it was a good idea to leave the car in a street next to the square and continue on foot. Guylaine nodded. Close to the exit of the piazza he nestled into a space and turned off the engine. The parking lot had only two entrances; if the red car came in, they would see it from where they were. After twenty minutes, no suspicious vehicles had passed through. They came out on to the street through the pedestrian exit and lost themselves in the crowd of people shopping in the surrounding streets.

Rome was a large enough city not to bump into anyone by chance.

* * *

The brisk walk back to the hotel took them almost an hour, which they spent discussing how such an awful coincidence as running into the two men in the Basilica of Saint John could have occurred.

'It's not by chance,' said Guylaine, without taking her eyes off the pavement. 'Those criminals are after us and they know exactly where we're going.'

'But how did they know we were in Rome? Who could have told them?'

'That really is a mystery. We only decided to come here yesterday and we arrived in a private jet. Nobody saw us at the airport collecting our boarding passes for Rome, neither could they have seen us boarding. We've even come on a direct flight from a city that doesn't offer commercial flights to Italy. How could they have got here so quickly?'

'Only if they had been given a tip-off.'

They looked at each other; the only person who could have done such a thing was the young archaeologist, who was, at present, working with Dubois in the castle. That instant, Guylaine desperately wanted to pick up her phone and warn the Count, to make him see that Bruno was a traitor, an accomplice of the thugs who were still following them. But Marc grabbed her hand, insisting it was not the right time to call, and they should choose their words calmly and carefully before rushing into a confrontation. Above all, they had to stay away from rash emotions.

When they reached the hotel, the detective stopped and told Guylaine that, given the circumstances, they should probably sleep in one room for safety. If the men managed to find out where they were staying, it would be dangerous for her to be on her own. Guylaine paused for a moment then agreed with him. She would get her things and bring them over straight away.

* * *

Marc's room had two large, comfortable beds and spacious wardrobes for each of them. Before putting her clothes away, Guylaine found her father's number and picked up the phone. It rang five times, but the wait felt like an eternity. On the sixth, Bruno's voice greeted her politely. Guylaine told him to put her father on and asked why he hadn't answered the call himself. The young man told her that the Count was very busy working with the information they had found in Medina Azahara and that he couldn't interrupt him at the moment, as he was on the verge of obtaining something very important. He said he would give her father the message as soon as he finished.

Guylaine hung up angrily. She looked for the butler's number and waited for him to answer. The call rang and rang and then cut out. She tried again and the same thing happened. The staff at the castle were usually so vigilant; something like this had never happened before.

CHAPTER 51

Guylaine's eyes welled up with tears and she leant on Marc's shoulder, crying openly. The situation had got out of hand. He consoled her and asked her not to worry; everything would work out if only they could put things into place.

'I think we should fly to Paris straightaway.' Guylaine was desperate now.

'I don't think we should do anything at this time of night. It's too late to go to the airport and we can't even be sure we'll get a flight. Let's calm down and make a solid plan of action for ourselves. What do you reckon?'

Guylaine agreed and went to the bathroom. When she returned, she found Marc sitting at the desk, putting all his ideas down on paper. She looked at what he was writing and saw a series of boxes, diagrams and other symbols that represented what had happened to date.

'What's all this?' she asked.

'I'm trying to see how and when everything in this case happened, because there are things that I don't understand. I'm trying to piece together the order of events, like the disappearance of your father, the arrival of the thugs, the possible abduction of Renaud in Córdoba and the appearance of that supposed archaeologist. Am I forgetting something?'

'Yes, you're forgetting my mother.'

'That's right. The Countess also disappears. And she does so exactly here.' The detective pointed to a mark in one of his diagrams. 'I can't say for sure, but I believe that there's a connection between all of this. There must be.'

'Do you think that if we can establish what the link is, we'll know what's going on? I'm starting to think that things aren't what they seem to be.'

'There's no doubt about it. We must have missed something important. Incidentally, I think that your mother could have something to do with all this.'

'And what do you think about the call to my father?'

'Before we make any assumptions, I think that you should call him again to check if your suspicions are right. Phone him right now.'

The Count's phone rang out clearly but no one answered. Again, the same thing when she tried to get through to a member of staff at the castle: no answer. She anxiously headed over to the window to see how light it might still be. She was at once tempted to rush to the airport for that one possible, available place on a flight.

Marc tried to console her, sharing her frustration and knowing how difficult the situation must be for her. Just when everything seemed to be falling into place, she had lost her father again.

Just then, Guylaine's mobile rang. On edge, both jumped at the loud tone. The number on the screen nearly made her eyes pop out. Someone she knew very well was trying to get hold of her. It was Jean Luc Renaud.

CHAPTER 52

Guylaine looked at Marc, not knowing whether or not to answer. Marc insisted that whoever was on the other end, it was important they find out what had become of Renaud. She pressed the button to answer the call.

'Is that you, Renaud?'

'Yes, it's me.'

Recognising his voice, she even thought that he sounded unharmed. She had half expected to hear weary moans, the tarnished voice of Renaud having suffered at the hands of the two thugs.

'Where have you been? We've been really worried about you.'

'I know. Those men in the mosque took me to a terrifying place to interrogate me. I was glad that you were able to get away from the two of them.'

'And where have you been all this time?'

'Locked up. They imprisoned me and when they didn't need any more answers to their questions, they let me go.'

'Thank God!' she exclaimed. 'Who knows what they could have done to you.'

'I'd like to see you straight away,' said Renaud, 'as I have some very important things to tell you.'

'We're in Rome; we left Córdoba this morning.'

'And so am I. They left me here a few minutes ago, in the middle of the city at the San Calixto Catacombs. I've telephoned the Count but he isn't answering and there doesn't seem to be anyone in the castle either. That's why I turned to you.'

'Well, don't go anywhere. I'll call you back in a few moments.'

She hung up and relayed the conversation to the detective.

She could tell from Marc Mignon's look of surprise that he wasn't too pleased by the news of Renaud's reappearance. Something strange was going on and he was dubious.

'Don't you realise that it's a trap?' the detective warned her. 'This isn't normal—you don't just kidnap someone and leave them stranded thousands of miles away, just like that, with no explanation.'

'There must be an explanation. I think that Renaud is an honest man. He told me that they brought him here from Córdoba, I guess in a private plane. I'm inclined to believe him.'

'And your plan is to go there and get him? I think that's very dangerous. How can we know that the men aren't with him, waiting to catch us too?'

He started to pace nervously around her. He had to think fast if he wanted to act with any apparent decisiveness, as a good private detective would, or should, he thought.

'This is what we'll do. But remember that we must follow these instructions to the letter. Agreed? First, we must not, under any circumstance, reveal the hotel we are in. Secondly, we'll tell him to walk to...' He looked at a map of Rome and found a point near to where they were that he thought was a good meeting place. '…the end of the Appian Way and to wait for us there, at the end of the road. It's very important that he does exactly that. Finally, explain to him that, for his own good, he had better be telling the truth.'

'All right.'

She followed Marc's instructions point by point. When she had put down the phone, she promised him that her father's assistant had understood their directions perfectly.

They left the hotel and caught a taxi to where they had left the car earlier. Walking around it several times, Marc checked and double-checked that the car hadn't in any way been tampered with. When the car park attendant saw that the detective kept inspecting his car, he came over and offered to help.

'Don't worry, Sir, your car is well taken care of here. I can wash it for you if you'd like.'

His accent sounded Romanian, although Marc wasn't expertly familiar with East European languages.

'Thanks very much. All the same, we're off now.'

'OK, but take a card with my telephone number and call me if you ever want anything.'

Marc put the card in his pocket and thanked him. Before getting in himself, he asked Guylaine to climb into the back seat. He drove out of the car park and headed in the direction of the Roman catacombs. When they were on their way, Guylaine asked him what their next part of the plan was.

'We'll drive up to the end of the Appian Way and, when we see Renaud, you'll open the back door and ask him to run as fast as possible and jump in behind you. If we even suspect that anyone is following us, we'll simply go without him. If what he says is true, even better, but I don't believe him. I wouldn't be surprised if they are using him as bait.'

She gave him a grateful look into the rear-view mirror and thought carefully about the plan the detective had hatched.

* * *

Marc drove cautiously the whole way to the catacombs, a very well-known site on the tourist circuit of Rome that no doubt would be deserted at this time of night.

Renaud's call plagued him as he drove. If he was telling the truth, which Marc doubted, they must have tortured him, as they had done to him. Jean Luc would carry the marks from the blows and bruises; Marc's left cheekbone still hurt even though several days had passed since his own unpleasant encounter with the thugs. If Renaud was lying, he had been deceiving them all along. From the moment he took on this case, Marc had suspected that the Count's assistant had been involved in some wrongdoing and for that reason alone, he needed to remain alert. There was no way he was going to trust Renaud just because he seemed like a feeble eccentric. As they came closer to the end of the Appian Way, Marc ordered Guylaine to concentrate. He could sense the trap was getting closer.

'If don't see him straight away, I'll step on the accelerator and we'll get out of there. OK?'

'Fine by me. But let's give the poor guy a chance if we can; he must have been through a lot recently.'

Driving slowly, two pairs of eyes were trying to see if

on either side of the road there lurked the suspicious red car. They had gone halfway up the road and still didn't see anyone waiting at the far end. Guylaine squinted; the faint light given off by the few streetlights wasn't enough for her to see clearly further than a hundred metres or so. Marc slowed down even more and crept along the last stretch of road.

Sure enough, Renaud was there, leaning on a car parked on the right of the street, looking around.

'There he is,' Marc exclaimed. 'Let's go and get him in. There doesn't appear to be anyone here and I haven't seen the red car with those swines in it either. Are you ready?'

'Yes, but I'm nervous.'

'Try to keep calm; if anything odd happens, we'll be able to get out of danger quickly.'

'OK, let's go.'

Marc drove up to the assistant and flashed his headlights a couple of times. Renaud straightened up at the signal. He raised his hand and waved. Marc stepped lightly on the accelerator and told Guylaine to open the back door. She opened the door just as they were level with the assistant. She shouted at him to get in. With his heart racing, the detective sped the three of them away as fast as he could.

* * *

Once the boot was safely closed, Guylaine bombarded the assistant with questions. However, Marc asked her to hold off her interrogation until they were certain that they were not being followed.

'I can't be sure that they haven't used me, Mr Mignon,'

said Renaud, sorrowfully. 'I swear to you that everything I said to Guylaine before is true. They took me with them when you ran out of the mosque and they have held me all this time. They have asked me thousands of questions, although, luckily, I couldn't tell them how the damned machine works. Only the Count knows that.'

'And how did you get here today?' the detective asked.

'This morning they put a thick hood over my head, put me in the boot of a car and, after a while, I noticed that I was on a plane. The flight lasted a couple of hours until they bundled me into another vehicle and we drove for quite a while. I don't think we landed at the Fiumicino Airport; I think we landed somewhere less conspicuous. Five minutes before I phoned Guylaine, they threw me into the middle of the road without saying a word. They left me my mobile phone and my wallet. However, I don't have any other clothes than these, so I haven't been able to change since they kidnapped me. Please forgive me for that.'

Marc was still weighing up whether what Renaud was telling them was true or not, when he saw the red car in the rear-view mirror. Once again, it was hunted against hunters.

CHAPTER 53

Marc shouted out that they were being followed. The others craned their heads through the back window to see the red car gaining on them at great speed. The detective wondered whether it had been worthwhile collecting their cargo, who was probably in league with their pursuers and had put them in serious danger one more time. He tried to dismiss these thoughts to concentrate on losing that obstinate red car.

Heading flat out back towards the city centre, he imagined that there would be more chances here to shake them off. He prayed for a red light to block the way between them, but then remembered that people, including him, disregarded red lights all the time in Rome. What other ways could there be to distance themselves from their pursuers? It wasn't easy in a city as old as Rome, with its winding roads and cobbled, irregular streets. But then he remembered the lad in the car park. The offer he had made. Slipping the card with the parking attendant's telephone number out of his pocket, he handed it to Guylaine, a plan beginning to form in his head.

'Key in this number and pass the phone to me, please.'

She did as he asked and handed him the phone.

'Hey, mate. I am the owner of the blue sports car. We chatted briefly this morning. Do you remember me?'

'Of course, I knew you'd call me. With a car like that,

you've got to know how to take care of it if you want to hang on to that beautiful girl at your side.'

'That's right. I have a strange request for you. I'll give you one hundred Euros if you do as I tell you.'

'For that kind of money, I'll do anything.'

'I'm going to drive into the car park through the same entrance as I did this morning. But I want to turn around inside and exit without having to insert a ticket. I know it's a bit odd but I'll tell you why I want to do this. There's a guy in a car behind me who wants to steal my girlfriend from me. I want to shake him off by leaving quickly and unexpectedly. Do you understand?'

'Perfectly. We'll show him who's boss. And how will you pay me the one hundred Euros?'

'I'll leave it near the open barrier, where your little box is. Sorry but I can't stop.'

'I understand. Don't worry, consider it done.'

Seeing Guylaine's reaction, he promised that he would explain it to her afterwards.

He accelerated in the direction of the Piazza Vittorio Emanuele II, checking first his distance from the men hot on their tail. At the entrance to the car park, he asked his two passengers to hold on tight in the back; in a moment he would speed up rapidly. Clutching one hundred Euros in his hand, he swerved into the car park, trusting that the boy would keep his word.

Down the entrance ramp, Marc grabbed the ticket. The red car came in just behind them, racing towards the barrier. Marc span around the car park at top speed and headed towards the other exit by the control cabin. The attendant had been watching this spectacle since Marc came down the ramp and, as he had promised, he lifted the barrier just in time for them to slide underneath and out without a hitch. As he passed, Marc held his arm out of the window and dropped the cash on the floor. The lad shouted after him in thanks and, immediately after they had passed, slammed the barrier down. The red car tried to do the same and found he was blocked by the barrier. What surprised the thugs even more was that a lad of no more than fifteen was standing in front of them with his arms crossed over his chest and an unfriendly, impassive look on his face.

Marc drove towards the largest roads he knew in an attempt to get out of the city as fast as possible. After their success in getting away, he turned his mind back to Renaud. He couldn't throw him out of the car now because despite everything, he did seem sincere. But he was not going to risk taking the assistant to their hotel; if he were lying, he certainly wouldn't keep their location to himself. The sensible thing to do was to take him to another hotel and not give him any information on where they were staying. Could that guarantee their safety?

They arrived at a small hostel on the southern outskirts of Rome and stopped in the drop-off zone.

'Monsieur Renaud, how do you feel about us leaving you here for the night so that you can sleep?'

'Of course. Compared to the awful bed I have had for the past few days, this will be paradise.'

They let him go upstairs for a few minutes to wash and agreed to wait for him in the café where they could then continue their discussions.

* * *

At the most discreet table in the café, the detective couple sat down and began to discuss their next strategy.

'I still don't trust him,' said the detective. 'I bet he's in the pay of the criminals. He looks as if butter wouldn't melt in his mouth, all meek and sympathetic, but I reckon he's going to bring us nothing but trouble. You'll see.'

'Until now he has kept to his word. And remember that we were the ones who ran away and left him in the Great Mosque. We should thank the Lord he's still alive. I'd like to hear what he has to say. I want him to explain what has happened to him in detail, and about his strange journey to Rome. Above all, I'd like him to tell us what could've happened to my father and my mother. Renaud is a key part of all this mess.'

'Agreed; we'll talk to him. But remember not to tell him the name of our hotel. We'll be asking the questions.'

'Here he comes…'

Renaud walked towards them and sat down. He gave his sincerest apologies for his scruffy appearance, still dressed in the only clothes he possessed now.

'I'll try to get you something else tomorrow morning.' Guylaine was very familiar with the shopping areas in this city.

'Could you explain to us what has happened to you in the last few days, what you have seen, and anything else that could be of interest to us? I must say, I was very suspicious when you turned up unexpectedly in Córdoba like that. Now you have done the same thing here in Rome.'

'I think that everything you've mentioned can be

explained, Monsieur Mignon. I will be completely frank with you. Understand that I'm feeling quite troubled at the moment; I've been beaten, abused and am, above all, completely bewildered.'

'Then begin by telling us how you knew we were in Córdoba. We didn't tell the Countess. How did you find out?'

'I received a call from the strange people I told you about, the mysterious group who have helped us in our investigations for years. The afternoon you called the Countess from Ripoll, they found me and asked me to go to Córdoba to help the Count. I have no idea how they knew he was there, but I followed their instructions as I always do. I know that you found Pierre because the men who tortured me spoke openly in front of me about what happened in Medina Azahara and at the doctor's house site.'

'How strange. So that means that the brutes chasing us let us carry out the archaeological dig and then followed the Count through Paris to Reims and us to Rome.'

'The Count is in France now?'

'That's right,' Guylaine confirmed. 'But he's gone missing again.'

'Well, at least if he's there, the Countess will know his whereabouts.'

'Far from it. My mother also disappeared a few days ago. My whole family is missing.'

'Carry on, Renaud,' the detective insisted.

'In Córdoba, they took me to a remote place where they beat me and asked me thousands of questions.' He opened his shirt, revealing large bruises and gashes all over his body.

He rolled up his shirtsleeves so that they could see the burns from the cords that had been tied around his wrists.

'I honestly didn't tell them anything. As I said, I don't know anything about the machine and the Count's work. I'm the person who knows the least in all of this business. Please believe me.'

'Now tell us how they brought you to Rome and why they let you go,' demanded Guylaine, who was beginning to believe Renaud's testimony. 'It sounds like they have used you as a decoy. For your own good, I hope you're telling the truth.'

'Mademoiselle, you have known me since you were a little girl. How could I lie to you? Why would I lie to you?'

'I have to be honest, Renaud, I don't trust you. I'll have my eye on you,' added Marc.

'I'm not deceiving you, I assure you. I'm very fond of the Dubois family. I have dedicated my life to serving them. In these tough times, the only thing I want to do is help them. I will do all it takes, anything necessary.'

It was impossible not to believe him; his imploring and wavering tone would win anyone over.

'Well, we'll trust you, but let's see how things develop,' Guylaine said. 'Now the most important thing is to decide whether we go to Reims immediately or try to complete what we came here for first. We're here because in Medina Azahara we found what my father went looking for and the reason he left Reims weeks ago. But what we found there is incomplete. Next to a large text written in Arabic we found a strange inscription with three simple Rs. My father interpreted them as standing for Reims, Ravenna and

Rome: the three cities the monk Gerberto gained access to with the aid of his mysterious books, which he probably found in Córdoba. That's why my father has gone to Paris; he's taken a young archaeologist we met in Córdoba to help him. We have come to Rome to try to find the last part of the puzzle.'

'And you say that he has disappeared again? How bizarre! He should be safe in the castle, I would imagine.' Renaud seemed as surprised as the other two.

'The thing is that even the butler isn't answering my calls,' added Guylaine. 'Nobody seems to be there and we don't know why.'

'That's unheard of.'

'I know. That's why I wonder whether we should go home as soon as possible or carry on looking for the third part of Gerberto's legacy.'

'Could I have a look at the text you found in Medina Azahara? Perhaps I can help.'

'Yes, we've made copies of the complete text and we also have photos. I have them all here in my bag.'

She rummaged through the various papers in her handbag and soon found the right scrap, which she handed to the assistant.

Showing a solid grasp of Arabic, he scanned it quickly.

'I have an idea. Here it refers to the Campus Martius, an area in ancient Rome that extends to the north of the wall built by Servio Tulio and is bordered to the south by the capital and to the east by a hill. There was a large plane in the middle of these borders, fringed by the curve of the River Tiber. I seem to recall that it is named after an altar dedicated to the god Mars that no one has been able to find for centuries. Not even the Romans knew who built that temple. In the golden age of Rome, the Campus was used as an entertainment area for the soldiers and also as a camp for the troops. Today, it's a very urban area of Rome. As the empire grew, they built many glorious buildings there that still survive to this day. I think we should take a look at some of the buildings that were around when Silvestre was pope and lived there, in the Basilica of St John of Lateran.'

'That's where we were today,' said the detective, joining the conversation.

'Well, if you want, I will prepare a plan tonight so that we can look into whether the pope magician left anything important in any of the buildings of the Campus Martius. Can I keep hold of this text to read it more thoroughly?'

CHAPTER 54

Jean Luc Renaud waited patiently at the hotel's entrance for the car to arrive at the time he had agreed with Marc. He had studied the document the Count's daughter had given him repeatedly and had found several parts worthy of discussion. On his first reading of the complex text he had found some interesting details, such as the reference to the Campus Martius in Rome, but after studying it in more depth, he had found a number of clues that had kept him awake all night.

He saw a car turning to the left of the hotel. It was Marc and Guylaine. Renaud let out a deep sigh and walked out to meet them.

'You're not going to believe what I've found,' he said, overwhelmed with excitement.

'Get in then, give us some good news for a change. We've called the castle again and there's still no one there. My father isn't answering calls and neither is my mother. Could it get any worse? We need to make quick progress so we can fly to Paris and get home as soon as possible.'

'I think we've struck some luck. I'm only guessing, but I think the text you left me could be invaluable. There are many things I can't get my head around, and I imagine the Count has been inputting this data into the machine, but some of the information has kept me up all night.' The assistant said the last words very loudly.

Marc turned to the back seat.

'Don't get worked up. First of all, tell me where we should go.'

'Well, we should start in the area that was the old Campus Martius. Let's head towards the famous Piazza Navona and talk more as we drive. The traffic seems to be moving quite slowly.'

After two or three readings during the night, Jean Luc could explain the contents of the text with precise detail. The whole text was a web of interconnected ideas and concepts that would take dozens of years to analyse in its entirety. For now he would get straight to the point, ignoring many subjects that no doubt the Count would want to study when this was all over. For now, Renaud had to prioritise. He focused on clues relating to the third part of the transcendental information's location that they must find.

'I want to tell you a very old legend that, for some reason, is reflected upon in the Arabic text. The historian William of Malmesbury was born around the year 1080 and died in 1141. He spent his whole life working in Malmesbury Abbey in Wiltshire, a county in England, and wrote a series of works about the scholarly but mystical French pope. In one, he describes in detail how Gerberto stole a book from the Arabs, was persecuted, and then made a strange pact with the Devil in order to become more supernaturally powerful. Apparently, the spell was effective; the young monk rose to the archdioceses of both Reims and Ravenna, followed by the pontiff in Rome. Allegedly it was at this time that he made an oath to the Devil for a second time and discovered a magnificent treasure near the capital of the Roman Empire.

'The legend has it that Gerberto, who was by then Silvestre II, heard of this incredible treasure hidden near Rome and, since nobody knew where it was hidden, he asked Satan to reveal its exact location. It was the Devil who showed him a bronze statue in the Campus Martius with an extended index finger on its right hand and an inscription on his head leading to the treasure's hiding place. For many centuries, people had mistaken these clues and brutishly attacked the statue to try to access the precious treasure they believed to be hidden inside. But the pope realised their mistake and interpreted the effigy's inscription differently. According to him, at midday, when the sun is at its highest point, the shadow of the finger extends to a specific point. He marked the spot and studied it for several days.

'When he was sure about the right course of action, he recruited several servants to come to the site one night under full moon. He ordered them to dig and, after a while, they found a wide staircase that descended underground, beneath the Campus Martius. There they found an extraordinary palace, whose walls and ceilings were full of rich materials and elaborate metalwork. The building was also full of gold ornaments and objects. At the centre of the palace was a sculpture made entirely of gold, in which statues of a king and queen—flanked by a small army of attendants—presided over a large, set table. On the ceiling of the palace, a great lamp lit the sculpture. Standing in one of the corners, was a golden statue of a boy armed with a bow. Indeed, the entire place was adorned with beautiful objects that were impossible to describe.

'The strange thing is that no one could touch anything that was there; when anyone tried to so much as gently brush an object, the statues started to shake and emit strange sounds. One of the servants put his hand on a knife on the grand table, seeing that it was set with precious stones and thinking that, among so many riches, the absence of one small object would go unnoticed. But just as he took it, the statues straightened up and the boy shot an arrow at the lamp. Everything was plunged into complete darkness and they had to leave hurriedly. Later that night, Silvestre went back alone and, somehow, was able to take some precious metals from the cavern, which he then fused together to create the talking head.'

'Well, it is certainly a fantastic story,' Marc reflected.

'I think it's a very interesting starting point for the search we have ahead of us,' Guylaine added. 'If Malmesbury's legend is true, we should be able to find the missing element we need in order to get to the bottom of this affair somewhere in the Campus Martius.'

'That's right; this is what the text points to,' said Jean Luc.

'And where exactly could it be?' asked the detective.

'The old Campus Martius is in the area of Rome today known simply as Campomarzio. Now it is full of buildings from various ages, constructed before and after the end of the first millennium. We need to focus on the renowned monuments that were standing when Silvestre II was pope, between the years 999 and 1003.'

'So how many places shall we reduce the search to?' Marc wanted an idea of how much work lay ahead.

'As I told you, the original site lies at the bend of the River Tiber. It was a public field where the Romans practised sport, carried out military exercises and even celebrated victories. A number of roads passed though it and still do so today. There used to be a large road called the Via Lata, which crossed the entire area and carried on towards the Milvian Bridge. This could be the present-day Corso Umberto and Via Flaminia. There are a good many places that have been conserved since Roman times that were still around when our pope lived here; for example, the Circus of Domitian is now the Piazza Navona, where we are headed. Other buildings that we should examine are the Theatre of Marcellus, the Mausoleum of Augustus, the Baths of Nero and the famous Pantheon.'

'But that will take us days!' exclaimed Guylaine.

'It might not take so long. Many of these marvels are ruins now and we may be able to determine quickly whether or not they hold anything of interest to us. I think we should take a look at each of these buildings; if we don't find anything useful we'll go back to France and study our findings there. Generations of the Dubois family have dedicated their lives to investigating the work of Gerberto d'Aurillac, so we cannot expect to decipher all this complex history in just two weeks.'

'You're right,' the detective agreed grudgingly. 'Don't get used to this, Monsieur Renaud, but I must say that your proposal sounds reasonable. We'll stay here for one day to investigate and, if we think it is going to take longer than expected, we'll go back to Paris tonight on the first flight we can find. Do you both agree?'

His proposal was met with a murmur of approval.

Almost at their destination, they left the car as Renaud suggested it was best to go on foot.

'This is the Piazza Navona. The old Circus of Domitian from the first century is here; that's why this beautiful baroque piazza maintains its elliptical shape. I don't think we'll find anything relating to the pope magician here. Let's go and see Bernini's Fountain of Four Rivers.'

Guylaine felt at home in one of her favourite parts of ancient Rome and was beginning to enjoy the tour. But she quickly snapped out of this mood; she knew she couldn't afford to lose even a second in contemplation, as she had to think rapidly about what she was observing.

'I think it's clear that we aren't going to draw any conclusions here,' Marc decided, looking at the fountain. While he recognised that he wasn't the most equipped to draw such conclusions, he felt that they weren't going to achieve anything there.

'Then let's go to the Pantheon because it's right here, very close,' proposed Renaud.

They walked to the magnificent monument. Seeing it reminded Guylaine of the good times she had spent in that very square with her parents, when there was still some intimacy between them. The last time they were in Rome, she must have been about ten, yet she remembered it perfectly; it had been a very pleasant trip. She had watched her parents frolic next to the Trevi Fountain, the Piazza di Spagna and

many other locations where no one could fail to fall in love.
Ever since then, the relationship between her mother and
father had visibly and, she feared, permanently stagnated.

Guylaine wondered whether this crazy adventure
might ultimately be positive for her parents' relationship.
She certainly knew that things would never be the same
again.

CHAPTER 55

Marc Mignon passed through the imposing front portico with its eight massive columns into the Pantheon, or the Rotunda, as it was commonly known by Romans. As soon as he stepped into the spectacular circular space, he thought that there must be at least one millennial secret hidden inside. If anyone wanted to leave a message for the future, he felt this was the perfect place. He expressed his thoughts to his companions and awaited their reaction. Were they as impressed as he? he wondered.

'I don't know,' said Renaud. 'We now know that the original temple of the Pantheon was destroyed and that what we see today was built in the emperor Hadrian's time. It is, without doubt, an impressive building but I can't think why anyone would leave millennial secrets here.'

'I agree,' Guylaine said. 'From what I know, originally the Pantheon was a temple consecrated to seven Roman celestial divinities: the moon, the sun and five planets, which were Mercury, Venus, Mars, Jupiter and Saturn. The Earth, the element that, as we have seen, is the central axis of Silvestre's discoveries, is not among them. I don't think there is any connection between this place and what we are looking for.'

'Moreover, the splendid dome above us represents the remote cosmos, not the world we inhabit. I think you're

299

right, Guylaine,' Renaud commented.

'There's nothing here we can use; this temple became a church in the Middle Ages, and in the Renaissance, long after Silvestre had died, it was adorned with different decorations. King Vittorio Emanuele II and his family are buried here.'

The detective believed them, their knowledge overwhelming his own. 'Then let's go somewhere else,' he proposed.

* * *

Seen from the outside, the Theatre of Marcellus had always caught Marc's attention whenever he had visited Rome.

'I've been to this city many times but always for reasons other than culture. Every time I have gone past here, I've wondered why such an old building has relatively modern homes above it.'

'It was built by Caesar and finished by Augustus, who dedicated it to his nephew Marcellus. It is the only theatre of its kind that still stands in this city, and when it was built it had a capacity of over fifteen thousand people,' explained Renaud. 'In the sixteenth century, the Savelli family decided to build a palace on the ruins. Those are the homes you are pointing at, which, if you look closely, are quite similar to a Renaissance palace.'

'I've been inside several times and remember seeing the later part,' Guylaine interjected. 'I can guarantee that there is nothing there that could have been added by the French pope in the tenth century.'

'Without doubt,' said Renaud, 'I agree.'

'Let's get on then,' suggested Marc again. 'If we do manage to see every monument before the end of the day, we can probably still catch the last flight to Paris and get back to Reims.'

* * *

Standing in front of the ruins of the Mausoleum of Augustus, they all fell into silent reverence. The brown brick walls, many of which were covered with thickets and bracken, nevertheless looked like a sufficiently prominent location for Gerberto to hide the third part of the legacy.

Seeing as no one was speaking, Guylaine continued to demonstrate her historical knowledge, speaking first this time.

'This magnificent sepulchre was once covered with white marble. In the entrance, two enormous obelisks stood, but they are now in different locations in Rome. Originally it would have been a spectacular mausoleum. As far as we know, it was built to guard the urns that contained the ashes of the imperial family, and was built in the Campus Martius because that's where the temples dedicated to foreign gods were erected. The first to be buried here was Marcellus, the nephew of Augustus, who was poisoned by his second wife. She wanted the throne for her son, Tiberius. But it doesn't end there; murders by poisoning throughout that dynasty's reign filled this mausoleum with more than fifteen urns.

'When Caesar Augustus died, his ashes were moved to the central part of the sepulchre, which changed considerably in later centuries. It went from being a fort with a moat in the tenth century, to an ornamental garden in the sixteenth, and then in the seventeenth, a wooden amphitheatre was built around it. Subsequently, it was transformed into a circus in the nineteenth century and, I seem to remember, at the end of the twentieth century it was used as a concert hall.'

'Exactly,' Renaud backed up. 'It has been through so many transformations that I doubt we will be able to find anything of interest here. However, we should look inside, in case we have overlooked something. Shall we go?'

'You go in,' said Marc. 'I have a phone call to make.'

While they proceeded towards the mausoleum, the detective took out his mobile phone and dialled Marcos's number. The time had come to resolve another matter that was bothering him.

CHAPTER 56

Despite all the events that had taken place in the last few days, Marc hadn't been in contact with his uncle Marcos at all. Strangely, the opposite was also true: the man who had entrusted a young amateur to solve the case of the missing count on behalf of his agency had not checked up on him. Perhaps he had blind faith in his nephew.

The deep voice on the line brought Marc's thoughts back to his call with a start, as if he didn't know how to react towards the presence at the other end.

'It can only be one of two things,' declared Marcos Mignon, laughing. 'Either you've already solved the Dubois case or you're calling me to throw in the towel. How are you? How's it all going?'

'Actually…,' he paused, 'I'm good. Lots of things have happened in the last few days, so many that we feel like we've been on a rollercoaster.'

'Welcome to the world of private investigation! But tell me, have you found the Count?'

'Yes, I found him, but now I've lost him again. Many things have happened and, if I'm honest, I still don't entirely understand the situation. Suspicious people are interested in the Count of Divange's studies and are willing to do anything to get hold of his discoveries.'

'Be very careful. Your life comes first, before anything. A detective must look after himself, whatever happens. Our clients don't pay us to die.'

There was a brief pause in the conversation. Marcos decided to tell his nephew about the strange appearance of the Countess in his office.

'Véronique Dubois called me while I was in Strasbourg on business and made me return to Paris as soon as possible. She wanted me to help her with something that could be connected to her husband's disappearance. While I went downstairs to the basement to investigate something, she left without saying a single word, stealing a load of my papers.'

'Well, her daughter is desperately looking for her. Now not only is the Count missing again but the Countess's whereabouts are also unknown.'

'Is this what you called me about?'

'Actually, no,' Marc managed to say, as a large lump formed in his throat. 'I have access to information that could be relevant to my parents' death.'

'Are you serious? What kind of enquiries have you made? What's going on?'

'I'm going to tell you down to the last detail. But first, I need you to do something for me. Right now.'

'Ask me anything.'

'I want you to go to Pierre Dubois's castle and see what's going on. You have to leave right now.'

'I'm just finishing up some important matters in the office, so I won't be able to leave for Reims until the afternoon at the earliest.'

'Fine. It's highly likely that I'll fly to Paris tonight and so will see you at the castle. But before you go, let me tell you about the extraordinary things that have happened to me.'

* * *

After the call, Marc felt a weight lift off his shoulders. Telling his uncle about the strange interrogation by the thugs who had beaten him up and his subsequent conversation with the Count about the Baumard case had been a huge relief. The return of his companions brought him back to reality. Their disappointed faces confirmed that the mausoleum didn't appear to have any connection to the end of the first millennium and Gerberto's prophecies.

'So now what?'

'We still have a couple of monuments left to inspect,' explained Renaud. 'If we're being thorough, we need to check the Baths of Nero and the Ara Pacis, and we should take a look around the Temple of Isis.'

'My patience is running out,' declared Guylaine. 'Can we get the car and go to the airport straight away? I can't take this any more. Sorry, but my nerves for my parents' sakes have reached their limit.'

'I've spoken to my uncle, the director of the agency, and I've asked him to go to your home as soon as he can to find out what could be going on there. In theory, he should arrive in Reims this afternoon or tonight at the latest.'

'What a good idea! In that case, I am prepared to see one more ruin, on the condition that we go back to Paris later today.'

'That seems like a reasonable proposal. Also, I should tell you that your mother called Marcos to ask him to investigate something. She went to see him but then took off without a word!'

'Really? At least that means she's probably safe.'

'So it would seem. And now that's been said, what is our next destination in the Campus Martius?'

'If you agree,' Renaud started, 'since we are in a hurry to get back to France, we could overlook the baths. I don't think that anyone in their right mind would think to leave millennial secrets in public baths. What do you say?'

His companions agreed.

'In the Campus, another of the most famous archaic buildings of the millennium was the Altar of Augustan Peace, better know as the Ara Pacis, which dates back to 13 BC. It aimed to demonstrate the leadership of Rome in securing world peace. So the Ara Pacis was designed as a sort of museum, where the most spectacular reliefs filled the walls, carved in marble from Carraca. In the galleries, portraits of the emperor's family hung, as well as those of soldiers and distinguished figures of the time. There were friezes of great battles, with military and victory processions. The monument was used as an altar to make offerings to the pagan gods. Unfortunately, the centuries have not been forgiving to such beautiful carvings. They have progressively deteriorated and the magnificent works of art have disappeared completely.

'In the sixth century, Italian art-lovers recovered fragments of the lost reliefs, now decorating the Villa Medici. Subsequently, pieces of marble from the Ara Pacis, found during different excavations across the city, kept appearing. In the nineteenth and twentieth centuries, they recovered a significant number of the treasures found under the foundations of the palace of the Via Lucina. In addition to the other remains rescued from various European museums, a good part of what was once the Altar of Augustan Peace has been reconstructed, as we can see.'

'You clearly know the monument well,' commented Marc.

'Indeed. I did my doctoral thesis on this subject and spent several great years here in Rome, studying the friezes. But that was before I met Pierre Dubois; from then on, I dedicated my life to studying the late French Middle Ages.'

'And so you can confirm that we are not going to find anything useful in that altar?'

'That's right,' the assistant responded despondently. 'I would really like the Ara Pacis to contain a secret of interest to us but I can emphatically say that it does not hold what we are looking for.'

'And so?'

'We are left with one last possibility before going home.' Renaud's eyes were wide open. 'If you remember, we are looking for something related to Mother Nature, are we not? We still have to visit the Temple of Isis, one of the most famous buildings here.'

'Exactly.' Guylaine had kept very quiet; she was thinking about the journey home. 'What we're trying to find must be connected to the ancient world, way before Roman culture.'

Renaud was striking his head repeatedly. 'Oh God, why didn't I see it before?'

Guylaine and Marc looked at each other, neither understanding what the eccentric could be thinking. When he finally stopped hitting himself, he adopted a serious tone of voice.

'In the Arabic text that you let me read, mademoiselle, it referred to two significant elements, two points of reference to find our objective. One was the Campus Martius, where we are now, and the other was a clear reference to the forces of nature.

'I don't know why I couldn't see this until now, but if there is something connected to the matter we are concerned with, it must be inside the Temple of Isis, Isis being the goddess of nature, fertility and maternity, also called the "great sorceress".'

'Of course!' Guylaine exclaimed. 'Isis is one of the oldest divinities, I believe, taken from Egyptian myth by the Greeks and the Romans. I haven't been thinking clearly enough to recall that either. I think we could be getting somewhere!'

'Let me think. The Temple of Isis is located in the Campus Martius because she was a foreign goddess. She has been venerated by all the ancient cultures that we know of – Greek, Egyptian, Roman and many others. But one thing unites all the places in which she has been worshipped: an acknowledgement of her power over nature. She has been given a number of names over time: Mother Goddess, Lady of the Heaven, Earth and the Netherworld, Queen of the Gods…'

'This is all very convincing,' said Marc. 'And where is the temple?'

'That's the problem, Monsieur Mignon. The Temple of Isis disappeared from Rome many centuries ago. There is no trace left of it today.'

CHAPTER 57

For a moment, the detective thought about getting the car, heading to the airport to catch a flight to Paris that afternoon, just as Guylaine had suggested, and forgetting this fruitless search. While he was still entertaining the idea, Renaud took control of the conversation.

'That doesn't mean to say that we can't find remains of the temple in the city. In fact, elements from Isis are spread all over Rome. The first thing that we have to do is go to the original site, identify the perimeter of the temple and see if that helps us come to any conclusions.'

Without waiting for an answer, he walked quickly around the back of the Pantheon towards the top of the Via del Seminario, ordering them to follow him. From there, they carried on towards the Piazza di Sant'Ignazio.

'As far as historians know, this temple was built in 43 BC and was vast, about 250 metres long. All these buildings before us are built on the site of the ancient Temple of Isis.'

Marc was disappointed by the array of modern buildings that occupied the space where they hoped to find the last part of the complicated puzzle.

'We're not going to get anything out of this. Do you have any other brilliant ideas, Monsieur Renaud?'

'Yes. We need outside help.'

* * *

Renaud explained that, when he was in Rome writing his thesis, he met a young historian who was working on a book about the heritage of Isis. The remains of the pagan divinity had ended up in museums all over the world, including some in Rome.

'And do you have this man's address?' asked Guylaine.

'Of course. We keep in contact over the Internet and, every so often, we send over questions about little things we are investigating. My friend is a professor at Sapienza University and every time the Count and I have needed anything whatsoever from Rome, we have turned to him. He is, without doubt, a scholar who knows these lands better than anybody. If you agree, we will call him right now.'

Renaud didn't wait for his companions' reply; he was already dialling the number from his mobile phone.

* * *

The sun began to descend in the blue, cloudless sky. Guylaine kept looking at her watch, constantly reviewing how much time they had to catch their flight; if things carried on as they were, they would never get to Reims that night as she so wanted. For the umpteenth time, she tried to call the Count, the Countess and the castle staff. When no one answered, she became even more worried, reprimanding Renaud for deciding to go to his friend's office at the university without consulting her. The assistant realised that his determination to unearth the secrets of Isis had forced him to take a course of action that was, perhaps, not in the best interests of his master's daughter.

Standing in the Piazza Aldo Moro, under the large entrance to Sapienza University, he apologised profusely for the mistake he had made.

'Please forgive me, mademoiselle. I got carried away with this prospect, but, if you want, I'll cancel the meeting with Luigi Colarossi and we will go straight to the airport.'

'That is what I wanted but since we are already here, we might as well see the professor and then hurry on to the airport. I promise you that, whatever happens, I hope to catch the six o'clock flight. That means that we can be here for an hour at the most and not a minute more.'

The two men nodded obediently.

Marc couldn't see how they would have time to find this chap Luigi's office, let alone study the matter in question and be on their way at the necessary time. At the most, they would have time to talk to the man for a few minutes and leave to find the third part of Silvestre's legacy yet again.

Much to his surprise, a large black car with tinted windows pulled up. An impeccably dressed chauffeur got out to open the back door and asked them to come with him. They could see from the look on Renaud's face that he was as surprised as they were by his old friend's gesture. The driver stopped in front of the rector's office. A pond with a bronze statue of the goddess Minerva, the symbol of Sapienza University, stood over the main quadrangle. Luigi Colarossi was waiting for them with open arms at the rectory door.

Marc laughed. He couldn't help himself. The professor's appearance was an exact replica of Renaud's: large, checked bow tie, trousers with braces and a bottle-green jacket, equally extravagant.

Guylaine noticed that the detective was laughing and asked him politely to control himself. Without saying a word, Colarossi embraced his friend with a greeting that seemed never-ending, and then, when the group had exchanged pleasantries, they were invited up to his office. Gathered in a large, spacious room full of books and various computers, Marc thought that this must be the rector's office. He soon realised that he was mistaken.

'You can see, Jean Luc, that I have been promoted and now have a very important position close to the rector, although you know that what I like to do best is research in this tidy office. We are the same in that way, as I remember; you also like things ordered.'

The detective remembered the day he found Renaud's office in the castle and recalled the Count's disorder in comparison to his assistant's organised precision.

'First, let me congratulate you on your career,' said Renaud to his friend before introducing Marc and Guylaine.

After listening to what had brought the French party here to Rome, the Italian professor paid his respects to the Count and his excellent investigations, which he had been following closely since they had met many years ago.

'In fact, I have had the chance to visit the castle you live in on various occasions. It must be exciting to live in such a place, with more than a thousand years of history behind it.'

'It can be frustrating at times, but I shouldn't complain,' Guylaine replied. 'I appreciate your kind words about my father. In light of your friendship with him, please listen to what we have to say about his investigations. There's a flight to Paris this evening that we cannot afford to miss.'

'Then let's get on. How can I help you?'

Renaud explained the background of the investigations to his former colleague. He informed the professor about what had happened in Reims and Córdoba, explaining the incredible finding of the talking head as well as the discovery of a text carved into the hidden room in a house buried in Medina Azahara. Over the course of his speech, the eyes of the Italian grew progressively wider, as though he were doubting what he was hearing; when it looked as if they were in danger of popping out of his head, he asked his first question.

'Are you aware of how important your discoveries are?'

'Absolutely,' Guylaine confirmed. 'However, the thing is, we can't appreciate our findings because my father disappeared some days ago, briefly returned to us, now is missing again, and my mother is nowhere to be found either. So, we haven't stopped to think about our achievements.'

'Yes, I see. Well, how do I come into all this?'

'We're missing the last part of Pope Silvestre II's legacy,' Renaud explained. 'To conclude a life full of success, the discoveries of Silvestre were transferred to his marvellous talking head. That knowledge was believed to have been lost but the machine seems to contain information that, when projected forwards, would point to our planet's uncertain future. The head is an artefact capable of creating mathematical models that can predict the future.

'After discovering the head in his own castle, the Count went off in search of parts of the legacy that the pope couldn't bring back himself from Andalucía. I wasn't able to participate in the remarkable discovery of the carved wall in Medina Azahara, but I have been able to read the text the Count transcribed and it contains messages that I can't get out of my head and have been pondering ever since. Honestly, this find is almost impossible to describe.

'In the text, there are riddles that would take years to decipher. Among them, we have been able to confirm that the last part of Gerberto's legacy lies in Rome – to be more specific, in the Campus Martius. We have scoured the Pantheon, the Mausoleum of Augustus, the Theatre of Marcellus and other monuments built outside the walls of the imperial city. In all of these, we concluded that there could be nothing of interest to us, but they did bring us back to the subject in question: Mother Nature. That's why we've come to the conclusion that what we're looking for must be contained in the Temple of Isis, the goddess of the earth, the mother of fertility and the ancient divinity who symbolises nature. But since the temple no longer stands, we have no way of finding our last clue.'

'I don't know what to say. First and foremost, I want to thank you for contacting me and I am, of course, honoured to be of help in such an important matter. That said, I have to tell you that the Temple of Isis's remains are spread all over the world. There are obelisks in various squares in Rome itself and the sculptures are in many museums, including the Vatican and the Louvre in Paris. I can't tell you where to start looking because the pagan sanctuary of Isis has been so thoroughly pillaged.'

'I expected that response. What we're looking for is a text

or a message that could be interpreted to provide information about the millennial knowledge, which we imagine would relate to the earth, or the power of our planet and nature.'

'A temple that disappeared centuries ago and a lost text!' said Colarossi. 'Christ, this would sweep any archaeologist, historian or adventurer off their feet.'

'Please, can you help?' hurried Guylaine, checking her watch.

'I understand that you're rushed. We have very old texts here that decorated the walls of the Temple of Isis in its day and that have never been published. Perhaps that is because, before now, no one has understood what they mean.'

CHAPTER 58

Once they had taken in Professor Luigi Colarossi's words, the three companions threw themselves forward in their seats and begged him to show them the texts containing the inscriptions on the temple's walls. Renaud now realised that they were on the verge of resolving the mystery that had occupied his entire working life and Marc Mignon smiled to himself at the thought that he was nearing the end of the first case of his new career. For Guylaine, the Italian's words made her deeply happy; her priority was to get home as soon as the professor had seen the texts.

'That's brilliant!' Renaud exclaimed. 'We finally have the last part of the legacy within our reach, and that will allow us to bring our investigations to a close. My dear friend Luigi, do you realise what a big moment this is for us?'

'Of course,' answered the professor, 'and it's an honour for me to be able to contribute to your work.'

'And how can we get hold of these drawings, inscriptions or whatever they are?' Guylaine asked.

'Well I have kept them somewhere safe. Now let me think. Fortunately, I'm very organised. Back when we were simple postgraduate research students, Jean Luc and I always liked to keep the things we found systematised. And I remember one day when—'

'Please, may you just give us the texts,' said Guylaine in exasperation. 'Sorry, but I'm losing my patience. You already know that we're in a real hurry and that we have to fly to Paris in a little over an hour. In fact, we ought to leave for the airport immediately.'

'Honestly, don't worry. I know exactly where I've put the information you need. If you wait one second, I'll give you a disc containing the texts, which, if I remember rightly, were bas-relief engravings found on some marble plaques. There are some drawings as well. My car is waiting for you downstairs to take you to the airport.'

'We must thank you for all your help and assistance,' Marc commended, cupping his hands together. 'You have been a great help. All we've done is come to your office and pester you. Please, forgive us. Thank you for the offer of your driver, but we have a hire car and must return it today.'

'You can tell me where you've left it and we will see it back to the rental office. That way you'll get to the airport in less time; my chauffeur knows many short cuts. What do you think?'

'I don't know how to thank you, Luigi,' said Renaud.

'Well, I would like you to call me in a few days and tell me how this all ends. The information that I'm going to give you really is very strange. I have read it and reread it thousands of times and I have never worked out what on earth the author of those texts and drawings was trying to say. It amazes me that you have come here asking for one of the most bizarre documents I have ever seen in my life.'

Colarossi took out a folder from the top drawer of his desk, removed a CD and inserted it in the computer. His fingers tapped away quickly at the keyboard and he brought up a mass of complicated hieroglyphics on the screen.

'The Temple of Isis was built in 43 BC,' explained the professor. 'However, in a sanctuary built by the Romans, someone engraved a text into the walls in an ancient language – to be more precise, in Demotic Egyptian, a language predating Coptic Egyptian.'

'Well, that is odd,' Renaud commented. 'Although Isis is one of the oldest remembered goddesses, and was venerated in Egyptian culture, I can't think of a single reason why they would put a demotic text on the walls of a sanctuary designed for worshipping a divinity. Who in ancient Rome was going to understand that language? Whoever was responsible obviously didn't wish to recruit followers of the pagan goddess.'

'There's more still,' added Colarossi. 'Next to the text there's a large quantity of numbers in Egyptian mathematical notation.'

The Italian's words took root in the mind of the Count's assistant. Guylaine still looked serious and didn't want to get deeply involved, her mind still on their departure, which she was beginning to see as increasingly unlikely. To calm her, Marc took one of her arms, holding her in an offer of reassurance. He asked Luigi to give them the disc, insisting that they should be on their way.

'OK, just one more comment and I'll stop.'

'Go ahead. All this news really is extraordinary.'

'Well, that's not all that strange. To end this mystery, I must tell you that next to the simplified, cursive texts are authentic Egyptian hieroglyphics. However, I'm not talking about the signs written in classical Egyptian, which was used between the years 2000 and 1300 BC, but the language of ancient Egyptian, from the archaic period between 3000 and 2000 BC. I mean that, regardless of what this strange choice of language says, I think it strange that it includes extremely old hieroglyphics.'

'And why does no one know about all of this?' asked the detective.

'Perhaps because, until today, nobody thus far has been interested.'

CHAPTER 59

The departure of the Air France flight was delayed by several minutes. As soon as they took off, the pilot announced that he would try to make up the lost time during the flight and that, if the weather at Charles de Gaulle Airport permitted, they would still land on time. Thanks to the university driver's familiarity with the roads, they had reached Rome's Fiumicino Airport without difficulty and by taking an unusual route out of the Italian capital, he had managed to reach their destination in half the time. Throughout the journey, Marc remained watchful in case someone was following them. When they drove through quiet areas of the city, he had a good view of the area and could see that, for once, no one was on their heels. At the end of the drive, their chauffeur even took them through the authorities' entrance and so, at the boarding gate, the team of three breathed a deep sigh of relief and managed to relax for a few moments.

* * *

Sat next to each other, Marc, Guylaine and Renaud discussed the ideas put forward by the Italian professor. Guylaine had chosen the window seat and the detective, the aisle. Sitting between them, Renaud took out the papers his friend had handed over.

To be on the safe side, Marc had chosen to take the disc himself, while the Count's assistant had kept the hard copy so that he could look at the strange hieroglyphics en route back to Reims. Guylaine's mind, however, was occupied with getting home as soon as possible.

'Ancient Egyptian is from the Afro-Asiatic language family, which the Semitic, Berber and the Cushitic languages also pertain to,' Renaud explained, his eyes glued to the text he was reading. 'However, the use of Demotic Egyptian in a Roman temple is exceptionally unusual. All of this is astonishing. I didn't expect to find anything like this.'

'Do you know how to read this language as well, then?' asked Marc, amazed that the man seemed to be able to read the bizarre characters fluently.

'Yes, Monsieur Mignon. The system of demotic script is a very advanced written form of hieratic, abridged hiero-glyphics, in which the graphic signs are hard to recognise because they have evolved over time. I have dedicated my whole life to learning dead languages and to reading all kinds of texts. Demotic Egyptian is not so unusual, as it is found in lots of texts, papyrus books and other art forms. The strange thing is finding something like this in ancient Rome, written with ancient Egyptian hieroglyphics. I think all of this is connected to the investigations of Pope Silvestre and, therefore, I would like to suggest we combine these magnificent revelations with those found in Medina Azahara and gathered from the talking head.'

'Then carry on reading to see what it means,' suggested the detective, who was deep in his own thoughts and needed a few minutes to consider what he would say to his uncle when he got back. He had no idea how to move forward in his personal investigation that would hopefully lead him to discovering the truth behind the events on the awful night that he was orphaned.

First of all, he had to head to the castle of Divange, where he would try to find the Count. This latest disappearance didn't worry him too much, as he imagined Pierre Dubois was preoccupied with handling the horrific talking head and indifferent to the world around him. He knew that the Count would dedicate all his energy to the completion of this project. From his point of view, that was the most reasonable explanation for the Count's sudden absence. From now on, Marc's work must focus on finding out who had captured him; he felt a knot in his stomach whenever he thought about those villains. If they had taken the trouble to chase them through four different cities—Reims, Ripoll, Córdoba and Rome—it was clear that they were not going to give up and that they would, once again, try to get hold of the secrets the Count had obtained from wherever his search parties moved on to. Surely the people who had tracked the nobleman were the same as those who had been involved in the Baumard case, thought Marc.

He put his thoughts together and observed the progress Renaud was making, the Count's diligent assistant doing his best to interpret the signs that were unrecognisable to Marc. They were less than half an hour into the flight and Renaud had already transcribed more than three sides of paper.

Marc sat up in his seat and leaned over to see what

Guylaine was doing; she was looking out of the window, staring at some tiny point on the earth's surface more than a thousand metres below. He tried to imagine what she was thinking. She must be wondering where her father, and, even more so, her mother could be. Every time he remembered Véronique, the night he committed the huge but only error he believed he had made during the case came to mind. There was nothing he could do about it now except force himself to forget that ill-fated act and keep the truth from Guylaine's ears. After so many days by her side, he was going to try to see her once the case had been concluded; obviously, though, his indiscretion with the Countess made this difficult. If her daughter found out about what had gone on between them, she would never want to see him again.

A severe storm was raging over their destination. The captain switched on the seat belt sign; the weather, it seemed, reflected Marc's tempestuous thoughts.

* * *

The turbulence didn't seem to affect Renaud, who continued reading, interpreting and writing without hesitation except, every so often, he looked up to the ceiling, seeking inspiration that would always come to mind quickly. With barely thirty minutes until landing, he let out a sudden cry that startled a good many of their fellow passengers.

The Count's assistant stared at the back of the seat in front of him, his eyes popping out of his head and his mouth agape. The stewardess came over straight away and asked him if he was feeling all right. When he didn't answer, Marc told her not to worry because he was taking care of Renaud. The detective asked Renaud what was wrong. The shout had also taken Guylaine by surprise and she asked him the same question. It took him a few seconds to snap out of it and say something.

'I've deciphered the text,' he stammered.

'And? Are you going to tell us what it says?' the detective questioned.

'Judging by the shriek, it must be something important. You look terribly out of sorts all of a sudden,' Guylaine added.

'Do I? That's because this text contains revelations that completely subvert what we have studied until now. I should tell you that the Count is wrong; his analysis is incorrect.'

'What the hell are you talking about?'

'He mustn't turn the machine on. That monstrosity hides a very different secret to what we thought. Mademoiselle, if your father operates the talking head fully, he could be in grave danger.'

CHAPTER 60

The pilot addressed the passengers again: their arrival at the airport was going to be more complicated than anticipated due to a bad front in the north. Consequently, they must expect a slight delay.

After Renaud's words, Guylaine cursed their bad luck. She was now more anxious than ever to get back to the castle. Out of the window she saw that the sky had darkened and she watched as the thick clouds were sporadically torn open by bright bolts of lightning.

'I never thought we would be returning home under such extreme conditions,' whispered Guylaine. 'Can you explain what you meant a bit more?'

Renaud continued to decipher the ancient hieroglyphics and every so often scribbled down observations in the margins of the drawings, annotations that they still couldn't read. When he finished, he gave some brief explanations.

'I still have more than half to translate but, even at this stage, I know that the Count is unaware of the risk that this artefact contains.'

'As we now gather,' said the detective. 'But can you tell us why?'

'Until now, we believed that the talking head was something very different. We thought it was a rudimentary

325

machine created by the pope simply to store ancient scholarly knowledge that was thought to be lost, and that the monstrosity was capable of making calculations in order to respond to basic questions following formulae. But we were wrong.'

'In what way?'

'I still haven't worked out what is says just here but I can already confirm that Baphomet is a machine that grants access to something very destructive. I don't mean to say that it's a weapon or a bomb or anything like that, but that it must contain information that could cause a great deal of damage if used incorrectly. It could also seriously harm anyone who tries to gain access to it. I believe it is some kind of unknown force.'

'You haven't clarified anything for us,' said Marc, visibly nervous and not only about the turbulent landing as the storm raged around them. 'Can you be a bit more precise?'

'Look, Monsieur Mignon, these documents, like the information found in Medina Azahara, could take years to study. In a few minutes, I have been able to offer you a preliminary but accurate explanation.

'Everything points to the fact that its contents are remnants of a very old civilisation, which we have no familiarity with. It is, in short, a door to an underworld that was believed to be closed. If anyone opens this door, the consequences could be fatal.'

CHAPTER 61

Reims, via Paris

Guylaine's eyes welled up with tears. Renaud's words terrified her. What he had said could explain her parents' sudden disappearance. What could possibly have happened? Marc noticed the grave concern in her eyes and so wanted to be seated next to her to comfort her, but he couldn't move because of the captain's orders. Finally came the announcement; the weather conditions had improved enough for landing. Marc looked over Renaud at Guylaine and caught her eye. At least they would be on French soil soon, his wink said.

* * *

The detective had left his car at the airport the day they flew out to Spain; he found it hard to remember how long he had been away because of all that had happened. In moments, he was driving out of Paris, towards Reims. He glanced at Guylaine and realised that she was calmer, hopefully because at last she was going home.

Marc picked up his mobile phone and while he was driving dialled Uncle Marcos, who had promised to go to the castle that afternoon. The line went straight to the agent's voicemail but he supposed the call could wait. In fact, Marc had forgotten all about his second case when he heard the alarming deductions of Renaud, who was still deciphering the texts in the back seat of his car. He focused instead on their most immediate priority: finding the Count and Countess.

The rain fell heavily on the motorway and lightning bolts filled the heavy sky with incredible displays of colour. The windscreen wipers could barely clear the sheets of rain falling over the car like drapes, obscuring Marc's vision of the road. The silence in the car helped his concentration; only the rustling of papers in the back caught Marc's attention as he thought about Renaud's discoveries.

In no time at all, they saw the exit for Reims was marked only one kilometre away. The detective pointed out to Guylaine how close they were to their destination, at last.

'Yes, I know,' she replied. 'I have done this journey twice a week for the last ten years, so I could find the castle with my eyes closed.'

'Then show me the way through the vineyards. Whenever I've been here I have always found this part confusing.'

The road between the vines, laden with grapes, once familiar to the detective, now felt inhospitable in the midst of the storm, caught up as he was with his dark thoughts. However, thanks to Guylaine's instructions, he managed to get there in a few minutes.

The lightning bolts striking the Champagne region illuminated the imposing medieval building, creating a sinister silhouette; the outline of the grey stone cast a ghostly shape against the horizon.

'I would never have imagined returning here under these

circumstances, and on a night like this,' muttered the detective under his breath.

They parked right in front of the small mansion attached to the castle. Even this more modern extension looked different now. The dozens of windows were shuttered and there was no sign of light from the bedrooms inside.

'I've never seen the house as shut up as this in all my life,' whispered Guylaine, who couldn't believe her eyes.

Although Marc Mignon had only been resident in the Dubois family home for a few days, he hadn't imagined it to be like this either. Renaud was the last to emerge from the car, clutching all of the papers in his hands, and when he looked up he exclaimed:

'Holy Christ! What's happened here?'

The detective walked up to the door and checked that it was locked. Guylaine looked in her bag and took out a bunch of keys, which she offered him after selecting the right one. She wanted him to go in first, afraid of what they might find in her own house.

CHAPTER 62

The key creaked loudly in the lock. It must be because of the size and age of the door, Marc assumed. He stepped inside. The cold and gloomy air sent a shiver down his spine as he walked into the entrance hall; the rain falling outside was the only noise that broke the deathly silence. He gestured for Guylaine and Renaud to follow him. Guylaine noticed that the staircase and upstairs landing were pitch black but a flicker of light, which didn't seem to come from an electric light, shone from the main living room. Marc told her to follow behind him.

The light was coming from some candles left in the middle of the enormous reception room. Guylaine was anxious to check the Count's bedroom to see if they could find any trace of her father, so suggested they search the first floor. The detective nodded and, asking Renaud to remain at the foot of the staircase just in case, they made their way upstairs. This floor of the building felt equally cold and empty.

'It smells a bit stuffy, as if no one has opened the bedrooms in days,' observed Guylaine, heading towards the Count's room without hesitating.

The windows were closed and the shutters bolted. She peered round the door nervously and the only light was that afforded by the flashes of lightning, still raging through the dark night.

She was about to turn on the light when Marc grabbed her hand. They must go undetected until they had finished checking the castle. He half opened the shutter and let in a little more of the gloom. Inside her mother's wardrobes, Guylaine saw that the Countess's favourite clothes were still hanging. If she had chosen to leave the castle and her husband, surely she would have taken all her clothes, but nothing seemed to be missing. The thought comforted Guylaine; at least one of her fears could be discarded. Now she just had to find out where her mother had disappeared to over the last few days. Where was a woman who changed outfits several times a day without a full suitcase?

She closed the door and headed to her own bedroom where everything was just as she had left it. The detective walked up behind her and stood staring over her shoulder—she slept, read, dreamed and lived there, he thought. He had no idea what she dreamed of, as she had not once shared her thoughts with him, but it was no good to ponder this now. He must concentrate on the search; if there were candles lit, there must be someone somewhere in the castle.

He asked Guylaine to follow him, as there didn't seem to be anything out of the ordinary upstairs. Renaud was still standing at the foot of the stairs, waiting patiently for them, when Guylaine followed the detective back to the entrance hall.

'The only sign of life in this part of the castle seems to be in the living room,' said Marc. 'We should go back there.'

They walked into the middle of the room where only moments before they had seen the candlelight.

'This is very strange. Don't you think?'

Neither Guylaine nor Renaud answered the detective.

Then, a man's voice came from the back of the room.

'Well! I didn't expect you so soon.' The outline of a figure appeared from among the shadows.

Bruno slowly came towards them.

CHAPTER 63

They all looked in the direction of the voice. The silhouette of the young archaeologist moved forwards, out of the gloom, and he ordered them not to move.

'What are you doing here?' barked Guylaine. 'Where's my father? Answer me!'

Marc whispered to her not to lose her temper. Looking closer, he had spotted a silver gun glinting in Bruno's hands.

'I'll ask the questions! Stand against that wall with your hands above your head. Is that clear?'

They obeyed silently.

'What have you done with the Count? Where are you keeping him?' the detective dared to ask.

'Stay quiet unless I say!' he shouted, pointing his gun straight at the detective's head. 'Have you brought the documents from Rome? Give me them now, otherwise this goes off.'

Renaud looked across at Marc to see what he should do, as if seeking permission to concede to this madman. When the detective nodded, the assistant retrieved the folded papers from his jacket pocket and handed them to the man with the gun.

'You must be very careful with those papers,' Renaud said as he handed them over. 'The information they contain is very sensitive and could be catastrophic if misapplied. Do you understand me?'

'Are you all stupid? I know much more than all of you about this; I've been investigating this subject for years. You have no idea.'

'What are you talking about?'

'You'll find out in due course.'

'At least tell me where my father is. I beg you,' pleaded Guylaine.

'I'll take you to him and we'll start entering the new findings into the machine. Get down to the basement!'

* * *

Obediently, they started to descend in single file down into the underground belly of the castle. In the blackness, Marc could just make out the narrow entrance to the cavern where the talking head was found. A faint, flickering beam of light came from the room, suggesting that someone was in there.

'You go first,' Bruno ordered Guylaine, who squeezed her torso and then her legs through the narrow opening. In the shadows she couldn't see more that a few metres ahead of her.

Marc followed her through the doorway. As he approached the monstrous machine, he tried not to look directly at it. He could not forget that fearful face and he had no desire to have such an evil image etched on to his memory.

It looked like no one was there. Guylaine moved deeper into the room.

'Are you there?' she said very softly, calling for her father.

A visibly exhausted Pierre Dubois emerged from behind the enormous artefact, his hands full of papers.

* * *

Father and daughter held each other in a tight embrace for several minutes. When they separated, the others were already standing by the machine.

'What have they done with you, and where have they kept you, Father? Have they treated you well?' Guylaine asked him. 'I've called you dozens of times but you never answered.'

'I haven't moved from here since I came back from Córdoba. I haven't stopped for so much as a second; what we found in the Arab doctor's house was an exceptional discovery that has taken up all my time. My guess is that you have had plenty of luck in Rome and have managed to find the last part of Gerberto's legacy.'

'That's right. We have also got Renaud back, after he was kidnapped by the awful men who were chasing us. The poor man has suffered a lot since then but he has played an essential part in finding the information we were looking for. What we have found is astonishing, believe me.'

The assistant stepped forward and greeted the Count. After so many days without seeing each other, they exchanged a few pleasantries with a cordial hug, asking about each other's health.

The detective realised that Bruno was behind him, with the gun in his hand. Marc wanted to know if the archaeologist whom he had never trusted had mistreated the Count.

'Has this man hurt you, monsieur?'

'You have no idea,' Bruno laughed. 'The Count's more implicated in this situation than anyone else. Who do you think is the brains behind this whole operation?'

Bruno looked round at the three incredulous expressions.

'Go on then, Pierre. Explain your role in this whole thing. Tell them who you really are.'

'Yes,' said the Count. 'I believe the time has come to explain.'

CHAPTER 64

With his head bowed, Pierre Dubois sat down on the enormous trunk that contained the rare artefacts they had found that first day in the hidden room. He knew the time had come to explain what was really going on, since the end of the case was so near.

'I must confess that, for generations, my family's objective has been to find not just the talking head, the mythical Baphomet, but rather what is enclosed in this great machine. This contraption is a means, not an end. In pursuit of this, I have done things that perhaps I shouldn't have.'

'What are you talking about, Father?'

'It is a long story, my child. It started back in the eleventh century, or it might have been before, although my research points more or less to that date.

'When Silvestre died, many people wondered what became of the awful prophecies that had been predicted for the end of the millennium, since nothing happened during the transition from the year 999 to 1000. That's why there were those who awaited the year 1033 for the possible new coming of Jesus Christ, the Parousia, only to find that nothing significant happened then either.

'However, the prophecies still stood and the Book of Revelation spoke clearly of the apocalypse, or at least with as much precision as any ancient writings can offer. The pope dedicated much of his life to recovering supporting documents but no matter how learned he became, there was evidently something occult behind all of his achievements. Why did he have such an obsession with those manuscripts? Where did his determination to gain access to prohibited books come from? What was behind those mysterious trips to lands occupied by the Arabs?

'After the death of Silvestre, our family had access to the best-kept secret of his life: the truth that the pope had built a machine that could give unlimited power to the person who possessed it. In the archives of the Divange castle, which I inherited from my ancestors, there are a number of papers that refer to a great force that is simply called the Power. This was the reason the old lineage of the Dubois toiled for centuries in the search for this enormous thing that we have before us.'

The Count looked up at the massive talking head.

'In order to find this monstrosity, my ancestors used every method at their disposal. Yes, my dear Guylaine, you should know that this means our family has been involved in practically all of the conspiracies, revolts and wars that have shaken France and Europe to date, just to remain close to the knowledge. And that's not the worst of it.

'We participated in the crusades because the Knights Templar adored the Baphomet, the head that contained the sought-after ancestral knowledge. The Templar Knight, Gaucerant, was the first to speak of it and therefore we had to be there in case they managed to find it. When the Order of the Knights Templar fell and all of its members were put on trial, this elusive idol was mentioned on a number of occasions. Out of a total of two hundred and thirty-one men executed, twelve, all of them high ranking, admitted to worshipping it. And the strange thing is that the tribunal of the Catholic Church interpreted this idol as a symbol of the Devil, a satanic adoration. How did they know that it had this appearance, which we can now see is true, if it was hidden here the whole time?

'And that's not all. Our ancestors were also part of the Priory of Sion and, since then have been members of a number of hermetic societies—the Illuminati, the Rosic-rucian Order, as well as becoming followers of ritual magic and collaborating with French occultists. For generations, our family has actively participated in these secret organisations. It was in this last secret society that the occultist and magician Eliphas Lévi, in the middle of the nineteenth century, put forward highly accurate theories about the talking head. Lévi wrote extensively about the subject, raising our family's hopes at the time. In one of his books he speaks of Baphomet in a degree of detail not seen for centuries. He even drew it as a figure of Satan, as a goat with horns.'

'Who was this Eliphas Lévi?' asked the detective, intrigued by this talk of the Devil. For some time now, he had been convinced that the people associated with the Count and Renaud belonged to some sort of satanic cult.

'Eliphas Lévi was a very strange gentleman. He was the first person ever to publicise a horrible drawing of this millennial beast.'

'But Father, there must have been some connection between this monstrous idol and Satan. Lévi could not have been the first to connect the two; you only need to look at the pentagram drawn on the marble pedestal that supports this immense machine to see that.' With an index finger, she pointed to an image etched into the base of the talking head.

'The pentagram, an image that has been usurped by satanic groups recently, was always considered to be a sign of magic, but it was not originally designed for that purpose,' explained the Count, still staring in the direction of Guylaine's finger.

He continued.

'I seem to remember that its first documented use was some three and a half thousand years ago in Mesopotamia, in the origins of written language. In ancient inscriptions, the icon was symbolic of royal power. It later appeared in ancient Greece. There, the drawing of five points was called the "pentalpha" and it was so famous that Pythagoras himself used it as the symbol for his academy; they considered it an emblem of perfection due to its exact geometric dimensions.

'And it doesn't end there. The first Christians connected the pentagram to the five wounds of Christ until the Holy Catholic Church decided to replace it with another, more direct symbol: the sign of the cross.'

'That's why it's surprising that something that was once a strong Christian symbol is now connected to the Devil.' Guylaine found this complexity fascinating.

'But nevertheless it is,' Marc pointed out. 'There are people out there who use this sign to represent evil.'

'I have to say you're wrong, Monsieur Mignon,' the Count corrected. 'The pentagram with one point pointing up symbolises summer and with two points at the top, winter. Before Eliphas Lévi drew the head of Baphomet with the goat and this symbol, nobody had associated it with evil. Of course, he did it with one important detail: he drew the inverted pentagram, with the apex pointing down. Today, that is the symbol of Satan.'

The detective turned towards the pedestal, focusing on the engraving.

'If you look carefully at this pentagram, it's not inverted. Therefore, it is a very old sign that represents wisdom.' Looking at the marble, they found the Count was correct. 'The Church always took it upon themselves to demonise pagan symbols but signs change in their use and context over time.'

Growing increasingly frustrated, Marc questioned the Count directly. 'Do you mean to say that this has nothing to do with the Devil?'

'That's right.'

'Then who the hell has been chasing us all this time? During this case I'd always assumed that two groups were following us: a couple of Arab men and members of a satanic sect.'

'You're wrong I'm afraid,' the Count told him, still avoiding the detective's gaze.

'And how can you be so sure?' Marc interrogated him, raising his voice this time.

'Because I am familiar with them. The truth is, I know all of them quite well.'

CHAPTER 65

The atmosphere in the room was icy. The nobleman's expression made it clear that he felt the time had come to explain the truth.

'We belong to the Francmasonery,' he murmured faintly. 'I have been party to different secret societies for many years, among which this one stands out, and so have these others you speak of. Our family always had the firm objective of obtaining any type of information that could lead to obtaining Silvestre's invention and legacies that we knew were spread across numerous countries, so were members of every possible kind of hermetic sect. Within these various circles they had a lot of power because among their fellow members there were a number of influential and well-known names, believe me. As a result, we have been fortunate enough to come across the papers that contained the information which led me here to find the talking head in a hidden room in my own castle, but which my ancestors were unable to find for centuries.'

Renaud, perturbed by the confession he was hearing from his master, agreed with a slight nod of his head.

'Some time ago, I and the men who are still strangers to you made a pact to find Baphomet,' the Count continued. 'We knew that this complex contraption contained a special force, an enormous power that was of interest to both them and me. That's why we made a deal and, for many years, it has worked quite well. But it came to an end in the last few days.'

'Why?' This time it was his daughter questioning him.

'It is simple, my darling. As soon as we found the machine and began to put it into motion, I realised that in order to complete the puzzle I had to rely on the invaluable help of this young man who is keeping quiet over there.'

They all turned their heads to see Bruno grinning, still pointing the silver gun in their direction.

Guylaine didn't understand what her father was trying to say and felt she had to put pressure on him to explain what he was implying more clearly. As the Count was preparing to resume, he was interrupted by the supposed archaeologist.

'Well, well, well!' exclaimed Bruno. 'Finally something links me to your dear French nobleman. That's right, mademoiselle, your father and I made another pact on top of the one with your pursuers because I had something that he needed in order to solve his puzzle. Without collaborating with me and my men, he would never have got this far.'

'Please, tell me why,' she begged.

'While for years your father had a pact with those villains who have been following you, the very same who beat up this useless detective you've contracted, we—another group after something specific—in fact had the key to the secrets hidden in al-Andalus.'

'I'm pleased it wasn't you because I would have pounded you right now,' Marc Mignon reacted. 'Who are you? What group of people are you talking about?'

'We are a group of Arabic descent but were all born in Europe,' explained Bruno. 'Our clear, simple objective, set out about thirty years ago, is to elevate the image of our people in this continent through a number of initiatives we put in place. Beforehand, we were children of immigrants mistreated by the French, Germans, British and many other nationalities. But now we have completed our aim to raise the power of our people. That's why we vindicate the glorious past we had centuries ago, when Islam ruled the whole world and everyone spoke of the Arabic race.'

'And what exactly do you get out of this personally?' enquired Renaud, who had, until that moment, remained undaunted, not believing what he was hearing.

'We know that this machine could provide a power of unimaginable proportions. Although we don't know the exact background of the force that it hides, what we do know is that our people, and more specifically, the Córdoban Caliphate at the end of the first millennium, had control of this secret, before a certain Frenchman stole it from us. Therefore, we are simply reclaiming what is ours.'

'The reality is that I knew for sure that Bruno and his men had the map, with the exact location we needed in order to find the legacy contained in Medina Azahara,' explained the Count, who seemed to have a second wind now that the worst of the confession was over and those present now knew about his role in the twisted affairs. Free from this burden, Pierre Dubois looked ready for the end.

'Do you mean the map that you showed us at the site with the location of the doctor's house?' asked Guylaine.

'That's right. And furthermore, they brought in an expert

archaeological team for us, with a license to excavate those particular buildings. We never could have even thought about getting this far without the help of Bruno's men. Therefore, there was no alternative but for me to betray those I had been travelling with so that I could join with the new forces who provided me with the essential details I needed to get to where we are now.'

A deep silence took hold in the basement of the castle of Divange. When nobody else could speak, the Count resumed his explanation.

'I have to add this was the real reason why I disappeared from the castle a few days after discovering the talking head. I needed to finish the investigations in Ripoll, Córdoba and another place. But I couldn't reveal where I was headed, because in doing so, they would have chased me relentlessly and that is why I was forced to leave a brief letter addressed to you, my family, so you couldn't reveal my whereabouts.'

'So you have been behind this confusion all along, then?' remarked Guylaine, scorn showing in her voice for the first time. 'That same lot have beaten up Marc and abused Renaud to limits that don't bear contemplating. In fact, we have all suffered.'

'I am truly sorry,' her father responded. 'I didn't know that your mother was going to contract a detective to follow me, nor did I know that Jean Luc was going to come after me. Fortunately, we are here now and we don't have to bemoan any misfortunes.'

'Yes, quite, but emotionally our search has been almost unbearable,' she reminded him. 'I ask myself whether it has been worthwhile—'

'Of course, my child. Now comes the moment we have all been waiting for. We are finally going to get the machine working to full capacity and release the millennial secrets that can change humanity. Great revelations await us and, moreover, we will be able to solve the terrible riddle the machine holds predicting an imminent global catastrophe.'

'We mustn't turn this monstrosity on!' cried out Renaud in the strongest voice he could muster, given that there was still a gun very close by. 'The words we found in Rome clearly say that, if we use this knowledge, the consequences could be dire. Sir, I beg you to be very careful.'

'I will, Jean Luc. But I think that I am in charge of this situation and, therefore, I will decide how and when we do things.'

The sound of a gunshot came from the back of the room. When they looked around, they saw that the bullet had not come from Bruno's gun. In the shadows stood the two men who had been on their heels constantly. Now, their presence was no longer distant but immediate. Their order was clear: for everyone—even Bruno—to raise their hands.

CHAPTER 66

The echo of the shot, fired in an enclosed room, resounded off every solid stone wall, not dying down, the noise throwing them all into a confused state of shock.

Marc's expression changed as he became aware of what had happened. That voice, coming through the blackness from the makeshift doorway, was without doubt the same one indelibly imprinted on his mind. He sharpened his eyes and saw at once that this was one of the men who had pursued them through Ripoll, Córdoba and Rome. An unwanted knot formed in his throat; this was the closest he had been to him.

Bruno, from whom they had taken the gun, was apparently now one of them. Marc swallowed and made up his mind to ask them a question.

'What are you doing? A bullet fired in here will ricochet for sure and could kill someone.'

'Shut up, or you could be the first to die,' one of them answered. 'I don't know if you're aware that you're now in our hands until we get back what's ours. So, if you don't want another beating or something worse, keep your mouth shut.'

Marc remembered—and now hoped—that his uncle had yet to arrive. Something must have happened to him, he thought, as the storm still whistling through the castle walls around them was unlikely to be enough to delay him. There must be a simple explanation. If he had reached the castle approach, he could have seen the armed men and most likely someone else guarding the main door. Marc imagined his uncle, in this case, crouched behind one of the cars in the entrance, or even hid behind a tree, waiting for his chance. He was sure that Marcos was not going to leave them in the lurch. Until then, that confined space felt like a dreadful dungeon.

He glanced over at Guylaine, straining his eyes to keep his head still. She was lost in thought, probably in disbelief about what was happening. Poor Guylaine. In a short space of time, she had found out that her father was not, in fact, who she thought he was and the dirty traps he had laid went beyond the usual limits for a man who had always been an example of rectitude. She would, Marc predicted, be worrying about her mother, the only person missing from their unglamorous gathering of family, 'friends' and 'colleagues'.

'You'll listen up now, is that clear?' shouted the man with the gun.

When they all nodded in silent agreement, he gave the first instructions. 'I want everyone against the back wall, except you,' pointing at the Count, 'and your assistant, who are going to work here, on this table. The papers from Córdoba and Rome should be on it, within my reach.'

'Do you mean to say that we are going to set about entering all this information into the machine?' asked Pierre Dubois. 'That could take quite a few hours.'

'Our big boss is going to be here soon and you, Monsieur Dubois, have deceived us and lied to us, but this time we are not going to let it go. The secret enclosed in this device is going to be ours, so you will do as you're told.'

Marc immediately thought that that was why his uncle still hadn't arrived. If someone important—the leader of their group—were on his way, there would probably be a number of men awaiting his arrival outside. If this was the case, Marcos, who would perhaps come alone, might have great trouble passing them. Even though Marc knew that his uncle was one of the best private detectives in Paris, he wasn't very hopeful that he would appear to save them soon. He tried to relax, or at least, not to appear tense in front of their captors, as there was no way out of this situation.

Pierre Dubois and Jean Luc Renaud sat down at the narrow worktable that they had used in the days following the discovery of the machine and on which they had carried out their first investigations. The Count had already looked at the material found in Medina Azahara, so he now started to work with what the others had found in Rome. His assistant spread out the papers that his friend, Professor Colarossi, had given him at Sapienza University. He quickly explained to the Count the initial analysis he had been able to undertake on the short flight to Paris.

Pierre Dubois's eyes grew wider and wider as Renaud narrated the fabulous details of the decorations of the Temple of Isis, the Mother of Nature, the goddess among gods. He was very surprised to hear about the demotic texts written inside the Roman temple.

'That is, quite simply, incredible. The only reasonable explanation is that someone deliberately wanted to leave that extremely old knowledge in a clear form in imperial Rome.

That someone made a record in a public place more that two thousand years ago seems impossible to me. What was the real reason?' asked the Count.

'Well, the mysteries continue. If you look at these other drawings that Luigi gave me, they correspond to hieroglyphics written in ancient Egyptian. It is probable that those engravings were made between 3000 and 2000 BC. Therefore we are faced with new evidence because we always knew that the pope read sources from many ancient cultures like Persian, Greek, Hindu and Arabic books, but we never thought that his studies could stretch back some seven thousand years from the present day.'

'Thousands and thousands,' whispered the Count. 'How old must the discoveries Silvestre made be? What civilisation does this knowledge come from?'

'We are, of course, now moving into uncharted territory,' Renaud admitted, though his voice sounded unfazed. 'From what I have read in the inscriptions from Córdoba as well as those from Rome, it must have been from a culture previous to all those known, one that had more advanced technology than we presumed of that age.'

'I have no doubt about it. Look at this!' The Count gestured to a group of hieroglyphics that seemed to represent instructions to access a remote place.

'I think that we should start here,' he said, pointing to a strange sign. 'This symbol could be the first in an operation that, if put into the machine, might lead us to something important. Let's try!'

He went over to the machine and, using the guidelines he had extracted from the document, inputted the formula. The talking head didn't react, as if the data hadn't had an effect, so the Count moved around the positions of the bars on the abacus, yet the monstrosity still didn't alter. The huge artefact seemed to be stalling, or blocked.

With the gun still pointing at them, the taller, more imposing thug threw them a warning.

'You'd better finish before our superior arrives. Do you hear?'

All this while, Guylaine, Marc and Bruno remained seated on the floor with their backs leant against the cold, stone walls on which the castle was founded. The detective considered proposing to the archaeologist that they try to do something together to free them from those people, as, deep down, with every minute that passed, he became more convinced that his uncle was not going to arrive. He edged closer to whisper but Bruno asked them not to rely on him, for reasons that he was not willing to reveal.

Guylaine looked at Marc with a little wink, reassuring him that surely they would get out of this situation even though at the moment it seemed complicated.

The Count walked away from the machine back to his assistant at the table. They were doing something wrong. In the pause, Renaud reminded him that they should be careful because, in one part of the demotic text, it alluded to great danger if that information was used badly.

'If indeed we are now in charge of something great and powerful, it is clear that whoever wrote these hieroglyphics had to ward off third parties who were not wholly dedicated to the mystery, just like notices we put on doors of houses, saying that the property is guarded by a burglar alarm,' said the Count. 'The entrance has to be protected.'

'That's it!' exclaimed Renaud. 'The machine isn't responding because it requires the password needed to access this information. It's the key to a most complex unity created by Silvestre. We're getting close to finding out what he really built it for and why he protected it with some kind of code.'

'You are absolutely right,' agreed Pierre. 'In every other operation I have done, as much in the days following the finding of this thing as in the last few days, I haven't had any problem making this decrepit artefact function. Why doesn't it react now? Our pope must have encrypted a password in order to gain access to the most confidential nucleus. What could it be?'

'Over a decade ago we found a text which said that to work the talking head one had to call it by its name. At that time we didn't have the machine, but now, we can try the simplest option. Let's enter Baphomet.'

The Count proceeded to combine the appropriate letters with the abacus and waited for a response. However, the machine still did not react. The Count looked blankly at his assistant, waiting for an idea. They entered other possible names that they were aware of for the biggest invention of the first millennium, but neither 'talking head' nor any alternatives worked.

From her seat on the floor, Guylaine asked their captors for permission to assist in the analysis being undertaken at the other end of the room. The thug conceded with a simple tap of the gun, gesturing vaguely towards the table.

'I think that, if Silvestre really put a password on the

final secret that this incredible machine supposedly contains, he must have done it thoughtfully. Coming from such an intelligent man, I can't imagine that he would choose a key as simple as the name of his invention.'

'And what do you suggest?' her father asked.

'Try variations of Baphomet. I understand that no one has ever known the meaning of that strange word, even though many possible explanations exist. What do you reckon?'

'Sensational!' exclaimed Renaud. 'Let's make a list.'

The Count explained first that the widely accepted belief was that Baphomet alluded to the union of the words *baphe* and *meteos*, probably meaning 'baptism' and 'adoration'. Neither had an effect on the machine. Renaud contributed another, more complex idea.

'Many historians over the centuries have thought that the word meant *Tem Oph Ab* coming from an anagram of *templi omnum hominyn pacis abbas* or "the father of the temple, who provides universal peace to men".'

'That is a cabalistic phrase, which, in my view, is very forced and must, in fact, have been adopted after the death of Silvestre,' countered the Count. 'But I am prepared to try it for you.'

He went back to the artefact and entered each word of the phrase mentioned by the assistant but, once again, there was no reaction. The three of them lifted their eyes to the ceiling, searching together for divine inspiration. Guylaine saw that her father had got up from his seat to walk around machine. After a few minutes, the Count returned to the table with an explanation he thought was reasonable.

'I remember I once read that someone had the idea that the name Baphomet came from Greek words *baph* and *metis*, meaning something along the lines of "baptism of light".'

'Yes, now I remember that too. Try it!' Renaud encouraged him.

Yet, once again disappointment washed over the Count's face.

'Well I can't think of anything else,' murmured the assistant.

Now it was Guylaine's turn. 'Perhaps we ought to think through the idea from the academic who worked with the Dead Sea Scrolls. Do you remember it? I'm talking about his theory that the word Baphomet was written in the Atbash cipher.'

'Yes, but when I first read about it, back in its day, it seemed a little strange,' her father answered. 'Do you know it well?'

'It's very simple. The Atbash code is written by substituting the first letter of the Hebrew alphabet for the last letter, the second for the penultimate and so on. When this man applied the code to Baphomet, the result he obtained was a surprising word: six of the letters spelled "Sophia"...'

'Which means "knowledge" in Greek,' recalled Renaud.

'Then it could be the key.'

Faced with a new chance and renewed sense of hope, the Count went over to the talking head, longing for this to be the correct password. However, to add further disappointment, the complicated machine did not accept even this option.

From his hard, wooden seat at the table, Marc wondered whether or not it would actually be better if they never found the password. In his desperation, he feared that, if they found the final answer, whatever it was, their captors could use extreme violence to take the result of so much work and flee without a trace. Or even worse: they could finish them off so that nobody would know what had happened. The fatal premonition was still resonating in his mind when the Count let out a sudden shout that alarmed everyone, as the echo reverberated around the room.

'Sorry,' he muttered in a suddenly low voice. 'I have just remembered that there is a rather strange theory about the meaning of Baphomet we have not yet considered. According to an eccentric historian, a friend of mine whom I met in America more that forty years ago, it could mean *Bafmaat* —in lost, archaic language—"the opener of the door".'

'Well, that would be the perfect word to get that hideous thing to say what it has to say once and for all!' exclaimed one of the thugs, speaking for the first time that evening. 'Our boss is on his way, so you must get on with whatever you're doing quicker because, if you don't get it in time, I'll shoot the lot of you. Do you hear me?'

He fired the revolver and once again they were temporarily deafened by the piercing echo that resonated in the cavity serving as their gaol. With the end of the pistol, he violently pushed the Count towards the head to make him try the new idea.

Pierre Dubois sat down on the stone floor in front of the frightening face and began to feed the appropriate instructions through the abacus as usual. As he entered the last letter, the machine emitted a strange sound, one which he had never heard before. A loud crunch came from deep inside the bowels of the machine. He looked anxiously into its gaping mouth, among the hundreds of wires, springs and cogs. Something had opened inside the invention of Silvestre II.

CHAPTER 67

It was an effort to calm the great commotion that broke out in the dungeon; the thugs threatend to fire their guns if their prisoners didn't get into their places. Soon everything was back to how it was before, with the exception of the wide smile that spread across the Count's face. He did not move from his place in front of the machine but immediately started to enter the dozens of descriptions featured in the hieroglyphics. Every time he tapped in a sequence, the talking head seemed to respond with the same force as the first crunch and at one moment, the force broke off a significant part of the artefact's face, causing some very deteriorated wheels, tubes and cords to fall to the ground.

After a few minutes, when Pierre Dubois thought he had entered roughly half of the information, a new and surprising sound came from deep within the monstrosity. A deep, hollow groan. Unsettled by what was happening, Renaud approached his master, begging him to proceed with caution.

'I have a feeling that Silvestre II built this apparatus for a very different purpose than what we thought.'

'Why do you say that?' asked the Count without pausing.

'Because if we carry on like this, the machine is going to

be destroyed.'

'Dear friend, there's no going back now. It's clear that the pope didn't construct this monstrosity for the purpose we initially thought and that there is actually something inside. I believe that the true use of the talking head was to guard something—I don't know what but it must be his best-kept secret.'

The assistant moved away and sat down in a corner to consider what his boss had said. From where he crouched, he watched obediently as the nobleman seemed to have lost his mind: Pierre Dubois carried on moving the bars at a frantic pace, making the machine collapse at an alarming rate. By the time he was nearing the end, the talking head was in pieces. Only the monster's face and the heavy marble base remained unaltered. The greatest enigma of the first millennium had been reduced to a medley of cords, tubes, wheels and levers, partly by its own energy.

* * *

The dust that had gathered over hundreds of years on each and every one of the thousands of pieces of the talking head had been disturbed, and the blanket was so thick that the others, at the far end, couldn't see what had happened.

'I've finished my part,' said the nobleman with a touch of solemnity, his voice muffled by the cloud.

Guylaine, Marc and Bruno rushed forward to look at the ruinous appearance of the pope magician's greatest scientific achievement.

'Oh my God!' Guylaine exclaimed. 'So many centuries of

searching to end up with this!'

'And the worst thing is,' added the detective, 'we could have died in this crazy adventure for nothing.'

'And now what?' shouted one of the thugs impatiently.

'I think that it all ends here,' Renaud said with chagrin.

'And what's the great secret you have to give us?' pestered the other armed man.

'We don't know. I think that we are all equally perplexed. The machine has been destroyed and left us none the wiser about the final legacy of the pope.'

There was a long silence. The particles of dust suspended in the air settled. After a few minutes they could see the pile of battered pieces strewn across the bare floor.

'Perhaps we should tidy up this deplorable mess to see if there's anything useful among this rubble,' proposed Renaud.

'Good idea. Let's clear this up.'

A frenetic collection of disordered segments from the previously sophisticated machine began. Guylaine realised that the large size of the bronze head and the solid marble base had made the talking head look like an enormous bust when Silvestre built it, but now, as they went about collecting fragments, the face of the monstrosity seemed less fearsome. She was still entertaining this thought when she noticed that her father looked very solemn, disheartened. It didn't surprise her because a whole life of studies, investigations and work ended here, on the flagstones, wasted. She wanted to console him but she remembered what he had said about his shady role in all that had happened, so instead she continued silently gathering pieces of material, practically rubbish, which had accumulated on the floor of the room.

The coming and going of people was interrupted by Renaud, letting out an ear-splitting shout.

'Look, come and see this!'

He was standing on the black marble pedestal that had served as the neck of the talking head and, with a bit of tube still in his hand, he pointed to a clay vessel.

'It seems to contain liquid of some sort, although I can't say what it is, because it won't open.'

The Count went over immediately. Before he had even got to his assistant to look at the receptacle, Bruno's voice came from the other side of the room.

'Well, there's another one here.'

'I've found one here too,' added Marc.

Three somewhat deteriorated vessels made of brown clay were adhered tightly to the solid block base of the talking head. The three containers were joined by thick iron bars that formed a triangle.

'They all contain a liquid,' the Count pointed out. 'How strange.'

When Marc tried to remove one of them, the nobleman shouted at him.

'Don't move a thing! I think I already know what it is.'

* * *

Raised on the enormous marble stone, they gathered around the Count and waited for him to explain what had been found. The nobleman stood still, pointing at something that seemed to be underneath the vessels. Guylaine saw that her father's expression had changed and now revealed a mixture of excited happiness and trepidation.

'Well, tell us please, because my heart is bursting.' She smiled because there was still a chance that all her father's investigations could reach a favourable outcome after all.

'The true secret of Silvestre II is under our feet and these receptacles are the best safeguard, so that only someone who really cares will find the legacy.'

'Now I understand,' said Renaud. 'These vessels contain some kind of liquid that, if spilt on the marble, will destroy whatever is below.'

'That's right – it is a rustic system of protection. If anyone had found the talking head and dismantled or manipulated it without doing what we have done, these receptacles would, probably, have broken, making the contents of whatever is below us disappear.'

'So can we take it apart now without any danger?' asked Guylaine.

'I think so,' her father replied.

They dismantled the metallic structure and the vessels came out easily.

As a test, the Count bent down and broke one of them on to the paved floor. When he smashed it, it broke into dozens of pieces and a black viscous liquid spilled out and immediately started to corrode the stone under his feet. The relief allowed a smile to emerge on each face in the dungeon; whatever had been protected, they had managed not to destroy so far.

Clambering back onto his soap box, the marble pedestal, with an energy surpassing his age, the Count confirmed that there were some slats of wood, blackened by the passing of time, on which the pots of corrosive acid had been resting. He asked for an iron bar and singlehandedly proceeded to peel back the planks one by one, revealing yet something else.

* * *

Decades of study had passed, or centuries including those of his ancestors, and now Pierre Dubois, the Count of Divange, finally had the millennial secret within his reach. After the savage epoch of the first millennium, Silvestre II had been able to capture its legacy and preserve it for humanity. And just at that moment, for the first time, and after such a long time, the Count was going to be the one to clamp eyes on that incredible heritage. He slid the iron bar underneath the first slat and levered it forcefully.

A piercing sound almost shattered his eardrum. He thought that the deafening noise had been caused by his action, but when he turned his head, Pierre saw that it had been due to a series of gunshots fired from an automatic gun. In the doorway, another armed man could just be seen pulling the trigger and shouting orders to his companions. He started to shout at the group crowded around the plinth in the centre of the room.

'Stop!' he screamed. 'Stop what you're doing. Our great master will be here in a couple of seconds.'

Pierre Dubois, whose ears were still ringing, climbed down from his position and rushed over to join his daughter and Renaud, glancing at Bruno and Marc, who stayed next to the farthest wall. Everyone was waiting for the person who would have to enter through the narrow opening of the underground dungeon. Even from a distance, the detective could see the silhouette of a familiar figure.

Marcos Mignon entered with a gun in his hand.

Marc threw himself at his uncle, intending to greet and embrace him. Never before had he been so pleased to see his father's brother.

'You have no idea how much I have missed you.'

The amateur detective wrapped his arms around his boss, who reacted tentatively, still holding up his gun.

'I knew you would come sooner or later,' Marc said to him, noticing that everyone else there was confused by the enthusiasm with which Marcus had been received. 'How did you get around the guards upstairs?'

The laughter of the two thugs who were still there got a rise out of him.

He didn't understand why the thugs were still not putting up any sort of resistance and, to top it off, they were laughing at what he had said.

'What's going on?' he murmured.

'Marc, we have to talk. There are a lot of things I must tell you.'

'Then start by telling me how you are connected to these people.'

'For some years now, I have been the Great Master of a secret organisation, called the Logia of the New World Order, which you can call the Logia.'

CHAPTER 68

Given his nephew's expression, it was clear that the impression caused by his words had left him bordering on collapse. Marc had frozen and realised he didn't know how to react, so he stepped back, allowing the other men who came behind his uncle to pass. The entourage was composed of three men and each of them, on entering, could not avoid staring impulsively at the hideous head. Even though its size had been notably reduced, the face of the ancient machine, now wearing a villainous mask, a shocking face stripped of its former majesty, was still enough to frighten.

Not even Marcos Mignon, the leader of the Logia, had imagined it would look like that. Wisdom, esotericism, cruelty, hereticism and a long list of adjectives could, only with difficulty, describe the icon.

Mesmerised by the image of the darkest revelation in humanity for a thousand years, he knew that, from this moment on, he had to take control of the dungeon he found himself in before accessing the secret that Silvestre II had hidden. There were too many people waiting to see what could happen. The final revelation could only be seen by a few.

'Upstairs! Everyone upstairs! Now!' shouted Marcos Mignon, ordering his footmen to see that the captives were herded out. As his nephew passed in front of him, Marcos stopped him with the tip of his gun and Marc's right arm flinched at the touch of the cold metal.

'You stay, Marc. We've got lots of things to talk about.'

The young detective couldn't decide what to do, to stay or to continue upstairs with the others, so he stood still, giving his uncle the chance to lightly push him so that he separated from the group and stayed behind.

Pierre Dubois muttered under his breath, but just in earshot of the detectives, that he should have the honour of seeing the final millennial legacy of the pope magician for the first time.

'No! You don't deserve to!' snapped Monsieur Mignon senior. 'You've betrayed us and we'll never forgive that. The Order has decided to expel you from the organisation.'

One by one they left through the narrow opening guarded by the armed men. Marc gave Guylaine a lasting look as she passed him. Despite the mess they were in, she felt sorry for the detective, as his eyes expressed the barrage of contradictions that must be going through his head, which, in a single moment, had swept away all of his expectations for solving this case.

The room where ten people had been confined soon returned to the silence it had held over the previous months. Even the temperature had dropped quickly, and the stone room now gave Marc a chill. The atmosphere was icy, his uncle, unnerving.

* * *

Marcos looked at the talking head face on, rather than

sustaining his nephew's gaze and, without checking to see whether he was listening or not, started to explain.

'It's a long story, so you can sit down if you'd prefer.'

'I'm fine as I am. Please begin.'

'The truth is that it's difficult to pinpoint the beginning because it gets lost around the time your grandfather came to France, to settle in a country he didn't know. Although his move opened lots of doors for him, he had yet to know how to grab the opportunities. The thing is that, at a time when the Agency was forging its reputation, someone gave him the opportunity to join a society that aimed, among other objectives, to improve the world. This, to a man who had suffered a lot, seemed out of his orbit. But, when he declined, the company took an unfortunate turn. We began losing our connections and contracts at an alarming rate, which is why I threw myself into a solitary adventure, unaware of the consequences. Fortunately it put us back in the circles we had lost and brought us case after case. We mentioned nothing to your grandfather, and your father and I continued collaborating with various societies so that we, as an agency, became increasingly well connected with an exclusive section of our country's society.'

He paused to clear his throat.

'Twenty years ago, when both your father and I were fully fledged members of one of the most important logias in Paris, we ran into conflict with the descendants of another family that was very active in these hermetic circles: the Baumard family. At first, our relationship with old Monsieur Baumard's children was very good and, in fact, we worked on a level of mutual understanding. However, after a couple of years, the position of ambassador of our organisation to other logias arose. It was at that point that your father came face to face with Daniel Baumard for the leadership. Their competition didn't end well.

'You know the story that we have told you all these years; well, a good part of it is true. The old man started to see that his children were being led astray, as they were unenthusiastic about directing a two-hundred-year-old family firm. Before he handed it over to them, Baumard entrusted our agency with the task of finding out if his children were involved in drugs as he feared. In a company that dedicated itself to importing and exporting to exotic regions, it was highly likely, he thought.'

Marcos paused to light a cigarette, took a long drag and slowly exhaled, the smoke invading the room, adding to its sinister atmosphere.

'The relationship between your father and the Baumard heir, who really should have minded his own business, got out of hand.'

'Did he kill my parents?' Marc asked the question directly, as he needed to hear the truth.

His uncle took a deep breath. 'Yes, he did. The idiot organised the car chase.'

The silence seemed to weigh down on both of them, neither being able to manage a single word for several minutes. When he finished his cigarette, Marcos decided to finish the story.

'I knew exactly what had happened and I had two options. If I found him and took him to the police, he would be in prison for a while but would be out again sooner or later.

That's why I chose the second: I killed him some years later, when no one could connect him to the death of my brother and sister-in-law. I was very calm when I saw that imbecile suffer and I can assure you that he suffered a lot. Yes, I admit I did it myself, with my own hands.'

He threw his stub to the floor and stepped decisively on it, then turned his head to see two silent tears rolling down his nephew's face.

Marcos loved his nephew like his own son. He went over and waited for a reaction, a response of some sort. Marc swallowed and dared ask one simple question.

'Why did you send me on this case?'

'Can't you see? I already knew more or less how this would end and it was about time you knew the real reason for your parents' deaths. Putting you on a case in which, indirectly, the Baumard matter was going to come to light, was a good way to tell you. Now all that is left is to know whether or not you have enjoyed investigating and if you are ready to dedicate yourself to your father's profession.'

'How dare you think so selfishly, acting for your own interests? Those criminals you're in charge of beat me up and nearly killed me.'

'Sometimes that happens. But you have to understand it was because they had a mission to complete and I had told them to spare no means in getting here. They never would have killed you, believe me. In all of this, the only mistake has been made by the Count when he made a pact with the Arabs in Reims. If the foolish Pierre had simply carried on in the footsteps of his ancestors, none of this would have happened.'

'And why are you personally interested in the secret hidden in this machine?' enquired Marc, pointing to what was left of the head. 'What is a man like you doing controlling thugs like that?'

'I can explain everything. Over time, I have been progressing well in my work within the Logia and have reached this point. It hasn't been easy, but the end justifies the means, Marc. We are on the verge of revealing one of the greatest millennial secrets of humanity. Doesn't that seem like reason enough?'

The young man didn't respond and his silence was interrupted by a muffled yet distinctive sound—the sound of gunshots, coming through the thick walls of the castle. Marcos told his nephew to follow him. Something was going on upstairs.

CHAPTER 69

When the two Mignons arrived in the residential part of the castle, they didn't believe their eyes and couldn't understand the commotion in the huge entrance hall. Suddenly, for some reason, it had become an improvised battleground. There was one group of men positioned on the first floor landing, behind a white marble banister, directly attacking another group sheltered behind the hall furniture, but for what reason Marc couldn't tell. On instinct, Marc presumed, Marcos Mignon removed a gun from his waist and starting firing upwards, in the direction of the balustrade.

Protected, from behind a door that led to the basement, Marc shouted at his uncle, demanding to know what was happening.

'Those people are Bruno's henchmen, the Arabs with whom the Count made a pact. I don't know how they got in here.'

'Can you see Guylaine?' Marc asked.

'Yes, I spotted her in the next door room with Renaud and Pierre, tied to chairs. They don't appear to be in danger, though.'

The young man sighed. Shocked by the shower of bullets that crossed in front of his eyes, he thought about how crazy this whole situation had become and how the men were going to destroy the castle if they weren't careful. Marc returned to reality when his uncle suddenly launched himself towards where his men were in the hall. His move was a dangerous one, as the director of the Mignon Agency now stood in the most vulnerable position, although it did give him the most advantageous angle to shoot the men overlooking the staircase.

Without revealing himself completely from behind the door, Marc saw a man get hit and start rolling down the stairs. His uncle must be a good marksman because, a few seconds later, another gunman came crashing to the ground. None of Marcos's men had been hit but Marc watched stunned as the man who had beaten him up and chased them in their journey around Spain and Italy was shot in the chest. He saw his uncle try to help him and lift him out of the crossfire but the intensity of the shots made it impossible to move from where he was, so Marcus stayed until he thought he could organise his men to help their comrade. Only when he knew he could provide cover did he signal for them to come to the rescue.

The attempt was a disaster. The relentless fire raining down on them caught the other two men on his team. Marcus knew what would happen if it carried on like that. He also knew he had to move forward in order to get a better angle from which to shoot Bruno's men hidden on the staircase. So, swiftly he lunged forwards, holding his gun with both hands. Right on target, several shots hit two people positioned in the middle of the stairs, behind the marble banister. He kept pulling the trigger and began to climb the stairs to where the men he had shot had fallen, but, when he reached only the third step, one of the men stationed on the first floor stood up and, with an automatic weapon, started a sweep of the area below him.

Without blinking, Marc witnessed the impact the older detective received. It threw him down the steps with such force that he came to a stop in front of the entrance door of the castle.

* * *

'Stop! Stop!' shouted the Count who, unable to bear hearing the violence next door, had managed to escape from his bonds and was desperate to end the madness.

He heard Bruno's voice telling his men not to shoot, a gesture which Marcos Mignon's men took advantage of to get their master out of the line of fire.

Marc hastily tried to get to the vehicle into which they were putting his uncle, but all he could see were the tail-lights of a car speeding away down the drive when he reached the front door. Back in the hallway, there was no longer any danger. The men stationed upstairs had come down and he saw them talking to the Count and Bruno over the bodies of their injured men on the ground. He slipped into the room next-door. When he saw Guylaine struggling in the chair, his pulse confirmed what he knew he felt for her but had tried to ignore so far. He fumbled with the ropes and freed Renaud and Guylaine from their bonds.

* * *

The Count of Divange stood in the middle of his entrance hall and stared in astonishment at the state of the oldest part of his castle, which looked as if it had been hit by a hurricane. Once he had got over the shock of this sight, the Count asked after the injured. The pact that the nobleman had made with Bruno and his men made Marc uneasy; he couldn't understand what lay behind their union. His look of distrust did not go unnoticed by the young archaeologist, who decided he ought to explain.

'We're not assassins. We don't try to kill people and neither do we want to resort to violence, except if it is in legitimate defence of our interests,' he announced.

'Our union with Pierre has been very clear from the beginning. He wanted to obtain the legacy of Silvestre II and we only wanted our role in the history of civilisation, the important role that Arabic culture has played in humanity's past, to be recognised. Marc, I believe the time has come for my race to receive recognition for the enormous contribution we have made to the world over time.'

'That's right,' corroborated Pierre Dubois. 'You can rest assured, Marc, that the people left here are going to collaborate in the final resolution of this issue.'

'And are you really an archaeologist?' Marc asked Bruno.

'Yes, I have spent my life studying.'

'And is everything my uncle told me before true?' Marc asked the Count this time.

'I'm afraid so. I have belonged to the same logias as him and we have collaborated on many matters to enable us to find the talking head. But there is one thing you should know and it's that the organisation to which your uncle belongs, the Logia of the New World Order, is a group of people whose objective is to change the world. Its origin dates back to the Illuminati, whose initial idea was developed by a German Jew in 1776. Over the centuries they have enlisted into their ranks individuals from very high levels in governments, institutions and multinational companies. In fact, since this particular logia was founded, it has been greatly assisted by presidents, ministers and multimillionaires, all pulling powerful strings within the world economy.

'To give you an idea, if you look carefully, you can see the signs of its tentacles in places as well known as the American dollar bill, which has the pyramid of the Illuminati—a truncated pyramid with an eye at the top part—on the reverse side with the phrase *Novus Ordo Seclorum*, which clearly reveals what these men are pursuing. Their power is so far-reaching that it is even said that they are behind many of the great events of recent times. I am sure that your uncle is a very powerful person and that he has infiltrated deep inside the most influential circles, some rather sinister, we can imagine.'

'But he can't be,' Marc responded. 'He's just a private detective.'

'I'm afraid not. The Mignon Agency is a brilliant cover-up. Have you been to your uncle's offices?'

'Of course, plenty of times.'

'Then it must have dawned on you that such a luxurious and well-located building doesn't seem justified by a profession such as investigation. The Mignon name is a synonym of influence and control in political, military and business spheres.'

'And what does my uncle want the contents of Silvestre's

machine for?'

'The secret society he represents has known the legends of the pope magician and the magnificent legacy he left for the future for centuries, so finding the talking head has, for them, been as important as finding the Holy Grail or the Ark of the Covenant. It has always been presumed that there are great occult mysteries inside the machine. However, unlike those present here, your uncle wants "the Power" that the great work of our pope refers to for very different uses. Do you understand?'

'Yes, and I suppose that's why you made a pact with these other men, even though you should have kept your word with the Logia. But why did Bruno meet us with a gun in his hand when we arrived earlier?'

'For one simple reason,' said Bruno. 'I didn't know what your arrival would bring and it was important that I control the situation as I did. You had to go down, hand over the papers from Rome and help solve this problem. Everything would have worked, were it not for the arrival of those ruffians.'

'I think the time has now come to put an end to this long story,' said the Count. 'The night still has some big surprises in store for us.'

* * *

Pierre Dubois, accompanied by his daughter, Renaud, Bruno and Marc, returned to the cavern. A hint of displeasure crossed his face when he once again saw the machine completely dismantled; those tubes, springs, wheels and pieces piled in one of the corners of the room. At least there was a positive side to the chaos: that was the intention of the pope magician.

The time had come to reveal the great secret that Silvestre II had hidden not inside but underneath the head. The Count lifted himself on to the marble base with unexpected dexterity, encouraged perhaps by what it might contain; but once he was on it, he realised his limited physical strength, so he requested the help of the other two younger men.

'We are going to take off the wooden planks. Help me please.'

Bruno and Marc started to remove the heavy planks and added them to the pile of debris already accumulated. A few minutes later, the work was done. The men had uncovered an enormous hole in the pedestal, which appeared to have something at the bottom. Marc jumped down to rummage inside and, because he was kneeling on the contents, nobody could see what he was handling.

'Tell us what you find,' said the Count.

'Of course,' said the detective. 'Take these.'

He lifted up a series of marble plaques. The nobleman took the first and began handing them to Renaud, waiting patiently on the sidelines. Guylaine was placing them neatly on the floor in order, and counted them—Marc had extracted more than twenty slabs.

'Is that everything?' enquired the Count from above.

Just before he lifted himself out, Marc shouted, 'Wait, there's something else here and it's much bigger. I'm actually standing on it and it looks like an enormous plaque made of some kind of metal. Bruno, can you come and help me?'

The young archaeologist came over. Marc told him to reach his hand down and pull directly upwards. He did the same from the other side. Nothing moved.

'Whatever it is, it's incredibly heavy,' the detective explained. 'Guylaine, please bring us two of the iron bars we took off a while ago.'

She handed one to each of them. Bruno understood what Marc intended to do: make a lever to try to lift the object. They wedged the improvised tools into various nooks and started to apply all the force they could. The men managed to dislodge the enormous slab, creating a big cloud of dust in the air. With a firm grip on the levers, they took hold of it and, using all their combined strength, slowly raised it up.

'It feels like it is stuck to the bottom. Can you take it from above?' he asked the others.

Between the four men they managed to lift it out and set it against the wall. As Renaud wiped the surface, a shining image appeared, leaving them dazzled. When all the dust was cleaned off, a metallic plaque, covered with characters that no one recognised, was revealed.

* * *

Renaud could not conceal his surprise: despite the many ancient languages he knew fluently, he was unable to decipher a single one of the characters engraved on the metal. The Count looked equally shocked by the object, as he too had never imagined finding an unknown language.

'I don't understand dead languages in the same way as you,' said Marc, 'but those characters seem extraordinary even to my eye.'

'Indeed,' corroborated the Count. 'It is a type of script that must come from a civilisation older than Silvestre's.'

'Also,' added his assistant, 'the material used to make this slab, which I would describe as a plate, looks metallic but is not iron. It could be some type of alloy, but not one common to ancient cultures. What do you think as an archaeologist, Bruno?'

'I've never seen anything like this. Before you wiped it, it looked no different from a number of artefacts that have been recovered from ancient worlds. However, now that we have dusted the surface of this…monolith, the quality of the craftsmanship, its excellent state of conservation and, above all, the extraordinary precision of the script surprises me. Obviously, it is not easy to etch with such accuracy into a metallic material that appears to be as hard and resistant as the one we have before us. This is all…simply incredible.'

Guylaine, who had been listening silently to the conversation between the men, broke the long silence.

'Well, these appear to be an instruction manual that explains what it is and how to interpret the language,' she said, pointing to the little marble plaques that they had taken out before.

'And how do you know?' her father asked in surprise.

'Because these pieces of marble are written in Latin. But the most surprising thing is…'

'What?'

'The author of these plaques is Silvestre II himself.'

CHAPTER 70

Her words caused a great stir among the men. Her father demanded to see the first small board which she had read. Guylaine showed it to him and, straight away, he began to summarise it as he read.

'Yes, my child, you are indeed right. These marble plaques have been engraved by the firm hand of our pope. There is no doubt about it. The legacy of Silvestre II is absolutely exceptional.'

Renaud picked up another plaque. 'It says here that he decided not to make this great discovery public because nobody would have understood it in his time. According to him, in the tenth century, people would not understand the deep concepts and revelations contained in this—'

'This what?' his boss demanded.

'I like the word you said before. I think we should call it a monolith. Anyway, this monolith the pope found is a survival from an ancient civilisation that no one remembers now and that brings together a series of hermetic principles relating to nature and how our planet works. Let me read Silvestre's first words addressed to whoever finds his legacy.'

Renaud translated aloud:

I hope God looks kindly on humanity and this prodigy that I leave here falls into good hands, because its use is destined to save life on earth and not destroy it. I believe that it has been sent by our God but I cannot be sure that it is not an invention of Lucifer, as it represents both sides of the same coin.

Ever since I was born, I have been an enterprising man, always interested in science and, above all, mathematics and astronomy. During the search for manuscripts and old texts, I found this prodigy and I want to leave it as a legacy for the future: a metal board on which is written unprecedented revelations. When I discovered it and found out what it contained, my first reaction was to destroy it due to the danger it presented. I hit it very hard but, in doing so, I only managed to break the tool. This, among other things, determined for me the value of my discovery and allowed me to confirm that it was constructed by a civilisation that no longer exists; but, judging by this remnant, a civilsation prior to my own which must have been considerably more advanced.

I have studied the cultural heritage of our ancestors, particularly those of the Egyptians, Greeks, Hebrews and, of course, the Arabs. Many people have used languages of signs to leave information to other generations. However, this is very different. I think that the chronology of humanity is not what we understood it to be and that, in remote times, long before the civilisations we today take to be the earliest, people existed who accumulated vital knowledge and lived in very close contact with nature.

Those people, whose name we don't even know, possessed an advanced control over the ground on which we walk on through their understanding of natural phenomena.

In my era, men are suffering the siege of Mother Nature. Heavy rains, droughts, bad harvests, violent movements of the earth and countless disasters constantly kill the beings that populate this earth.

Although we have always thought that these are punishments sent by God, the truth is that this metallic board allows us to control and solve those problems.

Therefore, whoever lays their hands on this prodigy could become God. In my case, I cannot understand everything it contains, as my knowledge is not sufficient for me to understand many of the things that it says. For this reason, I leave this divine board here so that people wiser than I can make use of it for the benefit of those that populate this world in years to come.

Put it to good use, as it will be needed for the disasters that are impending in the second millennium and, above all, at the beginning of the third millennium, around the year 2033—if a remedy is not found, that could be the end of the world.

When Renaud finished reading, a look of complicity passed between him and his audience. No words could highlight sufficiently the importance of the find. Guylaine was the first to reflect.

'I wonder how we're to interpret these words? I can't imagine how humans can control the earth to avoid natural catastrophes.'

She looked at the other-worldly script.

'The answer is right here.' Renaud lifted his right hand in which he held one of the small marble boards.

'Silvestre didn't understand what the monolith, or the "metallic board" as he calls it, meant, because he admitted that he lacked the basic notions necessary to understand the scientific mechanisms of our planet. But what he did know was how to translate this bizarre script. We know that our pope had an exceptional brain for mathematics and the interpretation of occult signs. However, it is highly likely that, when he discovered the monolith, he also found some sort of guide to its translation. The truth is that we will never know, but at least we have its complete instructions.'

'Evidentially, questions that modern science has been investigating for many years were resolved by other civilisations in a much earlier stage of human life,' said the Count. 'I wouldn't know how long ago, but it's clear that this discovery belongs to the mists of time.'

'Can we read any part of what is on the monolith?' asked Bruno.

Renaud placed each of the small plaques in order, and was ready to tackle the first translations.

'Well, here I go,' he said. 'Forgive me if I make mistakes but it would take me weeks of studying to become fluent in this very special language.'

'This man's gift for strange languages will never cease to amaze me,' commented the Count.

Renaud began.

A long time ago, the seed of life was sown on our earth by someone unknown to us. Some say it was a being from the stars and others that it was our God, the only one we believe exists, even though other people from far-off lands think that they are many gods.

Not even the oldest people know one way or another when or how we received the most valuable of our treasures, the one that puts us in contact with our fields, seas and the sky.

'There is a word here that is difficult to translate, but it must mean something similar to Mother Nature, so if you let me, I will refer to her whenever I see it.'

Our people evolved very quickly, and this threatened to destroy the ground on which we walk, the fields that give us fruit and the animals, and the seas that provide fish to feed us. This stage of humanity has lasted a long time and the damage is now irreversible: hunger, droughts, storms and desperation continuously threaten. The end of our civilisation is marked and there is nothing we can do now to avoid it.

All that is left for us to do is write this warning, so that other people may learn from our mistakes and may be able to apply the knowledge which we received but could not apply. We did not act on what we heard because we did not believe that Mother Nature was capable of turning against us with such violence, causing irreparable damage to the beings whom she used to treat with tenderness. When we stop feeling a harmonious contact with nature and throw ourselves into systems of exploitation and progress and do not respect the place in which we live, we start to die. Men cannot be criminals and looters of the space that accommodates them.

Those who read this must listen and understand what we have understood too late: Mother Nature has a life of her own, she is alive and, if her children harm her, she will seek vengeance.

Do not commit the same mistake as us in thinking that Mother Nature is inanimate and that she is only here to provide us with everything we need but nothing more.

Mother Nature, like the mothers of our race, is fertile, benevolent and generous. But she can also be savage and destructive when she is hurt because she has to defend herself against her children.

Renaud cleared his throat and looked up at the faces of

his listeners. Just as he expected, each and every one of them stared back, shocked.

Given all this, we must leave this legacy, which we received from those before us and which we don't know how to use, to other civilisations of the future. The laws and principles that follow next could give great power to the people who manage them appropriately. It is very important that they are used wisely because, if not, there could be disastrous consequences for mankind.

The power that emanates from here must be known and put in use only by a council of wise men who know to keep it quiet and secret.

I have here the principles...

The Count's assistant then began a list of declarations that would leave any scientist speechless.

'These include effects of the marine currents on the climate, conditions of self-regulation of the atmosphere by biomass, compositional data of the air and many other elements related to planet Earth.'

He paused. 'It is simply impossible that a lost civilisation knew this thousands of years ago.'

'Except if they weren't from this world,' murmured the Count.

'Listen to this part.'

We inhabit a living organism and we are a part of it. In ancient times there was no life on this huge being, but some initial conditions gave life to animals, plants and even humans, all of which have been changing its environment from their inception. Our world is a very complex entity, where the seas, lands and air we breathe all rest on a balance, a balance on which the very existence of the earth which houses us depends.

'This is, quite simply, astonishing,' Guylaine exclaimed.

'And here I have the jewel of the monolith,' Renaud went on. 'The relation between all the elements that make life on earth possible is written here in the form of a mathematical equation. There is, in so many words, a formula that governs the equilibrium of our planet.'

'Oh my God! Think how we could use this to lessen the problems that threaten our world!' exclaimed the Count. 'I believe we owe ourselves congratulations, after everything that has happened in recent days.'

Pierre Dubois went up to his assistant and, with a huge smile on his face, took his hand and firmly shook it: this outcome was worth their lifetimes' work. Renaud returned the handshake with equal gratitude and, for a few minutes, they devoted themselves to an exchange of mutual praise.

'I can't believe what I'm seeing,' Guylaine snapped. 'Don't you realise that we can't celebrate yet?'

The two men looked at her in confusion.

'Where's my mother?'

'When I arrived at the castle there was no sign of her,' the Count responded. 'My butler told me that she had left with a suitcase and I thought that she must have gone to Burdeos, to her mother's, as she has a habit of doing once in a while. To keep the work we were going to do as confidential as possible, I gave all the staff a couple of days' holiday. Call your grandmother,' he said.

'I already have; she's not there.'

'Then,' reflected the Count. 'What could have become

of her?'

He looked over first at Bruno, who went unexpectedly red, then turned towards Marc, who also appeared inexplicably nervous. Guylaine was about to question the two men about their reactions when Marc's mobile rang.

It was a call from his uncle. His men had the Countess. If they didn't hand over the legacy of Silvestre II that very night, Véronique Dubois would never be seen again.

Her heart beating violently, Guylaine grabbed the phone from Marc's hand and demanded to speak to her mother. She needed to hear her voice, to make sure she had come to no harm.

'My child, please get me out of here,' said a withered Countess, her voice trembling.

The words hit Guylaine like an arrow. 'Have they hurt you?'

No response. Instead, Marcos Mignon came on the line and said that they had spoken enough. Guylaine must now bring everything they had found since he left them to the door of the cellars and hand it all over if she didn't want the Countess to die.

CHAPTER 71

The Count's expression, twisted with agony, barely hinted at what was going through his mind: relief that they had solved the riddle; guilt at even thinking this; and a terror that those brutes might get hold of the legacy. The threat to kill his wife was too much to bear.

He was quiet for a couple of seconds and then asked the detective to tell him exactly what his uncle was demanding.

'He demands that we take all of this to the entrance of the cellars where we are to leave it. Once that is done, he wants us to close the door and disappear.'

Pierre Dubois thought about this strange request. Why would someone want to take the monolith inside the Dubois cellar? Suddenly, in a rush of clear-headedness, the idea came to him.

'Now I see,' he exclaimed. 'Their strategy is simple. The Logia members want us to leave our discovery in a safe place in the cellar because they know there are kilometres of tunnels down there to get lost among. It's impossible to guess which way they would go and there are so many exits where they could load the head into a vehicle waiting in one of the twenty loading bays which we use to transport the champagne. Each exit has its own bay. The tactic is brilliant because, that way, it's practically impossible to know where they will go. All of the trade exits are in very different places that lead out to different secondary roads from the estate.'

'Can't we use the secret tunnels?' asked Guylaine.

'What tunnels?' Marc inquired.

'There are several underground passageways that leave from here and link the castle to the wine cellars,' explained the Count. 'Our castle is much older that the first bottle of champagne created by Dom Pierre Pérignon. That's why, when the cellars were built, they linked both parts directly to avoid going outside in bad weather.'

'Then we could take them by surprise,' proposed the detective. 'Bruno, how many men do you have upstairs?'

'There are four but only three are in a state to fight as one of them is injured. What's your plan?'

'To attack them from behind, by surprise. If we can get to the entrance of the cellars without making any noise, I think we would have a chance to rescue the Countess without being forced to hand over the monolith.'

'A masterly move, Monsieur Mignon,' said Pierre Dubois. 'I can tell that you have the same talent for strategies as your uncle.'

'You shouldn't joke about that, Monsieur Dubois,' Marc answered. 'Today has been the worst day of my life, after the death of my parents: finding out that the only member of my family is a despicable criminal, who has kidnapped your wife.'

'Please forgive me. I didn't intend to upset you.'

Guylaine came between the two of them. 'I think it is time to get going,' she said. 'Who is going in the tunnels and who to the door of the cellars? My mother can't wait any longer.'

* * *

Bruno and Marc, followed by several henchmen, went through a door into an impenetrable darkness where the atmosphere was heavy with damp. They would go to the cellars through the tunnels while the Count and his daughter, helped by Renaud, would carry the monolith to meet the thugs' demand.

The detective had asked for a gun, which he tucked into his waistband, taking hold of a torch in one hand, the other free to guide him through the narrow passageway. They moved forward cautiously, through spiders' webs so thick that they thought no one could have passed through for decades. One of the men tripped when he didn't notice a small step in the gloom. Bruno reminded them not to make even the slightest bit of noise, as they approached what they expected to be the end of the passageway.

At the bottom of a stone staircase they came to a thick, black wooden door that seemed to give way to a different passageway or room, evidenced by the strong smell of wine that wafted through the doorframe. Marc told the others to wait at the top of the stairs.

'We should be careful when we open the door,' murmured the detective. 'If the hinges are as rusty as I'd imagine, just looking at the age of it, they'll creak and give us away.'

'Yes,' Bruno whispered back, 'but all we can do is try. You can't hear anything through the thickness of this door, so if we don't act quickly our presence here will be worthless anyway.'

Gesturing in agreement, Marc asked Bruno to hold the torch.

* * *

The Count of Dubois's hands were trembling when he slid open the door to his enormous champagne cellar. What he couldn't work out was whether his fear was for what could be happening to his wife or the possibility of losing the incredible discovery.

In any case, the strategy chosen by Marc Mignon worried him, because entering this underground world exposed them to many kilometres of tunnels, down any of which their enemy could be lurking. If the Mignon Senior's men escaped into the labyrinth with the monolith, he was sure that they would find one of the loading exits and disappear forever.

However, trusting Marc for the time being, he went inside, breathing in the intense aroma of the sparkling wines and ensuring the door didn't slide closed behind them. He reached for the light switch on the wall to his left and was taken aback by what he saw. Not only was the leader of the Logia, the same society to which he belonged himself, standing inside the cellar; Pierre also saw his own wife gagged and held by Marcos Mignon's two accomplices.

* * *

Surrounded by their family fortune, the Count demanded that they release the Countess. Loud laughter was thrown back at his face as they told him to leave the legacy of Silvestre II in front of them if he didn't want his wife to suffer irreversible harm. Renaud helped the nobleman heave the heavy monolith over the threshold and lay it on the ground near the armed men.

'Now, let my wife go, please,' begged Pierre Dubois.

Marcos, who now had an enormous bandage on one side of his body, waved at one of his henchmen with his good arm to check that there was no one outside the entrance. Only when the coast was clear, did he give them permission to release the Countess and pick up the slab. Just as they were preparing to leave the cellar through a back door, another group of men armed with guns started appeared, and ordered them to drop their weapons. Marcos told his men to shoot without hesitation, and an intense crossfire broke out between his men and the five strangers. Somehow, they had managed to station themselves behind a row of bottles stacked a dozen high at the back of this cellar. The racket from the gunshots, as well as the deafening cracks of exploding bottles hit by the rain of bullets, reverberated through the very cores of those present.

Marcos soon realised that his opposition had the advantage as they were better protected, so he fired a long series of shots in an attempt to reach the Countess and recapture her as hostage. As he rushed over to where Véronique was standing, he saw for the first time that one of the men firing was his nephew. Enraged, he rushed forwards and positioned himself behind the Countess. There was no time to react, and both Bruno and Marc watched in horror as their men carried on shooting at Marcos, who had grabbed Véronique around the waist.

A couple of seconds later, both bodies had crumpled to the floor, leaving a trail of blood where they fell. Guylaine's cries resonated around the high ceilings of the cellar and could be heard over the gunshots. Marc ran towards the entrance, using a wooden crate that he had found on the floor as a shield but before he got there, he realised that no one was shooting any more, because his uncle, the leader of the Logia, was lying motionless on the floor. Only when he had ordered Bruno's men to see to his uncle's accomplices, and they had been disarmed, did the detective cross what had become a battleground to see what had happened to his uncle and the Countess. Both were lying in an enormous puddle of clear, pink liquid, as their blood mixed with a flow of champagne, spreading across the flagstones.

* * *

Guylaine also went to help her mother, followed by the Count and Renaud. There was a red circle spreading on Véronique's chest: proof that she had been shot. Bruno took off the light cotton jacket he was wearing and pressed it on to the wound firmly, trying to stop the bleeding. Surrounded by her daughter, Marc, the Count and Renaud, Véronique prepared to say the only words that her meagre strength allowed.

'Please forgive me for what I have done to you. I don't think I have been either the mother or the wife you hoped for.'

'Don't say anything. Save all your energy for now. The ambulance is already on its way,' urged her daughter, not able to hide the tears streaming down her cheeks.

'No! I have something to say. Pierre, I have always been

fond of you and I have even been very happy by your side, but I had to fill the gap you have left in my life these last years somehow. And that's why—'

A small trickle of blood escaped from the corner of her mouth.

'That's why I was with this young man.'

Marc's eyes opened wide all of a sudden. He had never expected her to say such a thing, least of all at a time like that. Blushing uncontrollably, he cast his eyes down at the floor and endured the uncomfortable silence around him, wishing the situation undone.

* * *

Guylaine looked up and stared at the detective, who still had his head down, as if inspecting the paving. A torrent of thoughts flew through her mind. She didn't doubt her mother's behaviour, whose actions she had not been able to understand or predict for quite a long time now. What most outraged her, though, was that Marc had tried to get close to her having committed the unforgiveable act of sleeping with the Countess. Each time he had come on to her, Guylaine had systematically spurned his attempts and now she knew she had done the right thing by continuously rejecting him.

Guylaine was still waiting for Marc Mignon to look up so that she could reprimand him, when she realised that her mother wanted to continue.

'Bruno has been my lover for some years,' the Countess explained, addressing her husband. 'He filled all of those afternoons you spent travelling and studying abroad.

Please forgive me.'

'I already knew,' replied the Count. 'You are the one who should forgive me. All this time I have spent dedicated to something that distanced me from you and I threw myself into something that was outside of the family. I admit it and am sorry for my misdoings.'

Guylaine looked at Marc, who had finally managed to lift his head. She wanted to apologise to him for distrusting him but, instead, she furiously reprimanded the archaeologist, venting her anger at him. Not only had he got her father into trouble but he had also deceived her mother. Had he not still been putting pressure on her mother's wound, she would have kicked him without a second thought.

When he heard the sirens of several ambulances approaching, Marc suddenly felt guilty, as he had neglected his uncle, who seemed to be in a more critical state than Véronique. He went over and knelt down next to him. A bullet had entered his stomach and he had lost conciousness. As the others took the Countess away, Marc raised his arm and shouted for someone to help the only relative he had left in the world.

CHAPTER 72

Paris

Marc pulled the blind up completely in order to let the sunlight of a beautiful autumnal Parisian morning flood into the massive office.

Sitting in the large leather chair that months before had belonged to his uncle Marcos, Marc mindfully watched the busy traffic circling the Trocadero, although his eyes were quickly drawn to a leafy garden area below where a number of couples lay peacefully on the lawn. It was the last day he would see this view, because the building had been sold to a construction firm who planned to convert it into luxury apartments.

This was the patrimony that the Mignons had left him. His uncle never recovered from the shooting in the Divange cellars and before he died, had confirmed that the detective agency was not his only source of income or business. Marc was forced to sell the building as the Agency alone would never generate enough money to maintain it.

However, despite all that had happened, there was one thing that comforted Marc: his new profession as a private detective. Since the Dubois case had closed, he had turned his attentions internally, discovering that there was a small group of employees in the agency who were worth keeping and, above all, whom he could rely on to solve the broad range of cases that came in. Without expecting too much, he had realised that this new stability in his life filled him with satisfaction. Consequently, Marc had chosen to follow in the dignified footsteps of his father. The next decision was easy: get rid of the building and liquidate his uncle's dodgy assets. It was time to redirect the business from a new starting block.

He stood up and gathered the last of his items. He had resolved to get rid of a pile of documents that compromised quite a number of clients and other noteworthy Parisian names. As he looked over the papers before destroying them permanently, he sighed when he saw the dirty methods that Marcos had employed to solve his cases.

In contrast to this destruction, Marc then organised with utmost care each and every one of the documents he found that made reference to his father and his grandfather. He had gathered, through reading his father's notes, that he was the son of one of the most upright detectives in Paris and, now he must re-establish the name and brand of Mignon, as it deserved.

He pulled the blinds down for the final time, blocking out the light which now only peered through the slats, casting slicing shadows across the room. Marc looked at his watch and realised that it was time to go. He had been invited to lunch with a member of the French nobility. Pierre Dubois wanted to thank him for everything the detective had done for him.

* * *

As Marc drove out of the car park, he looked back to the

times he had been a target and chased in numerous cars and felt a sudden frustration when his thoughts still included Guylaine. She had rejected his calls time and time again, and had not even bothered to reply to an affectionate note he had sent her a few weeks ago.

He was aware that, after the Count's discovery of the greatest secret of the pope magician, Silvestre II, the stir that had come about had to be keeping her father very busy; the least his daughter could do was be at his side for the endless public appearances he had to make to announce the incredible revelations of the talking head. After all, it was a machine that had captured the amazement of the whole world—its remains had been removed from the basement of the castle to be exhibited in the Louvre Museum. It was undoubtedly the greatest discovery in recent centuries and probably, due to the nature of the metal with which the monolith had been made and the extraordinary information that it contained, the new text called into question everything that had been presumed about ancient civilisations.

Marc bounded into the restaurant with a smile on his face, pleased to be seeing the Count again. He asked the maître d' for Monsieur Dubois's table. Following the waiter, he made his way to a table in a comfortable, secluded part of the restaurant and there he was met with a great surprise. Where he expected to be met by a single person, Marc Mignon found a table for four. Guylaine and her mother had come to the meal.

* * *

The detective greeted the nobleman warmly and kissed both women. He took a seat and told them how happy he was to see them.

'I thought I would never see you again. It is such a pleasure for me to be with the Dubois family again.'

'Why do you say that?' asked the Countess.

'Well, let's say that I have tried to contact one member of your family recently, without success.'

'Please forgive me,' said Guylaine. 'I have been rather busy with my mother, coming and going from the hospital for several weeks, and then came the fuss with my father and the media. It has been a marathon that we have all now luckily finished, it seems.'

'I have seen the press. They don't stop praising the legacy of the pope magician,' said Marc. 'Isn't that right, Monsieur Dubois?'

'Indeed. Thanks to the fabulous discoveries we made— the whole world is starting to call it the 1000 Effect—I have more than fifty appointments and the opportunity to write for various publications ahead of me. The consequences that this finding is going to have on the planet, climate change and, mainly, the understanding of the environment and our surroundings are exceptional. And part of that we owe to you.'

'I didn't do anything. Just my job.'

'Don't be so modest,' returned the nobleman.

Marc changed the subject. 'And how is the Countess?' he asked, addressing Véronique.

'I'm very well. I have lost an organ but that doesn't stop me from living my life. Perhaps as a result, I have reconsidered many things. Now I go with Pierre to all his conferences and we are having a sort of...'

'Second honeymoon,' Pierre completed his wife's sentence. 'We have all made mistakes but our good sense has put them right.'

'I'm very happy for you. Honestly, you deserve this new opportunity. Was that the reason for this lunch, may I ask? Have you called me to tell me about your happiness?'

'It will always be an honour to have you among us and to share our well-being with you', the Count said to him. 'But we want you to do something for the Dubois family.'

'Of course, my attention is all yours.'

'As I said to you before, I am going to spend more time with my wife. That's why I have decided to sell all of my businesses that are not directly related to the production of champagne.'

'That seems like a wise move. And where do I fit into that matter?'

'I don't want to be far from Véronique whilst she is still recovering. That's why I have transferred legal powers to my daughter so that she can travel abroad to carry out the necessary formalities to liquidate my companies. Most of them are in Central America and, as you speak Spanish fluently, you would be the ideal companion for someone working in those countries.'

The detective looked at Guylaine and saw that she was smiling.

'Given the circumstances, I think I ought to accept this assignment.'

'Good,' said the Count. 'As I knew you would not decline

my proposal, I have brought you the tickets. You leave for Costa Rica tomorrow.'

Marc opened the envelope that the nobleman offered him and took out what was inside. He could not believe what he saw. Of course, the flight number could have been none other.

Air France flight 1000 departed tomorrow.

**Beautiful
Books**

Charterhouse Library

64179